To ~~████████~~ Whomever it may concern,

Enjoy!

[signature]

SNAKE ISLAND

By Marilinne Cooper

Real life inspires fiction – and who wouldn't be inspired by real life on Culebra? Interesting people evolve into colorful fictional characters who then develop personality traits, flaws or perfections beyond reality. Actual events and beautiful places find their way into a plot, but can change as the story progresses. In the end, it is all an invented tale meant to entertain, not exploit.

So Culebra friends, please remember – this story is a work of fiction. Names, characters, and incidents are either the product of the author's imagination or are used fictitiously for the purpose of storytelling only. Although resemblances to actual persons, business establishments or events may not be entirely coincidental, they have been used solely to evoke the atmosphere and quirky appeal of this one-of-a-kind tropical paradise.

CHAPTER ONE

"Tucker, look. Down there. I think that's it."

Straining against his seat belt, Tyler leaned forward to tap his son on the shoulder. Tucker turned his head, the white cord leading from his ears to his Ipod explaining his lack of response. Pulling one earbud out, he asked flatly, "What."

Tyler pointed through the scratched window of the plane, past the whirling propeller to a crescent of white sand framing an aquamarine bay. "Flamenco Beach. That must be the campground."

From fourteen hundred feet above, the amber light and slanted rays of the rapidly setting sun gave an ethereal other-worldly quality to the island. Any feelings of awe were quickly replaced by the thrill – or sheer terror of the plane's sudden descent and sharp right turn. Entering a narrow pass between two hillsides, the aircraft dropped to sea level with a couple of breathtaking lurches and then the wheels met a paved runway that seemed to run the entire length of the valley.

Tyler glanced at the only other passengers on the small plane, an elderly couple who seemed unfazed by the death-defying landing they had just lived through.

"Please stay seated until the plane has come to a complete stop and I get out to open the door for you," the pilot announced as they motored to a standstill in front of a tiny terminal. "Oh, and welcome to Culebra."

It had seemed like a good idea back in Vermont. Some father/son hanging out time, camping right next to the beach, doing some tropical hiking, water sports and relaxation. But after walking the half mile to Section E of the campground, dragging a large rolling suitcase along a soft sandy road, and then setting up a tent in the dark at the end of a long day of travel, Tyler thought he must have been delusional to imagine this might be fun.

Drenched with sweat, he flopped down on his sleeping mat and opened a bottle of water. He was glad they had stopped at the kiosks by the gate and grabbed a couple of pieces of pizza before heading out to their campsite; at least he wouldn't have to deal with the parental guilt of not providing dinner on their first night in paradise. A few feet away, Tucker's frowning face was illuminated by the light of his cell phone.

"Shit," he muttered. "I can't believe it. There's almost no signal here."

Despite his exhaustion, Tyler found himself grinning in the darkness.

"What do you say we go for a night swim?" he asked. His body felt hot and claustrophobic in the jeans he had been wearing all day. He wriggled out of them and then felt around in the suitcase for his trunks. "Hey, shine that light over here, would you, so I can see what I am doing."

"But we can't go in the water after dark." Tucker held up the phone to illuminate the interior of the tent.

"Why not?"

"You know. Sharks."

For some reason Tyler was annoyed that his son was so cautious, but he had to admit that he himself didn't know what the dangers of Flamenco Beach were. "Well, we can at least go down there and get our feet wet, maybe take a walk." Pulling on a pair of shorts, he unzipped the screen door of the tent and crawled out.

Soft glowing lights from other campsites shone in the wooded area around them; back along the road where they had come in, a much brighter light was the beacon to the bathroom quad. The rhythmic crashing of small waves against the shore was an endless background soundtrack that acted as gentle white noise, blocking out the sounds of the residents in Section E and creating a surprising sense of privacy.

Despite its proximity, Tyler realized he had no idea how to get to the beach without bushwhacking his way through the tropical underbrush of the campground. There had to be a path, but in the unfamiliar embrace of the warm velvet darkness, he didn't know where to begin looking.

Suddenly Tucker's slim body materialized beside him, unnerving Tyler with the silence of his approach. "Here." He flicked the switch of a small flashlight and put it in Tyler's hand. "This might help."

When they emerged onto the soft sand a few minutes later, Tyler could immediately feel his tension start to unwind. The breeze coming off the bay made the air several degrees cooler. In the distance, where the cloudless night sky met the horizon, the flashing beams of a few freighters were visible as they made their way through the Caribbean, headed for San Juan or St. Thomas or beyond.

Despite the signs of life in the campground behind them, the beach seemed deserted. While Tyler reveled in the solitude of the moment, he knew his son was probably a bit disappointed, or at least bored. He looked over his shoulder at him – the boy's troubled face was lit by the phone again.

"Only one bar," he said.

"You might as well put that thing away before it dies," Tyler suggested. "I don't know when you'll get to charge it again."

Tucker quickly shut his cell off and shoved it in his pocket. Tyler had a fleeting flash of sympathy for him – but only briefly. "Come on, let's take a walk. See if we can get any sharks to bite our feet."

Tyler headed to the water's edge and reluctantly Tucker joined him. "Warmer than Lake Willoughby ever gets in the summer," Tyler remarked. "I love swimming in the Caribbean. Do you have any memories of it from your childhood?"

Tucker shrugged noncommittally. "Kinda. I remember playing with a bunch of kids at that beach in Bequia; we used to go every day after school. Somebody found an eel one day. Once there was a hurricane and the waves came all the way over the road, washed right through that bar where they had bands sometimes." He was quiet for a few seconds. "It was like more than ten years ago, but, yeah, I do remember some things."

Of all the experiences he had weathered in his life, relating to his son was the most challenging by far. Tyler had never wanted children and had not known he was a father until Tucker was already six years old. He had returned to rural northern Vermont to be part of his life; it hadn't been a tough choice to make at the time, but the last ten years had been far from easy.

His relationship with Tucker's mother, Lucy, was more than complicated and, for lots of reasons, he did not move back in with her, which made it that much harder to find his own road with Tucker. Tyler had rented a bungalow in the neighboring town of Jordan Center and then tried to find rewarding employment. There was no going back to the investigative journalism career he had left behind several winters before. It took a few years of scrapping at construction jobs (which he was not good at), waiting tables (better), cooking in restaurants (best), before the Jordan Ledger had gone up for sale.

The work of writing, reporting and editing a small weekly newspaper was as close as he was going to get to a career in the Northeast Kingdom, and with one employee who handled advertising sales, he settled in as a self-employed business owner. And for the first time in a long while he felt good about himself. He even began to look the part. His hair, sun-bleached from years as a Caribbean fugitive from his own life, evolved into a thick silvery-gray mane, his eyesight degenerated to the point where he had to wear glasses all the time and not just for reading, the lines on his face became creases, and his lean muscular limbs turned sinewy. When he stood up after sitting at his computer for hours, his lower back took several minutes to recover from its stiffness. And yes, he was quite a bit older than the fathers of Tucker's classmates, but he could still climb a mountain and ride a bike with the best of them.

Although always a bit awkward, the father/son relationship had been easier when Tucker was younger. Tyler had recognized much of himself in the boy and it had felt natural to share the wonders of the world, from reading Harry Potter aloud to skiing at Burke Mountain to playing Angry Birds. It got harder when Lucy took up with a burly Gulf War veteran who took Tucker bird-hunting and ATV-ing, but luckily that romance hadn't lasted very long. Still it had worried Tyler how long a father figure who preferred doing the New York Times Sunday crossword could compete with drag racing and tracking deer. But as it turned out, Tucker wasn't much interested in those things.

Now, as they walked in the darkness along the edge of the bay, Tyler realized that Tucker matched him for height, maybe even surpassed him by an inch. At sixteen he suffered from the sudden growth spurt syndrome that affected so many teenagers destined for tallness; the uneasiness of not knowing what to do with the newfound length of his limbs was combined with unchecked rushes of testosterone, giving him a vulnerability that was counterbalanced by his adolescent defensiveness and innocence. His unruly sandy hair had darkened in the last year and freckles had been replaced by some random zits and thickening whiskers. It was unnerving to watch how rapidly the changes took place and how easily the boy could be mistaken for a man.

A sudden burst of laughter made them stop for a brief second. The yellow glow of a lantern and some strings of colored Christmas lights illuminated what appeared to be an elaborate campsite on a little bluff above the beach. A brawny man wearing a bandana on his head and a large gold earring was sitting at a picnic table talking loudly and gesturing wildly with a beer can in each hand. In the shadows, a female companion with long bushy hair wore only a bikini top and running shorts over what, in the half-light, appeared to be some extensive body ink. Another couple seemed to be saying goodbye, indistinguishable as they disappeared into the shadows leading back to the campground.

"Pirates," Tyler whispered conspiratorily.

"I doubt that."

"You never know."

As they moved on they could hear the man yelling angrily – "You gotta be fuckin' kidding me, right? Tell me you are kidding." – followed by a maniacal outburst of hooting and hilarity.

Tucker stopped walking suddenly.

"What's wrong?"

"I think this is the end, I don't think we can go any farther, unless we want to do some rock climbing."

Tyler played the flashlight across the unfamiliar landscape in front of them. It would be easier to negotiate the nighttime when the moon was full. But they would have to wait several days for that. "Okay, let's go back. I'm beat anyway."

"Beat?" Tucker snorted a little. "Tyler, nobody has said that in like a hundred years."

Tyler was more amused than offended and decided not to comment on the fact that his son had called him by name. Maybe this was just another assertion of adulthood that went along with the rest of Tucker's recent stand-offish behavior.

The zippered tent was airless and stifling inside, at least by northern Vermont standards. But in the exhausted wake of all-day travel, opening the screened vents and stripping down to their boxers was enough to alleviate their discomfort. Lulled by the relaxing repetitive soundtrack of breaking surf, Tucker and Tyler both slipped quickly into sleep.

At some point in the night, Tyler awoke to the timbre of angry voices from a nearby campsite. He could not make out what they were saying and he didn't really care, more concerned with how cool his flesh had become with the dropping temperatures of the predawn beach environment. Pulling on a t-shirt and drawing up the sheet, he curled up and threw one arm protectively over his ear. He wasn't used to neighbors.

It seemed like he had barely drifted off again when the sound of the tent zipper caused him to bolt upright. "Who's there?"

A beam of light blinded him momentarily. "It's just me. I had to take a whiz. Didn't think you were supposed to do it in the bushes here so I went over to the john."

Tyler realized that he hadn't even been aware that Tucker was not in the tent when he had been rooting around for his shirt a few minutes earlier. The idea that his son could sneak out without his knowledge was unsettling, but not worth losing sleep over. Heart still pounding rapidly, he settled back down under his sheet.

A few hours later he came out of his now restless sleep to strange scratching noises a few inches from his head. Disoriented, he sat up, unsure of what he was hearing. The crunching and scuffling of leaves on the other side of the rip-stop nylon wall could be anything; the gray light filtering through the tent screen gave an ethereal quality to the emerging landscape outside. Cautiously, he peered through the mesh. A couple of clucks and a few peeps later, he relaxed and lay back down, grinning. Chickens. In the campground. How Third World.

Tyler glanced over at Tucker. His long body was curled into a fetal position against the coolness of the air and he snored lightly. Tyler knew from experience that he wouldn't be up for hours, especially not after being forced into wakefulness for their airport trip the previous day. Covering Tucker with his own sheet, he dressed quietly and crept out of the tent, thinking how nice it was to have

11

nothing on his agenda for the morning except a walk down the beach in search of a fresh cup of coffee.

By the time he returned with a bag of empanadillas and his second coffee, he felt infinitely wiser and more curious about his surroundings. Section E was definitely exceptional in comparison to the rest of the campground; its inhabitants had clearly settled in for the long haul, making it their home for however long they were lucky enough to stay at Flamenco Beach. Some had set up outdoor living areas with comfy folding beach chairs; there were elaborate kitchens under tarps with propane stoves and sinks. He saw a few solar showers. From what he could see of the tent interiors, most were furnished with real air mattresses and bed pillows. One of his closest neighbors had what appeared to be a three-room cabin tent that was bigger than some apartments he had lived in. It was situated under the trees on the edge of the beach with a million dollar view of the water. It was arguable whether that location was superior to another that was nestled into a grove of trees that offered ultimate privacy within this public space.

In the daylight he saw that the better sites at least came with a picnic table and he made plans to move camp to one of those as soon as possible. Scoping out the landscape around him, he saw a gray-haired couple that appeared to be breaking down their extensive camp nearby. They gave him a friendly nod and he ambled over.

"Looks like you've been here a while," he commented.

"More than two months. Since New Year's." The very tanned woman was packing up their food supplies. "Do you want any of this? If not, it will all just go to the free store over by the bathrooms."

In just a few minutes time, Tyler learned a whole lot about the ways of the Section E world and came away with a Styrofoam cooler full of perishable food and a bag of non-perishables. Apparently people liked to leave the campground a lot lighter than when they arrived and many of them opted for ditching most of their gear. These two had been coming to Flamenco for decades and kept their tent and equipment with friends who lived on the island. Unfortunately, their desirable site had already been claimed by some other campers who had arrived a few days before Tyler, but the man pointed out a couple of other sites that would soon be vacant.

As Tyler made his way towards one of these locations, he heard an angry shout coming from the three-room palace tent. Moments later a darkly tanned and wiry man stumbled out onto the screened porch spewing Spanish invectives.

"Yo, Alejandro, dude, what's going on?" another camper called out to him.

"Those fuckers – they slashed through the wall of my tent and ripped through the side of my air mattress." His words were slurred and hard to understand, as though he had been drinking all night rather than sleeping. "I woke up sleeping on the fucking ground. I will fucking kill that motherfucker." His words were punctuated by the sound of a beer can popping open.

Tyler paused on the path, not sure he wanted to explore any campsites close to this unfolding drama.

"Don't worry, it's not really like this here most of the time." He looked over his shoulder to see the man, who had just spoken to Alejandro, standing behind him. He had the appearance of a classic salty sailor, wispy blond hair and moustache bleached by the sun, wrinkled and leathery skin the color of a tequila sunset, watery blue eyes that had seen a lot of horizons. "That's his personal shit going on; this is actually a very friendly and safe place. No worries, mate." Hitching up his low-riding, faded board shorts, he extended a hand – "I'm Cassidy, I live here. Right over there actually," he indicated with a thumb over a mottled shoulder – "if you got any questions."

Tyler's eyes registered a well-worn cabin tent under a dark blue tarp and a picnic table cluttered with the detritus of camp living. Blackened pots shared space with toothbrushes, battery-powered lanterns and solar cell phone chargers. A bright Mexican hammock strung between two sturdy mangroves completed the homey scene.

"Thanks, Cassidy. Tyler Mackenzie," he replied as he returned the surprisingly gentle handshake.

"Oh, we already got a Tyler here. I'll have to call you Mackie." Cassidy shifted to Tyler's left. "Sorry, man, I only got one good eye and I can't see you from over there."

Behind Cassidy, Tyler could see Alejandro speaking rapidly in Spanish to someone and gesturing wildly. "I better go smoke a bowl with him, calm him down," Cassidy said. "I'll catch you later."

He moved away, still talking as he walked comfortably backwards over the uneven surface of dried leaves and roots. "Oh, and you see that little orange tent there – those guys are leaving today, if you want a really sweet campsite."

Tucker was awake when he returned, but Tyler chose not to share all the details of the scene he had just witnessed. They rooted through the free food with the delight of inexperienced scavengers, treating themselves to a few oatmeal raisin cookies and a couple of oranges. With plans to move, they chose not to unpack their suitcases.

"So how's this for today." Tucker did not know why he felt the need to lay out a schedule on their first day in paradise, but there was something about traveling with a teenager that seemed to require it. "We go down and swim for a couple of hours and then we move camp to the new spot and then head into town to buy some stuff, charge phones, check emails, etc."

Tucker shrugged. "Cool," he said, and Tyler understood that this was actually a sign of enthusiasm. Zipping shut the tent flaps, they headed towards the beckoning turquoise waters of the Caribbean Sea.

It was already mid-afternoon by the time they caught a "publico" from the campground to town. As they waited for the bus, Tucker was ecstatic to realize he actually could pick up a decent signal from the parking lot, and despite his private disappointment that the boy would not have to forgo his phone addiction for a few weeks, Tyler knew this would make their stay easier.

For three dollars apiece, they got a ten minute ride in a minivan that dropped them off in Dewey, at the end of a sleepy main street by the ferry dock to Fajardo, the port on the mainland of Puerto Rico. There was the usual somewhat sleazy bar and restaurant across from the landing, some souvenir shops and banks with ATMs, and a handful of cafés that would not be open until evening. Traffic consisted of a steady and noisy medley of open golf carts, ramshackle all-wheel drive vehicles and a variety of pickup trucks.

Tucker and Tyler were directed to head "over the bridge" which turned out to be a strangely oversized orange steel structure that seemed out of place in such a small town. But as they walked across it, they saw that it ran over a slow-moving green canal that connected the sea to a large calm bay full of moored sailboats; clearly the bridge could be raised and lowered to allow oversized yachts and other floating means of transport to pass through. On the other side, Tucker went off to the library to charge his phone and Tyler went to "Milka's," the local grocery.

In the typical island way, there were some basic staples that you could not buy (decent bread) and some gourmet delicacies (French brie, Greek olives) that could be in abundance for as long as they lasted and then maybe never again. Also lots of general supplies that nobody wanted but had to buy for lack of other options (premade Oreo pie crusts, raspberry-and-cream granola bars) were available. There was a room with a butcher's counter and bins of the usual moldy potatoes and onions as well as sad-looking apples from some faraway overseas land. Despite the steep prices, customers had their small rolling baskets piled high with groceries, many of them apparently restocking their boat larders before heading off to other tropical harbors.

Overwhelmed by the crowded aisles, long line and lack of food choices, Tyler wandered outside and decided to check his own phone for messages. There were a few desperate texts and motherly voice mails from Lucy, wondering if they had arrived safely and how it was going. He toyed with the idea of not answering her and making her worry, but then realized that Tucker had no doubt already texted her, letting her know they had arrived. He had no interest in checking in with his job or friends back home. He decided the only thing he would use his phone for while he was here was to keep track of where Tucker might meander off to.

Around the corner he found Tucker sitting on a bench in an airy outdoor pavilion that connected what appeared to be the animal rescue center and a small library of recycled books. His phone was plugged into a wall outlet and he was intently texting away. Tyler turned his attention to the public bulletin board and while his eyes were reading about yoga classes and movie showings, his ears tuned into a conversation between a couple of women a few yards away.

"...not saying who it is but it happened at the campground. Jose found him in a tent this afternoon."

"Oh, my god, that is so awful. Things like that don't happen here. This could ruin our tourist economy."

"We don't know that – maybe it was just a heart attack or something natural."

"Well, I'm heading over to the dinghy dock, maybe somebody will know what's going on."

With a quick glance at Tucker, who was still engrossed in his phone, Tyler turned to the two women whose gray hair, deep tans and worn flip-flops identified them as local expatriates. With an effort, he switched on the charismatic personality he had used to his ultimate advantage back in his younger days as an inquiring journalist.

"So sorry, my son and I are staying at the campground and I couldn't help overhearing your conversation." He flashed what he hoped was a warm but worried smile. "What did you say happened?"

16

The two looked at each other, clearly unsure of how much to share with this stranger.

"I'm Tyler, from northern Vermont." He stuck out his hand. "And that's my son, Tucker. You both look like you must live here."

After a few seconds more of checking him out, one of them took the bait. "Lila – my husband and I have a house out in Zoni. And this is Maura; she spends the winter on a boat in the bay."

"When the manager of the campground checked the site tags this afternoon, he found a man dead in one of the tents. That's all we know," Maura blurted.

Tyler swallowed. "That's really disturbing. It seems like such a peaceful place."

"It is! You have no idea how terrible this is for us – Culebra prides itself on having almost no crime," said Lila. "We're headed over to happy hour at the dinghy dock. Do you want to join us? Maybe you can find out more." As quickly as they had been suspicious of him, now they were his new best friends.

"Um, my son–" He nodded in Tucker's direction.

"Oh, he'll be fine there. It's just around the corner. What'd you say his name was, Tucker?" asked Maura. "Tucker, we're taking your dad to the bar on the other side of the bridge. You cool with that?"

Tucker's eyes came up from his phone and his reconnection with the real world around him was visible to all. Confused for a few seconds, he took in the situation, and then suppressed a grin. "Uh, sure. Have fun," he said, before refocusing on the device in his hand.

"You know they have a charging station at the campground kiosks," Lila whispered as they descended the library verandah steps.

Tyler laughed. "Nope, and I still don't know it."

The "Dinghy Dock" turned out not to be a public boat wharf but a popular bar and restaurant on the edge of the bay where sailors could motor in with their dinghies to tie up and have a drink. Even at this early hour, there was a good crowd of people already starting to unwind or wind up, as the case might be. The open air design with a beautiful view of the bay made it appealing to locals and tourists alike.

"What are you drinking?" asked Lila.

Ha, thought Tyler. A simple but loaded question. Ten years earlier on another Caribbean island, he had spiraled into the alcoholic depths of a love affair with Mount Gay rum. After a dangerous escapade had forced him into unexpected detox, Tyler had drunk only sparingly and on an irregular basis.

"Um, a beer is fine." He did not want to get too intoxicated while he was responsible for Tucker. A moment later, a can of Medalla was pressed into his hand. Closing his eyes, he tipped it to his lips, relishing the first instant the cold liquid touched his taste buds. Alcohol...yes, he would always love it.

"Okay, guys, so, here's what I found out." Coming out of his reverie, he registered Maura leaning towards them. "It was a guy who was staying out at the campground while he was trying to buy a house over in Muñecos. I guess there were some problems with it not having a title and he'd been pretty stressed about it. Guess there were a couple of bad late night bar scenes with the realtor, lots of shouting."

"So natural causes?" asked Tyler.

"They don't know yet. Probably have to take the body over to the big island to figure out how he died."

"Guess he won't get the house now." Lila laughed darkly.

Feeling refreshed by the beer making its way through his system, Tyler relaxed and surveyed the local characters around the bar. At the far end was a man with an untrimmed gray beard that reached halfway down his chest, wearing round wire-rimmed glasses and a hat woven of palm fronds. Next to him stood a deeply tanned sailor whose short hair, polo shirt and boat shoes screamed prep school and yacht club. He was talking to a short woman

18

whose facial features were so distinctly Native American, almost Navajo, that they seemed out of place in the Caribbean. A booming voice at the other end of the bar belonged to a towering lunk of a fellow whose wild silver curls and startling blue eyes contrasted sharply with the sun-bronzed hue of his weathered skin. A pale, bespectacled man in a navy captain's hat sat a table next to the water, staring intently at his laptop.

"That's your boy, isn't it?"

Tyler looked up, trying to dismiss the sense of guilt he felt. Tucker stood on the stairs that descended from the street, surveying the scene below with casual bewilderment. He tried to conceal the relief that suffused his face as he caught sight of his father in the crowd. "Hey," he said, his eyes immediately drifting to the beer in Tyler's hand.

"Want something to drink? I mean, you know, a soda or something." This should not be as awkward as it felt.

"Sure, I'll have a Coke."

As Tyler tried to get the bartender's attention, he heard Lila chatting Tucker up.

"So is this your first time to the Caribbean?"

"Not really. I lived here until I was five."

"Is that so? Here on Culebra?"

"No, no, down in the Grenadines – on Mustique and Bequia."

Tyler suppressed a grin at Tucker's offhand cool at throwing island names around. He'd been nowhere but West Jordan, Vermont, for the last ten years, but he had managed to exude the air of an experienced cosmopolitan traveler.

"Mustique – that's a pretty chi-chi place, right? Rock stars live there, don't they?"

Tyler stiffened and glanced over his shoulder to see Tucker's response. He didn't know exactly how much his son actually knew about what life had been like for him and his mother on Mustique when he was a baby.

"Yeah, I guess so. I don't remember much; I was really young."

19

"There are a few boats here that are headed all the way down to the Leewards," he heard Maura chime in. "See that young Danish couple over there; they're sailing around the world and going that way soon."

Their small talk continued until Tyler finally returned with the soda – and another beer for himself. Then the two women drifted away to socialize with their local compadres.

"They told me about the dead guy in the tent and a good taco place over the bridge," Tucker commented to Tyler. "Can we go there to eat?"

Tyler choked on his Medalla. "Sure. Let's go."

A couple of hours later, they were back at the campground, relaxed and satisfied, just as the light was beginning to fade from the sky. Compared to the lively afternoon atmosphere of the beach, it was quiet and peaceful now, with just a few campers moving around through the trees, cooking on camp stoves, laying in hammocks, and quietly socializing. If you didn't know someone had died there in the last twenty-four hours, you wouldn't have guessed.

In Section E, the scent of ganja smoke intermingled with the smell of barbecuing fish somewhere nearby. A few campsites away they could see people on a picnic bench laughing and talking. One of the group detached himself and came towards them – it was Cassidy.

"You guys want to join us? Leo and Sam caught a snapper out past the reef today and we're just hanging around while they cook it up, smokin' a little weed, playin' some music."

Tyler hesitated, once again feeling his parenting skills were being challenged, but before he could say anything, Tucker spoke up. "Sure. Why not? We haven't got anything else to do tonight."

His easy agreement made Tyler realize he had no idea what kind of social life his son had with his friends back home, and whether smoking pot was part of it. If he sat there and watched Tucker get high, would that make him a bad father? Could he or should he disassociate himself from that responsibility while here? Maybe they could agree that what happened in Culebra, stayed in Culebra...

"So you heard about Ivan, the guy who died, right? You missed them taking the body away a little while ago," Cassidy informed them. "Man, he was laying in that tent right over there for most of the day and no one even knew. Kinda creeps me out thinkin' about it, you know?"

They approached the small cluster of campers sitting around a picnic table; two very tanned young men in their late twenties wearing only swim trunks and flip flops were kneeling over a fish cooking on a small open fire; both sported kinky hair pulled back into man buns and some impressive tattoos. On one of the benches, two young girls in bright bikinis and sarongs were chopping cucumbers and drinking red wine out of plastic cups. They had pretty eyes and warm smiles as they greeted Tucker and Tyler.

There was nothing harmful here, he decided, as he sat down in a folding camp chair and watched his son flirt self-consciously with one of the girls. As they talked, she tossed her gold hoop earrings and flicked her long blonde braid back and forth over a sun-burned shoulder.

Well, almost nothing.

Cassidy was from the mountains of Utah. He'd been a white water rafting guide in places like Chile and Brazil, and apparently even on the Zambezi River in Zimbabwe, before he'd settled down to start a river rafting tour company not far from Zion National Park. Tyler learned all this and much more – Cassidy loved to talk, and especially about himself. He knew the dead guy, of course, Ivan, nice fellow but a mean drunk and he'd rubbed more than one person on the island the wrong way in his pursuit of a piece of sweet property in town. Apparently Ivan had entertained more than a few Culebresa senoritas at his campsite during his stay. So yeah, there were all kinds of people who might like to see him dead.

After a while, Tyler excused himself to go back to his tent and read. Cassidy had assured him that Leo and Sam had already gotten into the pants of the two cute little British girls and that Tucker probably wasn't going to get lucky tonight. Tyler didn't know if his son had ever "gotten lucky," but he didn't think he had to worry. At least about that. So far Tucker had refused the dope pipe that was being passed around, but Tyler had a feeling his behavior was about to change shortly. He didn't care – his son was now having a good time on Culebra; hadn't that been the point of this trip?

After a day of sun, the beers followed by cheap red wine had definitely affected him more than he had realized. Stretching out on his mat, he fell asleep reaching for his Kindle. He did not hear Tucker slip in a few hours later, nor see him pass out fully dressed a few feet away.

CHAPTER TWO

By the following evening they were settled into a new and improved beachfront campsite with a picnic table and a view. Even with only one good eye, Cassidy was an expert scavenger and by the end of the day their tent was equipped with an inflatable air mattress ("You might have to blow it up a little every morning but it holds air pretty good.") and a couple of slightly broken folding canvas chairs.

"End of March, lots of the long-termers are leaving and they don't want to take nothing back home," he informed them. "You might even get a nice big cabin tent if you keep your eyes open."

"We're only here for ten days. This is luxurious enough," Tyler assured him.

"Well, you could probably use a little camp stove and a few dishes. Makes it easier than walking the half mile to the kiosks and at night they're not even open." Cassidy lit a cigarette and coughed a little. "Shit, I gotta go get a bag of ice for my cooler. See ya later, dude."

Tyler was glad to see how much Tucker seemed to be enjoying himself. After saying goodbye to the British girls who tearfully had to return to university because spring break was over, he had hiked around the cliffs at the end of the beach with Sam and Leo while they went spearfishing. Sunburnt and sleepy, he had flopped into one of the camp chairs and was checking his phone for the first time all day.

"I heard they have live conga music tomorrow night at the Dinghy Dock," he told Tyler. "We oughta go."

"Definitely. That sounds cool." Tyler gasped a little; he had been slowly blowing up the air mattress, breath by breath, for the last hour.

"Leo says he heard that guy was murdered."

"Murdered?" He had been glad that Tucker had been away during the afternoon when the police had come around questioning campers, but apparently he was already on the inside track of island gossip.

"Well, you know, like he didn't die naturally. He was killed."

"Really. How so?"

"They think maybe someone drugged him and then smothered him."

"Or maybe he just took too many sleeping pills and then stopped breathing?"

"Well, that's not what they're saying." Tucker's phone dinged in his hand suddenly. "Oh, a message from Mom got through."

Tyler exhaled slowly into the mattress. "Hey – don't tell her about the uh, murder, okay? We don't want her worrying."

"No problema, amigo." He scratched his ankles. "Did we bring any bug spray?"

After dark, when Tucker went over to Sam and Leo's campsite again, Tyler took a walk down to the kiosks. He knew his son was going to get high with them and if he didn't watch, he could pretend he didn't know. Classic dysfunctional parenting behavior, but he didn't care. He felt even more dysfunctional when he discovered the bar at the kiosk stayed open late on Friday nights. He stood for a couple of minutes, staring at a bottle of local rum sitting on the shelf, imagining the gold liquid coursing its warmth through his veins. The pull was too strong – he couldn't go there.

"Buenas noches," he greeted the bartender finally. "Una cerveza, por favor."

He held the frosty can of beer to the side of his cheek for a second before downing it in a few hearty gulps. "Una más, por favor."

Yes, he was acting recklessly, but he was on vacation. And it felt so good.

A short distance away, he could see the blue lights of a police cruiser circling the parking lot. There was still a murder investigation going on.

"Una Pain Killer, por favor. Gracias, Wilfredo." Tyler recognized the wiry camper whose tent and mattress had been slashed the other night. Despite the casual atmosphere of the campground, he wore a jaunty Puerto Rican style straw hat with a flashy t-shirt and black cargo shorts decorated with rivets and D-rings. "How you doing, man?" he nodded to Tyler. "Beautiful night, isn't it? I love every minute of my life here."

Tyler agreed with him cautiously. The last time he had seen this man, he'd been angry and swearing a blue streak.

"Didn't I see you out by Section E? I've been coming there for 20 years. You might have seen my big tent." The more he spoke, his accent displayed a distinctly New York character. "I'm Alejandro. They call me the king of the campground." He laughed.

"Where you from?" Tyler asked, in the way of all travelers.

"Originally Spanish Harlem, but I've lived a lot of places recently."

"Oh, I spent a lot of time in Manhattan myself at one point." His journalism career in the city seemed like ancient history; he could not even remember how long ago it had been.

They bantered back and forth for a while about favorite uptown and downtown places before their conversation came back around to the campground and Culebra. They exchanged the rumors they'd heard about how the dead man had been murdered – Alejandro said Ivan had been a son of a bitch who pissed a lot of people off, may he rest in peace.

Alejandro seemed sufficiently inebriated that Tyler had no trouble declining his offer to take a ride into town to visit another bar. "Thanks, but I've got a son back at the campsite I need to keep an eye on."

"Maybe tomorrow night then; you know about the Saturday night conga music – I'd be honored to take you and your son to the Dinghy Dock to experience some of the real partying on this island." With a cordial tip of his straw hat, he moved away with a loping unsteady gait, dragging one leg at an awkward angle. There was definitely some back story there for another time, Tyler thought.

He watched Alejandro, drink in hand, stop to chat amiably with the police cruiser on the way to his car. Apparently there was no problem with driving drunk on Culebra. At least not if you were Alejandro, the king of the campground.

The surf was up the next morning on Flamenco and the beach by the campground had virtually disappeared. The usually peaceful crescent of white sand was a roiling sea of breakers and rollers that looked more like Malibu than the Caribbean. There would not be any day-trippers strolling to the campground end of the beach today to take their selfies on the half-sunken tank that stood as a testament to Culebra's infamy in U.S. military history.

Tyler had learned that, throughout the first part of the twentieth century, into World War II and even beyond, Culebra had been used as a bomb testing ground by the Navy, making the island an undesirable destination for tourists to visit and a less than pleasant place for the natives to live. Back in the day, many locals had been relocated to St. Thomas, a scant twelve miles east but worlds away, and the few that stayed were hardscrabble poor, their beautiful beach area becoming the site of live unexploded grenades, making it dangerous to traverse. As the rest of the Caribbean became a vacationer's paradise, Culebra stood still in time, without the colonial character of more southern islands and without the resorts or development. Finally in the 1970s, President Nixon gave Culebra back to its rightful owners. Local residents were given a "parcela" to build a house and as long as they lived there for ten years they could buy their property for a dollar. Today their funky ramshackle structures were worth a small fortune when marketed to the right prospective buyers. A few tanks still remained at Flamenco Beach as reminders of less happy times, now flamboyantly painted in colorful native designs and photographed many times a day by indiscriminate tourists from San Juan to Beijing. More disturbing were the signs that said "Peligro!", warning of the dangers of unexploded mines that apparently still lurked in the jungle like a dormant demilitarized zone, however, most people seemed to ignore them.

Fortified by early morning coffee and an egg sandwich from the kiosk of a petite, pretty woman named Rosita and her elderly mother who sold fresh fruit protected from insects by a mesh strainer, Tyler walked back to camp with the "pirate" they had spotted on the first night. Despite the swashbuckling appearance of bandana, earring and tattooed chest, Tom was actually the owner of a restaurant in Ann Arbor, Michigan who continued to run his business via cell phone during his extended stay in Culebra. He carried twelve cans of beer on one burly shoulder and a bag of ice in the other. When they passed Alejandro limping unsteadily on the path in the other direction, Tyler asked Tom about him.

"Oh, Jandro has quite a past. He was a medic in Vietnam, got shot up and left for dead in a rice paddy — some serious damage there. When he came back he joined the Black Panthers and got jailed for a murder he didn't commit. But that's only the beginning of his story." Tom coughed harshly. "Get to know him — he'll be happy to talk about it. The man loves to impress people with tales of his life."

Tyler glanced over his shoulder at the friendly little man who called greetings to everyone along his way. No, nothing was ever as straightforward as it might seem. As they approached Section E, Tyler reassured himself that among the unexpectedly unique long-term characters there were also the usual backpackers, retired couples and families, all of whom went about their own business and

27

doled out their friendship in reserved helpings. But the yellow police tape surrounding Ivan's tent seemed to challenge that assumption.

"What about this guy, Ivan?" Tyler asked him. "You have any theories on him?"

Tom spat derisively in the leaves along the path. "He was an asshole. Whatever happened to him, he had it coming. Stop by and have a beer later, man." He turned off the trail towards his campsite.

Tyler and Tucker spent the day at the other end of the beach, bodysurfing the big waves and swimming in a calmer man-made cove that had apparently earned the ironic name of the "Shark Tank." In the early afternoon a big pleasure boat motored in and dumped forty tourists wearing only bathing suits and waterproof neck pouches into the rough waters to make their way to shore. Tyler watched from the shade of a palm tree as the pale men and women staggered onto the sand, some looking stunned and seasick, like refugees after days at sea. A few carried snorkel equipment and some of the less confident swimmers wore life belts. They wandered the beach for an hour or so until the boat horn sounded and then they all scurried back from their "deserted island" rest stop to flounder or swim from shore to their ride home. A couple of last minute stragglers barely made it back in time to climb the ladder before the boat departed, playing loud salsa music as it headed towards Fajardo on the big island.

As he dozed in the mid-afternoon sun, Tyler wondered how many of those tourists got left behind and whether the tour company actually kept track of how many reboarded. It seemed like an easy way to sneak off or on to the island...

"Tyler. Tyler!" He shaded his eyes to see Tucker's lean silhouette hovering over him. "Sam is lending me his snorkel gear and I'm going to swim out around the cliffs with Leo while he looks for some fish for dinner." His boyish face was pleasantly sunburnt and relaxed in a way Tyler had never seen before. He realized that Leo was also

28

standing there, wearing the top to a wet suit and carrying a menacing-looking spear gun. This did not seem like a particularly safe arrangement for a kid from Vermont who had never snorkeled before, but he did not want to seem like an uncool dad.

"Okay. Probably a good idea to put your t-shirt on so you don't burn out there?"

Luckily Leo agreed and Tucker ran off a little distance to where his backpack was stashed.

Tyler sat up. "You know he's never snorkeled before, right?"

Leo laughed. "Yeah, no problem, Sam gave him some fins and we aren't going out very far." He indicated some shallow waters at the end of the beach where they could see the air pipes of two or three snorkelers moving along the surface of the water.

"Okay. Have fun. If I'm not here, I'll be back at the camp." As he watched the two of them move towards the water's edge, he reassured himself that Leo seemed extremely capable and experienced and that Tucker was probably safer learning to snorkel with him than with Tyler. Besides, what was an adventure without a little risk?

The sun was already behind the western hills by the time Tucker and Leo made it back to the campground. To keep from worrying, Tyler accepted Pirate Tom's offer of a beer. During the time Tyler had consumed one can, Tom had easily downed four as well a shot of whiskey.

Exhausted but happy, and with no harpoon wounds in his arms or legs, Tucker went back to their tent to take a nap before they headed out for the Saturday night conga music. While they were gone, Sam hooked up with a couple of long-limbed Danish girls who were helping him cook up a pot of chili. The boys certainly didn't seem to need to go out on the prowl to attract women. Leo said he was just going to smoke a bone and settle in for the night with them – going to town was just too much hassle and he'd seen the drummers dozens of times. But he assured them it was definitely fun.

"Alejandro always goes and he has a car in the parking lot," Tom confided. "Check with him and you can probably catch a ride. You'll be able to get a taxi to bring you back."

The outing was starting to seem more complicated than the usual demands of island life, but Tyler decided it was probably worth it. Apparently it was pretty much the only music that happened on Culebra.

Tucker would most likely have slept all night, but a few hours later Tyler roused him from his nap and after a quick open-air cold shower he was awake enough for anything. They walked the half mile to the parking lot and found Alejandro outside the bar with a colorful blended drink in his hand and an amiable shit-faced smile on his face.

"You sure it's safe for us to ride with him?" Tucker whispered.

"Yeah, I don't think he's really as drunk as he appears. He's got some war injuries that make him like that." It was definitely against his better judgment to get in the car with this man, but so far pretty much everything they had done here was against his better judgment and it was going pretty well.

"Buenos noches, amigos! Estamos listo?" Alejandro stood up and swung his hips in a circle. "Let's go dancing, ey? You want to get a drink to go?"

"Oh, I think we're all set." Tyler avoided Tucker's eyes. This was hardly different from getting stoned senseless in a hammock at the campground. Well, maybe a little different.

At 9:30 on a Saturday night, the Dinghy Dock was crowded with drinkers and diners and the atmosphere was alive with the anticipation of the music to come. The drummers were setting up their equipment along the water's edge, against a backdrop of twinkling sailboat masts in the softly lapping bay. Attracted by a light trained beneath the surface, an impressive school of large fish made an exciting display for onlookers and Tyler and Tucker

30

spent several minutes watching them swim and swarm in the dark waters.

"You see anything like this today when you were out snorkeling?"

Tucker shook his head. "No, the fish were smaller and more colorful in their natural reef environment. This is a little weird, like a fish farm or a zoo."

And then, at the sound of the drums, their interest in the fish was replaced by the colorful local scene that began to take shape. As the rhythm of the congas took hold, bodies began to move in time to the pulsating beat, shaking and stamping, hips rolling and writhing. Starting slow and sexy, the throbbing tempo began to increase, getting faster and faster until the quick feet of even the most experienced dancers could not keep up with the lightning speed of the thumping hands of the drummers, finally ending in a crescendo of staccato taps accompanied by shouts of satisfaction from the audience.

Another number began, this one more Latin in its rhythm, and two very slim dark dancers leaped to the floor and began a practiced series of movements that made it almost impossible for the rest of the crowd to keep up. The man wore a tight black tank top and skin-tight jeans; his partner wore short sparkly booty shorts and a tiny half shirt of some loosely crocheted material – their lack of clothing accentuated the litheness of their lean bodies. After a suitable period of admiration, the other dancers could restrain themselves no longer, and moved in again. Blonde women in bright island prints, barefoot sailors in shabby khakis, even members of a wedding party, overdressed in sequins and heels, all merged as one pulsing primal unit as they whirled and gyrated to the heartbeat of the island.

Tyler looked over at Tucker; transfixed by the drummers, his eyes were dark and shining, and his feet kept time to the music. "Want something to drink?" he asked loudly. "I'm going to get a beer. And, no, I am not buying you a beer," he said in response to the half-grin that dimpled one of his son's cheeks.

While he waited in line to get the bartender's attention, he watched the interaction of the people around him. The drumming seemed to inspire primal urges – there was more touching now, more flirting, heads closer together, mouths pressed to ears to be heard over the rising loudness of voices, drumbeats and chanted songs. It was easy to tell the local Puerto Ricans apart from the tourists. Their clothes had a distinctive style; he saw sheer black lace leggings over meaty thighs, a horizontally striped miniskirt worn low to reveal a jeweled bellybutton piercing, bedazzled tunics, studded shirts and hair dyed or streaked in a multitude of Crayola hues. There were skinny Italian women in short chic dresses and brawny Scandinavian men in t-shirts emblazoned with American place names like "Missouri" or "Cleveland, Ohio." He recognized a couple of young Americans from the campground by their elaborately tattooed arms and Alejandro sitting at the bar grinning broadly in an alcohol-induced haze.

When he finally turned around, beer in hand, Tucker was no longer where he had left him. Making his way to the other side of the dancing throng, he saw his son standing along the edge of platform by the moored dinghies. A young girl now held his rapt attention as she chatted animatedly to him, waving a slender hand out toward the bay and laughing. She wore a pale yellow halter top and white running shorts that displayed the muscular physique of a swimmer or basketball player and the deep tan of someone who had spent more than a few weeks vacation in the islands. When she turned her face, Tyler saw big eyes and angular cheeks framed by a swingy chin-length curtain of dark hair and a large smiling mouth. His parental fascination would not let him look away as he watched Tucker warm up to her overtures.

Someone tugged at his arm and a moment later he was on the dance floor, bumping and grinding with a petite redhead he'd never seen before in his life. It was fun – he could not remember the last time he had felt more lighthearted – or lightheaded for that matter. Closing his eyes he gave himself over to the beat.

By the end of the first set, he was sweaty and exhausted and ready to head back to camp. Searching vainly for Tucker, he eventually found him sitting at the far end of the "dock" with the dark-haired girl, their feet dangling over the edge, still engrossed in conversation. He felt some premature panic at the possible outcome.

"Hey, how you guys doing?"

Tucker glanced up briefly at him. "Fine," he shrugged. "Looked like you were having a good time kickin' it up out on the dance floor."

The girl glanced over her shoulder at Tyler and giggled. "Now I know what you will look like in thirty years," she said playfully to Tucker.

His cheeks flushed as he turned back to gaze at the bay. "Not really."

More like forty years, thought Tyler, but he didn't say it.

The girl extended her hand. "Hi, I'm Chloe."

"Tyler. Hey, Tucker, I hate to say it, but I am ready to call it a night and go back to Flamenco. What do you say?"

Tucker's eyes darkened defiantly. "Really? Because I'd like to stay a while longer."

Tyler swallowed the last of his beer and looked across the room to the bar where Alejandro slumped a little as he chatted with a friend. "Well, let me talk to Alejandro – maybe he can bring you back."

"Yeah, I don't think so. How are you getting back?" His tone was a little accusing.

"I'm going to find a taxi. I suppose you can do the same." He did not feel good about this conversation.

Chloe held up her phone. "I have the numbers of at least five cab drivers right here. I'll make sure he gets back. Want me to call you one right now?"

"Uh, yeah, that would be great." The knot of responsibility in his stomach tightened sickeningly and he leaned over Tucker's shoulder. "Buddy, can I talk to you privately for a moment?"

Reluctantly the boy got to his feet and looked down at Chloe. She waved sweetly to him as she held her cell to her ear.

"I'm not going yet." His whole posture hardened into a rebellious stance.

"Okay. Okay. I just want you to be smart. Make good choices. Do you have money?" Tyler dug in the pocket of his shorts and handed him a twenty dollar bill.

"Thanks. Don't worry. I'm not stupid. I go out by myself all the time in Vermont." As the defensiveness slipped from his face, Tucker's youthful innocence surfaced again and Tyler felt his heart muscles tighten.

"Okay," he repeated. "You have your phone, right?" He wanted to ask him if he had a condom, but it was not like he had one to offer if the answer was no. He was probably assuming way too much. Tucker had only met Chloe an hour ago. "Be cool and have fun. I'll see you back at the campground."

Chloe jumped lightly to her feet and joined them. "They're coming right now – you should go wait outside," she told Tyler.

A warm-up drum roll on the congas announced the next set was about to begin. "Thanks, nice to meet you, Chloe. Make sure my boy gets home safely."

"No, worries, amigo." She gave him a sweet smile and put her arm through Tucker's. "I'm really good at getting home safely. I do it every night."

When he reached the steps up to the street, Tyler looked back. Tucker and Chloe were still standing, faces close together, laughing like old conspirators. Or young people just hooking up for the first time.

The campground was as quiet as it should be at midnight and he enjoyed the light breeze as he walked silently along the sandy road to Section E. He was grateful for the comfort of the air mattress, although it did seem to be losing a little air. His last thought was that he would have to blow it up again in the morning.

It was already hot when he awoke, the sunlight streaming in through the open tent window at an angle that fell across his chest. The scuffling of the chickens scratching and clucking in the dirt outside sounded familiar and pleasant. With a satisfying stretch he sat up.

He was alone. Had he really overslept so long that Tucker had actually got up before him? The unlikeliness of that happening was so extreme he knew it wasn't true.

Bolting out of "bed," he unzipped the door and stepped out into the yard. A short distance away, he could see Sam and Leo making breakfast on their camp stove. "You guys seen Tucker this morning?" he called. They shook their heads.

"I don't think he made it back last night." He walked over and sat down heavily on their picnic bench, realizing that he had a bit of a hangover. "Either of you know a girl named Chloe?"

CHAPTER THREE

Neither Sam nor Leo knew a girl named Chloe. They were both pretty nonchalant about the fact that Tucker had not returned from the previous evening's adventure, Leo grinning and murmuring quietly to Sam, "So maybe he got some."

Tyler walked over to Alejandro's oversized tent but there were no signs of life there yet. Silver duct tape gleamed where it had been used to repair the slash in the side of the wall. Peering in one of the screen windows, he saw only a couple of empty air mattresses with disheveled sheets but no people. He wondered if Alejandro had made it back last night.

Other campers were moving about their sites, eating, washing, or just hanging around. He talked to Jane, a rugged single woman from Vancouver who had spent the winter on Culebra, and rarely left the campground. Jane gave him a cup of black coffee and her sympathy. "Teenagers are tough – just remember how you were at that age."

Ned and Kate, an older couple with white hair and stooped shoulders, who were heading off with their snorkeling equipment, also reassured him. "It's an island – he can't go far. Don't worry – he'll show up when he gets hungry."

He was relieved to see Cassidy shambling down the trail – he seemed to know a little something about everyone and everything on Culebra. "Chloe? Let me see – what's she look like, man? Sorta skinny and muscular with a cute butt?"

Tyler had not noticed her butt. "Tallish with dark hair cut around her face like this?" He made some angular motions with his hands.

"Yeah, yeah, I know who you mean. I think she's L's daughter."

Tyler flushed with relief for this smallest amount of information. "L? What's that stand for?"

"I don't think it's the letter L – I think it's more like French or something. E-l-l-e."

"Elle. Okay. Do you know where she's staying?"

"Well, they kinda live here, I think. She was housesitting for a guy in Zoni for a while, then she was boat-sitting, now she rents a cabin, I think she might be trying to buy a place. Elle's a cool older chick, we've hung out a few times."

Right now Tyler didn't care to find out what this might mean. "So if you were looking for Elle, where would you start?"

Cassidy took off his worn yellow canvas cap and scratched a spot on the back of his head where his blond hair had thinned to almost balding. "Dude, in the daytime, I haven't got a clue what she does. But at Happy Hour you can usually find her at the Sand Bar in front of the ferry dock. The drinks are super cheap there."

At the look on Tyler's face, he clapped a long stringy arm around his shoulder and gave him a companionable squeeze. "Now don't you be worrying about your boy – Culebra's a good place to be sowing some wild oats. My boy visited a few years ago and had the time of his life. He couldn't thank me enough for letting him go a little crazy here."

Tyler took a deep breath. "You seen Alejandro this morning?"

Cassidy nodded his head towards the sandy road. "At the kiosk having a little Sunday morning hair of the dog. I'm sure he's still there."

In his haste and worry, Tyler did not realize he hadn't even put on any footwear until he stepped on a sharp stick near Section B as he moved aside to let a large Puerto Rican family pass by. The father carried a heavy cooler and an umbrella, children in bathing suits had inflatable water toys around their necks, a couple of plus-size women in spangled bikinis carried overstuffed leopard-print tote bags with towels and gear. Another man with a couple of folding chairs over one shoulder, gripped a small boom box which played lively salsa music. It was Sunday – the day for local outings to the beach. Although he could not understand their rapid-fire Spanish, he could hear the distress in their voices at how the high waves made navigating this section of the beach virtually impossible. Before he realized what was happening, the whole group turned around and followed Tyler back to the parking lot where there was access to a wide, sandy and crowded stretch of public beach.

Approaching the kiosk area, he began unconsciously scanning the customers and beachgoers for signs of Tucker. He tried to remember the color of the t-shirt his son had been wearing last night – he thought it had been a faded royal blue one with a store logo, maybe Abercrombie or Aeropostale. He chastised himself mentally for not remembering. However, he did recognize the cocky little straw hat and orange camp shirt at Wilfredo's bar.

"Alejandro, que pasa?" Tyler felt a bit breathless – he had not realized how fast he was walking.

"Good morning, my man. How are you on this beautiful day?" Alejandro gave him a beatific smile and took another sip of a drink in a strangely turquoise hue.

"Not so perfect. I'm looking for my son. Any chance he came back with you last night?"

Alejandro shook his head and laughed a little. "Not that I remember. But I was feeling no pain by then." He reached out and touched Tyler's wrist with forward familiarity. "I wasn't supposed to bring him back, was I?"

"No, no. I just thought maybe –"

"Good, good." He patted Tyler's hand and let go. "So you haven't seen him since then?"

"Um, no." Tyler eyed the bright drink, wondering what made it that tropical shade. "What is that?"

"They call it a 'Horny Margarita.' I don't know what's in it but it is damn good. You want one?"

"Probably better not." But he was going to need something to steady his nerves soon. "He was with a girl named Chloe. Elle's daughter?"

"Oh, yeah, yeah, I know who you mean." Alejandro nodded enthusiastically.

"So you know where they live?" he asked eagerly.

"No, no, I just know who they are, I don't really know them." Alejandro lit a cigarette. "Just chill – he'll show up sooner or later."

Everyone advised him the same thing – no one seemed to understand his anxiety. This was not usual behavior for Tucker, but then, this was not a usual place.

"If you want to find Elle – just go to the Sand Bar. Someone there will know where she is. You'll like her – she's a pretty woman." Alejandro put on a pair of very dark sunglasses, blew out a puff of smoke and then sipped his drink. "Life is good, amigo. No problemas."

He sat on a bench for a while, watching the crowds and the parking lot, expecting at any minute to see Tucker's familiar long limbs unfold themselves from a vehicle and come striding towards him. He told himself he would not be angry, he would not yell; he made a mental picture of himself being casual, concealing the worry and relief in his voice, asking Tucker if he'd had a good time. After a while one of his legs started to jiggle nervously and he decided he probably ought to get something to eat and walk back to camp. He would do better staying calm in a less charged-up environment.

A white bagel with cream cheese had seemed as if it would be comfort food, but it sat like a rock in his tight stomach by the time he reached Section E. What would he do if this happened at home, he wondered. And then, of course he knew what he would do.

Diving into the tent, he searched for his cell phone, finding it finally in a front pocket of his daypack. Dead as a doornail. It took a little longer to find the charging cord. He headed back towards the kiosks, this time wearing his flip-flops. Before he'd gone too far, Cassidy waylaid him.

"Mackie, let me show you a secret." He motioned him over to the toilet quad building. "Only us tall guys know about this one." He walked into one of the stalls and pointed above the door frame where there was an electrical outlet. Someone else's phone was resting on top of it and already plugged into one side. "We try to keep this under the general radar, so don't go advertising it to everyone."

It only took a few minutes for the screen to light up. The service was weak but he didn't need much to send a text. "*Where are you? Everything okay?*" he typed into the phone as it dangled from its wire. Then he balanced it on the top of the door frame to let it charge.

He waited for about ten minutes but there was no immediate reply. Could be the message hadn't really been sent, it was hard to tell out here. Restlessly, he strolled out to the beach and watched what were now breakers crashing into the sand. The sea seemed to be as agitated as he was today.

When he retrieved his phone an hour later, there was still no reply message and now he was beginning to feel pissed off. How could Tucker be so irresponsible and not check in at all, even by mid-day. He reminded himself that sometimes the teenager didn't even wake up until noon and if he had been up until dawn boffing some broad – he stopped himself in the middle of that reflection, appalled that he was thinking of his son in those terms.

He was not sure what to do with himself. He tried reading to pass the time but he could not keep his mind on the narrative, looking up every few minutes to see if maybe Tucker was walking down the path. When Pirate Tom and his girlfriend Lisa invited him over to do a shot of whiskey with them, it was hard to turn them down. But he felt he had to keep his wits about him, just in case of whatever.

An hour later, however, he returned to their campsite. In the still inertia of early afternoon, the fiery liquid burned its way down his throat and sent a pleasant numbing rush to his racing brain. It was just enough to help him think a little clearer. He knew he could not accept the eagerly offered second shot; even after ten years this slope was too slippery for him, especially in what might be a time of crisis.

"Elle – do you know a woman named Elle?" he asked them.

"Yeah, yeah, she comes around the campground sometimes." Tom lit a cigarette and stared out to sea, his expression hardening. "We know Elle. She was friends with Ivan, wasn't she, Lise?"

Lisa took a drag of Tom's cigarette before answering. "Yeah, she was." She looked sideways at him, her eyes narrowing. "Might have even been lovers – she spent the night a few times. But maybe she was just too wasted to get home."

"Ever meet her daughter, Chloe?"

She shook her head. "I've heard Elle talking about her though. Guess she is like a genius or something and she got expelled from some fancy-ass expensive boarding school so now she lives here doing a ...what do they call it when you don't go to college or something..."

"Gap year?"

She took another hit off the whiskey bottle and pointed her finger at him, squinting. "Bingo. Give the man a prize."

He needed more than a prize right now. Thanking them, he wandered back towards his own campsite but was distracted by the delicious aroma of cooking food coming from the direction of Jane's tent. He found Jane and Cassidy there, raptly watching a pan of frying bacon over a propane camp stove. "BLTs, man. You want one?"

As crazy as some of them seemed, the long-termers in Section E were generous to a fault. Resting in a swinging

41

hammock with the buzz of whiskey still in his head and a delicious sandwich in his hand, life couldn't have been more perfect – if only the phone in his pocket would vibrate with a check-in from Tucker.

By four o'clock, he could stand it no longer and headed at a fast clip towards the parking lot where the publicos were filling up with day-trippers headed back to the Fajardo ferry. Jammed into a seat between beach gear and a mother with a baby and a folded stroller, he tried to keep his eyes focused on the vehicles passing in the other direction, just on the off chance that he might see Tucker's familiar silhouette in one of them.

After baking all day in the sun, the asphalt and pavement of "downtown" Dewey radiated a heat that felt almost suffocating to Tyler in his keyed-up condition. He found Hotel Kokomo, one of those ubiquitous low-budget establishments present near every ferry dock around the world. Beneath its oversized sign were three doors; the middle one advertised itself as the "Sand Bar." Across the street people were crowded into lines waiting for the boat that would take them to the big island, away from their weekend outings and back to everyday existences. In the distance the skylines of two islands could be seen – to the north, the more mountainous one was Puerto Rico, to the south lay Culebra's sister island of Vieques.

Outside the Sand Bar there were some cast iron tables and chairs that accommodated an eclectic mix of backpackers with dreadlocks and computers, disheveled sailing types and a few very inebriated locals. One man was selling mangos and plastic baggies of bush peas, which he shelled as he sat. For their listening pleasure, the strident strains of some unidentifiable electric rock music blasted from a loud speaker above the door.

He paused momentarily, dredging up the investigative journalist persona that had been his heart and soul for so many years. His former identity was now buried beneath the small town politics and high school basketball scores

42

which were the breaking news in his Vermont world. A few slow dances with death-defying experiences had dulled his appetite for the cloak-and-dagger drama of criminal exposés or the zipline-like thrill of missing person discoveries. He reminded himself that, back in the day, he had been really good at it. Like really good.

The interior of the Sand Bar seemed almost blindingly dark after the brightness of the late afternoon sunlight. It took a moment for his eyes to adjust to the shadowy atmosphere lit by a blinking display of multi-colored laser lights against the rear walls. At the back of the space was a narrow bar where a few patrons sat watching a football game on a TV, despite the deafening music. The only woman was the bartender, a plump blonde in a sequined tank top and cut-off denim shorts that showed a little too much of her soft thighs, at least in Tyler's opinion.

"What can I get you?" she asked smiling tentatively, her pale blue eyes doing a quick experienced bartender's assessment of his character and the sobriety of his condition.

Forcing a grin, he gave her his best imitation of his former self. "Actually I'm looking for a woman named Elle. Have you seen her?"

Her smile became tight-lipped. "Not yet. But she'll probably be along soon. She always is."

"What about her daughter, Chloe?"

The smile faded. "What about her?"

"Do you ever see her here too?"

She shook her head. "Hardly. She's only seventeen. Drinking age is eighteen in Puerto Rico. You won't see me serving her." Her words seemed to hold some double meaning which he didn't care to interpret. And the only bizarre thought that filled his head was that Tucker had been hanging out with an "older" woman.

With a cold can of Medalla in his hand, he went outside to wait for the arrival of Elle, taking a seat at a table with a couple of young Germans who busily typed on their iPads and ignored him. Nervously he checked his phone again. No message from Tucker. He tried actually calling him this time but after a single ring, it went right to voice mail. "Hey, sorry I missed you, bro. Leave me one and I'll catch up with you." Tyler shook his head at the"bro" part, but when the beep went off he could not control himself. "Where the fuck are you, bro? This is so uncool. Call me as soon as you get this message."

Down the street he could see a slim young woman approaching. She wore a beat-up straw hat and big sunglasses; her gauzy green and yellow sundress billowed a little in the late afternoon breeze coming in off the sea and wisps of long sun-bleached white blonde hair blew lightly across her face. As she got closer, he realized she was not so young at all — at closer range her tanned limbs appeared wiry not willowy, a map of creases ran through the dark freckles of her cleavage, her cheeks were weathered with deep laugh lines and crow's feet that only came with experience and time. When she removed her sunglasses, her kaleidoscopic green eyes took his breath away before they met his with reproachful mirth.

"Are you checking me out?" He felt suddenly self-conscious as she did a frank and open assessment of his looks in the same manner he had been appraising hers. He could see her adding up the sum of his parts — unruly gray curls, tawny irises behind expensive titanium glasses with transitional lenses half-darkened by the lengthening rays of sunlight, the three days' worth of stubble on his unshaven chin, his faded t-shirt with the legend "It's Better at Burke" over a graphic of a skier on a mountain, right down to the golden hairs on his sunburned shins and the sand stuck between his toes. She returned her gaze to his face, one hand resting defiantly on her hipbone, waiting for his answer.

"Yeah," he said. "I am." Despite the overwhelming stress of his situation, he felt a spark of something for the first time in a while. "Are you Elle?"

"Yeah. I am." She repeated his words with a crooked smile, a deep dimple appearing among the other fine wrinkles of her face. She was beautiful in a way he felt he had only recently begun to appreciate. "And you are…"

"Tyler Mackenzie." He sat up straighter and stuck out his hand which she squeezed gently (and in his mind, provocatively) with slim strong fingers before releasing it. "I think you have a daughter named Chloe?"

Her pleasant grin instantly became a frown. "Why – is she in trouble?"

"I don't know. Have you seen her today?"

She shook her head, peering at him even more suspiciously from beneath the brim of her hat. "No, I don't need to watch her every move. She's a grown girl."

"Well, she was the last person I saw my son with last night when I left him at the Dinghy Dock. And he hasn't been in touch with me since."

Her face softened into a smirk. "So maybe they're a bit smitten with each other. No crime in that. And maybe you're being too overprotective as a parent."

"I think that's a bit unfair – I'd say it's just the opposite. I left my sixteen-year-old son at a bar in a strange place and haven't seen or heard from him in almost twenty-four hours. I don't think there is anything wrong with being not entirely comfortable with that."

They stared at each other distrustfully for a few seconds.

"He's only sixteen?" she said finally. She took off her hat and set it down on the table. "Hold on, I need a drink. You want another?"

The Medalla can in his twitching hand was empty, he realized, and nodded his thanks. As he watched her go inside, he again thought how youthful she looked from behind, with her small stature and easy movements. But something about her presence scared him as much as it intrigued him.

She was gone a long time – if she hadn't left her hat, he would not have believed she was coming back. But eventually she emerged from inside carrying a pale pink drink in one hand and a beer in the other. Vodka and cranberry, he surmised. The preference of all skinny women.

"Sorry," she apologized. "I just heard some really disturbing news."

"What's that?" he asked after a satisfying swallow.

"A local real estate agent was found dead this morning. That's two people in less than a week." She had a grim expression on her face.

"Natural causes?" He knew the answer before she shook her head.

"They're not saying how, but no." She took such a deep sip of her drink that half of it disappeared.

"Did you know him?"

"Perry? Yeah. He was my real estate agent. I've been trying to buy a house here." She sighed. "First Ivan, now Perry. What a fucking mess. Doesn't feel like a safe place to live anymore."

Tyler was even more worried now about Tucker. "So would you do me a favor and give your daughter a call? I just would like to know my son is with her, that's all."

With another sigh and a dark look, she dug a smart phone out of her oversized woven handbag. After a few quick strokes, she held it up to her ear. "Chloe, it's Mom. I've got a guy here with me looking for his son, named..." she glanced questioningly in Tyler's direction.

"Tucker. Tucker Brookstone."

"...Tucker. He says you were with him last night. Give me a call if he's with you or you know anything. The guy is kind of, uh, desperate." That flirtatious grin flickered across her lips again. "Anyway, whatever, call me. I haven't talked to you in a few days. Let me know what you are up to. Love you." Elle put the phone down. "I don't know if she ever even listens to her voice mail. You know how kids are."

Nervously he drummed his fingers on the steel grating of the table. "Yeah, would you do me one more favor and text her? Tucker tends to respond that way more often."

46

With a gesture of slight annoyance, she picked the phone up again and typed a short message into it. "I'm sorry you're so worried," she said. "I'm sure they're fine."

"So can I ask you—" he hesitated a moment and then decided he didn't care if she thought he was prying. "Does Chloe live with you? Or does she stay somewhere else?"

"Yeah, she lives with me. If you can call it that. She's hardly ever home, doesn't wash dishes or pick her clothes up off the floor, usually sleeps wherever she ends up for the night. She's been here for the last nine months, since she got kicked out of school in the states. Her father couldn't deal with her anymore. There's nothing wrong with her, she's just a little wild. Can't say I was any different at her age."

Under any other circumstances, he might have just laughed and agreed with her. Now he felt like he needed every detail. "So what does 'a little wild' mean on Culebra?"

She laughed. "Not much. There isn't a road long enough or straight enough to drive faster than 50 miles an hour. It's not easy to find drugs harder than weed – maybe a few hallucinogenic mushrooms that grow in the cow patties. And even a cow is hard to come by here. You could definitely drink too much or party too hard with European tourists. Maybe sail off with a Caribbean pirate who put into the harbor for a few days. Just kidding," she said at the look of alarm on his face. "Well, maybe not – I did it once years ago." Elle sipped her drink, staring off into the distance of her own past for a moment. "I'm not worried about Chloe. She's super smart; she'll find her stride soon enough."

Tyler wished he had the same carefree confidence in his child that she had in hers. With his eyes still noting every pair of passersby that came around the corner, he asked, "So where was home?"

"Originally, western Pennsylvania. Then California for a while, New York City for some years, until I took my first trip to the Caribbean. I've been kind of a world-traveling island vagabond ever since. Except for the part where I fell in love, got pregnant and got married, in that order. Settling down in the New Jersey suburbs nearly took my sanity away – I take that back, it did take my sanity away."

"Ever get it back?"

"Not really. Finding Culebra six years ago made me feel a little less crazy." She sucked on a few ice cubes which was all that remained in her plastic cup.

"Let me get you another one of those." Tyler got to his feet, glad for anything that would keep him occupied. "Vodka and cranberry, right?"

Elle put two fingers to her lips and blew him a kiss. "Thank you, sweetheart."

But as soon as he was inside the bar, he felt antsy again, afraid that he might miss Tucker walking by, even though there was nowhere he could walk by to. He knew he should not have another beer, not if this was really a crisis where he needed all his wits about him, but Elle's casual manner was starting to make him feel that maybe he was over-reacting. It had not even been twenty-four hours yet. And what could happen on sleepy Culebra?

At the counter, the blonde bartender was pouring a line of shots from a bottle of Jose Cuervo. Four crusty-looking patrons raised them in unison. "To Perry," one of them said loudly. "Rest in peace, amigo."

A chorus of "Amens" followed, tequila was swallowed all around and the glasses were slammed hard against the bar. "Another round. I'm buying this one," said the tall dark man with wild white curls who Tyler recognized from a previous night out. He managed to get his drink order in between the second and third refills, and went back outside, his false sense of calm shattered by the toast to the second dead man in just a few days. What could happen on sleepy Culebra...apparently a lot.

Elle was talking on her phone when he returned. "Gotta go, sweetie. My drink just got delivered by a handsome man. Talk to you later." She slipped the phone back into her bag.

He looked at her questioningly and she shook her head. "Just a friend. Thanks for this."

He checked his own phone again, just on the unlikely off-chance that he had not felt it vibrate in his pocket. Nothing. He sat down, feeling helpless and frustrated.

"So what about you? Besides losing your son on a tropical vacation, what's your sad story?"

"The short version? Grew up on Long Island, had a career in the city as an investigative journalist, followed a story to northern Vermont, fell in love, lost my job and stayed there, fell out of love, moved to London with an old girlfriend and started working again. Then I almost got killed because of a story I was doing. And a couple of innocent bystanders did get killed. So I moved to Grenada." He stopped to take a breath and a swallow of beer.

Her eyes narrowed with interest. "Really — Grenada in the Grenadines? How long ago was this?"

"Sixteen years ago." He nodded. "Yeah, do the math."

"So what did you do there?"

"Tried to drink myself to death."

"Because...?"

"Because I was still alive." He grinned ruefully. "We're straying into the long version here."

She arranged herself more comfortably in her chair. "Let me check my calendar. Sunday night? I don't have anywhere I need to be."

"You have no idea what you're asking for, lady. For now, I'll just tantalize you with the high points. After five years, through the deviousness of some good friends, I ended up on the island of Bequia, tangled up with the same bad guys who caused me to leave London. And yes, they tried to kill me again, but I got the better of them the second time around. Along with an unexpected detox and a return of my dignity. As well as discovering I had a six-year-old son. Who was living in Vermont with his mother and another ex-girlfriend. I moved back to Vermont. Where I currently run a small newspaper and lead an uneventful life. Until now. End of short story."

"Huh." Her eyes were shining, a tapestry of blues and greens, almost iridescent like a peacock feather. Or a snake skin. "Who woulda thunk it. When do I get to hear the chapter book version?"

"Maybe someday." Just the brief mention of Lucy in Vermont had re-jangled his nerves again. If Lucy found out he had left Tucker at a bar and had lost track of him for nearly a day... It had been hard enough to get her to agree to let Tyler take him back to the Caribbean on vacation. She'd even agreed to sign a notarized piece of paper in case there was any legal trouble with him traveling as a minor with Tyler, who was not actually named as Tucker's father on his birth certificate.

"I think I need to get back to the campground before dark, in case he returns." He stood up abruptly, looking around for a taxi.

Elle pulled gently on his arm. "Relax, sailor. I have wheels – I'll drive you. Just let me finish this drink."

On the way to her vehicle, they stopped at Heather's Pizza for a couple of giant slices topped with spinach and goat cheese, which tasted way better than Tyler would have imagined. He ordered a couple more to go. Just in case Tucker was at the campsite. Or for when he returned.

Elle's 'wheels' turned out to be a blue golf cart, which was not unusual for Culebra. Unlike the shiny new rentals that tourists rode around in, hers was dusty and dented with worn-out seats and a shattered side mirror. "Put on your seat belt," she admonished him. "Really. They don't care if you drive with a drink in your hand, but they will fine you seventy-five dollars if you don't wear your seat belt."

As they bounced along the road to Flamenco Beach, she told him she had been trying to buy a house here for the last several months, but had been frustrated by multiple obstacles along the way.

"So you really want to live here permanently? I've only just met you, but somehow that doesn't fit your profile."

"Home base," she said. "And yes, Culebra totally suits me. When I first came to Puerto Rico, I had an apartment in Fajardo. The man I was – seeing – brought me here for a weekend and I fell in love. With the island, not him." There was obviously a lot more to the story that she wasn't telling.

Dusk was closing in as they crossed the last gully and speed bump into the campground parking lot. Again he wished the circumstances were different – he would enjoy spending a few more hours with this free-spirited woman – but given the situation, his feelings seemed inappropriate. They exchanged cell numbers and she promised to call if she heard anything from Chloe.

"If they don't turn up by morning we can spend the day worrying together tomorrow," she giggled. "I'm sorry, I know you don't think that's funny." She leaned out of the golf cart and gave him a quick squeeze and a kiss on the cheek. "And even if they do turn up, maybe we can spend the day together. After you finish spanking your son."

Despite his frame of mind, he laughed. "I'm in Section E," he said. "I know you know where that is."

"E for End of the World," she called. Pulling a U-turn, she drove away.

And Elle, he thought, as he walked hurriedly back to camp.

It was almost dark when he arrived at his tent. "Tucker! You in there?"

His hand shook as he unzipped the door flap. The tent was as empty as when he had left it, with no signs of anything having been disturbed.

"Fuck." He threw himself down onto the picnic table bench. "Fuck, fuck, fuck."

CHAPTER FOUR

He was awake most of the night, going over the what-ifs and wherefores. He laid out several strategies in his head of what he would do in the morning, ranging from absolutely nothing to calling in the National Guard. He needed to talk to someone who had been at the Dinghy Dock on Saturday night who might have seen or talked to Tucker and Chloe; Alejandro was an obviously poor choice but at least a place to start.

Just before dawn he made his way over to the outdoor showers, where he stripped off his clothing and let the cool water run over his sticky body and shock his numbed and exhausted brain back to life. There was no hot water or privacy for bathing at the campground, and most people washed with their swimsuits on and a few even brought collapsible shower tents. But right now none of these issues mattered to Tyler. He stood with his eyes closed, letting the steady stream run over his head, wishing he could stop time and never have to deal with his new reality.

When the sound of flip-flops on cement next to him indicated that he was not alone, he quickly shut off the water and reached for his towel. He nodded good morning to the young woman who looked away demurely, waiting for him to leave so she could have her own few minutes of privacy before full-on daylight.

Fortified by a cup of strong coffee from Rosita's kiosk, (which he was astonished to learn opened at 6am), he went back to Section E in search of Alejandro. Surprisingly, the man was up and sitting in a lawn chair on the screened porch of his fancy tent, loading up a pipe with his first hit of weed for the day. He wore only a pair of striped pajama bottoms and Tyler could see a couple of faded old-school style tattoos on his arms and torso.

"Buenos dias, my man," he greeted Tyler warmly. "Come join me in my humble abode and enjoy my beautiful view." Taking a deep toke of smoke into his lungs, he held the pipe out.

Tyler shook his head, wondering again how these people functioned as well as they did being high all the time. Although this morning, the idea was almost appealing – it would be an easy way to forget about everything and just be in the moment.

"Your son get back okay? What – he has not returned?" Alejandro appeared genuinely concerned. "Did you find that girl you were looking for – what was her name, Zoe?"

He recounted what little he had learned the night before. "So do you remember seeing them on Saturday night? Were they with anybody else?"

Alejandro smoked another bowl before answering. "Forgive me if I don't recall." His response was almost formal. "I have only the vaguest image in my mind of two beautiful young people leaning against the far wall on the other side of a crowded room."

Tyler felt an emotional catch in his throat. "So who should I talk to?"

"You might start with Carson; he's one of the owners of the bar and he is usually down at the end by the kitchen. Who knows – he might remember something." Alejandro rubbed his tattooed tricep muscle which Tyler now saw was imprinted with the image of fierce black cat.

"You a Panthers' fan?" he asked, nodding at the arm.

Alejandro laughed harshly. "No, I was a Black Panther for several years, back in the sixties and seventies, after I returned from Vietnam. I did good work back in the day, until I was wrongly imprisoned for a murder I did not commit."

For a moment Tyler thought he was joking, but Alejandro gazed out at the sea and went on.

"Spent some more time in the federal pen years later and I've been claustrophobic ever since. Being out here in the open restores me. And most of my enemies would never look for me here." He grinned broadly. "Just kidding you, man. All of my enemies are dead. Matty the Horse made sure of that before I got out."

"Okay. Well. Glad to hear that." Tyler didn't care if his disbelief was evident. He was pretty sure that Matty the Horse was a made-up character from the musical *Guys and Dolls*. "So where would I find this Carson?"

Alejandro shrugged. "Dinghy Dock, I guess. You'll know him – tall skinny guy, gray hair down to his waist, designer glasses. Speaks Spanish like a son-of-a-bitch."

It wasn't much of a lead. But at 8am on a Monday morning, it was something.

As he left Alejandro's campsite, his phone buzzed against his thigh and dinged softly. He could not get it out of his pocket fast enough. A text message from Elle: "*Good morning. Any signs of teenage life yet?*"

"*Nothing. You?*" he wrote back.

"*Nada. Calling a few of Chloe's friends. Text you if I learn anything. Hasta luego.*"

So even she was a little worried now.

Back at his own tent, he dug through Tucker's suitcase, searching for the boy's passport, eventually dumping everything onto the floor and emptying all the inner and outer pockets. He did the same with his backpack but again came up with zilch. Tucker's passport was not there – had he actually carried it with him that night? He found the charging cord for his phone, fifty dollars in cash and a wrinkled sheet of paper that turned out to be a vacation homework assignment from eleventh grade English class called "At This Moment." *"In a hundred words, describe what is happening around you. Use all your senses. What do you smell? What do you hear?...."*

His heart sank a little more as he held the phone cord in his hand. It had been thirty-six hours, more than that

54

since Tucker had last charged his cell. How many hours would the battery work? Obviously it all depended on usage. Of course he could probably use another person's charger, if it came to that.

Repacking all the clothes and gear, he tried to think where he had a photo of his son. He probably had one on his own phone somewhere; if not he could probably find one online on Facebook or Instagram. In the side pocket of his own duffel, he found the notarized letter of permission to travel and a photocopy of Tucker's birth certificate. Sitting crosslegged on the air mattress, he unfolded this document.

He had forgotten that Tucker was not even legally an American citizen. His birth certificate had been issued in London, naming Lucy Brookstone as his mother and Kip Kingsley as his father.

Tyler had never spoken to Tucker about why a celebrity known for his heavy metal music and decadent lifestyle was listed as a parent on his birth certificate. He was not sure how much Tucker knew about those aberrant few years in his mother's life, when she had gone off to write a magazine piece about the has-been rocker and ended up as his live-in lover, eventually as abused as every other substance in his debauched existence. A one night reunion with Tyler had produced Tucker, but it had taken six years before Tyler had caught up to them. It was not an era that either of them, Lucy or Tyler, liked to talk about, and he doubted that Lucy brought it up very often, if at all, with her son.

If it came down to him going to the police and having them put out an APB, there was a good chance that this hidden info would come to light. He knew he had to do everything possible to keep this from happening, even if it meant conducting the search himself.

A buzzing against his leg indicated another text from Elle. *"Coming to get you. Meet me in the parking lot in twenty."*

Cassidy walked with him, offering advice in his unhurried and casual manner, which Tyler only half-listened to. "Elle, she's a good girl," –" Cassidy called women of every age "girls" – "we were pretty close for a while when I first came to this island," – Tyler could easily guess what this meant – "hey, she was pretty good friends with Ivan, you know, the camper who died, you oughta ask her what she knows about that, I mean, after you find your boy, maybe."

But Tyler did not want to think about the dead men on Culebra right now.

Elle came driving up just as they hit the pavement. She and Cassidy greeted each other with the obligatory island kiss on both cheeks and then he asked her if he could catch a ride into town, swinging himself into the open back seat of the golf cart before she even replied.

She and Tyler did a simultaneous once-over of each other; today she was wearing a little lightweight dress stitched together of colorful embroidered t-shirt patches that showed off her tanned shoulders and sinewy legs. Her straw blonde hair was caught up in a clip and in the stark light of morning he could see a few strands that looked more white than yellow; her sunhat was stuffed into a bag at her feet.

"You checkin' me out?" he asked.

"Yeah, you not lookin' so good today, brudda," she replied, feigning a Caribbean accent. "Like maybe you didn't sleep?"

"Well, you are as lovely and candid as ever, sister. No, don't tell me." He held up a warning hand and then buckled the ragged ineffectual seat belt around his waist.

"Nothing I like better than a quick learner." As always, her words seemed to imply something other than what she was saying.

"So where are we going?"

"To find a guy named Spencer. They tell me he was seen with Chloe on Saturday night." He looked at her, but behind her sunglasses, her eyes stayed focused on the road.

"Are you worried yet?"

"Don't judge my parenting style, Tyler Mackenzie. Yes, a little. Just because I can't get in touch with her, not because I don't believe she is fine."

Neither of them spoke the rest of the way into town, both lost in their own preoccupation with the situation, but Cassidy filled most of the silence, shouting over his shoulder to Elle about the latest campground news. After they had finally dropped him off at the post office, Tyler turned to her. "So who is Spencer and where do we find him?"

"All I know is that he lives on a boat. Let's head over to the public dock and ask around. Oh, and he's a black man with dreadlocks. So that eliminates most of the other sailors on this island."

It took a couple of hours during which Elle exercised all her island connections before someone pointed out the little sailboat that Spencer was caretaking for an absentee owner. Then it took more than a few drinks at the Dinghy Dock to bribe a local sailor to tender them out to it, at which point they discovered that Spencer was not at home. At Tyler's suggestion, Elle climbed aboard and left a note stuck to the hatchway asking him to call her. They returned to the bar, no more enlightened then when they started.

"Is that Carson?" Tyler asked, nodding towards a lean man with Nordic features who was carrying boxes of liquor into the store room. "Alejandro said I should talk to him, he may remember them."

Elle pulled a pair of glasses out of her bag and peered across the room. "Yeah, that's him. Always makes my heart throb a little, he's still so cute." She tossed the glasses back into her bag. "And talented too. He was an artist for years before he bought into this place – you can see his work in the gallery upstairs."

Tyler felt nervous as he approached Carson and introduced himself. Carson was pleasant, friendly and sympathetic, apologizing profusely for not having any clear recollection of the young couple from a few nights before.

"You know, after a while it's all a blur, we have crowds every evening and Saturday nights especially. I could tell you I remember them if that's what you want to hear, but I probably can't really distinguish them from a dozen other pairs of kids I've seen in the last few days."

"Well, Chloe actually lives here, you might know her, she's Elle's daughter..." Tyler nodded toward Elle who was by the bar but Carson shook his head.

"Sorry, I don't keep track of the teenagers on this island, I have a couple of preschoolers so my social circle is a slightly different crowd. Yoga for toddlers, play groups, nap time – the only social life I currently have is serving customers here." If his kids were that young, his wife must be from another generation, Tyler thought distractedly.

With an experienced motion, Carson pulled his long silver hair back into a ponytail and then bent at the waist to rip open a carton. He began removing bottles of wine. "But I feel for you, man. I don't know what I would be doing if one of my kids disappeared."

Tyler had never really known what the expression "his heart lurched into his throat" meant until that moment. Swallowing hard, he asked hoarsely, "So who do you think I should talk to?"

"I would say the police, but they're pretty caught up in this double murder thing –you've heard about that, haven't you? Worse thing to happen on this island in years. A couple of runaway teens probably won't make their radar right now." A frown creased his brow suddenly and he stood up. "You say they were last seen on Saturday night? That was the night Perry was killed. I'm sure it's just a coincidence," he said quickly, seeing the look that flashed across Tyler's face. But it was pretty clear that maybe he didn't think so himself.

"How do they think he died? Any word on that yet?" Despite his innate desire to bury his head in the sand, Tyler's investigative instincts told him he should know as many facts as possible about that night.

"Don't know. They took his body over to San Juan for the autopsy. All I can tell you is that he was found yesterday morning floating face down in the bay around the back of the building. Captain Zeke found him when he rowed in for coffee." There was a sharp dinging sound and the next moment Carson was speaking rapidly in Spanish into his phone.

Tyler waved his thanks and wandered over to the edge of the wood-planked restaurant floor to stare into the water, its calm aquamarine surface playing counterpoint to a cloudless azure sky. The picture perfect view of paradise. If only. He assured himself that there was a bright side to his conversation with Carson – only one body had been found.

He returned to where Elle was sitting on the steps checking email on a battered iPad, a half-empty plastic cup of vodka and cranberry juice at her side. "Starting early?" he asked, as he moved the drink to sit down next to her.

"Don't judge me. And it's never too early on Culebra."

"Hey." He touched her bare arm and her eyes lifted to meet his. "I am not judging you. I get it."

Their gaze locked for a moment. "Okay, then." This time she affected a nasal Minnesotan twang; she obviously had an ear for accents.

"Can I borrow your device for a minute? I want to check Tucker's Facebook page."

"You betcha," she replied, still in her "Fargo" persona.

Years earlier, against Lucy's wishes, Tyler had been the one to help Tucker set up his social media accounts; it had been one of the weekend activities they had done together, son teaching father, father giving permissions and advice. He hoped the user names and passwords had not been changed since then. He was in luck; he watched the spinning icon as he connected to Facebook as Tucker Brookstone. A couple of keystrokes brought him to the profile page and then he sucked in his breath sharply.

"What?" Elle leaned against him, straining to see the screen.

59

"Look." He pointed to the most recent photo, posted Saturday night at 11:10pm. It was a selfie of Tucker and Chloe, heads close together, mugging for the camera against a backdrop of Dinghy Dock nightlife. The picture had almost 200 "Likes" and several comments from Vermont high school friends that Tyler scrolled quickly through. "Way to go, bro." "Looks like a hot night in the islands." "Score!" "Ever coming back?" "Who's the beautiful babe?" And then a few messages from unfamiliar faces that seemed to be Chloe's friends. "Chloe, been trying to reach you, amiga. Text me!" "So that's where you disappeared to on Saturday night. Let me know when you come up for air!"

Tucker pointed to the last comment from a girl named Salina, whose profile pic showed her doing a cartwheel in a white bikini on Flamenco Beach. "Do you know this one?"

"Salina Rodriguez. Yeah, she's Chloe's good friend. I already messaged her – she hasn't heard from her either." Elle swiped a finger across the screen to return to the photograph, peering intently at Tyler and back again, grinning. "He's cute – definitely has your good genes. Did you look like that at sixteen?"

"I guess so. Except unfortunately he's got his mother's English complexion. Burns easily. Chloe doesn't look much like you."

"No, takes after her dad. She got the long legs and height I always wanted. Her hair is not really that dark – she colors it. Likes the drama of black. At least she's kind of over her Goth phase."

Tyler clicked on Chloe Erickson's photo tag and up came a different profile page. Chloe did not seem to be a prolific poster, at least not recently – there were only random statuses from the last few months. "Erickson – is that your last name as well?"

"No, that's from Hans. I kept my own name. Keller. Elle Keller was already my personal brand and it had more of a ring to it." She downed the rest of her drink and stood up. "Let's go, I want to show you something."

"Hold on — let me email the photo of them to myself so I can have it on my phone to show people."

"Will you save it to my iPad also? I'd like to send it to a few friends too."

He quickly sent himself the Saturday night picture and saved it to her photo gallery also. Then, taking her outstretched hand, he rose with a groan from the wooden steps. "Getting old sucks, doesn't it." He handed her the iPad and she slipped it back into her voluminous bag.

"I wouldn't know. Apparently I've never grown up." She gave his fingers a quick squeeze before letting go. He followed her up the stairs, chastising himself internally for enjoying her flirtatious overtures at a time like this.

"Where are we going?" he asked as they climbed back into her golf cart.

"Do you have to know everything? You'll see." They drove through the traffic of town and headed towards the beach. By the airport, she turned off onto a side road into a neighborhood of low flat-roofed houses constructed of cement or wood; most of them had traditional louvered windows and front porches crowded with the debris of everyday living. Some had yards shaded by mango trees and palms, while others were dusty and desiccated with weeds and dirt that passed for lawns under the heat of the sun. Brilliant bougainvillea and hibiscus blooms added bright spots of color along chicken wire fencing and peeling picket fences. Aging pickup trucks and rusting jeeps were parked in front of a few residences and a rooster crowed loudly from the top of one vehicle, marking his fiefdom.

Elle pulled to the side of the road and turned off the engine. Perched on a slight rise there was a simple cottage painted in a warm orange hue, like the inside of a papaya. A wide wooden sundeck extended across the front, from one end to the other, shaded by a tall tree with long gnarled branches and thick green foliage. A sign tacked to its wide trunk read, "Se Vende."

"This is it." She gazed dreamily at the property. "The house I am trying to buy."

"Nice. What's stopping you?"

He could see her jaw muscles tightened. "I'm working on it, I'm working on it. It's not as easy as you might think. Most of these houses don't have titles. A lot of people end up owning the structure but not the land itself. And affordable houses are getting harder and harder to find."

"Who owns it?"

"A Puerto Rican guy who moved to Brooklyn. His father built it when the 'parcelas' were being handed out back in the seventies. Ten years and a dollar and you could be a land-owner. Only the deeds were never actually written. At least not the way we expect."

She had climbed out of the vehicle and was walking towards the building now. He followed her cautiously, picking his way across the untended path that led to the steps of the deck. Up closer he could see that the wooden struts were rotten and missing in places.

"Looks like it needs some work."

Elle was already perched on the edge of the deck, roosting happily like an exotic tropical bird. "Of course. Anything worth having takes work."

"Speaking of work—" he moved carefully to a place next to her that looked fairly sturdy. "How do you make your money? Or are you independently wealthy? If you don't mind my asking."

She gave him a sideways glance. "Are you a golddigger, Tyler Mackenzie? Looking for a sugar mama who owns a beautiful mansion with a seaside view?" As she spoke, a chicken strutted across the yard followed by several half-grown chicks and then disappeared into the bushes.

"If I were, I wouldn't be hanging around with you, Peter Pan, talking about redecorating a tree house you don't even own yet."

Her laughter loosened the tension that was starting to build between them. "I was pretty down and out by the time I got to Fajardo. My – uh – landlord helped me out for a while, letting me work off my rent. It was a less-than-perfect arrangement, but I was near to broke. When I first got to Culebra, I did a lot of boat and housesitting so that I at least had a place to live. Then my father died a few years ago and I inherited a small amount of money. Not enough to live on forever, but if I invest it wisely, it might be able to support me modestly. Even a rundown bungalow on this island can be rented in season for a tidy little income."

"So what did you do before that?"

"I was a freelance stylist for fashion photo shoots. Made enough money working a few days a month to live comfortably or travel during my time off. It was a good gig for a long time. But no pension and pretty much no Social Security."

Tyler nodded knowingly. His situation was not so different. "You really want to be tied down to a house on Culebra?"

She jumped up. "No, I don't want to be tied down to anything. But it makes a great home base. Believe me, I will get this place." There was a dark undertone to her voice that made him uncomfortable. "Are you hot? You want to go for a swim?"

Her mercurial change of mood and subject was hard to keep up with. "Yeah, but I want to find my son more."

Her fingers grazed his arm lightly as they made their way back down the ramshackle stairs. "I know. But I always find that a quick dip in the ocean can change my perspective and make me think clearer."

They stopped by her casita so she could put on a swimsuit. It was a tiny little place with a bedroom, kitchen and screened porch furnished with Puerto Rican basics — plastic furniture, plastic dishes, a folding lawn chair, a hammock. "Where does Chloe sleep?" he asked curiously, when Elle emerged from the bathroom; beneath her dress, the sea-green strap of a bathing suit was visible around her neck.

"There are two beds in there but usually she prefers to sleep in the hammock out here." She shrugged. "Yeah, it's tight. The house I am trying to buy actually has three bedrooms."

She tossed him a couple of bananas and a towel. "Here take these out to the cart. I'll be right there."

A moment later she joined him, a plastic tumbler in her hand. She handed it to him with a warning look as she swung into the cart. He took a swig before putting it into the drink holder next to the steering wheel. "Mmmm, refreshing," he commented. "Tangy with just enough buzz to keep the pain of life at bay."

"Sassy bitch." She punched him in the arm and stepped on the gas.

An hour later, he had to admit that she was right. Stretched out like a lizard in the hot sun at the east end of Flamenco Beach, the salt water drying on his back, he could almost forget his troubles. Behind his darkened lens, he observed Elle, who sat cross-legged beside him on a purple sarong. Despite her petite stature, she was surprisingly buxom, her full breasts spilling over the neckline of a one-piece swimsuit that showed a still trim waistline above the inevitable rounding of her belly. Her well-weathered arms and legs were crisscrossed with a fine web of tiny wrinkles and a spattering of freckles and age spots that at one time he would have found unattractive; now he thought they added distinctive character and mystique.

"I know you're looking at me." She adjusted the brim of her straw hat as she gazed out across the bay. "Yeah, I'm old."

"I was thinking experienced. Age appropriate. Very fit." He kept himself from adding, "and very sexy" – this was not the time for that. "These days I find older people are so much more interesting – we have so many life stories to tell."

"I used to be a lot fitter."

64

"Well, didn't we all." He sat up and shaded his eyes. At the other end of the beach, more than a mile away, he could see the painted tank that indicated where Section E was located in the campground. "Someone told me you were friends with Ivan, the other guy who was murdered."

She snorted and laid back, tipping her hat over her face. Except for the soft sloping rise of her chest, she seemed small and childlike, her hip bones jutting out of the damp fabric, a line of pale ivory flesh showing at the top of one leg where her suit had ridden up. "I would hardly call it friends. Ivan was a jerk."

"So I've heard." He really wanted to run his fingers over that white skin, see how soft it was. "I heard he was also trying to buy a place here on Culebra."

"Yeah, all he ever wanted to talk about was real estate. Always trying to squeeze a better deal out of someone or get a local to sell their place to him for peanuts. Nobody trusted him."

He forced himself to look elsewhere, focusing on her toenails which were painted a dark red shade; his exhausted mind placed the color somewhere between a fine pinot noir and dried blood. He had to think of something else. "So where was the house he was trying to buy?"

"He was looking at a few of them. I don't want to talk about him. The man was a snake." She sat up and dug her toes into the sand, effectively ending his reverie. "That's what it means, you know."

"What. What means?"

"Culebra. It means 'snake.' It's a kind of cobra that lives here."

They walked the length of the beach back to Tyler's campsite, just on the off chance that something in the status quo might have changed, but everything seemed eerily the same. The stopped-in-time feeling that he had so enjoyed at first had now become exasperating and discouraging.

He introduced Elle to Sam and Leo but it turned out they already knew her, Sam giving Tyler a thumbs up behind her back until he heard what their connection was. "You guys are resourceful," Tyler commented, trying not to sound as desperate as he felt. "Short of going to the police, what would you do?"

Sam looked up from the picnic table where he was smashing an avocado with a fork to make guacamole. "I guess I wouldn't freak out. When I was sixteen I hitchhiked from Charlottesville to Santa Fe." He began peeling an onion. "I was gone for a month. But I came back, finished high school, even went to college for a year. And hey, I turned out okay."

Leo laughed at him. "In your opinion."

"So, Spencer, do you know him?" Tyler asked. "He supposedly was seen with them on Saturday night."

Sam nodded. "Yeah, I've met him. Nice set of dreads that dude has. Lives on a boat. Is working construction on a crew at some billionaire's place out by Zoni. You know where they hang out after work? That place at the end of the airport runway. Happy Landings. I bet you'll find him there in an hour or two. You want to stay for some guacamole?" He directed his question at Elle, which Tyler found amusing.

"Delighted to." She hung her straw hat on a branch and tipped her sunglasses up on her head, her smile accompanied by a flash of swirling psychedelic irises.

"Wow, you have such crazy amazing eyes, lady." Sam stared at her with unabashed youthful interest, rubbing a sunburned spot in the middle of his rib cage. "I didn't notice them when we were playing cards the other night."

Leo gave Tyler a "can you believe this" look and then, with a smirk, pulled a six-pack of beer out of a cooler. "Help yourselves," he said. "I'm going kayaking for a while."

Elle settled herself into one of their collection of cast-off camp chairs and popped open a Medalla. Tyler stared restlessly at the sea for a few moments before deciding there was nothing he could do right now but join her.

They were still there a few hours later, pleasantly buzzed and almost relaxed, enjoying what Elle termed as the "frat house atmosphere," when Leo returned. "You oughta get going," he said to them. "I mean, if you want to catch Spencer at Happy Landings."

Tyler would have liked to take a shower, wash the day's sweat and sea salt off his skin, but they had lingered too long at this point. The two of them walked back to the parking lot at a swift clip, Elle's woven bag swinging in time to their steps. Again he felt that pit of dread growing in his gut. He wished so much that right now he would see Tucker loping towards them with his long coltish stride, earbuds plugged in to iTunes, oblivious to the beauty of the lengthening shadows and afternoon light on the water and the shoreline that appeared between the trees along the road.

Elle's phone beeped as they reached the golf cart. "Sorry, I've got to take this." She walked about ten feet away for privacy, then spoke rapidly with urgency, her head down and face covered by the brim of her hat. "You don't want to know," was all she said in response to his questioning look upon her return. "Let's go."

They moved slowly and steadily along the road back to town with top speed for the vehicle being only about twenty miles an hour. After passing the airport, they made a left and pulled into a paved lot next to a low building with a view of the end of the runway. Loud music of an indeterminable genre blared from inside. A small crowd of men stood outside smoking and drinking. Through the open doorway, Tyler could see a pool table in the darkened interior.

"That must be our man." Elle nodded to a small dark fellow recognizable by the long matted locks of hair that were held at bay with a green, red and black print headband. The tilt of his eyes and arch of his cheekbones spoke to a multi-ethnic background and his expression was blank as he watched them approach.

"Spencer?"

He nodded warily, clearly on guard as to whatever situation was about to unfold.

"You're a friend of Chloe's, right? I'm her mom."

The tension in his features eased for a second before tightening with anger. "Yeah, let's say I *was* a friend of Chloe's. Until she went off with my fucking dinghy on Saturday night and never brought it back."

Tyler leaned forward. "Say what now?"

"I said she asked me if she could borrow my boat for a little while and take her new young boyfriend out for a ride in the bay, and then she fucking never came back with it. I've had to beg rides back and forth, and believe me, that ain't easy when you have to be at work before dawn. When you see her, tell her I am super pissed. I just barely got that outboard working again."

CHAPTER FIVE

The next morning, Tyler sat on the beach with his coffee, watching the sunrise, still feeling as exhausted as ever. For the hundredth time he went over the previous days' events in his mind, looking for some clue as to what he should do next.

Like the good journalist that he was, he had taken down all the details about Spencer's missing dinghy, which he had apparently lent to Chloe around midnight on Saturday. "The thing is, it's not even mine, man. It belongs to the owner of the yacht I am boat-sitting and it's going to be my head that rolls if anything has happened to it," Spencer complained. "So when you see your little bitch of a daughter, you tell her she better get it back to me, plus she owes me fucking big time."

Elle had been ready to argue with him until Tyler coaxed her away, promising Spencer they would call as soon as they knew anything. "He has every reason to be angry," he reminded her. "But for now, please tell me that Chloe knows how to handle a small outboard motor."

She closed her eyes, breathed deeply and nodded. "Yes, she does. And she knows how to sail a small boat also. Stan, the old guy with the little trimaran gave her lessons." She gave a little sarcastic laugh, some of the color coming back into her cheeks. "I think he was trying to get into her pants."

Inside the Happy Landings bar, a loud disagreement in Spanish was escalating. "I think we ought to get out of here. Go back to the Dinghy Dock. Ask around."

The rest of the evening had been equally frustrating as darkness fell, the only small success being that the word had been passed from sailor to sailor, all of whom promised to be on the lookout for the nondescript gray rubber inflatable that two teenagers had motored off in two nights earlier.

Tyler eventually caught a ride back to the campground with Alejandro, who, even in his permanently inebriated state, seemed a safer bet than Elle. Now that she was acknowledging the fact that her daughter had not only disappeared but stolen a boat as well, she seemed intent on getting drunk.

His conversation with Alejandro on the way home had been no less disturbing. The usually smiling little man told him stories about pirates and drug smugglers known to traverse the waters around Culebra. Tyler's nerves were so rattled that he actually accepted a couple hits of weed from Cassidy in an attempt to fall into a few hours of restless nightmarish sleep.

Now he watched the sun as it moved through a narrow band of clear sky above the horizon and then disappeared into a threatening gray cloud cover. It did not look like a great day for hanging around the campground or for sailing around the bay looking for missing kids.

His head was pounding and he rested his forehead on his knees. Lucy had left him two voice mails late last night saying she hadn't heard from them for a while and hoped that no news was good news. At some point soon he was going to have to call her and either tell her the truth or a whopping lie. He knew which it would probably be – he could not face letting her know that he had betrayed her trust and lost their son.

Elle got in touch with him a few hours later. She told him that she had talked Stan, Chloe's sailing teacher, into taking one of his boats out and scouting the bay for the missing dinghy. Having lived and sailed on Culebra for a quarter of a century, he knew the coves and inlets better than anyone.

"Are you going with him?" Tyler asked.

"No, I need to go over to the real estate office, see if I can get things in motion with my house again. I'll let you know as soon as I hear anything. Are you doing okay?"

Her concern seemed like an afterthought.

"Yeah, sure. Good as can be expected, I guess."

"I'll come out and get you in a little bit, all right? Catch you later." Her island casualness put him off a little. Not knowing what else to do with himself, he walked the beach from one end to the other, eventually getting drenched in the inevitable squall that had been gathering in the darkening sky. He stopped for an empanadilla at the cluster of kiosks, paying with some damp bills pulled from the pocket of his even damper shorts. By the time he got back to Section E, his mood was almost as gloomy as the day.

He needed to change his clothes anyway, he reasoned. In his anxiety, he was becoming oblivious to hygiene and was still wearing the same sandy swim trunks and smelly t-shirt he'd had on for the last two days. As he rummaged through his suitcase, he came across the copy of Tucker's birth certificate again, along with a printout of their airline reservations. They were supposed to fly back in five days. In his current state of mind, it seemed both too long and not long enough.

As he rinsed the sand out of his shorts at the water tank, he noticed for the first time that the police tape was gone from Ivan's campsite. In fact everything was gone, nothing left but an empty spot on the ground, worn bare from continuous use. Even the picnic table was gone, probably scavenged by other campers in need. Soon enough the site would be occupied by someone new, oblivious to what had gone down there. The thought made him uneasy.

A short distance away he could hear Tom and Lisa shouting at each other — it was unclear from their tempestuous tone whether they were fighting or having fun; the line between anger and enjoyment was always so blurred with those two, they were just passionate about everything.

Out of the corner of his eye he caught a flash of bright blue coming up the trail from Section D. When an arm waved, he saw it was Elle – without her straw sunhat, she cut an entirely different profile from a distance and he realized how little he actually knew her. Friendships were forged so quickly in this island atmosphere. Today she was wearing a flowing dress in a deep royal color that draped in uneven diaphanous points below her knees; her pale hair fell freely around her shoulders and she carried her sandals in her hand. Again he was struck by how youthful she appeared as she approached, her age not becoming obvious until she had nearly reached him.

"Hey." She stood on her bare toes to give him a kiss on the cheek. In response to the obvious question in his eyes, she pulled her phone out of her bag and held it up. "He said he would call when he got back."

They walked back to his tent and as he hung the wet clothes on the branches of a nearby mangrove tree, she settled herself into one of the beat-up canvas chairs. "So this is home," she said, looking around.

"Hardly. If I lived here, home would be a bigger tent – like that one – with a few extra tarps and a nice campstove and maybe a solar shower." He indicated the various sites around him where the long-termers had established themselves with their creature comforts.

A gust of wind rattled the leaves of the trees as some large raindrops began to fall. And then, in the swift and sudden way of the tropics, a torrential downfall was upon them. Tyler leapt to his feet and quickly unzipped the door flap to his tent. "In here – quick."

He waited until she had climbed inside and then rapidly followed, zipping the vent and rain fly behind them. Elle surveyed the cluttered interior – she was short enough so that she could just barely stand up in the middle. Tyler had to stoop as he moved from one side to the other, securing the flaps over the window screens.

"Sorry if it smells like a boy's dorm. It kind of is." He cleared the air mattress off and smoothed the single sheet.

Stretching out along the side against the tent wall, he patted the space next to him. "Have a seat."

The rain was falling so hard now he almost had to shout to make himself heard. Elle sat down on the edge of the mattress, her slight weight displacing enough air that the surface became firmer. "Quite a storm!" she yelled back over the sound of drops pelting the ground and hammering against the tarp above the tent.

Unbelievably, the storm seemed to get stronger and louder, making conversation impossible. After a moment, Elle stretched out next to him, resting her head on one arm. They lay side by side, listening to the downpour, the unspoken awareness growing in the way their legs pressed against each other and the curve of her rib cage met his. When her fingers curled around his own, he knew there was no way this was not happening, that even in the uncertainty of his churning reality, the future was rock solid, inescapable, predictable and preordained.

Rolling onto his side, he gently brushed the hair away from her face before leaning forward to press his lips against hers. Her response was anything but tentative — she kissed him deeply and passionately, as though she had been waiting forever for this moment, rather than a mere two days. Before he realized what was happening she was sitting astride him, taking control of this preamble to lovemaking, searching his mouth with her tongue, the pressure of her body hot against the length of his own.

When she sat up and gazed down at him with her crazy swirling eyes, he felt dizzy with desire. Trying to suppress the sense of urgency that had overcome them, he gently pulled the straps of her dress down from her shoulders, revealing a faded blue bra that separated the sun-wrinkled flesh of her chest from the paleness of her untanned torso. As he reached again for this second set of straps, the top of her head grazed the roof of the tent and a trickle of water ran down the middle of her forehead and off the end of her nose. Her laughter lightened the growing intensity between them.

Leaning forward, she spoke into his ear so he could hear her. "Hey, are you checkin' me out?" She licked the rim of his ear and sucked on his earlobe with soft slurping sounds. The warm wetness she left behind was a tactile turn-on that invited him to slide further down the steep slope of intimacy.

"I hope you're not expecting any perky petunias here because that ship sailed a long time ago," she said as he reached behind her to unhook the bra.

"That would be unrealistic of me, don't you think?" As he ran his fingers over the full curves of her breasts, he tried not to imagine what they might have looked like once upon a time. Her nipples hardened as his fingertips grazed them again and again; at the flick of his tongue, she sighed pleasurably and closed her eyes.

It seemed like forever since he had made love to a woman; how had he forgotten how present and in the moment the experience could be, how did a person let this tactile sensuality slip away from his life? When had sex no longer become the driver behind everything... he could not remember when the transition had occurred. Actually right now he could not remember anything except the softness of her flesh against his, and how her body parts tasted in his mouth and the way his groin felt as it crushed against hers. Inside a tent pummeled by rain, surrounded by wind and whipping water, personal problems and difficult dilemmas fell away as their remaining clothing hit the floor and their cries and groans and moans were lost in the sounds of the passing storm.

The rain subsided before they did, and their last exclamations of emotional release rang out across the campground amidst the sounds of lingering drips and drops falling from foliage and protective tarps. Inside the now steamy tent, Tyler wasn't sure if the wetness he felt on his face was sweat or tears.

Elle curled into the crook of his arm as her breathing slowly returned to normal. "Well, I'd say that was an 8.5."

"Hmmm?"

"On the Richter scale of orgasms."

"Ahhh. Does that happen often?"

"No, if the earth quaked like that all the time, there would be nothing left standing." She shuddered a little and sighed. "Just an aftershock."

With his free hand, Tyler reached up to unzip the window screen flap and a welcome humid breeze blew over their damp bodies. Suddenly exhausted, he closed his eyes and let sleep take him away from reality for a few more precious moments.

Elle was still wrapped around him when the sound of voices roused him from the deepest sleep he'd had in days. The numbness of his shoulder and tingling in his arm indicated that he had been in this position for a while. He did not want to move – moving meant that this amazing afternoon episode in his life would be over and he would have to remember what it was that he had been trying to escape from...

A short distance away he could hear Leo yelling, "We need the butcher – get the butcher!"

"We need the butcher! We need the butcher!" Sam and someone else had taken up the chant. He could hear Tom and Lisa join in from their camp.

He tried to gently extricate himself from Elle's embrace, but she stirred and whispered, "No, don't go," tightening her grasp around his waist. He kissed the top of her head and struggled to a sitting position so he could look out of the open screen.

Through the trees he could see Cassidy coming up the path. He was carrying something metal that glinted in the sideway rays of the late afternoon sun; when he passed by Tyler's tent the shape of the object gave it definition – it was a big silver cleaver.

His curiosity got the better of him and he struggled to his feet. "I'll be back in a minute," he said when Elle protested. He found his shorts in a crumpled heap on the other side of the tent and slipped them on. Stumbling outside, he felt groggy from sex and sleep, but in a good way, satiated. "Yo, Cassidy!" he hailed him as he passed by.

"Hey, man. Havin' a good afternoon?" Cassidy's grin made him realize there were not many secrets in this neighborhood of Section E.

"Ha. Yeah, yeah, I guess I am. Whatcha got there?"

"Oh, this?" Cassidy laughed and waved the cleaver in a wide circle like an oversized tomahawk. "The boys speared a really big tuna and they want me to cut the head off of it before they grill it. So they called in a professional – I did tell you that I used to be the butcher of Telluride, didn't I?"

To Tyler's ear, it sounded more like the title of a grisly Western than an actual vocation. "No, I think you forgot to mention that interesting detail of your past."

Cassidy swung the oversized tool with professional ease. "Yeah, I was really good at it, could chop up just about anything – big, small, bring it on. I can turn your side of beef into hamburger or make your hog disappear into bacon."

Something about the way he said this – with a broad smile that displayed a few gaps in his back teeth – felt very unsettling to Tyler.

"And, of course, I'm not quite so skilled at it now with only one good eye. Anyway, we're gonna have a fish grilling party tonight – you and your little gal-friend ought to join us."

"Thanks – we might." Tyler experienced a sudden shift in his mood as the memory of responsibility settled over him like a dark cloud. "But first we need to find out if the dinghy was located and if there is any news. Of our kids."

Beyond the trees the cry started up again. "Butcher! Butcher! Butcher!"

"Natives are restless, gotta go. Good luck, bro."

Through the screened door of the tent, Tyler could see Elle moving around. When he went inside, she was standing naked under the ridge pole, her cell phone pressed to her ear, a grim look on her face. The sight of her, combined with the smell of sex now mingling with the other unwashed odors inside the tent, made him want to start all over again. He ran a finger lightly up and down her backbone, but she held up a warning hand as she listened to a recorded message. He was too aroused – he kissed her shoulder and pulled her back against him.

"Tyler." She stopped his hand as it slid southward below her belly. "They found the dinghy."

"What?" His erection was gone as quickly as it had come.

"They found Spencer's boat. But not them."

"What do you mean?"

"Stan found the dinghy tied to the back side of an abandoned purple houseboat that sits in a small cove of mangroves, just by the markers to the channel for Ensenada Honda. But there was no sign of Chloe and Tucker."

He still was not comprehending the situation. "So what does that mean?" He knew he was repeating himself. He watched in a daze as she turned her underpants right side out and stepped into them, hooked her bra and pulled on her dress. "What does that mean? Where are you going?"

She tossed him his t-shirt. "There's only about an hour until sunset. We have to get going if we want to get out to the purple houseboat. Stan is waiting for us at the Dinghy Dock."

Stan had a wild gray beard that stuck out in unkempt tufts and big serious eyes that contrasted with his easy giddy laugh. His rail-thin arms and legs were surprisingly pale for a sailor, and covered with random age spots and freckles. Tyler was sure he had lots of entertaining stories that would have to wait for another time.

"I think you would do better to go in a boat with a motor than in my sailboat," Stan recommended. "The wind is dying down and it might be a bit hard to navigate close enough to the houseboat for you to board. Manny said he would take you." He indicated a blond and bronzed man in a faded captain's hat who was undoing the rope that held his boat to the dock.

Fortified with the usual drinks in plastic cups, Elle stepped nimbly on board the metal skiff and seated herself in the prow without spilling a drop. Tyler followed, somewhat less surefooted, and then Manny leapt in and started up the motor. As they sped across the harbor, Elle told Tyler about the purple houseboat.

"A couple lived on it for a number of years and then the husband died suddenly and the wife couldn't take being out there alone, so she basically just abandoned it. It's super charming – if she had sold it right off she could probably have got good money for it, but now it's rundown and ragged from lack of upkeep. People who know about it will go there to party sometimes, occasionally some vagabonds will take it over for a few months, but it's kind of far out and you need a way to get there on the water." She shaded her eyes as they approached the end of the bay. "I've thought about it a few times myself. You'll see what I am talking about."

"So Chloe had been there with you before?"

Elle nodded, sipping on her vodka and cranberry. "And no doubt with her own friends a few times since. It's the perfect place for underage drinking."

Tyler surveyed the landscape surrounding the bay, trying to memorize the shape of the hills and the distinctive buildings. Behind them civilization was defined by the clusters of houses dotting the slopes, a handful of bobbing sailboats and the incongruous orange and white steel metal bridge. Ahead, beyond the channel markers, the open sea loomed, a vast horizon leading to the world outside of Culebra.

Off to the right, an ungainly two story boat-home came into view, distinguished by its peeling lavender paint and salt-clouded windows. It was moored by itself, a good distance from any of the permanently inhabited yachts or seasonal charters that found their way to the bay.

"So Spencer already got his dinghy back, I guess?" Elle asked Manny as he slowed the motor so that they could come smoothly alongside the houseboat.

"Ayuh. Stan towed it back." Manny's accent identified him as hailing from somewhere along the coast of Maine. He stood up in the bow and grabbed one of the houseboat deck railings to pull them close to it. Tyler was surprised to see there was still a metal ladder attached to the side for easy access. "You folks hop up and take a look around – I'll wait here for yuh."

Elle and Tyler scrambled barefoot up the rusting rungs.

"Wow, this is amazing." On the back porch swung a contemporary hanging chair of weathered wood and macraméd nylon boat line. Tyler stepped inside the open doorway to the main cabin. Cushioned seats lined the walls beneath large Plexiglas windows that were now too fogged with salt and moisture to display a clear view. Custom built cabinets and tiled counters formed what had once been a state-of-the-art sailing kitchen with weighted gas burners and a stainless steel sink. A few steps up brought them to an airy sleeping area covered with mattresses, edged with wooden shelving and built-in light sconces.

"Wow."

"You haven't seen the best part. Come on."

Tyler followed her back out on deck where a ladder built into the side of the cabin led to the upper level. Here there was a room with only three walls, the aft wall being open to a breathtaking view of the sea; big windows on both sides were propped open to take advantage of cross breezes. In the center was a king-sized bed, still outfitted with a worn fitted sheet in a faded seashell print and a mold-spattered quilt.

"Wow," he repeated, sinking slowly to sit on the mattress. "This is a place I might want to stay forever." He looked around. "Why aren't they still here?"

"They probably got hungry. From too much sex. On this big bed."

Tyler jumped up as though he had been stung. "Shit. You think so? Of course, they did. Of course." As hard as it was to digest, there couldn't be a more awesome place for his son to lose his virginity.

"It's going to be dark soon. Let's look around." Elle picked up the quilt and shook it, tossing it on the floor. There was not much else to do on this level. Tyler lifted the mattress and peered under it. A quarter, a pen, a lot of sand and an empty condom wrapper. Gingerly, he held it up between two fingers.

"Let's hope this was theirs."

Elle nodded. "Chloe carries them. I made sure of it."

There was more to explore on the first level. A plastic shopping bag that hung from a hook by the counter had been used for garbage. Holding his breath, Tyler started to poke through it and then dumped it out on the floor. An empty yogurt container, a cheesy popcorn bag, two granola bar wrappers, a plastic water bottle, and some curling tangerine peels told the story, as did a couple more condom wrappers – and the used condoms themselves.

"All right, all this tells us is they ate what little they could get a hold of and had protected sex." His eyes met hers. "Which their parents did not."

"Don't worry. I'm way beyond the possibility of pregnancy." She began opening cabinets, searching for any other clues. Tyler decided not to bring up the other reasons that maybe he should have thought about a condom. Not that he had any with him – getting laid had not been part of his father-son vacation plan.

"Elle. Look." Tyler pointed under the table. Two pairs of plastic flip flops were parked there, a small turquoise set decorated with dangling silver butterflies, and large brown ones with textured walking soles.

She stared at the shoes and blinked a few times. "So they forgot their shoes. What does that tell us? We came aboard barefoot – people go barefoot on boats." Her voice had an edge of hysteria to it.

"I don't know what it tells us!" He felt as distressed as she did, but he knew he had to stay calm and think straight. "They didn't leave their phones or their clothes so they probably didn't swim to shore. They must have left by boat. By a different boat. Which means somebody else is involved. Or has seen them."

"But why haven't they come home by now? Why would they run away?" He could see tears beginning to fill her eyes, her iridescent irises glistening. "Chloe likes to change her outfit every day, it's important to her not to wear the same stupid little shorts two days in a row." She put two fingers in the corners of her eyes, trying to stop the flow. "I'm trying to buy this house for us, I'm doing everything to make a perfect life, I was trying not to let anything or anyone get in my way..."

Tyler pulled her to him, wrapping his arms tightly around her, their heads resting on each other shoulders. Choking back his own fears, he stroked her tangled hair, still uncombed since their afternoon tumble in the tent. "We'll find them. Don't worry." He spoke as much to reassure himself as her. "We have to."

CHAPTER SIX

Chloe kept her eyes on the horizon even though it disappeared from view every few seconds as the sailboat rolled with the swells. Despite her sailing lessons in Fulladoza Bay and around the coast of Culebra, she had never experienced the waves of the open sea, nor the classic head-spinning nausea of seasickness. Until now. She knew that by staying on deck in the open air, keeping her eyes focused in the distance and never looking down or going below, she would do better. But right now the thirty odd miles to St. John in the Virgin Islands seemed as far away as Hong Kong, and the thought of sailing all the way from the Caribbean to the South China Sea made her feel even sicker than before.

She leaned back against Tucker and tried not to let sleepiness overtake her. When she closed her eyes it was worse. If they were really going to pull this whole trip off, she was going to have to get some drugs, or one of those patches that people wore behind their ears to ward off motion sickness. Tucker's long bare legs were wrapped protectively around her body and she held onto his knees like the armrests of an overstuffed chair, a very bony and uncomfortable chair, but it was as good as she was going to get for the next few hours. Tucker had seemed oblivious to the wild rocking of the boat; in fact it had lulled him off to sleep almost immediately, his back against the outside wall of the cabin, chin resting on chest.

The mainsail shifted slightly and she took the chance of shifting her gaze to Hendrik who was adjusting the line. The Norwegian sailor and his girlfriend Astrid were a matched set, all brown and blonde in that enviably beautiful way that Scandinavian people seemed to so easily achieve. They were sailing around the world, had already been at it for two years. Hendrik's ragged T-shirt and khaki shorts were bleached pale from sun and salt, Astrid's bikini top and fringed sarong worn thin from wind and weather. They were happy for the company of two young "adventurers," something to break the monotony of each other, and didn't question the teenagers about the dirty clothes they wore or the fact that their luggage consisted of a daypack and a pillowcase stuffed with a few random possessions pilfered from the purple houseboat.

The Norwegians had totally believed Chloe's story. She told them she and Tucker had been left behind on Culebrita by one of the large touring "rum boats" on a day sail from St. Thomas, because they had lost track of time when they had taken a hike to the lighthouse and the boat had left without them. Chloe did not even know if tour boats made the trip to Culebrita from St. Thomas like they did from Puerto Rico, but she figured Hendrik and Astrid wouldn't know either. Her tale of how two kids had gotten "stranded on a desert island" was anything but the truth. And the truth was anything but simple.

What had started as an innocent Saturday night hookup with a cute boy had gone suddenly and disastrously off course. During the second set of conga drumming and dancing, they had slipped around the back side of the Dinghy Dock into the shadows along the wall of the building and she had kissed him.

She had never really been with anybody younger before, usually the guys she hooked up with were older. There were also some way-too-old men that seemed perpetually after her ass whom she always rebuffed, wondering why geezers of their age would think she might be attracted to them.

So she was super surprised to find how much she liked kissing Tucker, how soft his curly hair felt between her fingers, how his chest was so lean and hard against her own and especially how passionately he kissed her back.

"Wow. Do this often?" she whispered breathlessly into his ear when they finally unlocked lips for a break.

"Sure, every time I go camping in the Caribbean." His laughter seemed like an unexpected release of tension and he pulled her face towards his again.

They kissed for a long time and she was starting to feel very turned on, but she had the feeling that he was unsure of what exactly should happen next. And certainly nothing was going to happen if they just kept standing here, or if it did, it would not be very romantic.

"Hey, I have an idea." Gently she slipped out of his grasp and pulled her cell phone out of her pocket, sending a quick text. Within seconds it dinged a response. "Come on." She took his hand and led him back over to the dock along the restaurant, stopping in front of a gray rubber dinghy. "Oooh, you feel kind of electric right now." She ran her fingers up his arm.

"Well, you've kind of electrified me." His eyes were wide and smiling.

"Good. So hop in." She knelt down to unhitch the rope that held the boat to the dock.

"What?"

"Spencer says we can borrow his dinghy for a little while. Go out into the bay. Come on, you'll like it."

He hesitated, but only briefly. Kicking off his flip-flops, he stepped carefully into the rocking boat and sat down.

Throwing the line in, she leaped nimbly into the stern by the outboard motor. Seconds later the engine came to life and she was maneuvering them away from the dock.

"You're really good at this," he said awkwardly as the sounds of the bar and the band faded into the distance.

"Thanks. So, Vermont boy, have you been on a boat before?" She cut the motor and the sudden silence was almost deafening, broken only by the soft lapping of the water against the sides of the dinghy.

"Of course. I spent my childhood in the Grenadines. Well, until I was five. I remember a few boats. We used to take water taxis from town to our village."

"Really?" She regarded him with new interest.

"Yeah, my father was a famous rock musician."

"What – that guy back there?"

"Well, according to my birth certificate, he's not my father."

She giggled. "That's pretty amazing. You look so much like him."

Tucker shrugged. "Stranger things have happened, I guess. I'll show it to you when we get back." He started to move towards her and the boat listed precariously from side to side.

"Whoa, whoa, careful!" she warned. "This is probably going to be a little tricky. Stay where you are; I'll come to you."

He moved over and she slid silently onto the bench next to him and then straddled it so they were facing. Taking the cue from her, he did the same, putting his hands around her waist and scooching her closer. She threw her legs over his and wrapped her arms around his neck and they kissed some more. The crotch of her shorts was pressed up against his and she could feel how hard he was growing.

He tugged tentatively at the hem of her halter top but the stretch fabric fit too snugly against her body to slide off easily. With a practiced movement, she crossed her arms in front of her and pulled it over her head. The untanned whiteness of her small firm breasts gleamed palely in the light of the half moon. Tucker sat back a little bit so he could look at her.

"Wow, you're so perfect." He ran his fingers over her curves, feeling how her nipples hardened under his light touch.

"Ha, not hardly. Wait until you know me better." She shivered a little and closed her eyes, enjoying how the whole experience felt, the bay breezes cool on her skin, the sensation of his gentle exploration.

"Oh, my god, I want to know you better." The moon disappeared behind a cloud and a brisk wind picked up suddenly.

Chloe opened her eyes and looked at the sky. All the stars were now hidden; the only lights that could be seen were on the bobbing sailboat masts and the houses along the shoreline. "I think," she said, leaning forward and kissing him quickly but deeply, "that we need to go back right now." A couple of large drops splashed off her forehead, confirming her suspicion. "We'll have to find a different place to hang out."

She could sense the intensity of his regret as she pulled away from him and moved to the seat by the motor. "Toss me my top, would you?" She started the engine, pulled the Lycra sports halter over her head and pulled hard on the rudder to turn the boat around. As they sped back towards the Dinghy Dock, it began to pour, thick, hard, driving rain, so dense that she could barely see where she was navigating.

And then, as quickly as it had begun it ended, leaving them soaked to the skin, hair plastered to their foreheads, water dripping off the tips of their noses. "That was ridiculous!" she laughed with him. "Maybe we're not supposed to do this tonight."

"Is there someplace else we can go? With a roof maybe?"

She pondered his question for a moment as they approached the bar. The music had stopped and the crowd had thinned out. To extend their trip, she turned off the engine and they drifted quietly in the semi-darkness several feet from the shore, floating towards the dark end of the restaurant where they had stood making out earlier. The flash of a lighter illuminated the faces of two people igniting the ends of their cigarettes as they hovered against the back wall.

"You can't do this, Perry!" The sound of a woman's voice carried easily over the water. "There's no way you're getting away with this."

Chloe gasped audibly and then clapped a hand over her mouth.

The man's reply was slurred and incomprehensible. He took a large swig of his drink and swayed visibly. "Hey. Hey! Where are you going?" he mumbled loudly, swatting his arm out at the woman who took a few steps out of his reach. "Shit, what the fuck is happening to me..." His silhouette slumped heavily to the ground.

The lighter flicked on again, illuminating a body sprawled awkwardly by the water's edge, the woman leaning over him. Out of the dark, a large square figure materialized beside her and the flame went out. "Listo," they heard her say. "Ahora. Rápidamente," and then her shadowy form disappeared.

Something heavy plopped into the water and then they heard a lot of splashing and choking. Someone gagged desperately, "What the – no – aah..." and then there was an ominous gurgling and finally silence.

"What just happened?" Tucker breathed the words into Chloe's ear.

Before she could reply, the dinghy bumped into something and then grazed the side of the dock. Somebody swore and the lighter flicked on again, briefly disclosing the harsh features of the big hulking man. "Shit. I know that guy," she whispered. "We have to get out of here."

She tossed the rope around the hitch on the dock and handed the end to Tucker. "Hold this. I need to grab my backpack; I left it under a table. Don't make any noise."

"What? What's going on?" Frightened, he froze in position as she leaped onto the wooden platform and scurried across the room. In a single fluid motion, she scooped the pack up by its straps and headed back towards the boat, finishing off with a graceful leap that turned awkward as the boat tilted crazily.

"Let go of the line. Now!" she hissed at him. As she started up the engine, the glaring beam of a flashlight suddenly lit up the rubber craft, temporarily blinding them. Shielding her eyes with one hand, she gunned the motor with the other, speeding away out into the harbor.

"Oh my god, oh my god, oh my god!" Suddenly she was crying so hard she had to stop doing everything for a minute. As the engine started to sputter, she angrily wiped the tears away with the back of her hand and then determinedly steered the boat out into the bay.

"Chloe, are you okay? Maybe we better just go back." In only a few words, Tucker's fear and uncertainty came through loud and clear.

"No." She sniffed one last time. "No," she repeated. "I'm fine. And we can't go back. Not now. But I know where we can go."

They didn't speak as the boat sped across the harbor, bumping and bucking across the newfound waves caused by the recent wind. Just before they reached the channel, Chloe steered the boat closer to the shore. After a brief one-handed search in her backpack, she handed a headlamp to Tucker.

"Shine that in front of us. I don't want to hit anything."

Nervously, he held the light aloft, its pale beam casting a narrow path ahead. The hull of a large boat appeared suddenly and Chloe navigated skillfully, slowing the dinghy to a halt alongside it and turning off the motor. "We're going to have to tie off to something," she said, standing up and grabbing hold of a metal ladder on the back side of the large boat. "I guess I can use this for now."

Moments later they stood on deck, both of them still breathing hard. "You won't be able to see it until morning, but this is a houseboat and it's purple."

"You're amazing." He pulled her towards him, holding her close.

She collapsed into his embrace, feeling suddenly spent. "Come on." She took his hand. "Let me show you the best part."

The first thing they realized as they fell onto the bed in the open upper deck was how wet their clothes were. "Oh my god, we are totally soaked. Forget the foreplay; let's just take our clothes off now." She peeled the drenched garments away from her skin, laying them out on the floor to dry. Her skin felt clammy and cold and she wished there was a blanket to cozy up in besides an icky stained quilt that was folded at the foot of the bed.

"Shit, I'm freezing. Come here." She wrapped her limbs around him, realizing he had managed to shed his clothing as fast as she had. "Wow," she giggled, suddenly self-conscious. "You are absolutely naked."

"And so are you." His hands ran up and down her back, rubbing her skin to warm it.

"Okay. I have to ask you this." Abruptly she sat up. "Don't get upset or offended. But this is your first time, right?"

He nodded, clearly mortified that she recognized his inexperience.

"It's cool. Don't worry." She stroked the side of his face. "If you don't know what to do, I'll just tell you. It'll be the best." Rolling on top of him, she sat up and took his hand in hers. "So... start here..."

When she awoke, the sun was hot on her face and across her bare breasts. Tucker had fallen asleep with one leg entwined over hers, his hand resting in the crevice between her thighs. She smiled a little as she remembered what she had taught him to do to her and how good it had made her feel. Kissing his shoulder, she sat up, pressing his hand against her for a moment before realizing how badly she needed to pee. She was going to have it hang it over the edge of the boat – there was no other option out here. Disentangling herself from his embrace, she made her way down to the main deck.

Seeing Spencer's dinghy tied to the ladder reminded her of the late night events that had caused her to flee so quickly to this hideaway. A nauseating pang of fear in her stomach made her double over with pain. What was she going to do? They couldn't go back. He would find her. And her mother ...

The thought was too much to deal with. It was much easier to go back up to the top deck and have sex again with that cute guy.

Their clothes still lay in the same damp heaps where they had dropped them the night before. She gathered them up to hang over the upper railing to dry in the sun. When she picked up Tucker's cargo shorts she realized that several of the pockets had things in them and rather than risk losing important belongings over the edge, she emptied the contents onto the floor.

It was hard to believe he had carried so much stuff with him, but she guessed that was the difference between girls and boys; her shorts didn't even have pockets, but she had a purse that could hold so much more. From one pocket came a handful of change, some crumpled bills, and a stick of SPF 45 lip balm. From another came his cell phone and a head lamp. There was a twenty dollar bill in the zippered pocket on the left leg and a small Swiss Army knife. Under a buttoned flap on the right leg emerged a plastic Ziplock bag with a British passport and some folded papers.

A British passport, really? Her curiosity got the better of her. Sitting cross-legged on a ratty cushion, she unzipped the bag and pulled out the little red book. A picture of a freckle-faced boy with tousled blonde hair and a serious expression on his face stared back at her. "Tucker Mackenzie Brookstone. Address, Lower Bay, Bequia, St. Vincent and the Grenadines, West Indies. Mother, Lucy Benton Brookstone." The expiration date was 6 years earlier. There were only a few stamps on the entry pages: a decades old departure from Kingstown, St. Vincent, followed by entry and exit to Barbados, and an immigration stamp into the United States at Boston, Massachusetts.

Stuck between the back two pages of the passport was a sheet of paper folded into eight squares. Carefully unfolding it, she spread the document out on the floor. It was a copy of a birth certificate from the United Kingdom. It stated permanent address as Rock House, Mustique, mother as Lucy Benton Brookstone, father as Quentin "Kip" Kingsley.

"Oh. My. God." She could not keep from speaking aloud. "What are you doing?"

Tucker was sitting up in bed, staring groggily at her from beneath lids still heavy with sleep. "Are you going through my shit?"

"Sorry. I'm so sorry." She jumped up guiltily, the paper still held out delicately between two slim fingers. "I was hanging up our clothes to dry and I didn't want your stuff to fall out or blow overboard. And then, when I saw your British passport, I couldn't help myself. Yes, I snooped."

He said nothing, still eyeing her suspiciously with a frown on his face.

"But, Tucker—" Climbing up on the bed next to him, she spread the birth certificate in front of them and put her arm through his. "When you said 'famous rock musician' I never thought you meant like mega-celebrity. Why didn't you say that Kip Kingsley was your father?!"

His defensive demeanor softened a little and he pulled her back down onto the pillows with him. "Maybe I wanted you to like me for myself?" he murmured suggestively. "Or maybe I've never even met him and maybe I didn't even know he was my father until I saw my birth certificate a few weeks ago."

"Really?"

Tucker frowned. "Yeah. When I asked my mom about it, she just said, 'Don't believe everything you read,' and she wouldn't talk about it. I knew we lived on Mustique until I was two, but I obviously don't remember anything about it. I've only seen a couple of pictures."

"Wow. This is really cool. I mean, you are already cool, it just makes you more so." She squeezed his arm "So did you look any of this up online?"

"Of course. I did my homework. I actually found an article that my mother wrote about touring with Kingsley and Boneyard like twenty years ago. She used to be a journalist in London then. And then there was some exposé about him being busted for drugs on Bequia; but that was after we left. I also found a couple of images of parties at his house on Mustique, and there was one ancient photo that looked like my mom with him but that was it. I guess the band broke up after the bust and he hasn't been on tour much since then."

"So there were no mentions of a baby boy." She hopped up suddenly and began rummaging through her backpack, eventually retrieving a bottle of water and two granola bars from its depths. She tossed him one. "Breakfast."

"Thanks." He devoured it in about thirty seconds.

"You ever think about going there?" she asked, nibbling her own bar more delicately.

"Where?"

"Mustique. To find him."

Their eyes met in the silence that followed. "Yeah." The answer came slowly. "I've thought about it."

Sex in broad daylight was different, she realized. It was more real, you could see everything, you could have eye contact or you could disappear into the blue of the sky when you were coming. It was like a celebration or a holiday party, where you gave presents and got presents and everybody was happy. Time could stand still or the hours could disappear into a sunlit pool of pleasure.

When they woke in the afternoon and found their bodies stuck together with sweat, they dove off the back of the boat and swam naked in the sea and then climbed the ladder to lie on deck and let the sun dry the salty water off their skin.

"Chloe."

"Mmm?"

"I'm starving. Maybe we ought to go back."

He propped himself up on one elbow and looked down at her. He traced the concaveness of her belly with his finger and played with the little sparkling jewel that pierced her bellybutton.

"Tucker. We can't go back. I don't want to go back. Look in my pack – there might be something else to eat. I always keep a lot of snacks in there, just in case."

"Just in case what?" He got to his feet. "Just in case you accidentally witness a murder and end up having killer sex with a hottie on a houseboat? Oh, sorry, maybe I shouldn't have used the word 'killer.'" He disappeared up the ladder to the upper deck.

His sarcasm stung a little – she hadn't seen this side of him before.

He reappeared, wearing his shorts and holding up a tangerine, a yogurt and a small bag of cheese-flavored popcorn. "This is it. The entire pantry. You think the yogurt is still good?"

"Yeah, they last longer than most people realize." She sat up and patted the deck next to her. "Come here. Let's talk."

"Let's eat first." He peeled the tangerine and gave her half. She took a few slices and handed the rest back to him.

"You take it. I'll get by." She felt lightheaded from hunger but she didn't want to lose him yet over something as dumb as food. She pulled the foil top off the yogurt container and fashioned it into a crude spoon. "This is how we do it here."

A couple of power boats sped by, their passengers waving gaily. "Where are they coming from?" Tucker asked.

"Culebrita, probably. A pretty little deserted island between here and St. Thomas where a lot of day trippers go. Good thing nobody decided to stop here and party today. Lots of local people know about the abandoned houseboat."

"So we can't live here alone forever then." His humor seemed to be reviving a little as his appetite subsided.

"Unfortunately not without another bottle of water." As they rocked in the wake of the passing boats, an idea began to form in her mind.

"Maybe if we go back to bed soon, we can last until morning?" He was smiling but his eyes were serious. "I don't want this to be over yet."

After nightfall they seemed to lose all track of time. It was maybe an hour after sunset, or maybe it was five, or maybe it was almost dawn, when Chloe brushed a curl off his damp forehead and whispered, "What if we went there?"

"Mmmm. Is there someplace we haven't gone yet? Haven't we done everything in the last twenty-four hours?" His voice was sleepy.

"To Mustique. To find your father."

"Sure. Sounds like a plan. We'll charter a yacht in the morning. And make sure it has a good cook. I want steak and eggs for breakfast."

She sat up and turned towards him. "No, I mean it. We'll hitchhike boats. If we can get someone to take us over to Culebrita, we can probably sneak onto one of those rum boat day tours back to St. Thomas and go on from there."

He laughed. "Do you even know where the Grenadines are? They're not exactly nearby."

"I know my Caribbean geography. I'm good with maps – I won the National Geographic geography bee in eighth grade at my school. Want me to name all the islands from here to there? St. Thomas, St. John, St. Croix, St. Kitts and Nevis, Montserrat–"

"So how long will this trip take? I have to be back at school next week."

He still thought she was joking. "Longer than that. And it will be a better education." She slid a hand between his legs. "Look how much you've already learned."

"We don't have to go to Mustique to continue these lessons." He put his hand over hers.

"I'm afraid of that guy. He knows where I live and he knows I saw him. WE saw him. I'm afraid for you too. And I can't go back to live with my mother. Not now." She pulled away from him and stood up. After pacing across the room a few times, she rummaged in her bag. "Shit. I thought I still had a little pot left. Oh, phew." She held up a tiny baggie. "You smoke?"

"Not usually. I mean, I have." In the shadowy light of night, she could see him sit up but could not make out his features. "Won't that make us hungrier?"

"Or maybe the opposite." The flash of a cigarette lighter momentarily lit up the room. She handed him a small pipe. "You want some?" He hesitated for only a fraction of a second before accepting it. "Be careful – it might make you cough."

"So you can't run away from this forever," he said in a tight voice, holding the smoke in his lungs in a way that indicated he'd had a little experience in this discipline.

"This is not running away. It is a solution to a problem. And an adventurous one at that." She was silent for a minute as she took a toke. "Look, we both are pissed at our parents here on Culebra. My mom is acting like a jerk and doing some really bad things and whoever that poser is who says he's your dad has not been telling you the truth. On top of that, there is some Puerto Rican thug who knows we can identify him as the guy who drowned a big-time real estate agent on this island."

"Hold on a second. That's who the guy in the water was? Shit." Tucker reached for the pipe. "This thing is out. Do you have any more?"

"No, that's it. It was just my emergency stash." She stood up again and stepped over to the railing, enjoying the way the breeze touched every part of her body. "Wow, I haven't worn anything at all for more than twenty-four hours. I love not having clothes on; they're so confining. Maybe I should be a nudist."

Tucker laughed. "I think someone has a little buzz on." He joined her at the rail and they stood there quietly together, looking out at the stars and the moving surface of the water. For several moments they stayed in that position, shoulders and feet touching, each alone with their private emotional struggles, feeling like they were the only people on earth.

"You know what?" Chloe straightened up. "I'm doing this whether you are or not. I'm done with this stupid little island and my mother and all her drama. I am just dropping out of sight, presto, change-o, disappear-o, not telling anybody, with only the clothes on my back."

"You're not wearing any clothes," he reminded her and then they both had such a bad case of the pot-smoking giggles that they had to sit down.

"So," she said after a while. "Are you in or not? Because if you're not coming, it would probably best if I take you back to town right now in the middle of the night so no one sees us."

Suddenly the situation got very serious and totally real. She could feel Tucker's pain at the idea of sudden separation after all their closeness and she was surprised at how much it made her heart hurt. If he did the smart thing and said no, it would all be over and she realized how much she didn't want to let him go.

Squeezing her eyes shut, she prayed that he wouldn't leave her. And then she remembered having heard somewhere that hope was not a strategy. So instead she straddled his lap, wrapped her arms around him for the umpteenth time and kissed him long and hard.

When they finally broke apart, he stroked her face and took a deep breath. "Okay," he said. "I'll do it. What's the plan?"

They stayed up most of the night talking. Tucker said he would only agree to Chloe's plan if they had some food, so just after daybreak she dropped him at a small dock just out of town with directions on how to walk to the nearest food store, which would not open for another hour. When he returned with her backpack and a plastic bag full of groceries and a gallon of water, she was out-of-her-mind jumpy with nervous energy.

"We have to get back before someone sees us. Boat people are up early and I am sure Spencer is looking for his dinghy by now." They sped along the open water as fast as the motor would go, feeling a sense of security and relief when they had once again tied off to the purple houseboat and were safely on board.

A couple of peanut butter and jelly sandwiches later, their whole perspective seemed to change, the outlook becoming less desperate and more intrepid. "We should pack up and be ready to go," she instructed. "Let's take the bed sheet and that snorkel and mask in the corner. We want to look like tourists when we get there."

A dinging sound made them both freeze and look up at the bedroom. "That must be your phone," Tucker said. "Because mine has no service out here and might have died by now anyway."

Chloe was amazed that she hadn't even thought to check her phone in the last thirty-six hours. It was the first time she had been satisfied enough with her present condition to not crave the constant stimulation and validation that she got from her cell. She made no move to get it and the reminder sounded again.

"It's going to go dead faster if it keeps ringing. You might want to just look at it and then turn it off," he suggested.

Reluctantly she climbed the ladder, returning a moment later, her eyes glued to the screen. "My mother wants to know where I am. She says she and your father are looking for us."

"What?! Really?"

She held the text message up for him to see. "I'm not answering it."

Tucker's mood changed abruptly. "My dad – Tyler – must be freaking out."

"Tucker." Chloe sensed she was losing him. "First of all, remember he's been lying to you about being your dad. Let him freak out a little."

She watched his jaw harden and his eyes grow dark. "Yeah, you're right. Let him worry for another day. Or two. I'm not a baby anymore. And I never was his baby anyway."

"Let's wait until we are like really away from Culebra, on a different island. Then we'll text them and tell them we

97

are okay. We don't want them sending the coast guard after us or something like that."

He frowned thoughtfully. "Right. They might do something like that. Call the police or something."

She snorted. "The Culebra police are worthless. Besides, I know my mother would never go to them. She says she doesn't want them poking around in her life." She looked around. "Are we ready? We better get out on deck and watch for a boat."

The plan hadn't gone as smoothly in reality as it had in her mind. It was noon by the time they had flagged down a boat and that one had been headed towards a different island. But about fifteen minutes later a pair of speedboats came by and the second one slowed for Chloe's frantic waving. The friendly passengers were Puerto Ricans who did not speak much English but they understood "Culebrita" and moved over to make room for the two non-threatening teenagers.

In less than half an hour they hopped off the boat into a picture-perfect bay, a pristine crescent of sand with calm turquoise water and a handful of boats. After a profuse amount of "gracias's" and "mucho gusto's", they shouldered their minimal possessions and began walking to the far end of the beach.

"Wow, this is an awesome place," Tucker commented enthusiastically. "I'm surprised people aren't camping here."

"You're not allowed to. It's kind of a state park or something. Everyone is supposed to leave by dark. Let's just stash our stuff up under those palms and go for a swim. Spread out the sheet on the beach. Act normal like we're just here for the day."

Once they had set themselves up like day-trippers, had gone for a swim and stretched out on the sand to dry, Chloe began to relax a little. Since getting that text message from her mother, she had felt wired and nervous. Despite her bravado with Tucker, the truth was she had never really done anything like this before.

It was a crazy plan but she thought they could pull it off.

The afternoon passed pleasantly. They hiked over the rocks and cliffs and swam in a place that people called "The Baths" where the sea came churning into a deep hole. They took turns using the mask and snorkel to view the underwater sea life and laughed at a wild goat and her kids they saw on a trail that ran into the interior of the island. With a stick, she drew a map of the Caribbean in the sand, taught him the names of all the islands and showed him the route they were going to take.

"Geography quiz tomorrow at 11," she told him. "We'll see how much you can remember."

From beneath the protection of the palm trees, they watched the sailing yachts and power boats leave the harbor one by one, until they were alone with the sunset colors of the darkening sky. They ate more peanut butter sandwiches and then made love in the twilight under the stars.

"This would be super romantic if I weren't being eaten alive by mosquitos," said Tucker, scratching maniacally at a bite on the back of his leg. "I don't suppose you have any bug spray in that magic bag of yours."

Miraculously she produced a small container of citronella spray. "This is some natural repellent a friend of my mother makes on the island. It doesn't work very well but the little bottle was convenient for carrying around." They took turns spraying it all over each other and then put their minimal clothing back on to protect as much skin as possible.

Still, somehow the mosquitos always managed to find the one spot where the repellent wasn't. Finally they wrapped themselves completely in the sheet and slept close together, bodies tightly spooned in a tangle of entwined limbs.

When they woke at dawn, the sheet was soaked through from contact with the damp sand. With stiff necks, itchy skin and wet shorts, the luster of the adventure seemed to be wearing off. Stripping down, they ran into the sea for a morning bath, the salt water both stinging and soothing their bites.

"If we stay in the water, they can't get us," Tucker said, reaching for her.

"That's true. They'll be gone in a little bit, as soon as the sun is up." She dipped her head back, her dark hair emerging from the surface in a sleek dripping cap against her scalp.

"Mermaid goddess, have you ever done it in the water?" He put his hands over her breasts, feeling the hardness of her nipples against his palms.

She laughed and pressed against him. "No, Neptune, I never have. Shall we see if your spear gun works?"

By the time the first sailboat of the day arrived, they were ready to play their roles as two tearful teenagers who had been left behind on a snorkeling tour the day before. "Let's just not choose the first boat that comes, let's check them out, pick a good one," Chloe suggested. They had found a protected place in the brush to scope out the day's arrivals.

"Well, let's not wait too long. You know that I could easily finish up all the food we have left by noon." Tucker buried a banana peel in the sandy soil beneath their feet.

Chloe could not believe how hungry he always was. Her own stomach had been in a tight little knot for the past few days, unable to digest much of anything.

To pass the time, she asked him, "What island is south of Antigua?"

"Uh...Guadeloupe?"

"Ding, ding, ding! Good job. And what little island group is off of Guadeloupe?"

"No idea."

"The Saints. And the biggest of the Saints is Marie Galante."

They went on this way for a while until he touched her arm and then pointed. "Look."

Another sailboat was gliding slowly into the bay.

"Geography whiz, what flag is that they're flying?"

She shaded her eyes. "Norway. They usually speak English pretty well. How many people do you see? I only see two."

"Yeah, a man and a woman. Hmmm, she's not wearing any top."

"She's European. And a sailor. That's how it goes on the water. She's probably not wearing any shoes either."

"Shit. Our shoes. We forgot our shoes on the houseboat."

Their eyes met. "Well, where we're going we don't need any shoes. We can buy some new flipflops on the next island." They watched the Norwegians moor their boat and throw out the anchor.

"Are you ready for this?" he asked her. "You're the actress, not me."

She stood up, brushing the sand off her legs and slinging the bag over her shoulder. "Come on, let's do this thing."

CHAPTER SEVEN

Tyler spent the night at Elle's casita, mostly in a state of numb disbelief. He did not understand how such a safe, carefully planned camping vacation with his son had gone so awry. Somehow he had to fix this situation and get Tucker back home, but he had no idea how or where to begin.

After a couple of hours of disjointed and rambling discussion centered around the current incredible circumstances, they settled into a dazed silence. The quiet was broken only by the sound of ice hitting the bottoms of their plastic cups every time a drink was set down, or by the soft thud of Tyler's feet hitting the floor of the screened porch as he pushed the hammock into motion again.

"Are you hungry? I can make something." Elle got out of her canvas chair and went into the kitchen. "I have eggs. Maybe some leftover something." She poked through the fridge.

Tyler had no appetite although he couldn't remember the last time he'd had a meal. "Yeah, we ought to eat. I'm not fussy, you choose." He stared listlessly out into the night, trying to think what he should be doing next.

As she clanked a few pans around on the stove, her cell phone chimed on the table and she moved swiftly to claim it. "Hmmm, I better take this," Stepping outside into the darkness, she said quietly, "Sí," and then walked down the driveway and out into the road.

Tyler stayed quite still, trying to catch her conversation. He was surprised to hear her speaking in what to him sounded like passable Spanish but she was far enough away that he could not make out any of the words. Within a few minutes, she had returned to the cottage, her lips set into a narrow line, her wild eyes fixed on some unseeable point in her mind.

"Everything okay?"

She nodded. "Yep. Sure. Everything's fine." She set the phone on the counter next to the cutting board. "You good with hot peppers?"

Her obvious unwillingness to share any information about the call piqued his curiosity and he made a mental note to look at her phone when he got a chance.

Full mouths gave them another good excuse not to talk, and they ate Mexican omelets in companionable quietude, their bare knees touching under the small plastic table, her feet resting on top of his. It was a rare moment of repose for her, he realized. She was like a butterfly or maybe a hummingbird, almost always in motion, occasionally alighting on a branch or wire for a brief respite before flying off again.

When she hopped up to clear the dirty dishes, he stopped her, his hands feeling the smallness of her rib cage beneath her dress. "Let me."

She stayed there for a second, holding the plates aloft, leaning into his grasp. "The dishes can wait until morning," she said. "But I can't."

It was hard to deny the desperation in their lovemaking, the void they were trying to fill, however temporarily, but they agreed that they were a good match sexually, sharing the best of two lifetimes of experience.

"This does feel a little weird," he commented afterwards, enjoying the feel of a real mattress and good bedding, which was as satisfying as a delicious dessert after a gourmet meal.

"What?"

"The idea that my son is probably going at it with your daughter at the same time that I am doing you. Crudely speaking."

"Yeah. I know. I was trying not to think about it." They lay on their respective pillows, eyes open, staring into the darkness.

"Does this make us bad parents?"

"Yeah, probably. But so does pretty much everything I've ever done, apparently. So nothing new on this end. But I'm sorry for your loss. Of virtue." She felt for his hand and gave it a heartening squeeze. "Now enough of this feeling sorry for ourselves. How soon can an old man like you get it up again?"

"Give me a few minutes," he said, returning her playful squeeze. But then he rolled onto his side, facing the wall, needing to be alone with his thoughts for a bit. And with the guilt in his heart.

A hot shower in the morning was even better than a real bed, he decided as the water streamed over his head. He tried to think of how many days he had been on the island now – a week, maybe? He washed his hair with some shampoo that smelled like coconuts and scrubbed his body with a loofah brush hanging from the faucet. It felt great to be clean and, for a moment, as he toweled himself dry with the fresh towel she had given him, he felt full of energy and hope.

Elle had her phone pressed up to her ear as she handed him a cup of coffee. "Yeah, I've called my bank," she was saying. "They said they were going to get in touch with you or you can contact them any time. It's all set. I don't need a Puerto Rican mortgage..." She held a container of milk out to Tyler questioningly. "I don't understand what the fucking problem is. Why can't I just sign today?...Okay, okay, bueno. I'll check with you tomorrow." She smacked her phone down on the edge of the stove. "Seems like every day is a holiday in this freakin' country. Or territory. Or whatever it is."

"Good morning." Tyler kissed her lightly on the lips. "You look beautiful after a night of good sex." Her disheveled hair was clipped up into a tangled mass on the back of her head, one stray, very blonde strand hanging loosely along one cheek. She was dressed in a long loose garment that tied behind her neck; at one time it had probably been elegant but the silky fabric was now faded to a pale washed-out gray and one seam was ripped from the hem nearly to her knee.

She laughed and relaxed a little. "You country boys have such low standards." She slapped the back pocket of his shorts. "That was a good time, honey," she said with a Southern accent. "Now what'd you say your name was again, sweetheart?"

"Floyd. You know. Rhymes with hemorrhoid. Because I can be such a pain in the butt–" He stopped joking as she held up a hand, cocking her ear towards the bedroom.

"Something's going off. Is that your phone?"

They both froze, motionless, listening. From somewhere in the house came a muffled dinging sound. In the next moment, she rescued his coffee cup as he flew by in search of his daypack. Rifling through the front pocket, he pulled out his cell, which lit up with the notification of "One new text message."

Taking a deep breath, he touched the screen. A message popped into view. Elle was at his shoulder now, watching with him.

"I'm OK. Don't worry."

That was it. The entirety of what his son had to say to him.

Instantly he hit the call button, waiting to connect, but was immediately sent to voice mail. "Tucker, where the fuck are you?" He could not control his anxiety any longer; he was shouting into the receiver. "This has gone on long enough. Call me NOW." He hit "Send" just before Elle grabbed his hand from the phone.

"Shit, I'm a bad parent. I shouldn't have left that message. I just couldn't help myself."

"You're not a bad parent, you're just a bad negotiator." She led him out to the porch and sat him down in a chair.

"Calm down and then call him back. And remember – you'll catch more flies with honey."

A vibrating noise from the kitchen made them look up. Elle's phone was making a humming noise against the metal stove top. She was there in two long steps, Tyler right beside her.

"Damn them." They both stared at the message on the screen.

"We're okay. And I know, Mom."

"What does she mean by that?" Tyler indicated the second line.

"Just an old mother-daughter thing between us. You know, be safe, use condoms..." Elle's eyes did not move from the phone, as if waiting for another text to come in.

"Text her back. Ask her where they are."

Her thumbs flew across the touchpad with a speed usually only associated with youth. *"Where are you?"*

They waited, watching the phone, sipping coffee, not speaking. After five minutes, she said, "They obviously have decided they don't want us following them. This is consensual manipulation." She sounded tough and angry, but her hand shook as she placed her empty cup on the table.

What now, Tyler wondered. Was there a possibility they had been kidnapped and were being held against their will? He looked down at the floor, where the two pairs of flip-flops they had brought back from the houseboat sat heaped forlornly in the corner, like sad dogs waiting for their owners to return. It was unlikely; there was something defiant about their purposefully short texts, a child-to-parent challenge to leave them alone.

Abruptly Elle stood up. "I guess I'll take a shower. There's more coffee if you want it."

Through the doorway he watched her go into the bathroom; the nightdress slid off her shoulders and onto the floor in one fluid motion and she stood there naked in full view as she waited for a brief instant while the water warmed up. Even at this distance, he could see a fading scar on one of her buttocks; it was curiously circuitous and he was surprised he hadn't noticed it before.

They had become so close so quickly – as intimate as they already were, there was still so much he didn't know about her. Suddenly her phone vibrated again, this time against the plastic surface of the table next to him. He looked at it; another new text message coming in. It might be from Chloe – he could not resist the urge to view it.

"*Lo necesito HOY*," he read. There was no name, just a phone number. Shit, could he mark it as unread? He didn't think there was a way to do that with a text.

He could hear the shower still running full blast. Quickly he scrolled down through her recent stored texts. There was nothing suspicious that he could see, but who kept dodgy messages in their phone – they were too easy to erase. He shifted quickly over to her call log; lots of times people would delete their incoming calls but would forget about getting rid of the numbers they themselves had dialed. Sure enough, the same number showed up a few times in her outgoing call list. A couple of times a day over the last few days, the most calls being on Saturday. There was even one at 1am on Sunday morning.

Guiltily he stopped himself. He was being ridiculous, snooping through her phone, trying to read suspicion into what were probably communiques from a best girlfriend or someone else close to Elle.

The water stopped running and he gently put the phone back down on the table, making sure to first return it to the new text message. Nervously he went outside, pacing the yard, watching a hen and a rooster as they pecked their way across the driveway, scratching in the dirt. He picked a brilliant red hibiscus flower from a bush and brought it back inside, letting the screen door slam.

Elle was already sitting at the table again, a towel wrapped around her, looking at the phone. "Sorry, I looked at that text," he said, tucking the bright blossom behind her ear and kissing her on the cheek. "I thought it might be from Chloe."

"No, just an annoying friend." Casually she deleted the message and stood up. "Can I take you back to the campground for the day? I have to take care of this."

"Yeah, sure." He did not know what to do with himself at this point – the campground was as good a place as any to sit down and collect his thoughts. He started to wrap his arms around her but she slid sinuously out of his embrace and disappeared into the bedroom, returning moments later dressed in a long, multi-colored skirt and tight purple t-shirt that hugged her womanly curves and showed off her tiny waist. Her blonde hair was brushed out into a wavy angelic froth around her shoulders and her eyes looked larger and wilder than ever; they seemed to be focused on something beyond him, like she had just dropped some awareness-enhancing drug.

"Ready?"

Flamenco Beach looked beautiful through the trees as he walked the road out to Section E. The wind had finally died down and the water was unusually calm and almost glass-like. Even the campers seemed affected by the lull in the weather, their energy transformed into a quiet inertia; they sat in the shade reading or rocking in their hammocks, staring out to sea, except for Cassidy, who knelt by the water tank, washing his clothes by hand with a scrub brush and rinsing them in a Styrofoam cooler.

"Hey, Mackie. Have a good night?"

It was a simple question without an easy answer and Tyler could not begin to think of how to respond. Before he even said anything, Cassidy continued the conversation. "Hey, so what happened with the dinghy last night? Did you find the kids at the houseboat?"

Tyler recounted the events of the last twenty-four hours for Cassidy, and then again for Alejandro and Tom and Lisa and eventually again for Jane and Sam and Leo and a few other campers that he did not even know. They were all very supportive, offering sympathy and assistance, although nobody really had any idea of what he should do.

"So what — they just went to this houseboat and then they just kind of vanished into the ethers? There has to be an explanation. I mean chances are they were not abducted by aliens." This observation came from a tall, long-termer named Sid with curly unkempt gray hair and a rail-thin physique that suggested an aging bass player or a former heroin addict.

"You might do better talking to sailors instead of campers," suggested Jane. "Most of us don't know much about that end of the island."

"I beg to differ," said Sid. "Some of us have done some sailing. Although I don't mean me."

"You might as well settle in — you could be here a while. There are a couple of ocean-front campsites opening up in the next few days." Tom offered him an open bottle of whiskey and when Tyler declined, he took a swig himself. "Might as well get yourself some beachfront property."

They were full of good intentions, but in the end not much help. Soon they drifted back to their own sites, leaving Tyler alone with Cassidy again. "So what does Elle think?" he asked.

Tyler shrugged. "I don't know. She's upset but she seems to be caught up in this house-buying thing."

"She's a hard one to pin down, that Elle. In a lot of ways." Cassidy stood up to wring out a bed sheet. "And just so you know, a lot of men on this island have been captivated by her uh, charms. Including our dead buddy, Ivan. She's a sexy old thang." He laughed and coughed and then lit a cigarette. "You just might not want to get too attached is all I'm saying."

Tyler thanked him for the unsolicited advice and went back to his tent. He knew what he should do next, but he would put off the inevitable call to Lucy for as long as he could. Instead he pulled a notebook out of one of the pockets of his suitcase and sat down in his reclaimed camp chair to work out his thoughts on paper.

Elle did not show up until nearly the end of the day. By then Tyler had drunk a few beers, walked the beach twice, stopped to check his email at the Villas and investigated what it would cost to extend two plane tickets. When she finally arrived he was sitting in a hammock, watching Leo prepare dinner from his catch of the day, which included a couple of conch and a spiny lobster. Regardless of age, all of the men in the campsite paused in awe of her presence when she approached.

"Hi, beach boys," she said, taking off her sunglasses and acknowledging them all around. When her gaze locked with Tyler's, an unspoken force seemed to pass between them. Before he even realized what was happening, he was out of the hammock and walking towards his tent with her.

They couldn't get their clothes off fast enough. It was too hot to shut the window and door flaps and it didn't seem to matter anymore – everyone in Section E knew what they were doing and hopefully they would look the other way if they happened to be walking by.

"Oh, my god," was all she said. And then, "What is wrong with us? Oh. My. God. Oh! Oh..."

Afterwards, as they passed a towel back and forth, wiping the sweat and other fluids from their bodies, she said, "As impossible as it seems, I think that was even better than yesterday."

And the best part, thought Tyler, was that for a few moments, everything else in the world slipped away except the pleasure of sexual giving and receiving. He buried his face in the warm moistness between her breasts and tried to keep the rest of his life at bay while he filled his brain with the scents and sensations of her. Lulled by the beat of her heart, for a precious short while, he escaped into the false security of sleep.

It was dark when he awoke to the pleasant feeling of her hand stroking him into hardness again. By turning his head just the slightest bit he could move his mouth to her breast; he loved how easily he could arouse her this way and how it made her moan and gasp. She leaned into him and then out again, enhancing the sensualness of the experience for both of them, pulling away and then pushing forward, rubbing and grinding against him.

"Animals," she whispered. "We're animals."

"Really sexy animals," he murmured, his breath hot against her.

"Use your tongue."

"Like this?"

"Yes. Oh, yes."

This time he wrapped the bed sheet around the two of them and they walked together through the shadowy trees to the darkness of the open showers. "Just warning you, it's not hot. Or even warm."

She gasped and shrieked as the water ran over her. "I'm awake now," she laughed, huddling against him as he scrubbed her with a bar of soap.

"You're having too much fun," yelled someone walking by. "Behave yourselves!"

Back in the tent they dressed slowly, prolonging the moment. "I'm starving. And I bet I missed the conch and lobster stew," Tyler realized regretfully.

"Let's go see." Elle led the way along the dark path with the skill of someone who knew the territory.

Sam and Leo were just finishing bowls of what smelled like an amazingly delicious concoction. On the edge of the site, Alejandro sat in a camp chair, drinking something green from a plastic cup, a beatifically stoned smile on his face.

"Oh, too bad you missed dinner, dude," Sam grinned at him knowingly. "We waited for you but the waiter needed our table for the next reservation. Just kidding – we left some in the pot for you. Here, you can use my bowl. One less thing to wash."

Tyler shared his portion with Elle, passing the spoon back and forth, savoring the rich flavor of fresh seafood mixed with potatoes and vegetables.

"What are we drinking tonight?" he asked Alejandro.

"Mojito. Full of fresh mint. But I think I'm in the mood for a Bushwacker." He staggered to his feet. "Anyone want to join me?"

Sam and Leo glanced briefly sideways at each other. "Uh, no thanks, man. We're playing Nines tonight with Sid."

"What's Nines?" Tyler's question hung in the air as they all watched Alejandro limp off in the direction of the road.

"Man, he is wasted tonight," Leo commented, shaking his head.

"Nines is a card game somebody made up here years ago. Elle is pretty good at it. But she hasn't played since we added the Joker rule."

"Pretty good at it? I beat your asses hard last time! We'll teach you, Tyler. This is what Section E does for a hot night of entertainment, before they go to bed at nine o'clock." The reflection of the candlelight gleamed in her kaleidoscopic eyes.

"Oh, really?" Sam threw all the dirty dishes into the empty pot and then shoved it aside to wash in the morning. "Because I remember Ivan kicking your butt last time you played with us."

"Yeah, that was the night he died. You guys go on without me; I'm going to hang here." Leo lit a cigarette and held it expertly between his lips as he put the remaining food safely away in a cooler, out of the reach of chickens and feral cats.

"Maggie is coming over after work," Sam said in answer to the unspoken inquiry. Maggie was a young local waitress who looked great in a bikini and had a crush on Leo. "Maybe I'll sleep in the guest tent tonight."

They walked a few hundred feet to Sid's campsite, where the picnic table was completely cleared off and illuminated by a solar lamp overhead. "We always play here – Sid is the only one who ever actually clears off his table." In contrast to the frat house atmosphere of Sam and Leo's site, Tyler noticed that Sid's area was immaculate, every item and tool stored neatly in its proper place. Tyler knew from his own limited experience how much energy it took to accomplish this kind of tidiness when camping.

Sid materialized out of the darkness nearby. "Oh, I see we have a few guest players tonight. Elle the Shark and some fresh bait." From a wooden box resting on a handmade counter at the end of the table, he produced a deck of cards.

Nines was way more complicated than Tyler had expected. Apparently new rules were randomly added as the campers got bored with the basic game. From what he could tell, twos were wild, tens and aces cleared the pile, as did four-of-a-kind. If a nine was laid down, the next card played had to be lower than a nine. The latest rule was that a joker changed the direction of play. In addition to all this, each player was dealt nine cards, three were placed face down, three face up, and three had to be in the hand at all times, until the pile was used up. First one to get rid of all their cards won. Card counting was key and both Sam and Elle had amazing photographic memories for who had picked up which cards and what had been played.

Tyler found the personalities revealed in the playing as interesting as the game itself. For all his compulsive orderliness, Sid was easygoing and couldn't care less if he won or lost. Jane played quietly and intensely, Sam put down his cards fast and hard, shouting and swearing over victories and losses, but Elle played only to win, stealthily, seriously, aggressively, her mood darkening swiftly if the game did not go her way, glowing with satisfaction when it did.

Tonight the cards were not in her favor, and with each new deal, she seemed to get angrier and more determined to sway the odds back towards her own triumph. When Sam passed around the pot pipe and the rest of them got giddy and relaxed, Elle became more tightly wound and more intent on winning.

"Too bad you don't have a big jug of vodka and cranberry juice like last time," Sam commented to her. "You and Ivan got pretty loosened up drinking that, as I recall. If they did an autopsy on him, they must have found a lot of that in his system. Sorry," he apologized when Elle gave him a cold look. "That was probably in poor taste," he added before laughing uncontrollably.

"Well, I'm ready for bed so that means game night is over, folks," announced Sid, unfolding his six-foot-four frame from the picnic bench. "Or you have to take it somewhere else."

"The evening always ends so early with you elderly people." Sam stood up and scratched at the tattooed skin on his bare chest. "And I'm being eaten alive."

Tyler touched Elle's elbow; he could feel the hum of angry energy buzzing through her flesh. "Elle – let's go."

"I need a drink," she proclaimed, getting abruptly to her feet. "Who wants to go to the Sand Bar?"

"I'll go," said Sam. "It would make Leo happy if I wasn't home for a few more hours."

Suddenly Tyler felt he needed some distance from this unpredictable, intense woman. "I think I'll pass. I'm tired. I'm just going to stay here for the night."

Her eyes burned like glowing candles as she stared at him almost hostilely. "Okay, then."

"Hey." He pulled her towards him. "I just don't feel like drinking," he lied. "Don't be weird about it. Come back later."

"Maybe. But probably not. I'll be back in a few minutes, Sam. I need to get my stuff." She glided off down the path in a strange silent way.

"Whoa. What just happened?" Tyler felt like his lungs had just been vacuumed.

"Yeah, she gets like that. She's not a great loser. Don't take it personally; she'll be over it by tomorrow. After a few vodkas. Luckily she's not out here very often at night." Sam pulled his tangled hair back into a ponytail and then up into a bun. "Guess I oughta put a shirt on."

"Guess I oughta call Tucker's mom. Been putting that one off."

"Maybe you should call his dad too. Just sayin'," he added in response to Tyler's quizzical look.

"What do you mean by that? Is that a comment on my sorry parenting skills?"

"No, no, not at all." Sam held up a hand. "You're a cool parent. But he showed us his birth certificate that night we got him really high – I mean, that night he hung out with us. Ha. I'm totally putting my foot in it, aren't I?" he laughed at himself as he headed towards his tent to get a shirt.

"He what?" Tyler followed him. "Why the hell would he show you his birth certificate?"

"Because we didn't believe him when he said Kip Kingsley was his real dad. His birth dad, I mean."

"Shit. He's not. He's just..." Suddenly it was all clear – how Tucker's behavior towards him had changed since they had left on the trip.

"Just what? I think I'll wear this vintage Hawaiian shirt that Mojo left me. It only has a small burn hole in the pocket." Sam looked like a different person with his hair tucked up and a real shirt covering his tattoos. "What do you think, will girls love me in this?"

"He's just a fucking abusive asshole who Lucy happened to be living with at the time she gave birth. He never cared a rat's ass about Tucker!" Tyler exploded angrily.

"Oh, ouch. Yeah, his music sucks too. Even if he did make millions on it. Anyway, your son seemed pretty worked up about it, like he thought somebody should have told him sooner. But then again..."

"Then again what?"

"It was some killer weed. Sorry, sorry. I had to say it!" Sam put a hand on Tyler's shoulder. "Look, I know I come off as a stupid stoner, but I'm not actually. I'll help you find him, I mean it. I don't know how we'll do it, but maybe you'll think of something."

"Sam, you ready to go?" Elle's voice came through the trees.

"On my way!" he responded. "So, let me know what I can do, really." Then he disappeared down the path.

Tyler slammed his fist down in the only free space he could find on Sam's picnic table. He could not believe this was happening. He had no idea what to do next – all he knew was, there was no way he could call Lucy now.

CHAPTER EIGHT

It was impossible to sleep. As he flipped from front to back and side to side, the events of the day churned through his mind – the torment of Tucker's abrupt text message, the primal afternoon sex with Elle, his final exchange with Sam about the birth certificate. By midnight he gave up and decided to go for a walk on the beach.

He had not gone fifty feet when he heard his name being called.

"Up here, amigo." Above the sand he recognized Tom and Lisa's campsite from the string of multi-colored Christmas lights that ran around their picnic area; not surprisingly they were still drinking, although the bottle of Barrilito rum that Tom held out to Tyler only had a couple of inches left to go. He accepted it gratefully – he could not think of a better time to completely fall off the wagon than now.

"Want some of this for that?" Lisa hospitably held out a rough-hewn chunk of lime before breaking into a spasmodic smoker's coughing fit.

The fiery combination of alcohol and citrus did a lovely tango as it burned its way across his tongue, down his throat and into his bloodstream.

"Thanks. That was excellent." He sank down onto their picnic bench to enjoy the buzz.

"What're you doing up so late?" Even in the darkness, Tyler could see Tom's eyes were heavy with alcohol and fatigue.

"Why you asking him that? You're up too." Lisa's voice held the argumentative late-night challenge for which the two of them were so well-known. Tyler recalled hearing them in the pre-dawn hours of his first evening in Section E before he had even made their acquaintance. The same night of the last Nines game, the night that Ivan died. All roads seemed to lead there.

"Yeah, but so what – he isn't usually up. Don't be such a nagging bitch."

In an attempt to break the building tension, Tyler said the first thing that came into his mind. "I remember hearing you guys at like three in the morning when I first got here. And then by the end of that same day they had discovered Ivan's body in his tent."

They both fell strangely silent which suddenly felt worse than listening to them argue. "Yeah. Son of a bitch, that Ivan. May the bastard rest in peace." Tom turned the rum bottle upside down and drank deeply.

"Oh, Tom's still pissed that Ivan thought I was hot and tried to put the make on me right in front of him." Lisa's throaty laugh rang out. "He really liked that jack of hearts tattoo on my left butt cheek. Said he was going to get a matching one." Lisa stood up, turned around and pulled down the waistband of her sweatpants to display the coveted design to Tyler.

"Pull your fucking pants up, woman. And I am not still pissed at a dead guy. Okay, maybe I am, but if so, it's your fault." He handed Tyler the bottle and then reached out to smack Lisa on the behind. Anticipating his behavior, she stepped neatly away at the moment before contact, staggering drunkenly only just a little.

These two were certifiable, thought Tyler as he swigged the last few mouthfuls of rum. This time the rush was hard and strong, like being on fast skis going down a steep mountain; his eyes watered a little from the intensity. "So did you guys hear anything suspicious the night that Ivan died?" he asked.

Again there was an abrupt silence. Tom and Lisa stared at each other fiercely with narrow eyes. "Nope. Nothing," Lisa said finally, her gaze still locked on Tom's.

Suspicious didn't begin to describe their behavior. Tyler wondered what they had actually been up to but he was not about to ask any more questions; the atmosphere was too charged now.

"Well, thanks for the rum. I'm going to head out." As soon as he stumbled a little down the sloping path to the beach, he heard them start up again in fierce whispers. He stopped and stood motionless, just out of sight, to listen.

"Shit. Is this going to follow us around now all our fucking lives?"

"What – what did I do? You would've done the same if you were me."

"This is the last thing we need right now, what with the tax audit of the restaurant when we get back, I don't want some petty island police force shining any other spotlights on us. We gotta come out of that audit smelling like roses."

"Well, the closest you'll ever come to that is smelling like a bottle of Wild Irish Rose!" Lisa's bitter laugh was only slightly louder than a wheeze. "You need to stop worrying, baby – our books are cooked perfectly and–"

"Our books are not cooked –they are completely legit. Remind me I gotta call work first thing in the morning." A loud yawn and then the thud of feet hitting the ground. "Now hide that friggin' glass bottle so we don't get thrown out of the campground and come to bed. Maybe I'll even let you call me Ivan."

"You asshole. Shut the fuck up."

They were definitely hiding something. Or maybe a few somethings. When he was sure they had gone inside their tent, Tyler continued cautiously down the beach. He had not gone much further when the flare of a lighter caught his attention. Quickly assessing his nighttime landmarks, he guessed this was Alejandro's site.

"Buenas noches?" he called out hesitantly.

"Ah, Señor Mackenzie. Ven aquí." The answer shot out into the darkness. The lighter flared again, briefly illuminating Alejandro's face, a small pot pipe and the inside of the screened porch of his oversized tent. Although Tyler made his way cautiously towards him, he still stubbed his toe on a protruding root in the path. "Be careful, my friend. Come inside quickly – I don't want any mosquitos in here."

He fumbled to find the zipper pull and then slipped swiftly into the protected space, which was dimly lit by a fading solar lantern. He could see Alejandro better now; he was wearing only a pair of striped pajama bottoms and a necklace of large white shells that glowed against his brown chest. The scent of insect repellent mingled in the air with the pot smoke.

"You're up late for an early riser," Tyler commented as he sank into a camp chair.

"I always take a long nap in the afternoon. Sometimes in the morning as well." Alejandro offered him the pipe and given the way the night was going, Tyler could see no reason to refuse.

"Must be tough being retired."

"Actually napping is a habit I picked up in the pen. Four out of ten years spent in solitary...you do what you have to not to go insane." It was such a leading response, that Tyler decided it was okay to pry a little.

"This was when you were a Black Panther?"

Alejandro smiled, showing his exceptionally pearly teeth. Tyler wondered if they were real. "No, this was many years later. When I got busted for being on the take for the Mafia. My life had been amazing until then – at one point I rented a yacht in New York Harbor for two hundred and sixty-five thousand dollars. I kid you not." His sudden laugh was surprisingly warm and infectious. "A boat like that, but no friends I wanted to take out on it for my birthday...That was July. Six months later, on December 16th, I got busted." The laughter faded from his voice.

"People didn't understand how a Puerto Rican could climb so high in the Mafia. How I could be sitting at a table and having Tony Salerno and Matty the Horse buying me champagne..."

Despite the hour and his inebriated state, Tyler found himself sitting up straighter in his chair. "No kidding."

The grin returned to Alejandro's face at the memory of it. "But when all the shit went down, they threw me under the bus first to try to save their own asses. I ended up doing ten years hard time, a total of four of which were in solitary. Since I was a big Mafioso, as soon as they sentenced me, the guards started harassing me. Like all of the sudden under my bed they found a shank – and it was six months in the hole for me. Five months here, eight months there. They were taking me to the prison hospital because of my paralysis – two guards and a lieutenant escorting me there, and I said to them, 'Where are your guns? Don't you think if these motherfuckers want to get me they would come after me with a gun?' And then it was ten months in the hole for saying that."

"And where was this?" Tyler asked in disbelief.

"Rochester, Minnesota. The federal medical prison. They did everything they could to make things as miserable for me as possible. But they couldn't break my spirit."

"Really. Huh." His story was wild. They passed the pipe back and forth a few times in silence, Tyler wondering how to corroborate the truth of what he was hearing. "So you must have made a lot of money before that time. Did you save any?" he heard himself saying. Shit, he was high – it was like he was looking down from the roof of the tent at the two of them having this conversation.

"Did I have money? They confiscated over a hundred million dollars in cash. They took that – they never reported it – and it went straight into their pockets. Then they took my property too, my brand new Volvo, my brand new Corvette..."

"You must have had some stashed some place safe. For a 'just-in-case' scenario."

Alejandro laughed again and nodded vigorously. "PVC pipes. In the ground. Yeah, I saved some. But that is a secret, man." He put his hand on Tyler's arm. "That is just between you and me. Now I am collecting Social Security – a least I am getting some of the money back that those sons of bitches stole from me!"

121

"So this is all separate from the jail stint you did for the Black Panthers?" Tyler's brain was definitely fogged now.

"The seventeen months I spent in jail in Ann Arbor for a murder I didn't commit? Yeah, that was decades earlier, after I went to Vietnam, got shot in a rice paddy and almost drowned. I was paralyzed from the neck down, had to learn to do everything all over again, which left me with the nerve damage you still see me with today. I am a scrappy survivor, man."

"Can't deny that." Tyler had lived through some things but nothing that compared to this man's stories. "You know, I was just starting out as a journalist in New York at that time – I don't remember your name in the news." Really, he didn't recall much of anything about the Mafia Commission Trials, but he wanted to see what Alejandro would say.

"Well, by that time I was already a doctor practicing at Mt. Sinai Hospital and there were people that paid a lot of money to keep my name out of the news."

"A doctor? When did you have time to get that degree in all of this?" Tyler nearly choked on the improbability of it.

"There were a good ten years in between – and the money I extorted from the gay bars of New Jersey helped me pay for my university bills. Hey, I am a very diverse guy; I was part-time a lot of things. During that time I even went to the Lee Strasberg school of acting for a while to become an actor."

Well, that could explain all of this, Tyler concluded amusedly. At the least, it had been an entertaining hour.

"Enough about me. What about your son? Any word?"

The sobering reality of Tucker's disappearance was an instant downer. Tyler shook his head. "We don't know where they are – they could be on this island or somewhere else. San Juan. St. Thomas. Anywhere."

"But at least you know he is not alone."

"What would you do? Call in your connections?"

"This is what I would do." Alejandro handed him the pipe.

They smoked without talking again for a few moments and then Tyler said, "I keep obsessing about the first night we were here, which was when Ivan died."

Alejandro's eyes became dark pinpoints and his beatific smile faded. "The same night my tent and mattress were slashed. Ivan...the bastard fucking hated me. Thought he was better than all of us. I'm glad I will never have to see his ugly face again."

And every one of them has a motive, Tyler mused. He remembered waking up that first night, being surprisingly cold, hearing people arguing in the distance. He suddenly also remembered that he had not known that Tucker was out of the tent until he had come back in. A chill crept through him. Had the boy been witness to something?

He realized he had no idea what Ivan even looked like, where he was from or anything about him.

"A Russian-American from Chicago I think," Alejandro answered in response to Tyler's inquiry. "Kind of a skinny motherfucker with long scraggly hair and this messy little goatee, always wore a cowboy hat. Probably to make him seem taller than he really was. He sure as hell wasn't no fucking cowboy." Alejandro's eyes closed suddenly and his head fell forward onto his chest for a second. "Whoa, I am falling asleep sitting here. Time for bed. Hasta manaña."

But Tyler stayed there for several minutes more, listening to the soft sound of Alejandro's snoring on the other side of the tent wall, before finally making his way across the campground to collapse on his own air mattress.

He woke a few hours later with a head full of cobwebs and a dry mouth to match. He had forgotten the feeling of the hangover funk, and at this time of morning, when the day was fresh and clean and full of hope, it was a path he did not want to go down again. A cup of coffee and a plan — that was what he needed.

123

Forty-five minutes later he was walking towards town, fortified by caffeine and breakfast from Rosita's kiosk. By the road to Tamarindo Bay, he gratefully accepted a ride from a tall woman in a golf cart full of bags of dirty laundry. She was all efficient energy.

"I'm Sadie," she introduced herself. "I own a guest house, care-take several cottages and snorkel every morning with the turtles at Tamarindo. I don't have time to take you any place that isn't on my way but where can I drop you?"

She drove as fast as she talked and a few moments later Tyler was walking down the crumbling sidewalk on the road into Elle's neighborhood. He passed small groups of school children on their way to the "Ecological School," which was a large newish building with solar collectors on the roof. He said good morning to a happy-go-lucky pink pig that was frolicking in a muddy yard with three big dogs and walked around a pair of exotic-looking iguanas that were copulating on the sidewalk.

He hesitated at the end of Elle's driveway, recalling the tension between them twelve hours earlier when she had left the card game, unsure of how she would react to him showing up unannounced. He searched for signs of life on the screened porch and then realized that her vehicle was not even in the yard. Striding confidently towards the house, he called her name a few times just in case. It was always possible she had been too drunk to drive home and that someone had given her a ride.

He let the screen door bang hard behind him to announce his arrival, on the off-chance she was in the shower or still sleeping. A quick walk-through of the tiny cottage showed an unmade bed and a coffee mug in the sink. He was about to make himself a fresh cup when, in his peripheral vision he saw a movement on the porch. A bulge in the hammock was wriggling and the hammock itself began swinging suspiciously.

Tyler froze and looked around for an appropriate weapon of defense. He was trying to decide between an aluminum frying pan and a bread knife, when a muffled voice mumbled, "What the fuck..."

A few seconds later the dull thump of a body hitting the cement was followed by "Ouch!" and "Fucking piece of shit!" Peering out of the doorway, Tyler saw Sam sitting on the porch floor underneath the hammock.

"Sam. What's happening, man?" Tyler held out a hand to help him up.

Sam's unruly hair was flattened against one side of his head and a tangled mass of knots on the other, a few strands stuck to his face with dried drool. The Hawaiian shirt of which he had been so proud the night before, was an accordion of wrinkles and appeared to be missing a few buttons. His bloodshot eyes blinked a few times, as he tried to reconcile exactly where he was, with who, and why.

"Tyler. Bro. Jesus, I feel like crap after sleeping in that stupid hammock. Is there any coffee?"

Tyler laughed. "Yeah, I was just about to make some. And there is also a hot shower."

"Really? Are you kidding me?" Sam's sluggishness disappeared and he was awake with the easy speed of youth. "Point me to it. Where's Elle? What are you doing here? What time is it?"

Instead of answering, Tyler grabbed him by the shoulders and turned him towards the door on the other side of the kitchen, where the rainbow seashell print of the shower curtain beckoned seductively. Sam moved forward like a hypnotized man, shedding his shirt and shorts along the way. He was soon groaning loud expletives of enjoyment as the steamy water ran over his skin.

"Okay, the shower alone was worth the agony of spending the night in that thing," Sam declared when they were back on the porch, sipping hot mugs of coffee. He looked around as if seeing his surroundings for the first time. "This place is nice. Maybe Elle will let me live here with her when I get a job as a waiter at Zaco's."

"Is that a plan?" Tyler asked amused.

"Yeah, I'm running out of money fast. If I don't work I will have to go home early. And it can be hard getting out to the campground at night after your shift. I mean, I haven't applied yet or anything. But I know I'll get the job."

The bravado of 'millennials' was amazing, he thought. They could brag about anything and there was nothing they believed they couldn't do.

"Did you see Elle this morning?"

Sam shook his head. "I can't believe she is already up and gone – that woman can pound them down. The main reason I had to stay here was that she was too wasted to drive me all the way out to the beach. I didn't think she could make it back on her own."

Tyler wondered where she was off to so early; probably something to do with buying "her" house. If Sam hadn't ended up here, Tyler probably would have not been able to control his inquisitive nature and lifelong addiction for snooping around. He would like to find out what was really going on with Elle.

The loud roar of a plane taking off from the airport a few blocks away made it impossible to converse for a minute. He had already learned that this was part of island life – the thirty seconds of obligatory silence whenever there was a departure from the tiny terminal.

"Sam," he said, when the buzzing died down, "I need you to think like a teenager for me for a minute."

"Ohh-kayyy..." Sam gave him a dubious look. "But you know that was a seriously long time ago for me, bro."

Tyler tried not to show his amusement at this response. "You're closer to it than I am, bro. So if you were a boy from Vermont on school vacation on a small island in the Caribbean..."

"I grew up in Virginia, but, okay, go on."

"And you're pretty much a straight A student and have never done anything really out of line in your short life. Then you go to this island and you meet this girl one night and you fall in love..."

126

"Okay, I can relate to that part. But I was kind of a C student who hated school."

"You can do this, Sam. So you go off with this girl for a night – and you have nothing with you. I mean, you have your phone but you don't even have your charger. All you have is the clothes on your back, a twenty dollar bill and your birth certificate. Where would you go?"

"Man, I don't know." Thoughtfully Sam combed his disheveled locks with his fingers. "I mean I don't know why you wouldn't just hide out on Culebra somewhere. There are some great deserted beaches here. Ever been to Brava?"

"Brava?" Tyler felt hopeful for the first time in days. "Where's Brava?"

Finding a ride out to the trail that led to Brava Beach had been a challenge. Finally they had just hitchhiked. The kindly older couple who picked them up gave them a ride all the way out past the museum to where the path began. It was a two mile hike on a path through an island forest that was not unlike trails Tyler had climbed in Vermont or on other Caribbean islands, winding its way down over rocks, dry stream beds and through gnarled branches. In a few places bevies of white butterflies created fluttering cloud covers in prickly bushes and dried wasps' nests warned of potential dangers.

Within half an hour they emerged onto a vast sweep of pristine beach that stretched for nearly a mile. Wild waves crashed against the shore with a fury beyond what Tyler had experienced at Flamenco. Beneath his feet, the white sand was soft and deep and hard to walk in, like trudging through fresh powder snow, except that it was hot and inviting, enveloping each step in its warm embrace.

There were just a handful of other people visible; a couple of kids surfing with boogie boards and two pairs of what appeared to be serious hikers with canvas sun hats, walking sticks and lace-up ankle boots. Tyler had to admit that he did have a small blister between his toes from

127

walking the path in flip-flops, but the gear of these people seemed over-the-top for Culebra.

"This is also a nude beach if you want it to be," Sam laughed when Tyler pointed out the overdressed tourists. "So I hope they're not offended, but I'm hot from that walk." He stepped out of his shorts and ran into the surf, disappearing under the next wave.

Shaded by a palm tree, Tyler sat and watched him. In the distance, he could see what looked like a couple of makeshift shelters farther down the beach. When he started to walk towards the first one, Sam materialized at his side, wet and dripping like a puppy. "Wait 'til you see this first place," he enthused. "You'll understand what I'm talking about."

Constructed of driftwood and other reclaimed materials and covered in a roof of palm fronds, the three-sided structure offered protection from wind, rain and sun with a picture-perfect view. A variety of colorful plastic buoys and fish netting decorated the outside, along with what appeared to be a large exploded (or perhaps unexploded) bomb casing from back in the day, now painted a cheerful red. Inside was a comfortable bench made from a couple of wooden shipping pallets and tables made from old coolers and recycled boat parts. The best feature was the two swings made of planks and rope; they hung sturdily from a branch that formed the main front-facing beam.

"If I were a kid on Culebra, trying to run away, this is where I would come." Sam hung his shorts on a buoy and then plopped down onto one of the swings. "Although it does get a fair amount of traffic during the day."

"I'm surprised no one is camping here." Tyler claimed the other swing and looked around.

"You're not allowed to. But people do. It's not like the police are going to come down here at night and check it out. Although the coast guard do swing by regularly. Bales of marijuana and pounds of cocaine have been known to wash up on Brava. Even a bunch of money once."

Tyler took a bottle of water out of his daypack and held it up. "But this would be the issue, right?" He took a couple of swigs and passed it to Sam. "You'd have to haul in lots of water if you were going to stay for a while."

"Yeah, and food too. Unless you were going to hike out every day and return at night." Sam stood up. "Come on, there's another sweet little shelter down at the end I want to show you."

The softness of the sand made for slow going and the stroll to the other beach shack took more energy than expected. When they finally reached the second structure, Tyler was ready to crawl into its shaded interior and sink down on the "couch," a makeshift seat created from a couple of boat cushions atop an old freezer. "This is amazingly comfortable," he admitted.

"If you really want to feel like you are on a desert island, this is where you go," Sam declared. "When I really like a girl, I bring her here. If she loves it here as much as I do, then she passes the test."

They sat in companionable silence for a while, listening to the sea crash against rocky shoals that formed the corner of the beach. "What do you think – were they here?"

Sam shook his head. "Nah. I don't think so. I can't explain why, I just don't feel it. There are a good number of hikers here every day – someone would have seen them by now and recognized them."

Although Tyler was inclined to agree with him, there was a part of him that just wanted to stay here for the day and wait and watch. And hope.

A few hours later, when they had snoozed and swum and hunger was setting in, they made their way back to the trail, which now felt hot and parched as it baked under the mid-day sun. Halfway up the trail, Sam turned to him. "So ask me the question again."

"What question?"

"You know, 'if I were a teenage boy...'"

Tyler tried to remember the exact words he had used. "So let's say you're a kid from Vermont vacationing on a small Caribbean island, a good kid, and you meet a pretty girl one night at a bar and fall in love, which makes you run off with her even though all you have is the clothes on your back, your cell phone without a charger, twenty dollars and your birth certificate. Where would you go?"

"It's the birth certificate, man. That's where your answer is. Can I have some water?"

Tyler passed him the nearly empty bottle. "What do you mean?"

"Tucker was pretty emotional when he showed it to us that night. He told us that he had lived on some island in the Grenadines when he was a little kid that he had never been back to. And we were all, 'Kip Kingsley, dude! You need to meet him.'"

Although Tyler was sweating profusely, he felt a chill pass through his chest.

"I mean, I don't know how far the Grenadines are from here, but they are still in the Caribbean. You know, it's like how some people will say stuff like 'I'm in Florida, so since I'm in the United States I might as well go to California.' This is gone." Sam held the water bottle out to Tyler who merely stared at it.

"So that's what I think. I think he went to meet the man who – whose name is on his birth certificate. I think he's gone to find Kip Kingsley." Sam wiped the back of his arm across his forehead.

Tyler looked around for something to lean against but there were no hospitable-looking tree trunks or rocks in the area. His secondary instinct was to lie down and curl up but the muddy red-brown dirt of the trail and insect-infested sawgrass looked less than inviting. When he swayed visibly, Sam reached out a hand to steady him. "Hey – you all right? We better get back to town and get some lunch, what do you say?"

He closed his eyes and took a deep breath. "I'll be okay. But you – you're a genius, Sam."

Sam beamed. "You think?"

They didn't speak much again until they had hitched a ride back into town and were seated at the Dinghy Dock bar, nursing cold beers and waiting for their fish burgers to arrive.

"So how far away is it actually?"

"What?"

"The island where Kingsley lives."

"Mustique? Probably about five hundred miles. But that's assuming he still lives there – it's more likely he's at his house in London." Tyler shook his head in disbelief. How could Tucker ever think...He stopped himself. Sam was right – this was exactly how he was probably thinking.

"So how would you get there from here? Can you fly?"

"Yeah, but not on twenty dollars. It's ridiculously expensive. You could sail. But that would take a couple of weeks at least, and that's assuming you didn't put into port anywhere for very long. Unless you had a private motor-powered yacht, that would be the only way." He stared out at the harbor full of boats, wondering how two teenagers without money would find their way down through the Lesser Antilles, from the Leeward to the Windward Islands.

"Maybe she's got money. Or access to a credit card."

Their food arrived and hungrily they dug in. "Chloe might have a credit card." Tyler realized he had never connected with Elle at all since the night before. "I wonder where she is."

"Hey, Maria!" Sam hailed the bartender. "Anybody seen Elle here today?"

Maria held up a full bottle of cranberry juice and shook her head. "Now that Perry's gone, we never seem to run out of this unless Elle comes by. I won't even tell you how many vodka and cranberry juices I served the two of them one afternoon last week."

Tyler pulled out his phone; he had not checked it all day. There was one missed text from Elle. "*Where are you? Nobody seems to know.*"

He texted her back. "*At Dinghy Dock with Sam. Come down?*"

"Well, I can tell you one thing," declared Sam, as he chewed on a French fry. "I know my mom would be freaking out if I were missing."

"You don't think I am freaking out enough?"

"I said my MOM. You said Tucker's mom doesn't even know." Sam's tone was more than taunting.

"Yeah, and she isn't going to if she doesn't have to. Here's one thing you should know about mothers – they won't worry about what they don't know." Tyler could feel his face shutting into grim lines. "Now be quiet and think about this next question – how would you get to Mustique if you didn't have any money?"

CHAPTER NINE

Chloe pulled up the hood of her sweatshirt and leaned back against the plastic cushions to look at the stars. Despite how good she was with geography maps, astronomy was another story entirely. She could only recognize a few constellations – the Seven Sisters, the Big Dipper, Orion's Belt – and there were so, so many. She was glad that sailboats had autopilot these days – there was an old guy on Culebra who had told her about how, back in the day, he had navigated a boat all the way from the States only using the stars. She wasn't sure if it was a true story, but she kind of thought it was; she knew that was how navigation used to be done.

Now that she had one of those seasickness patches behind her ear, sailing through the open channels wasn't so bad. She didn't mind doing a few hours of night watch for Hendrik if it meant they would get to their destination faster.

She had been surprised how quickly the Norwegians had become like family to her and Tucker after they had traveled together for the day sail to St. John. She had been so revoltingly sick by the time they arrived in Cruz Bay, that all she could do was sleep. Astrid had made her some tea and put her to bed in a narrow little bunk under the hatchway steps and she had slept for nearly twenty-four hours.

When she finally awoke, dehydrated and disoriented, she found that Tucker had already become their right-hand man. He was in a rubber dinghy tied off to the side of the sailboat, scrubbing the fiberglass outer walls. He grinned when he saw her and said something so garbled she thought maybe her hearing wasn't functioning.

"It's the name of the boat." He pointed to the prow he had just been cleaning. "Himinglaeva. It means 'the heaven-shining wave.' Kind of cool, huh?" He pulled the dinghy around to the ladder and climbed aboard. "So how are you feeling, my little Himinglaeva?" When he wrapped his long arms around her, she felt small and frail, enveloped by the fresh smell of salt and sweat that rolled off his body.

"Starving. And nowhere near as robust as you, sailor. What have you been doing?"

"Working for de man. De Norwegian man. Paying for our passage. I love these people." His sunburned visage glowed with a satisfaction she had not seen before. "This feels so right, this boat life."

"You think?" Chloe looked around. "Are they here?"

"No, they went into town to get some supplies. Took the motorized dinghy into the dock. Sooo also...they kinda know our story was shit. But I don't think they care. They like having us here. I think they're sick of just being with each other. You sure you're okay?" He steadied her as she swayed a little.

"I just need to eat." Her legs trembled as he led her down the stairs into the tiny galley kitchen and showed her the remains of a pot of chili that was still on the burner. "We've been saving this for you. Do you care if it's cold?"

She already had a spoonful in her mouth. "Oh, god, this is so good." She stood in front of the stove, trying to chew the cooked beans slowly. While she ate, he sat on a bench and gave her a nonstop report of his evening and day with Hendrik and Astrid; the education he had received about sails and rigging, the cooking lessons, the card game they had played last night. How they had met as young teachers at an alternative primary school and had decided to chuck a conventional lifestyle for an adventure at sea.

"So how much do they know about us?"

134

"They pretty much guessed we were not really left behind on a day cruise when we were not in a hurry to get onshore yesterday. I told them that we were kind of like them – that we had left school – well I said, college – and we were actually hitching our way south, headed to my father's place on Mustique and that we had run out of money. Really only a small part of it is a lie." Tucker scratched at the bug bites on his leg and then asked, "Did you check your phone? Tyler went totally whack job on mine."

Chloe had actually forgotten all about the text messages. When they had arrived in Cruz Bay yesterday, they had agreed they would both text their parents brief messages in the morning and then turn their phones off. But Chloe had felt so bad that she had typed hers in and saved it, so that Tucker could send it for her if she didn't wake up.

"What did he do? You didn't answer, did you?"

Tucker shook his head and looked away, scratching another bite on the side of his neck. "He left me this 'where the fuck are you?' voice mail like right away. But I just turned it off. Your mom sent you a message too."

He took a few steps across the cabin to retrieve the daypack from where it hung on a hook and fished their phones out of the front pocket. They sat side-by-side checking their messages, and for a fleeting moment it felt like they were just two normal kids doing what kids everywhere did.

"Shit, my mom sent me a text also," Tucker said. He read it aloud with a British accent. *"Haven't heard anything from you two in days – you must be having a fab time. See you in a few!"*

"So she doesn't know anything. Your dad – Tyler – apparently hasn't contacted her yet."

Tucker frowned. "He wouldn't. I'm sure he doesn't want her to know he 'lost' me because she will ream him a new one. What day is today – I'm sure he's going to have to tell

135

her soon; we must be due to fly back." He crossed his arms over his bare chest and bit his bottom lip, lost in thought.

"My phone says it's Wednesday. What do you think will happen when she finds out? Will she call out the National Guard?"

"I have no idea. But Tyler might have to hire them just to defend himself from her rage. She tries not to be, but she's a pretty overprotective mother. When I was small and we lived on the island, she never let me out of her sight. I don't ever remember being alone without her. Something went down when I was really young that she never talks about. That neither of them talk about." He stiffened and shook his head a little as if to rid himself of the memories. "What did your mom say?"

"Nothing really. Just that I needed to let her know where I was. She's harmless." Chloe shrugged and tried not to think about what she suspected about her mother now. "She's so caught up in the drama of her own world, she doesn't really worry about me. I think she felt really sorry for herself when my dad dumped me on her, so we worked out this way of living that didn't cramp her style. It probably would have taken her days to notice I was gone if it weren't for Tyler."

Suddenly she found herself blinking back tears. "I wish we could take a proper shower and change our clothes. I would feel so much better. I'm so sick of these stinky shorts." Her voice sounded childish and pouty and Tucker looked up at her with concern and surprise. She could tell that the priorities of personal hygiene had not crossed his mind. "I AM a girl, you know."

"I like how you smell." He leaned over and pressed his cheek against her bare midriff and breathed deeply. "Mmm, it turns me on." He pulled the elastic waistband of her shorts aside and buried his nose in her abdomen, inhaling all the funky scents of her unwashed female parts.

Despite her moment of self-pity, she laughed. "Stop. I feel so gross right now. I don't feel sexy at all."

He turned his head to make eye contact with her. "Yeah, but I know how to make you feel sexy." She felt his hand slide down between her legs and back up again to explore her crotch.

"Don't. What if they come back." Her protest was weak and pathetic because she actually did feel turned on and it felt good.

"What if. I had to listen to them do it last night. There's no privacy on a boat this small." He stood up abruptly and then in one swift gesture, he swept her up and laid her back on the galley dinette table and pulled her shorts off. "And there's not much space either."

"Tucker!" But she was giggling. and then she was moaning with pleasure and sighing with satisfaction and disbelief. She started to come almost immediately, and then he was inside her, filling her empty spaces, big and hard and she couldn't believe the waves of sensuality and desire that were washing over her, higher and deeper. She wrapped her arms and legs around him and held him as close to her as was physically possible as he shuddered violently with the power of his own orgasm.

They fell back against the polished wooden surface, panting, sweaty and smellier than ever. "That was freakin' amazing," he breathed into her ear. "Oh. My. God."

Holding each other, they enjoyed the now-ness of the moment until suddenly she tore herself away from him and sat up, sobbing uncontrollably.

"Chloe. Chloe! What's the matter? What happened?"

"We're such idiots." She pulled up her stained and filthy halter top to wipe her nose and her eyes." Of course it was amazing. We forgot to use protection."

Tucker had been really sweet to her that day, calming her down and then helping her take a bath with a gallon jug of water and a bowl. She did some mental calculations and decided her period was due any day and that they would probably be fine. But then the thought of what she would do when she got her period got her started crying all over again. "I'm gonna have to buy tampons. How do you do that on a boat in the middle of nowhere?"

"We need some money. How can we get some money?" He lifted her arm and poured a bowl full of water over the soap in her armpit.

"I have a debit card my mom doesn't know about. It's on my dad's bank in Pennsylvania. If we can find an ATM, I can get us some cash. Well, I can only take out $300, I think."

"Wow, that's brilliant. That changes everything, don't you think?" He dried her back with a dishcloth and then wrapped a sarong around the rest of her – it had been the closest thing to a real towel that he could find. "But we ought to do it right before we leave this island, just in case they are watching it."

"Are we leaving soon?" She felt so disoriented – in contrast, Tucker seemed relaxed and at ease with their entire situation.

"Tomorrow or the next day. They said they could take us as far as St. Kitts and then we would have to look for another boat. Or another way."

The thought of getting out on rough seas again filled her with instant nausea. "I've got to get something for seasickness before we go or I am going to mess up this trip."

As Tucker made a half-assed attempt to wash himself up a little with the remaining water, Chloe spread the sarong on the deck and stretched out on it to dry. The late afternoon sun combined with the light breeze coming off of the bay felt good against her semi-clean skin, even if her hair was still gross and greasy.

"They're not as old as they look."

"What?" Chloe thought maybe she had missed a piece of their conversation.

"Hendrik and Astrid. They're just wrinkled from spending so much time in the sun. I saw Astrid's passport. She's only like thirty something."

"Really?" The thought of looking twenty years older than she was made Chloe want to start crying again. She must be getting her period. "How'd you see her passport anyway?"

"They were putting their papers together to clear customs. Oh, right, and if any kind of coast guard boats come around, we're supposed to lay low. They aren't declaring us as being on board."

"Well, we're U.S. citizens. I think we're allowed to be in this country any time we want."

"You are. Remember I'm actually not. Plus, officially we're both underage." As he discussed the legal ramifications, he became quite still and thoughtful. Chloe worried about it when he got like this – he had much more of a moral conscience than she did. She could see that he struggled internally with things he considered wrong or illegal.

Voices and banging noises on the other side of the boat brought an end to their private conversation. Quickly slipping her shorts and top back on, Chloe went to help their hosts unload their purchases. When Astrid greeted her warmly and then transferred two plastic bags of groceries into her outstretched hands, Chloe realized she didn't care how leathery the woman's brown face was against the straw-whiteness of her long sun-bleached braids; she already felt more of a caring connection with the Norwegian than with her own mother.

By the following evening, Chloe felt completely renewed and ready to start on the next part of the adventure. She and Tucker had caught the ferry over to St. Thomas and gone to a big-ass Kmart where she had used her debit card to buy them both new wardrobes of cheap clothes, as well as toothbrushes, shampoo, tampons, condoms and all that basic stuff that she had always taken for granted. And new flip-flops for their tanned and dirty feet. Then, when they found a bank, she also realized that the purchase did not count against her daily cash limit at the ATM, and with $300 cash in her pocket, she felt like a queen. In the crowded streets of Charlotte Amalie, no one

139

paid the slightest attention to a pair of grubby teenagers on a shopping spree, carrying big plastic shopping bags and stuffing their faces with generic potato chips washed down with cheap cola.

As they sat cuddling on the last ferry back to Cruz Bay, Chloe appreciated the fact that they were able to be out in public together, not sneaking around, that there was no international alert out for them. Yet.

"I think your phone is going off." Tucker's fingers felt familiar and reassuring as they cradled the curve of her hip beneath her new tank top. She snuggled closer against him as she pulled her purse onto her lap to search through it.

"One new message," she said aloud. It was from a Puerto Rican number she didn't recognized. Her brow wrinkled as she studied the phone and then she gasped as the text opened.

"What is it?" Tucker could feel her body stiffen under his touch and he moved his head next to hers to read the message.

"Say nada to no persons or you are muerto también."

"WHAT?" he pulled away from her to stare into her widening eyes. "Who is that from? What are they talking about?"

"I don't know, I don't know!" she wailed. "It isn't from anyone I know. Oh, my god, how did he get my number???"

"Who? Who do you think it is?" He grabbed her wrists to make her look at him. The other passengers around them started to stare; self-consciously he released her and tried to appear casual again. "Chloe, tell me," he whispered loudly.

"Maybe – maybe it's him. The one who was fighting at the Dinghy Dock that night." She spoke in a tiny quiet voice and he leaned close to her face so he could hear her. "Remember he shined a light on us when we were leaving. He saw us and he knows we saw him."

She could feel him fill his chest with air and then hold it for a very long time, finally releasing the breath with a deep, deep sigh. "But you knew this, right? That's why we hid out on the houseboat in the first place, isn't it?"

"Well, yeah, but I didn't think he actually knew who I was. Fuck, I don't know his name – I'm not sure I would even recognize him if I saw him again. Would you?" She was scared and angry now.

"I never saw anything, I only heard it." Tucker spoke slowly and logically, working through the problem. "So this might mean that our parents have gone public, that our pictures are in the paper now."

"I don't think so. I think other friends would have texted me if that was the case. And your mom would not be sending you 'fab time' messages."

"True." He was silent again, thinking. "So what are you going to do?"

"Nothing." Then angrily she said, "No, wait." While he watched, she typed and sent a short furious response in all caps. *"FUCK YOU, MOTHERFUCKER."*

"What? Wait – don't. Jesus, Chloe. You don't want to antagonize the guy."

She was not even sure what that meant. "Whatever. I just wanted him to know that we're not scared of him. There's not a rat's ass chance that he knows where we are."

"Still." He lowered his voice to a barely audible level. "We heard him *drowning* someone."

"Tucker. No one knows where we are. Hendrik and Astrid don't even know our last names. We'll change our identities – what's a name you always wanted?"

He grimaced a little and snorted. "Anything that doesn't rhyme with 'fucker.' What was my mother thinking..."

During the next twenty-four hours as they worked hard at their new boat chores, it became a huge source of amusement for them to try out new names on each other. Heath and Isabelle took the laundry to town on the dinghy, Liam and Madison scrubbed down the head, Caleb and Avery chopped onions and garlic for fish stew. When they found themselves alone for a precious hour, it was Leonardo and Kate who made love on the narrow bunk under the stairs next to the engine, arms and legs flailing awkwardly over the edge and against the walls and ceiling. ("Now I can't get that annoying Celine Dion song from Titanic out of my head! Leonardo!" she had jokingly complained afterwards.)

But it was Chloe who stressed about how she was going to get through the next stretch of sailing and who nearly cried with thankfulness when Astrid produced a prescription box marked "scopolamine."

"They last for three days, but they take a while to start working. You better put it on tonight so that you will be good when we leave port tomorrow."

Chloe threw her arms around the tall Norwegian woman. "You've been so good to us, Astrid. I'd do anything for you."

"You have done almost everything for us today already." Astrid patted her on the back. "Too bad we can only have you with us as far as St. Kitts. But we are going to stay in that area for a while."

Now as Chloe sat by the tiller, alone at the helm, she found herself dreaming about a perfect fantasy life, where she and Tucker sailed onward into the sunset in the care of Hendrik and Astrid and there was nothing to worry about except whether the supply of condoms would hold out until they got to the next far-off port of call. She did not want to think about what would happen when they had to say goodbye to the Himinglaeva. These last couple of days had been the happiest in months for her.

When Hendrik came out to relieve her a few hours later, a rosy hint of light was just starting show on the eastern horizon. She thought she could make out the faint outlines of distant islands that her sense of geography told her should be Anguilla and St. Martin. She slipped quietly down into the cabin, shed her clothing and slid under a flannel blanket next to Tucker in their "bed" which was created each night when the dining table folded down against the wall and the two benches below pulled together to become a small and not very comfortable double sleeping area. But she was sad to think that they might only get to sleep in it another night or two; it was home now.

He stirred and threw the dead weight of an arm over her as she fit her cool body into the cozy curve of his long frame, his body heat curling over her like the hot flames of a blazing fire. She sighed with contentment – if only now could last forever...

She was wakened by the comforting smell of coffee. She loved the aroma of coffee brewing, even if she did not drink it; she loved it because it was still the classic indicator that somewhere a normal day was beginning for someone.

When she opened her eyes, she saw that Hendrik and Astrid stood a few feet away at the tiny galley counter, passing a steaming mug back and forth as they watched her.

"God morgen." She used the Norwegian greeting they had taught her as she sat up, discovering that the blanket had slid to the floor and that she had been spread-eagled stark naked in the middle of what was essentially the kitchen table. "Oh, my, god, morgen!" she laughed, grabbing the nearest corner of flannel and pulling it up to her chest.

"Not to worry, darling. We were just saying how beautiful you are asleep," Astrid assured her, but there was something in the way Hendrik avoided meeting her eyes, his gaze lingering on the blanket. She felt suddenly itchy and uncomfortable, like she had poison ivy in a place that was impolite to scratch in public. She hoped he wasn't really thinking THAT about her, but she kind of suspected he was. She'd seen that look on the face of more than one older guy in her life.

"Yes, very beautiful." He nodded stiffly and then turned abruptly to climb the stairs to the deck, saying over his shoulder, "We should be to Basseterre by afternoon."

"You want some, ya?" Astrid was holding out a piece of French bread smeared with some kind of thick dark jam.

143

Chloe realized her hand was trembling as she accepted the breakfast offering. The fairy tale seemed to be headed for a rapid and precipitous ending. Astrid reached out and gently pushed Chloe's hair off her face before grazing her lips across the girl's forehead. Then she followed Hendrik out into the air.

Chloe had to swallow hard before even biting into the bread. Thick crumbs showered the flannel covering her lap as she stared sightlessly at the blue square of sky that appeared in the open hatchway overhead. Nothing felt perfect and right anymore. They would have to get off the boat as soon as they could.

She choked a little on the dry crust, trying not to have a full-on coughing fit.

"What do you mean 'he looked at you weird'? How did he look at you?"

They were folding the benches back into place and setting the table up again.

"You know. Like – like he wanted to have sex with me."

"Ugh, don't be ridiculous. That's gross. He's like twice your age."

Chloe had gone quite still. "Don't tell me I am being ridiculous. I know what he was thinking. I am not being a narcissist when I say I know he was turned on."

"Okay. Okay. But you're a hot chick. He would have to be...impotent or like seriously gay or something not to be turned on by seeing you naked."

She did not know what to say. All she knew was she could not spend another night on this boat. "Whatever. Just don't leave me alone with him. With them. I don't feel safe. That's all I'm saying."

Tucker's eyes searched hers for a long minute, like he was looking for some insanity deep inside her. Then he said, "Okay. I won't."

Up above they heard the groaning of the mast as the mainsail shifted, catching the wind. Without even thinking, they steadied themselves as the boat listed to an even greater angle. "We're moving fast now," Tucker commented. "The wind seems to be picking up."

Peering out of the hatchway, Chloe could see that the sky was now a dirty white color; all signs of a clear and sunny day had disappeared. She perched on a step, leaning heavily against one wall to keep her balance. "Here's a question I was thinking about last night. Do you think they can track our location through our phones? You always see that in movies."

Tucker frowned. "Only if it's on and if we're online, for starters. I mean, if someone went into my computer at home and used the 'where's my iphone' app, they might be able to find it. Yeah, shit. They probably would. We ought to turn our location services off. Maybe delete any apps that identify where we are? When we dock, we are going to be in a foreign country; our phones might not even work there."

Although she had barely used her phone for days, there was something about being totally without it that made Chloe feel adrift and nervous. She liked being able to look information up online and even if she hadn't been able to respond, she enjoyed seeing other people's photos and posts on Instagram and Facebook.

She didn't want Tucker to see how unhinged she was feeling this morning. Suppressing her uneasiness, she said casually, "You know they use different money on St. Kitts and Nevis. They call it E.C., Eastern Caribbean dollars."

He nodded. "Yeah, I actually remember it from Bequia. It was the first money I learned to count with when I was little."

From up above they heard Hendrik calling their names. "I need your help up here with the sails, American kids! Don't be lazy."

By afternoon they were all in the larger dinghy, motoring into Basseterre, the capital of St. Kitts. Chloe's mood had lifted from the moment the island really began to appear; it had high magical mountains covered with green rainforests and a rambling community of buildings with

145

colorful roofs that sprawled from the harbor to partway up the green slopes. A long sandy beach ran the length of a peninsula on the outskirts of town.

"The mountain — it's a volcano," Hendrik informed them. "Only it is...sleeping?"

"Dormant." Tucker supplied the word.

"And there are... apes? The little ones, you know," Astrid giggled.

"Monkeys? Really?" Chloe leaned forward in the dinghy, as though she could possibly see them swinging from the trees on the mountainside.

"Yeah, I read that online when we were on St. John. They call them 'green monkeys' and there are actually more of them than people here. The French brought them for pets 300 years ago and they went wild." Tucker shrugged at the surprised look she gave him. "You do know I have kind of a photographic memory and a seriously geeky side."

She squeezed his hand. "You do know that I love that about you." Even though he did not take his gaze off the coastline, she could see him beaming with pleasure.

"Okay, kids, see you back here in two hours," Hendrik announced as he tied up at a concrete dock. "We have to clear customs and we are not declaring you, so go get lost somewhere."

"But not too lost," warned Astrid. "And I can already see you are real sailors — you forgot to bring your shoes. So be careful walking around."

"Real idiots is more like it. I can't believe we forgot our flip-flops again." Tucker climbed up onto the warm cement. "At least it's a cloudy day so we won't burn the soles of our feet."

They laughed at the way the ground seemed to roll beneath them as they reacquired their "land legs" after being at sea, staggering sideways sometimes as they wandered through the streets, marveling at the Caribbean charm of the city, so different from Culebra and the US Virgins. There was a French colonial character to the old buildings, with long louvered doors and wraparound

146

porches with painted wrought iron railings. The population was overwhelmingly Afro-Caribbean; schoolgirls in plaid uniforms, their hair plaited into tight cornrowed braids stared openly at the two barefoot American waifs; full-breasted women, wearing printed cotton dresses and bandanas around their heads, sat on benches and sold fish and cakes and bananas from plastic tubs on the sidewalk. A few men in dark suits and ties contrasted sharply with others in ragged t-shirts and ripped pants.

"We need to find a cheap place to stay until we can find a boat south," murmured Chloe.

"Why can't we just stay with the Norwegians? I'll protect you."

She was not going to have this argument with him. Proactively she went into a small corner grocery store and asked the man behind the counter where there was an inexpensive hostel or guesthouse. His lilting Caribbean accent brought to mind Bob Marley music and a Jamaican restaurant she had once visited in Philadelphia. He called a woman in from the back room and they spoke rapidly to each other in some mysterious dialect that made her think of New Orleans voodoo and then he turned back to her with directions to a place he recommended that local West Indian travelers frequented.

"You will get the best price and the real local culture from Miss Celestine, yes, miss," he promised.

Tucker's expression was seriously doubtful when they finally found the crumbling wood and stone structure, identifiable only by a flaking painted sign that read "Canne a Sucre" in ancient script letters faded from years of tropical sun. Tall French doors with peeling shutters ran the length of both floors; behind a few of the wavy old panes iron bedsteads and wooden wardrobes could be seen.

Chloe on the other hand, was completely enchanted, especially by the elegant elderly woman who answered the door. Even though she was quite stooped over, she was still nearly as tall as Tucker and her soft white hair was neatly combed into a twist on the back of her head. She was clearly of local descent, but the wrinkled and spotted hand she extended was of a lighter hue than Chloe's own very tanned skin. She glanced disapprovingly at their dirty bare toes, but welcomed them in and showed them to an upstairs room for 35 EC a night. "That's only like thirteen dollars!" Chloe whispered excitedly. "And there is a real shower down the hall!"

She could see Tucker take in the dark interior, the worn curtains and uneven flooring. Gingerly he sat down on the bed and the mattress sagged dangerously as the springs squealed. Reaching up he stuck a couple of fingers through penny-sized holes in the neatly knotted mosquito net that hung from a hoop above and raised his eyebrows questioningly.

For some reason Chloe was delighted by the decrepitude of the place. "We'll take it," she told Miss Celestine. "We just need to go back to the boat and get our stuff."

"It is compulsory that you pay in advance," the old lady informed her. "And breakfast is at 8am; if you don't rise until 10 you will not get breakfast because the kitchen will be closed."

She could see that even Tucker was impressed with the fact that they actually got fed as part of the deal. As they made their way back to the waterfront, she chattered excitedly, trying to make sure he was on the same page as she was. "We will make that squeaky bed sing tonight!" She squeezed his arm.

"I'm just sorry to be leaving Hendrik and – wow, look at that." Sailing into the harbor was an old-fashioned four-masted schooner with miles of rigging. They stood on the dock along with a handful of locals, admiring the beauty and complexity of the large ship as it anchored and brought down its sails. "Wouldn't it be fun to take something like that to the Grenadines. I'd like to learn to sail a ship like that."

"We'd have to stowaway – we'd never be able to afford it." Chloe turned to a couple of young tourists who had joined the crowd. "Excuse me, do you know where that ship sails to?"

They shook their heads, murmuring excuses in German, but a man in a uniform stepped forward. The gold tag clipped to his shirt pocket read "Customs and Immigration." "The Polynesia does a weekly circuit to St. Barts, Anguilla and St. Martin. It is one of the most beautiful of the Windjammer boats. Where are you two from?"

His question came so smoothly that it took them both by surprise. Chloe tried not to stutter before she replied, "California. San Francisco. The Bay Area. We're just island hopping."

"And how do you like our country of St. Kitts and Nevis?" he asked with sincere interest.

"Very much. We just got here." She was afraid she was going to say too much and she could tell Tucker was beginning to feel anxious about this conversation.

"Where are you staying?"

You couldn't just ignore a customs officer; otherwise she might have walked away. "At the Canne a Sucre," she was happy to be able to tell him.

Even though she knew he had been trained not to show any expression, he appeared mildly surprised. "Is that so? How did you find that place? The lady who runs it is an old friend of mine."

Without giving too much away, and against what was obviously Tucker's better judgment, Chloe continued the friendly repartee with "Norman the Customs Man" as he became known to them. By the time the first tender full of Windjammer passengers arrived on shore, Norman had invited "Kate and Leonardo" to come with him for a tour of the Polynesia while he conducted his legal business.

"You are so out of your cuckoo adventurous mind," Tucker breathed into her ear as they followed Norman up the gangplank. "And I so love you for it." He teased her earlobe with his tongue. "Because I can't wait to see this boat. Kate."

149

Although tired, happy and inspired, they were over an hour late by the time they met up with Hendrik and Astrid, and the Norwegian man was livid. Chloe and Tucker had clearly overstepped the bounds of the unspoken agreement with their hosts and it was time for them to go. Astrid did get a bit emotional at the goodbyes, kissing them both on the lips and hugging them to her brown chest, but Hendrik was all too happy to drop them and their few belongings back on the public dock. He shook Tucker's hand and thanked him for his help but only nodded curtly at Chloe, who was anxiously looking around to make sure Norman did not see them and their possessions just arriving on land now.

"I think he can help us find a boat off this island," Chloe had assured Tucker. "He really likes me."

"Okay, sure, Kate. What'd you say your last name was again?"

"Do you have a better plan?" she had demanded.

Finally settled into their new digs in the tattered old hotel, they relaxed on rusty metal chairs on the narrow landing outside the French doors and drank beer out of brown bottles while watching the rain that had been holding off all day finally come pouring down.

"Was that a rat? No, don't answer that. I don't want to know." Tucker squinted suddenly and held up a hand to his ear. "What is that sound? Sounds like a phone dying. You did turn your phone off, didn't you?"

Guiltily she leaped up. "I guess not. I thought I had. Shit."

She pulled the offensive devise out of the daypack, daring to give it a last look before turning it off. "*Three new messages,*" she read. She did not have any service here, but these must have come through before they left U.S. territory. With a glance over her shoulder to see if Tucker was watching, she quickly scrolled through them.

"It really is a rat, by the way," she heard him call.

The first message was from her friend Salina and for some reason it choked her up because it was just so...normal. *"Hey, GF. Where are you? No one has seen you in days. Beach party tomorrow at Flamenco for Davis. C U there?"* She felt like she barely remembered that Chloe.

The next one made her shiver. *"Chloe, this is Tucker's dad. Please tell him I am not mad. Just contact me. It's time to fly home."*

But the third one made her blood run cold. *"You I am find. CUNT. I come NOW."*

It seemed as though the phone fell out of her hand in slow motion. As it hit the floor, the back flew off and the battery fell out, skidding across the room and into the blackness under the bed.

CHAPTER TEN

The constant buzzing of the electric generator that powered the "Seafood Paradise" truck made conversation impossible. But Elle had insisted they had the freshest and cheapest grilled grouper on Culebra, so they were waiting in silence at a cement picnic table in the shadow of the food truck for their meals to be cooked, drinking from plastic to-go cups. Tyler almost thought it was a subversive move on Elle's part to postpone for as long as possible the impending discussion on their missing children, but the smell of frying fish was too good to walk away from.

With dinner secured in a big plastic bag, they drove back to Elle's bungalow, where finally, over an admittedly delicious supper, Tyler was once again able to broach the touchy subject.

"Mustique?" Elle stared at him in disbelief, her mouth full of rice and beans. "You think they could actually get there on their own with almost no money?"

"It's possible. From what you've told me about your daughter, it would not be out of character. For Tucker it's a big stretch, but I think he's impressionable enough that he could easily be influenced. And we know he's developed an obsession with this idea that he is the son of Kip Kingsley. He was carrying his birth certificate around in his pocket showing people."

"So have you been there? Do you think they could find his house?"

Tyler made thoughtful circles with a French fry in the ketchup on his plate. "Well, I did it years ago. Believe me, everyone on the island knows where he lives. But it is not easy to get to Mustique, there are no accommodations affordable enough for teen hobos and his place is a friggin' guarded compound. Assuming he even still lives there. And it is entirely possible that he no longer does." He did not go into the details of the sting he himself had helped engineer ten years earlier on the amoral abusive celebrity.

Her eyes narrowed into slits as she contemplated the potential scenario. "So if you wanted to get there fast, how would you go?"

"Well, I would fly. I think LIAT has flights from San Juan that eventually get to St. Vincent and then you could take a Mustique Air charter over to the island. Or go via Barbados. But I'm not sure they can do that as underage teenagers without proper travel documents."

She waited for him to go on. "Really you can get anywhere in the Caribbean on a boat and without documentation. Pirates do it all the time."

"Pirates?"

He gave her a 'don't be so naïve' look and continued. "If you can get to St. Vincent or Bequia on a yacht, you can easily sail or motor over to Mustique. Although local people don't travel much between Mustique and the rest of the Grenadines. But to sail from Culebra to the Grenadines? It is not an overnight trip. Even if you went direct, it would take you days."

"So it has been days. Do you think they could be there yet?"

"Why? What are you thinking?" But he knew what was running through her mind. He had already gone through this plan a dozen times himself.

"That we could fly there and retrieve them. Alert the authorities. Alert Kingsley."

Tyler snorted disdainfully. "Good idea, but I am the last person he ever wants to hear from. I think you're on the right track, but here's my first and biggest problem. Tucker and I are supposed to fly back to Vermont in two days. Lucy is super-pissed that we haven't contacted her. And she is going to be beyond super-pissed when I tell her the truth. And she is going to absolutely freak out if she thinks Tucker is headed to Mustique."

Elle put her weathered hand over his. His gaze fixated on the multitude of silver rings that she wore, all inlaid with a variety of sparkly and incandescent stones in shades of blue and green. They reminded him of her eyes.

"You know what you have to do." She squeezed his fingers, the metal bands of the rings pressing into the skin of his knuckles.

She was right. He could not put it off any longer. It was time to call Lucy.

"HE WHAT??" As he walked down the street holding the phone away from his ear, Tyler wondered if all of Culebra could hear Lucy's reaction. "When did this happen?! How could you not let me know? Oh, my god."

He said nothing, waiting for her to continue her outburst. "Why would he run away? Are you sure he wasn't kidnapped? Have you gone to the police?"

Tyler attempted to patiently explain the week's events to her but she kept interrupting. But when he brought up the birth certificate her angry barbs dissolved into the gasps and sniffs of a sobbing mother's breakdown. It pained him to picture her, with her masses of curly hair now faded from auburn to nearly white, the tiny dynamo firebrand turned into a fragile weeping waif at the news of her only child. "Why didn't we ever tell him the truth...only trying to protect him...how could he think...it's so insane, he looks just like you!"

Everything she articulated was something he had already said to himself. "This might be all conjecture," he reminded her. "But it's the only logical thing we can think of. And there really may be no logic at all if it is just two runaway teenagers in love."

"How can Tucker be in love? He's only sixteen. Okay, okay, I know that's a bloody stupid thing to say." He heard her blow her nose loudly. "He has to get back here – he has SAT testing next Saturday!"

The illogic of her reasoning reminded him of the contrast between the everyday routine he had left behind in

Vermont and the impulsive insanity that now seemed to dictate his reality. "And I have a paper to put out next week, but I am not coming back until I find him," he told her, making a mental note to himself that he still had to deal with his own business responsibilities.

"How could you have waited so many days to tell me?!" she wailed again. "He could be anywhere in the world. Pirates could have taken him to Columbia or Afghanistan by now... How could you be so inept to lose your son? I'm coming down there before you botch this up any more than you already have."

"Lucy – no – listen to me. LISTEN TO ME."

There was a pause on the other end of the line and he thought maybe she had hung up but he went on.

"I'm going to find him. I promise. I am going to book a flight to St. Vincent tomorrow or as soon as possible. We still have friends on Bequia I can stay with. You know it's not safe for you to go anywhere near Kingsley." The sound of a long sniff let him know she was still there and he blundered on. "But I need your help – you were always the best investigator I've ever known."

"Don't bloody bullshit me, Tyler Mackenzie." But the compliment seemed to help her focus. "You've got to move fast on this. I don't want fucking Kip taking out his aggressions towards me on my son – the man is a fucking irrational time bomb."

"We did get a couple of texts a few mornings ago..." Tucker felt dizzy from trying to remember how much time had passed since the brief messages.

"We? Who is 'we'?"

"Chloe, the girl's mother. I've been...working with her to figure this out." He knew how lame that statement sounded and that Lucy, who knew him better than almost anyone in the world, would know exactly what his relationship with Elle was.

"Tyler. Are you kidding me. You never change. It's like you still have adolescent hormones raging through you." He wanted to argue with her, remind her it had been years, that while she had her horny fling with her lumbersexual mountain man, he had been essentially celibate, but it didn't matter.

"Lucy, give it a rest. What I need you to do for me is get online and make sure Kip still owns the house on Mustique. After his arrest the government might have taken it away from him."

She was quiet for a few seconds and then she said, "Yes, he still owns it."

"You looked it up that fast?"

"No, I've been stalking him over the years. I felt like I needed to," she justified quickly. I've kept tabs on him, to make sure our paths would never cross."

Tyler realized he was actually not surprised by this revelation. "Are you still in touch with anybody down there?"

"No, I severed all ties when I ran. Really, I hardly ever look back at those times. I don't like to. Those years when I was hiding out on Bequia were idyllic in a certain way, but nerve-wracking, always looking over my shoulder, using fake names." He could hear her give an audible shudder. "What about you? Have you stayed in contact with anyone?"

"Not really." He did not want to admit to her that he also occasionally stalked someone from those days, a local artist whose sensuous beauty had overwhelmed him back then; she had since relocated to Barbados where she had a successful studio and gallery so there wasn't much point in reconnecting with her right now.

"So this girl that Tucker is with. She is only seventeen? So she is also a minor and can't be held responsible for abducting him?"

He wasn't sure what she was getting at, other than shifting the blame. "Yeah, they are just two kids. Apparently she is kind of wild."

"Tyler, do you think they're having sex?"

He could not keep himself from laughing aloud. "Lucy! Yes, I think they are having sex. In fact, I know they are. No, don't ask. Please – just remember how you were at sixteen. I'm sure you were out of control and look at you – you turned out fine."

His words did not have the effect he expected. Instead she burst into tears that were loud enough to hear over the tenuous long-distance connection. "I am not fine! My son has been missing for five days and he won't answer my texts or calls. How can I know he is safe and okay?"

"I don't know. I don't know. We just have to trust that most people are basically good at heart and that he will make smart choices. We made a mistake – we should have talked to him about this. But now we'll make it right. It's going to be okay. I promise." He didn't really believe anything he was saying, but just speaking the words helped him to imagine that just maybe it might be true.

As he approached the casita, he could hear Elle talking on her phone and was surprised when he could make out that she was actually speaking in fairly passable uncomplicated Spanish.

"Sí, a Mustique. A mañana. Buscar a mi hija y su novio. Qué? No, no vengas aquí, nunca, entiendes? Díme tu precio, señor. Adiós ahora." Suddenly aware of Tyler's presence, she abruptly ended her call.

"You speak the language pretty well, señorita."

She shrugged. "Más or menos. How did your call go?"

"As poorly as expected. Maybe worse. And yours? Who were you talking to?"

"No one. Just the man who looks after this place when I'm gone." He knew enough Spanish to know that was not exactly what she had been saying.

"Really? Where are you going?"

She smiled then and looked up at him demurely from beneath her long blonde bangs. "To Mustique with you, of course."

"You are?" He was genuinely startled; when they had discussed it earlier, there had been no talk about her coming with him.

"Honey, I'm not letting anything as sweet as you get out of my sight." She leaned forward and put her mouth on his, slipping her tongue between his lips; at the same time she took his hand and guided it under her dress. As he pulled her towards him, he realized she was not wearing any underwear.

"Mmmm, going commando tonight, are we?" He ran his hand over the soft skin of her bare behind.

"Mmm — we call that come-and-oh..."she leaned backwards into his palm and fingers as she deepened the kiss. "Ah...oh..."

"Oh?" She was totally sexually manipulating him but she was such a turn-on he didn't care. "Oh? Or ohhhh... Don't you think we ought to go inside?" he whispered.

How could he not want her to come with him to Mustique, he thought as he followed her to the bedroom.

Afterwards, spent and sweaty, they lay stroking each other in the semi-darkness, illuminated only by a flickering candle melting down into a saucer on the plastic chair that served as a nightstand.

"Tell me about these scars." Elle was running her fingers up and down the inside of his legs, tracing a row of faint welts that ran the length of each calf.

"A story stranger than fiction," he murmured, enjoying the sensation of her touch. "I was left to die at sea on a sailboat and I used the blood from those cuts to write an SOS on the roof of the cabin."

"What?" She laughed in disbelief. "No way."

"Yes, way. Nearly died from staph infection but I am here to tell the tale." He felt for the serpentine scar he had seen on her butt and made an outline around it with his pinkie. "Your turn. How'd you get this?"

She stiffened and moved away so that he could no longer touch it. "An accident. An error in judgment, you might say."

"Go on." He reached out for her again, his curiosity up. "It's such an unusual 'S' shape."

"It's a burn mark. Courtesy of a machismo boyfriend." Her tone was bitter as she sat up and turned her back to him. "It was sort of deliberately accidental. A hot piece of metal. On a boat deck. In the sun." The mood had definitely been broken and Tyler kissed the curvature of her spine, trying to regain the closeness they had just experienced.

"That's sick. What kind of person does that?"

"An insecure son of a bitch who enjoyed the idea of leaving his brand." His lips could feel the tremor that went through her whole body before she pulled away from him and stood up.

"I'm sorry." He was sorry that he had ruined the moment, but she was showing a vulnerability he had rarely seen and he wanted to know more. "What was his name?"

"They called him Serpentino." She spat the answer out in an angry hiss as she tightened the belt of her robe. "And this conversation is over."

Tyler sunk back onto the pillow, stunned by the sudden turn their playful exploration had taken. Serpentino...it must be Spanish for serpentine or snaky, he thought. He remember Elle telling him that Culebra meant snake also. He shuddered a little, as memories of the snake pit scenes from Raiders of the Lost Ark came to mind. He was not Indiana Jones, but snakes were still the last thing he wanted to think about before he fell asleep.

He heard the sound of the freezer door opening and then the familiar smashing sounds associated with breaking chunks off a large piece of ice. Another drink to chase away the nightmares. It was Elle's cure for everything.

"Make one for me too," he called, reaching for his glasses.

As it turned out, they could not arrange a flight schedule that would work the next day – in fact, flights in and out of Culebra were booked solid through the weekend and even getting out of Puerto Rico on an island hopper had dim prospects.

159

"It's the beginning of spring vacation week for Puerto Ricans," Elle explained to him when she realized the dates. "All the locals are traveling and all the snowbirds are headed back to the states. You can't even get on a ferry. Wait until you see what happens at the campground and the beach this weekend."

The soonest they could book a trip that made any sense in time and money was on Monday and even then, they would not get into St. Vincent until late in the evening. By the time he had finished the online ticketing process, Tyler was feeling helpless, antsy and impatient, and he still had to figure out how he was going to deal with his newspaper deadlines next week.

"You know what I always say – go take a swim. I would come with you, but I need to go into town and see what is happening with the title search for my property-to-be. But I'll drop you there."

It was sound advice and Tyler decided to walk the beach to the campground instead of the road. The midday sun was so hot and the water so inviting that he immediately dropped his belongings on the sand under a palm tree and ran into the waves. As he stood in the warm sea, looking back at the shore, he could feel himself instantly start to relax.

But as he headed towards Section E, he could sense the change in the season. There was definitely an increase in tents that were being set up in the sections of the campground that were closer to the parking lot but as he approached his own site, he was surprised to see some of the long-termers dismantling their camps. Jane's tarp was down and Cassidy was helping her fold up her tent.

"Do you want any of the food in my cooler?" she called from where she knelt on the ground. "I'm not sure what's left, Sid's been through it, but he's leaving Sunday so I don't think he took much. Sam and Leo will take whatever you don't want, but they've been collecting from people all morning and may be saturated."

It was an offer that was hard to refuse; he took half a dozen eggs, some mushrooms, a ripe avocado and some salsa and then realized how hungry he was and asked to borrow her frying pan. "Just keep it. Then I won't have to pack it. Here – take the spatula too."

"Hey, let me know when lunch is ready!" Cassidy shouted after him as Tyler carried his haul away. "I should be done here in a few minutes."

Over omelets and guacamole, Cassidy caught him up on the campground news of the day – gossip about people Tyler knew and some he'd never heard of. Enrico had gone back to the mainland, Doctor Dreadlocks had two friends coming in from Chicago who were great musicians, Tracy's daughter was here for the week and she was dropdead gorgeous. Leo had come back from his morning's spearfishing with three spiny lobsters and two conch. Tom and Lisa had another big fight. Alejandro was going to leave next week and he was giving his giant tent away because he didn't want to bother taking it down.

"Well, I hope you're going to be the one to score that." Alejandro was such a campground fixture, Tyler was surprised to hear that he was going so soon.

"Nah, I think it's too big for me. What the hell would I want with a three room tent? Just more space to sweep the sand out of every day."

"You could start an Air BnB, live in one room and rent the others. I'd bet you'd make a decent living."

"Sounds like a lot of work to me. I'm done with that much responsibility." But Cassidy agreed to keep an eye on Tyler's tent when he left on Monday, and then recommended he bury anything important, like credit cards and passports underneath it for safekeeping.

"I'm taking those with me." Tyler tried not to smile. "But thanks for the suggestion."

After lunch, he went to find Sam, who was impressed at how quickly Tyler had made the decision to go to Mustique. "Man, if Elle wasn't going with you, I'd go. It would be so cool to meet Kip Kingsley – even if he is a butt wad. Hey, maybe I'll sleep in your tent while you're gone – do you mind? Our quarters have felt a little close since Leo hooked up with what's-her-face."

Part of him wished Sam was coming too; he might be more useful at finding lost boys and girls than Elle. The unsettling thought passed through his head, and not for the first time, that he knew Elle's vagina better than he knew her mind.

"We'll stay in touch," he promised. "And if there is any sign of them back here, you should contact me any way you can – Facebook, Twitter, text message – okay?"

"Sure. Cool. When are you leaving again? You ought to come over to Tom and Lisa's tonight; they're having a big chili party. We think they're afraid to be alone together too much anymore. They invited a lot of people, like just to be sure."

Tyler knew he would have to remind Sam on Monday about what was going on. He remembered how strangely Tom and Lisa had acted the night he had drunk whiskey with them and decided it might be interesting to go to their party and see if he could figure out what was happening. And he had a lot of hours to get through this weekend.

The chili was excellent and the company was interesting, to say the least. But as happened at many gatherings on Culebra, most of the guests were gone by 9pm except for the hard core partiers and the nearby neighbors. There was some guitar music and some bongo drumming courtesy of Dr. Dreadlock's friends. Tyler had enjoyed meeting Dr. D, whose ironic distinguishing features were a shaved head and a large belly that hung out between his white t-shirt and green scrub pants. Tom and Lisa kept their distance from each other and were well-behaved until Elle showed up.

In comparison to the rest of the funky campground residents who were half-dressed in swimsuits and cover-ups, Elle swept in like a fashion icon in a flowing dress with revealing neckline, colorful bangle bracelets on her arms and her hair swept up in a large fancy clip. She kissed everyone on the cheeks with faux affection except Tyler who got a full-on mouth smooch and Lisa who insisted on a long lip-lock.

"We going out tonight, girlfriend?" she asked loudly, slipping her arm through Elle's.

"As long we can dress you up sexy. I'm not taking you anywhere in those tomboy beach chic gym clothes you wear." Giggling, the two women disappeared into the tent.

Tyler turned to Tom, whose face had disfigured into an unpleasant grimace. "So what's that all about?" he asked. "We're not invited, I guess."

"Tell you later." Tom handed him the bottle of whiskey. "I think you better hold onto this for a while, man. Keep it away from me until they leave."

Alejandro, sitting on Tom's other side, was wearing his straw hat and usual spacy smile as he passed his pot pipe over. "Have some of this instead, amigo. Even if you boyfriends aren't going, I am going downtown with those beautiful chicas." He adjusted his necklaces — one a gold chain, the other a seashell pendant — with a slightly effeminate gesture that made Tyler wonder idly about Alejandro's sexual preferences. At times his Latino machismo seemed overdone to the point of concealment.

With a theatrical shriek and a laugh, Lisa and Elle reappeared. Lisa was now attired in one of Elle's sundresses, a frothy yellow ruffled affair which was too small, too short and way too girly for her large-boned, boyish frame and contrasted outlandishly with her dramatic tattoos, particularly the rose vine that swirled over her left breast and a dragon that wrapped around her right thigh. "The old Lisa is a thing of the past," she announced, doing an awkward hula dance while humming the theme to "Ghostbusters." "And I ain't afraid of no ghosts..."

Tom choked on the pot smoke he was holding in his lungs as the rest of the group enjoyed the humor of the moment. Coughing violently, he wrenched the whiskey bottle out of Tyler's grasp and downed a long slug, glowering at the two women. Tyler could hear Lisa's parting words as she leaned over and spoke into Tom's ear. "Don't be such an uptight a-hole. We'll be back in a few hours."

Elle's gaze met Tyler's; she raised her eyebrows and mouthed, "See you later maybe?" as she led Lisa away. Alejandro loped along the path after them.

Tom's ill-tempered moodiness splintered the party's atmosphere and most of the guests followed the musicians a few hundred yards down the beach to Dr. D's campsite where they continued to play golden oldies accompanied by drums and bad singing.

"Mind if I have some of that?" Tyler poured himself a stiff shot of whiskey in a plastic cup without waiting for Tom to respond.

"Suit yourself." Tom scratched at a mosquito bite on his forehead and then swore as the bandana he always wore over his scalp slipped sideways and fell into the dirt at his feet. Without it his appearance changed radically from beach buccaneer to a balding business man whose scraggly gray locks were in need of a barber.

He decided to jump right in while Tom's defenses were down, and before he got any drunker. "So what's going on with you two? I've been wondering since I talked to you the other night and you guys got all weird when I asked you about Ivan."

Tom cleared his throat as he carefully untied the faded red print scarf and then secured it around his head again, reassuming his confident swashbuckling personality.

"Yeah, well things aren't always what they seem. Weird barely begins to describe it." He peered out into the darkness surrounding them, apparently looking for any potential eavesdroppers, before continuing.

"So that night when Ivan died — or apparently was fucking murdered—" Tom stopped for a fortifying swig of whiskey — "so he and Lise had been flirting like hell that day and when we started fighting she stomped off and said she was going over to fuck him. I was pissed off at her and went to bed and didn't even talk to her the next morning, I was still so pissed. Then later, when we find out that Ivan is dead, I say to her, 'what the fuck, you were with him last night' and she gets all weirded out and says 'actually, no, I wasn't.'"

Tyler waited for him to go on, but Tom held out the bottle instead. "I think you better have another hit of this before I tell you the next part."

"I'm good." He held up his cup. "So what happened?"

"So what she says is that she never got to Ivan's tent, that when she was almost there she met Elle on the path."

"And?"

"And then somehow they ended up down on the beach having girl-on-girl sex. Which, sorry, but I gotta blame it on Elle, because Lise is totally hetero and had never done anything like that before in her life. But since then all she wants is for me to go down on her every night and we fight more than ever. And hell, I can't stop picturing those two in my head."

As he tried to process this new information, Tyler's mind was also swirling with sexual images of the two women that had not occurred to him until now, as well as the idea that this whole scenario had been playing out a few hundred yards from where he had been innocently sleeping that night, a new camper unaware of the debauchery ahead.

"She swore to me that it was a one-off, that she wouldn't have done it if she hadn't been horny and mad at me and looking for Ivan. I asked her how she knew what to do and she laughed at me like I was some kind of freakin' idiot." His voice became high as he imitated Lisa's response. " 'She would do it to me and then I would do it to her and then we did it to each other at the same time.' I told her it was a turn-off and to shut up and turn over." He guffawed at his own joke until he went into another smoker's coughing spasm.

Tyler actually was not put off by the idea and tried not to feel guilty that he somehow was always attracted to

165

women who either a little over-sexed or promiscuous. He and Elle were not really a couple and he could not feel betrayed by something that had happened before they met, nor did he feel particularly possessive about her. But he could tell that Tom was traumatized by both the threat to his masculinity and the danger of losing his partner and best friend.

"Sorry if this is a bummer for you, but you asked." Tom lit a cigarette. "When I saw the two of them go off together tonight, my blood just started to boil. Her dressing Lise up like that, Elle is just trying to have control in her own sneaky way. She may not wear frilly shit, but my Lise is all woman."

As he transferred his anger from Lisa to Elle, his fury and resentment seemed to charge the air. Tyler didn't ask the obvious – were they parked in some dark corner right now, doing it in the back of the golf cart? And did he care? How was he going to react if Elle slipped into his tent tonight? But another question floated to the murky surface of this story.

What had Elle been doing in the campground at the time of night? There was no figuring that woman out – she did not fit into any molds or fall into any classic roles. She clearly did not accept the standards for a woman of her age, however old she actually was. Her mercurial mysteriousness was what he found most fascinating about her.

Tom seemed to be slipping into a darker and darker funk, chain smoking and muttering to himself. "You okay, man? Maybe you ought to go to bed."

"Nah, I'm waiting up for her. I want to see how late she gets in." But even as he spoke, he was beginning to slide sideways in his camp chair and having trouble keeping his head up.

"Why don't you wait up for her lying down?" With some effort, Tyler helped Tom get inside the tent and onto his air mattress. Despite his protests, he began snoring before Tyler had even zipped the door shut.

166

A little while later, he lay on his own bed, staring at a dim circle of light on the ceiling from the illumination of a cast-off Coleman lantern reclaimed from the free store, trying to sort out the important pieces of the tale Tom had told him. He was still awake when Elle slipped stealthily in, unzipping and rezipping the flap more silently than he would have believed possible. He breathed quietly, not moving as she hovered above him, assessing whether he was asleep. He felt the tiniest puff of a breeze as her dress fell to the floor and then the shifting of the air in the mattress as she carefully placed her body beside his.

A mix of smells filled his nostrils — the reek of vodka and secondhand smoke, something garlicky, the musk of human sweat — all evocative of her most recent history. Too bad her past was not as easy to identify.

"Tyler? You still up?" she whispered.

"Mmmm." He pretended that he had actually been asleep and rolled over heavily to wrap himself around her as though he could not wake up. He wished he hadn't fallen so hard for her before he'd gotten to know her better.

"Okay, talk to you in the morning." She turned her back to him and as she drifted off, his hands slid easily into the places they were already as intimate with as old friends. They fell asleep in a tangle of limbs that was as entwined as their lives had become.

CHAPTER ELEVEN

By Sunday night, Tyler was tired of Culebra. He should have been back home by now, relaxed and tan, delivering Tucker to Lucy's house and going home to his own little bungalow. Back to northern Vermont where there would still be dirty snow on the north side of the buildings, the roads would be muddy, ice would form on the puddles in the morning and the daffodils would just be starting to poke through the ground. Instead he bounced back and forth between the raucous Puerto Rican spring break atmosphere that now pervaded Flamenco Beach and Elle's tiny casita, complaining like a local that there were too many tourists everywhere and that it took forever to get a beer at the Dinghy Dock.

He checked his phone obsessively, hoping for a message from Tucker and even tried texting Chloe to see if that might bring a response. On Saturday night, he joined the last game of Nines for the season at Sid's (since Sid was leaving the next day) and then went with Alejandro and Sam to hear the conga drums. Whereas a week earlier he had been afraid of getting in a car with Alejandro, now he knew that the suspicious little man somehow drove around in a permanently inebriated state, but always got where he was going. So Tyler did not hesitate to accept a ride to the bar with him.

"You ever hear about his Mafia years?" he asked Sam while they waited for their drinks amidst a crowd of bridesmaids from San Juan, who were wearing glittery short skirts and stiletto-heeled shoes.

"Sorry, I can't think right now. I'm overpowered by female hormones." Sam was flirting shamelessly with the group of party-going girls, enjoying their coy attention. "I'm trying to decide which one of these babes will take me back to her hotel room tonight."

Tyler found a vacant seat at the bar and watched the drummers and dancers for a while, wishing that he could turn the clock back a week and refuse his son the right to stay out late. He could not keep his eyes from straying to the edge of the dock where the two teenagers had sat, and he found himself sinking into a deep sense of melancholy. Finally he left and walked back to Elle's casita. She was not home yet from wherever her evening partying had led her and he let himself in with the key she had hidden for him and went to bed alone.

On Sunday Elle convinced him to go out with her and some local friends on Sadie's boat and it helped to pass the time. But as they motored by the abandoned purple houseboat, he could not stop thinking that with every minute Tucker could be getting farther away. What if their instinct was wrong and their children were headed the opposite direction from Mustique? Or what if they were somewhere on the main island of Puerto Rico, working for their keep at some two-bit taqueria or slaving away at some ritzy resort in Condado? Or what if the two unsolved murders on Culebra had something to do with their disappearance?

He could not get this last thought out of his head, not while he snorkeled the reef off Luis Peña, or ate fresh lobster salad or watched the sun set into the exquisite turquoise waters of the Caribbean. By the time they got home, he could sense that Elle had picked up on his uneasiness and was beginning to get as anxious about their trip as he was, for whatever reasons of her own. She also checked her phone regularly, but hers seemed to have way more activity than his, and she seemed to be constantly stepping away to take calls or send texts. Only once had he casually brought up the subject of her night out with Lisa and Jim's stress over it; Elle had laughed it off with a "Girls will be girls," comment and "He has nothing to worry about." Tyler had let it go, but every now and then, between

169

images of kidnapped teenagers and dead men, an erotic fantasy would pop into his head and not go away.

For whatever reason —anticipation, fear of the unknown or mirages of erogenous adventures — neither of them could sleep and they made love at regular intervals all night long, restlessly, hungrily, as a diversion from rational thought and deep-seated worry. When Tyler reached for her at dawn, Elle winced and rolled away.

"Too much touch. We've overdone ourselves. Okay, gently, gently, one more time," she acquiesced as he coaxed her with his tongue. "Just like that ... everywhere..."

Tyler fell deeply asleep afterwards, just as the sun was rising. When he awoke stunned and exhausted an hour later, Elle was standing at the foot of the bed adjusting the front of a tight black knit dress. Without her bright flowing tropical attire, she looked like a different woman, one you might be afraid to do a business deal with — her usually untethered hair was pulled back into a tight ponytail; her full breasts were encased in some sort of bra that smoothed and minimized her womanly curves and hid the shape of her erect nipples under some padded surface. The close-fitting style maximized her tiny waistline and narrow hips and somehow hid the roundness of her small belly behind a gathered fold of fabric.

"Who are you? Where is the woman I just spent the night fucking like rabbits with?"

"Ready to take on the world. Get up, mister." When he curled up and covered his face protectively with his arm, she whipped the sheet off his body and tickled the soles of his feet. "It's time to pack your bag and go to the airport."

As with everything on Culebra, nothing happened like clockwork, even if you were dressed for success. Just the time it took to walk out to his camp site and collect some clothes and gear took up half the morning.

When he got back to the campground parking lot, he found Elle sitting at a table with Alejandro, both of them sipping their usual colorful cocktails, despite the pre-noon hour.

"Don't give me that disapproving look, Tyler Mackenzie," she said tossing her ponytail.

"You are a lucky man to be traveling today with this beautiful woman." Alejandro picked up one of Elle's hands and kissed it. "Look at her — she looks like a hundred million bucks. And believe me, I know what a hundred million bucks looks like." He laughed at his own joke and when Elle laughed with him, he leaned over to kiss her on the lips.

"I will be a lucky man when I find my son and her daughter." Their blatant flirting made him uncomfortable. "Are you ready to go, Elle? We need to catch that noon plane to San Juan."

"Relax. This is Culebra. We only need to get there twenty minutes before it takes off. Let me finish my drink with this handsome man." Her phone, which had been resting next to her drink, began to vibrate and all eyes went to it as the vibrations moved it towards the table's edge. Elle slipped it into her lap to look at the screen. "Oh, I have to take this, sorry. I'll be right back." She walked quickly away from them, her body language covert and intent as she spoke into her cell. In her black dress and patent leather sandals she seemed like an alien element to the beach scene, almost like a Jehovah's Witness who had just dropped in to proselytize to the campers.

Watching her with growing trepidation, Tyler sunk into the seat next to Alejandro, one leg moving up and down impatiently. He was suddenly intensely exhausted — and feeling incredibly uncertain about what it would mean to travel with Elle. "She gets a lot of mysterious calls." He hadn't meant to articulate his thoughts aloud but there it was.

"She is a woman — don't even try to understand her, amigo. She has more going on than you will ever know."

And, although he agreed with Alejandro's advice, Tyler's need to know felt stronger than ever.

"Nobody would ever guess we were traveling together."
He had to laugh as he stood in line next to her in San Juan,
waiting to board the first of the three LIAT flights that
would eventually get them to St. Vincent. He looked like
the classic beach bum in t-shirt, shorts and hiking sandals,
a worn daypack slung over one shoulder, his uncombed
curls standing out from his head, a few days of gray stubble
adding texture to his face. She appeared to be a world class
jetsetter, wearing nice jewelry and shoes, hiding her crazy
eyes behind large dark sunglasses. He was sunburned; she
was sleek and tanned. He was anxious to get into the air
and on their way; she stared out the terminal window at
the propeller plane on the tarmac with a bored expression
on her face. "Maybe that's a good thing."

"This is just my airport act." She responded without
even looking at him. If someone was watching them from a
distance, they would not have realized they were even
having a conversation. "And really it's all in the clothes. If I
were dressed in one of my usual funky Culebra flower child
dresses and straw hat, nobody here would take me
seriously."

Across the waiting area, he noticed a man in tight black
jeans and cowboy boots alternately eyeing her and the cell
phone in his hand. He seemed to be watching her as he
tapped on his keyboard, typing a message.

"Well, either way men can't keep their eyes off you.
Even if you are old as dirt."

If he wanted to get a rise out her, he didn't get it
immediately. Instead she too looked at her cell phone,
checking it for recent texts and calls. What was it with
everyone having to be on their phones all the time – he
glanced around the waiting area and counted half the
passengers who were staring at the small screens in their
hands.

"Did you just call me 'old as dirt' you decrepit ancient
blowhard?" she asked him without even moving her eyes
away from what she was reading.

"Took you long enough. Come on, the line is moving."
He handed the flight attendant his boarding pass and then
went out a door and down a flight of metal steps into the
hot sun. When he turned to speak to her again, he saw
instead a pair of sailors wearing matching blue polo shirts
and visors. She was the last one to come down the stairs,
carrying her small roll-aboard suitcase primly in one hand,
her large shoulder bag slung over the other shoulder. It was
disconcerting to realize that, if he hadn't known who she
was, he would not have recognized her right off.

There was no sense of déjà vu for him returning to St.
Vincent. It had taken a total of four connections – Culebra
to San Juan, San Juan to Antigua, Antigua to Barbados,
Barbados to St. Vincent – to reach the island and after the
previous sleepless night, his mental and physical fortitude
were at their limits. It was also dark by the time the final
plane landed so there was no being awed by the majesty of
the mountains or the verdant countryside. While waiting in
the Culebra terminal, he had booked an AirBnB guesthouse
for the night and the owner had agreed to pick them up at
the airport, so within minutes of landing they were on their
way to their accommodations for the night.

The swiftness of their immigration had not stopped him
from showing half a dozen airport employees the photo on
his phone of Tucker and Chloe, but no one remembered
seeing the young couple. Elle had seemed annoyed by this
action on his part and by the time they got in the car they
had already had an argument.

"This is what we're here for, get used to it," he had
snapped at her. "You might be dressed like some high-class
tourist, but that doesn't mean you are one."

Alice, who met them, was a pleasant older white
woman who had married a local man whom she'd met when
sailing thirty years earlier. She'd moved to the Caribbean
and had never looked back to her former life as a Yale
graduate with a degree in medieval history. She listened
intently and sympathetically as Tyler told her the purpose

behind their trip and offered helpful suggestions which included posting an ad in the Caribbean Compass, a monthly newsletter for sailors, and the Vincentian, which was the local paper. She also knew of some online message boards.

After swearing richly when she realized that her cell service didn't work in the Grenadines, Elle sulked in the back seat without contributing to the conversation. Tyler knew that most of her problem was that by now she must be jonesing for a drink and wondered how the rest of the night would go if she didn't get to quench her addictive thirst.

When they were finally settled into the little self-service apartment beneath Alice and Nelson's house, she had to satisfy herself with one of the complementary bottles of Banks Beer from Barbados that had been left in the fridge for them. Tyler took his beer out on the little deck that overlooked the lights of Arno's Vale and let his senses be assaulted by the sounds of Caribbean life at night – the constant barking of dogs and the crowing of disoriented roosters mingled with the thump of reggae bass lines and the occasional roar of a car engine. He slapped at a mosquito on his arm and then another on his neck. This was the Caribbean he had known in Grenada for six years, most memories of which had disappeared into the fog and sand of his rum-soaked days. It could be equally as warm and easygoing as it could be hard and dark.

What now...he wondered. What the fuck now...

Elle was already in bed and asleep when he finally came in, designer traveling clothes abandoned in a heap on the floor. With her pale hair spread out across the pillow and covering her bare shoulders, she looked more like her usual fairy-queen self than she had all day. As he slid in next to her, he realized that she still had her phone clutched in one hand. As he gently pried it from her grip, the screen lit up, displaying the message "Skype Click to Call is now downloaded and ready for use."

For some reason she was desperate without her ability to connect. As usual, his curiosity got the best of him, but before scrolling through her incoming and outgoing calls of the day he checked to make sure she was really sleeping soundly. Gently he stroked her cheek and brushed her bangs out of her eyes; she didn't move at all. Beneath the covers he grazed his fingers over the various sensitive arousal places that he had grown so intimate with in the last week; she stirred slightly, almost reflexively, made a small sighing noise in her throat but did not wake.

He had never seen her so unconscious and it occurred to him that in the absence of large quantities of vodka, she may have taken some drugs to help her sleep. In fact, the more he considered the possibility, the more sure he became. He shook her arm brusquely then lifted it in the air and watched it drop back to the bed like the limb of a dead person.

Quietly he slipped back out from beneath the sheet and moved noiselessly across the room to the dresser where her toiletry bag was. It didn't take much poking around to find the bottle of Ambien; he wondered how many she had to take to achieve her current state of oblivion. Searching a little deeper through the usual soaps and lotions, he unearthed two more pill containers with unrecognizable names – Flunitrazepam and Rohypnol1 – both of which made him uneasy. Unlike the Ambien, they were not in prescription bottles with Elle's identification; they were in pharmaceutical packaging. He needed to look these up online right away.

He realized that if Elle had been downloading a Skype app, she must have been able to pick up a wireless signal here. Sure enough, he saw there were three bars of service for 'aliceandnelsonwifi' and in seconds he had googled the two drugs. They were anti-anxiety medications, which did not really surprise him, that were also commonly used for date rape. His heart beat rapidly as he let his imagination run wild for a few seconds and then became more rational;

175

Elle was so tightly wound, it was no surprise that she might use medication to calm her down on occasion.

While he had the phone in his hand, he sat down in a straight-backed wooden chair to scroll through her calls, first glancing cautiously back at the bed to make sure she was still out. Her light snoring reassured him that her sleeping status was still quo. But as always, Elle kept her phone trail well-swept behind her, too tidy actually as Tyler noted that there were no incoming text messages showing for the last twenty-four hours and he knew how many times she had been on the phone today. In the Sent Message box he struck a small amount of gold – the last text she had sent from the airport in San Juan was still there.

"LIAT 561, 523, 569, 2pm-9:30. Scheduled charters SVD to MUS on SVG Air. Ferry at 2pm some days."

It was the flight numbers of the planes they had taken today and the possible means of transportation they would use to get to Mustique. Had she sent this to someone on purpose or was she just recording it for herself? It had been sent to a Puerto Rican phone number that did not belong to any of her contacts. He pulled out his own phone and jotted it down before carefully resetting her phone to its home screen and placing it on the nightstand next to her head.

Stretching out beside her on the mattress, he propped himself up on his elbow and contemplated this unique woman that fate had thrown him under the bus with. Only her chest moved, slowly, rhythmically, up and down with each quiet breath. In so many ways during the past week they had acted as irresponsible as their teenage children, using stress as the driving force that connected them in a primal way. He had not been paying attention to the big black holes in the rest of their relationship. Truthfully, he did not really expect it to last beyond the moment that Tucker and Chloe were located and safely ensconced in normal life again. If this love affair survived the challenge of this mission, then maybe it was meant to happen. But he had to focus – finding his son had to take priority; he could not let himself continue to be distracted by his sexual urges.

He turned off the light and wrapped himself around Elle's warm, still body, falling into an almost instant and exhausted slumber.

But before he awoke the next morning, his priorities had already veered off course. He thought he was having a sex dream, but as he came slowly out of semi-consciousness, he became aware that it was not a dream at all, that Elle was sitting astride him, slowly and erotically riding his erection, watching him with a mischievous expression on her face.

"Are you taking advantage of me?" he murmured, closing his eyes and giving into the pleasant sensation.

"It was an opportunity I couldn't pass up."

"Mmm, we need to talk..." but he couldn't remember why.

"Yeah, I don't think so..."

He had to agree with her; there was no need for conversation at the moment. In fact, they didn't speak until much later, when they were seated on the deck that overlooked the valley that spilled its humanity down to the sea, drinking coffee and eating fresh-baked croissants.

"So, good morning, lover." The sex had mellowed the intensity of his midnight intentions and made him feel quite fondly towards her. It was like some freakin' drug...and that thought brought him back around. "You slept pretty hard last night."

"Maybe, but you were the one who woke up hard." She licked some butter off her lower lip as deep dimples formed in her cheeks. He couldn't help himself, he found her irresistible. She had shed her uptight travel persona and was once again light and airy Elle, in a blue cotton sundress that kept sliding provocatively off one freckled shoulder.

"Well, nothing would wake you last night. Too bad you can't remember what I did to you," he teased.

For a brief second a fearful expression crossed her face and then she laughed. "Really? I did take something to help me sleep. So tell me what I missed. Was it great?"

177

"I guess you'll never know. Unless you find those pictures I took with your phone – just kidding," he added quickly seeing how alarmed she became. What was wrong with him – he should not have said anything about her phone. "So are you coming on the ferry to Mustique with me today?"

"Yes, of course. Are we just jumping into this? Heading right to Kingsley's house?"

"I think it's the best place to start. And to ask around." He tried to think what he might do differently if she were not with him. Maybe go to Bequia first, enlist the help of his old friend, Calvin. "Chances are they may not even have arrived yet, especially not if they are traveling by boat. Or by LIAT 'Leave Island Any Time' connecting flights through Antigua and Barbados," he added in reference to their own endless journey. "Have you been checking Chloe's debit card to see if it has been used?"

She nodded. "I looked yesterday while we were at the airport. She hasn't touched it since last week."

"What could they possibly be using for money? I hope they haven't done anything really stupid like –" he could even bring himself to say the word 'steal.' "Do you think Chloe would contact her father if they got really down and out? What is their relationship like?"

"Seriously broken. I don't think they've spoken more than a few times since he threw her out. But...I suppose it's possible."

"Can you call him?" He was surprised this thought had not come up when he had been struggling with calling Lucy.

She shook her head sadly. "No, he doesn't want to hear from me. I had already earned the Worst Mother of the Year award when I left Chloe with him to move to Culebra."

"But don't you think he would want to know his daughter was missing?"

"He hasn't cared where she was for the last nine months. Why would he start caring now." Her bitter rhetorical question seemed to hang like a cloud over the breakfast table. For a few minutes there was no sound but the brittle clanking of cups on saucers and then suddenly Elle swore. "Damn, she might have another card. She had one on a New Jersey bank when she moved in with me. It could still be valid."

"Well, can we find out? Elle, this could be really important."

She pulled the wayward strap of her dress up and crossed her arms defensively over her chest, slumping back in her chair. "I don't know. Let me think about it."

Tyler felt ridiculously frustrated by her behavior. If her daughter were anything like her, he feared for his son's safety. He stood up abruptly, the legs of his plastic chair grating against the cement floor. "What is there to think about? Why do I feel like you don't really want to find Chloe."

"Well, I can't call him anyway. I have no cell service here!" she shouted after him as he stormed off to the bedroom. "I'll send him an email, okay?"

"Everything okay down there?" Alice's friendly voice sounded like an alien radio broadcast in the charged atmosphere of the apartment.

"Fine." Tyler came back to the doorway and smiled at her warmly. "We were just wondering – what's the best way to get to the ferry dock from here?"

"Oh, I'll be happy to drop you off there. But the Mustique ferry is not until mid-afternoon so you would have to stay over. The schedule is designed so that the boat leaves from there in the morning and returns in the afternoon so that those islanders can do their business on St. Vincent."

"Okay." This was going to be a little more complicated than he had anticipated. He had assumed that, like Bequia, Mustique had a daily round trip ferry from St. Vincent.

And you do know that it pretty much costs a thousand dollars a night to stay on Mustique. There literally are no budget or mid-range options." Tyler's mood plummeted. In the back of his mind he had totally known how carefully Mustique guarded its high-class chi-chi-ness. He did not know how they were going to pull this off. Or why he thought his son would be able to.

Alice began putting their breakfast dishes on a tray. "You might find the least expensive option is actually to fly over and back in a day. But you will probably want to book it today for early tomorrow morning if you want to have some time there."

Tyler looked out at Elle, sitting on the porch, thumb-typing furiously into her phone. He hoped she was sending an email to Chloe's father. "Can I book it online?" he asked Alice. "And if so, do you have a computer I could use for a few minutes? I'm not sure I can do it from my phone and she seems to be caught up in something."

Alice showed him to an ancient desktop machine that sitting in the hallway that connected to the guest quarters. While he waited for it to boot up, he went out and sat down next to Elle to explain the situation to her.

She seemed annoyed. "I wish we'd figured this out sooner. We could have been on our way this morning."

He tried to ignore her attitude. "Are you online?"

"Yes, it took a while to put together an email to Hans, trying to explain what had happened." She brushed her hair out of her face with a nervous gesture and Tyler noticed that one of her eyes was twitching slightly. Her crazy irises seemed to glow with an array of luminous peacock colors today and as always he found himself mesmerized by their iridescence. "I don't know how he is going to react. He might be really pissed off or he might be apathetic. He may put out an APB alert. He might delete my email without even reading it."

A tiny ping sounded and she looked down. "Oh, my god, he already answered. Listen to this – he says the card was used on St. Thomas more than a week ago at a Kmart, as well as for a $300 cash withdrawal at an ATM. He wants to cancel it immediately – he is sure it's been stolen."

"No, tell him not to!" Tyler leaped to his feet and resisted the urge to jump up and down like a child. "This is the best news we've had in ten days. We can track them with this. Tell him to wait – I'll pay him back whatever they spend. Holy shit, we've finally got a break!" He pumped his fist silently in the air.

She typed a reply as fast she could and sent it back to Hans and then they both watched the phone expectantly.

Hans' typing skills must have rivaled Elle's because his answer was almost instantaneous. "He wants to cancel the card by the end of the day; he is contacting his bank now. He says he is not comfortable with this situation at all and recommends we seek the help of the coast guard or the local police."

"Ask him if he can just put an alert on it for a few days so that his bank can let him know when it is being used. We need to know if we are way off the trail here."

"You mean, like what if they are still in the Virgin Islands and we came all the way down here for nothing?" He could not read the tone of her voice but he knew he didn't like it.

"Did you have a better plan? Did you have a plan at all?"

She set her lips in a grim line and said nothing as she stared at the screen waiting for Hans' next response. "He says he'll wait twenty-four hours and then he is canceling the card and he is done with 'this nonsense. Chloe is your responsibility now; see if you can keep her under control for the next few months until she turns eighteen.' Bastard." She slammed the phone down on the table and crossed to the edge of the balcony, gripping the railing and staring out at the green valley below. "God, I wish I had a cigarette. And a big fat drink."

CHAPTER TWELVE

Chloe clutched her aching abdomen and moaned softly. She couldn't think of any worse fate than her own right now – rolling back and forth with the rocking of the sea on a wooden bench in the filthy galley of a West Indian cargo boat while she had menstrual cramps. She sobbed quietly – not that anyone would hear her over the constant rattling whir of the ship's engine – and wished she was back in her pink and purple bedroom in her father's house in the bland and boring suburban subdivision, snuggled under the hideous floral polyester comforter with a hot water bottle tucked into the front of her flannel pajama bottoms. Instead she'd had to change out of her blood-stained shorts in the most disgusting bathroom she'd ever seen in her life – she couldn't even think about it or she would gag again – insert a tampon and then try to put on a clean pair of shorts without them touching the walls or the floor, let alone the toilet without a seat.

On an adjacent bench Tucker slept soundly, his body moving back and forth with every creak of the boat over the waves. Like a baby, she thought, and then the term "robbing the cradle" popped into her mind and she thought about how young he was and wondered what would happen when she turned eighteen in a few months, could she be arrested for having sex with him?

Nothing made sense anymore; she couldn't remember what quest they were on or why it had sounded like the perfect opportunity when Norman the Customs Man had told them about the small freighter that, for a minimal fee, had agreed to take them as far as Dominica. She bet Norman got a percentage – of course, he did.

He had come to get them at Canne a Sucre the previous evening and had escorted them down to a dimly lit dock where they were handed over to Captain Carreterre, whose skin was as dark as the night itself and who had greeted them in a gruff patois that they could not understand. Norman explained that the ship would stop at Antigua in the morning to unload cargo and then sail on again the next night, reaching Dominica the following dawn.

In the weak beam of Norman's flashlight she could see that the boat had at one time been painted blue but large swathes of rust now obscured most of its color. Chloe and Tucker had hung close together as they were led down a short corridor past a narrow room with four nasty-looking bunks; in two of them men were sleeping with their faces to the wall, their sweat-stained sleeveless undershirts stretched across their backs. The captain flicked a switch on the wall and the buzzing of a fluorescent light fixture illuminated the blackened stove, metal sink, bare benches and laminate table of the ship's galley. He indicated to them that they could occupy this space and then left them alone.

"This would be depressing," commented Tucker, "if it weren't so fucking exciting."

Chloe felt scared and nervous and really glad she was not alone. As the motor started, they went back up on deck to watch Basseterre disappear in the distance and then it began to rain so they returned to the dismal little cabin, where, lulled by the whirring of the engine, Tucker put his head on the daypack and fell promptly asleep. And that was when Chloe started to feel sick and when she put her head down on her knees and noticed the dark stain in the crotch of her white running shorts.

Just thinking about her misery brought a fresh spate of tears on. Then Tucker was shaking her shoulder, speaking into her ear. "Chloe. Chloe! What's wrong? Are you okay?"

"I've got my period. And I'm in pain." She did not know why she felt guilty saying those words to him.

"That's a good thing, right? That you got your period, I mean. Because that means you're not pregnant." His face was flushed – either with visible relief or just with the effort of waking up on a cargo ship in the middle of the night.

He was right about that, but she hated him right now for being so positive.

"Don't you have some pills you can take or something in this magic bag of yours?" He handed her the pack he had been using as a pillow.

He was right again. She dug around in the front pocket and came out with a small bottle. Not only did she have some ibuprofen, she actually had a couple of sleeping pills she had stolen from her mother. There was nothing she wanted to do more at this moment than to go to sleep and lose consciousness of her pain and this place. A couple of Advil and an Ambien later, she curled up with her head on Tucker's lap and remembered nothing more.

She awoke alone with a stiff neck and a headache. The boat was no longer moving. Dirty light came in through the grimy glass of a porthole and the cabin was stuffy and steaming. She had to pee so bad that she endured the disgusting bathroom long enough to relieve herself. Back in the corridor she could hear voices on deck and the heavy thud of boxes being moved. Stepping out into the sunshine, she could see the crew unloading cargo onto a truck parked on a concrete wharf; Tucker was working with them, his shirt stuffed into the back pocket of his shorts, his back and shoulders glistening with sweat.

Her heart swelled with feeling as she watched him – she was envious of how he seemed to embrace every opportunity for a new experience in such an unconditional way. When he caught sight of her, he grinned and posed cartoonishly, flexing his muscles.

He was the one working, but she was starving. Returning to the galley, she dug out their plastic bag of provisions and spread some guava jam on two pieces of white bread. She ate this poor excuse for a sandwich slowly and deliberately, trying to make it last, washing it down with warm bottled water. She tried not to think about the fact that lunch and dinner were going to be pretty much the same. Then she made a sandwich for Tucker and took it out on deck.

"Thanks. This is my second breakfast. You slept through the first." With his mouth full, he nodded towards a fat man in a stained white t-shirt who sat smoking a cigarette, watching the others work. "Tito actually came into the kitchen and made coffee and bread for everyone and you never even knew. It was like you were drugged or something." He laughed.

"Really?! What time is it?" She squinted at the sky.

"Almost noon, I think. Another hour and we should be done here. They told me about a beach nearby where we can go swimming if we catch a bus. The boat doesn't leave again until just before dark, I guess. These guys are going to drink and sleep, they say, before they wake up the other shift. I guess there aren't really enough bunks for everyone to use at the same time."

Chloe was always amazed by Tucker's easy ability to assimilate and absorb information in any environment. "So what about Antigua?" she asked looking around at the shabby industrial buildings that surrounded the quay where they were tied up and the gently rolling green hills dotted with pastel buildings that rose behind them. "It looks kind of beat. No volcanos."

"I think we're on the un-touristy side of the island. Gotta get back to work. Thanks for the sandwich!" His put his sticky lips on hers for a brief second, holding himself a few inches away in an effort to keep his sweaty chest from rubbing against her. When he returned to help the crew, they grinned, their smiles showing pink gums with missing teeth while they made what she could only assume were sexually suggestive comments to him as they stole glances back at her.

185

She felt more like her normal self by sunset when they motored out of the harbor (which she had learned was in the capital city of St. John's and was often confused with the U.S. Virgin Island of St. John where they had spent a few days). Passing a few hours swimming in a beautiful white sand cove covered in a trove of exotic seashells and then eating a real meal of fish and chips in an open air restaurant had restored her mood, especially after being able to brush her teeth and take a quick sink bath in the very clean restroom.

They were both in good spirits as they sat on a pile of thick rope and shared a beer, the only low point being that the skin on Tucker's back was seriously sunburned from his hours of shirtless work. "Ow, ow, don't touch it. Oh, wait that feels good," he said as she gently moved the cold wet bottle of beer across his shoulders. "I'm going to have to sleep on my stomach tonight."

But he was so exhausted from his exertions of the day, that he soon went down to sleep on his wooden bench in the airless galley, leaving Chloe alone to finish the beer. She stayed on deck, until they reached open waters and the steep pitching of the ship made it hard to maintain her balance. Then, holding onto the steel riveted walls for support, she made her way inside.

She rubbed her butt bone which was sore from always sitting on hard surfaces and pondered the fact that, within an amazingly short amount of time, her life had become such that a cushioned seat seemed like an unattainable luxury.

Dominica was a dream island, lush and beautiful, with pure, raw Caribbean character. Like a place that had been stopped in time, it was as Chloe imagined it might have been maybe fifty or sixty years earlier. The bright buildings of the colorful colonial capital of Rousseau tumbled like a waterfall down from the mountain rainforests. At the recommendation of Tito, the ship's cook, they had made their way to another cheap and charming West Indian guesthouse, where Miss Zena showed them to a room on the third floor. The Cherry Lodge was what the Canne a Sucre might have been if it had been kept up; the wooden furniture was still polished, rag rugs covered the floor and the mosquito net had no holes. There were ceiling fans that softly moved the air in the hallway and the dining room.

When they left their room key at the front desk before going out to explore, Miss Zena had looked disapprovingly over her glasses at Chloe's scant attire. "In Dominica the girls cover up more." Her reprimand had made Chloe redden and protest.

"But in my country—"

She cut her off. "This is not your country. We welcome you but we would appreciate you more if you respect our local customs. Many women arriving on yachts do not understand this." She looked down at the ledger she had been working on, indicating the conversation was over.

Tucker wrapped his arm protectively around her bare midriff as they walked out the front door. "Maybe we should buy you a dress?" he murmured into her hair.

Dresses reminded her of her mother who she didn't want to think about. Her mother always wore dresses. "Maybe just a skirt – I have a t-shirt. Or maybe she is just an old prude. I can't believe I'm the first American to show some thigh."

"And a little bare cheek. You do wear really short shorts." As they walked along a narrow curb, he touched the place where the back of her leg began to curve into her butt.

"Don't do that in public!" she scolded, angry that she was now on the defensive. She loved the way it felt when he slipped his fingers inside her shorts to caress the soft taut skin of her backside. "Sorry – it just seems like as a boy, you have it so easy everywhere we go. It's always harder for us girls."

They did not go skirt-shopping that afternoon. Instead they hiked out of the city to Trafalgar Falls and marveled at the awesome natural beauty of their surroundings. They found a secluded place along the river and in defiance of local customs, took off all their clothes as well as their swimsuits and went skinny-dipping. "I love Dominica," Chloe declared. "Even if it doesn't love me."

On the way back to the guesthouse, they stopped at a restaurant so Tucker could try the local specialty called "mountain chicken" which was actually giant frog legs. Chloe spread the remainder of their EC dollars on the table. "We're kind of out of money."

"You should have said something before we had dinner."

"When are we ever going to be in Dominica again? You had to eat frog."

"I don't know, we might want to stay here forever." He stroked the back of her hand and she suddenly felt very much in love, in a way that she had never fallen before in her life. "Can you use your card again? I'll pay you back. Someday. When I can access my own bank account again."

She wondered if it was safe to use her debit card on this least touristy of Caribbean islands. By the time anyone could track her down they would be gone. But first they had to figure out how they were going to get off Dominica.

The Cherry Lodge actually had an ancient desktop computer for guests to use and the internet connection was way faster than expected. They sat shoulder-to-shoulder on a little bench as they searched the web. It turned out there was a ferry that left the island almost daily that stopped in Martinique and went on to St. Lucia.

"And from St. Lucia we can actually fly to Mustique. We could be there in a couple of days!" Her triumph at this discovery felt suddenly misplaced. What would happen to "them" when this adventure was over?

"Why don't we just stay here for a while?" Tucker's question was barely audible and she knew he was thinking the same thing. She turned her face and touched her nose to his. "Is your period over yet?" he whispered. "How soon can we have sex?"

"There are other ways to have sex besides intercourse." Their faces were so close she could just breathe the words into his mouth. "Haven't I taught you anything?"

It was raining when they awoke the next morning so they just stayed in bed, talking and touching, both of them feeling as though they just wanted to suspend time and reality for as long as possible. "I'm hungry. Do you think we missed breakfast?" Tucker sat up and pulled back the mosquito net, trying to gauge what time it might be by the lightness of the cloudy sky.

"I think we might have missed lunch. Let's go find an ATM so we can eat."

When they descended the two flights of polished wooden stairs, they were surprised to find another young American couple checking in. Their heavy high-tech backpacks and expensive hiking shoes indicated they were adventurers of a different sort than the vagabonds that Chloe and Tucker had become. The woman clearly had understood the dress code memo that Chloe had missed – she wore long cargo shorts and a baggy t-shirt; her bearded companion even had a belt on his pants. And a pair of binoculars around his neck; maybe he was a little nerdy, she thought. But as always when traveling, friend-making crossed cultural barriers and social fences and the four of them were soon engaged in warm conversation.

"Kate and Leonardo, where are you from?" The couple had introduced themselves as Flo and Joe. Flo seemed to do most of the talking.

"California. The Bay Area." Chloe kept their story consistent these days.

"Really? So are we. What part?"

Uh, oh – she thought they were fucked this time, but Tucker jumped easily to the rescue. "Actually we are not there yet, we just say we are – we're taking a gap year before college. That's where we're headed in the fall, so we haven't really spent any time there yet. We're actually from a small town upstate. Upstate New York."

"Very cool. Wish I had done that. Now we're always squeezing these excursions into our short vacations from work. Berkeley? Or SFSU?"

There was an uncomfortable pause while they tried to decipher what she was asking. "Oh! Berkeley," said Chloe. "I'm Math; he's going to major in English or Literature." She could see the relief in Tucker's eyes that she had understood the question. "So what island are you guys coming from?" she asked, desperate to change the subject.

"We just flew in from Guadeloupe. We were in Les Saintes for half a week." Chloe knew of the little untouristy French island group north of Dominica. "Joe is a birdwatcher so that's our focus on this trip. We're going to rent a car and drive around here – they say there are 365 rivers on Dominica, one for each day of the year..."

Flo continued to talk, seeming able to carry on a conversation without any response, probably because Joe was so quiet. By the time the two of them shouldered their backpacks and headed up to their room, Chloe and Tucker had been invited to join them on their tour of the island the next day, an invitation they had been excited to accept. They just needed to get their story straight; the Bay Area thing had almost tripped them up big time.

She typed in the pin number to her debit card and then held her breath until the Eastern Caribbean money magically materialized out of the slot below the key pad. "It still works," She checked the account balance on the receipt. It showed that there was still over 900 EC in the account – nearly $300. "If we are going to buy airline tickets we ought to do it soon. Maybe when we get back to the hotel."

"But that would mean actually making a plan," Tucker commented lazily as they flattened themselves against the ATM machine, huddling beneath its small overhang as another sudden downpour splattered against the streets of the small city.

"Sometimes having a plan is good. I like looking forward to things."

"Well, I do have a plan for what I want to do to you when we get back to the hotel this afternoon."

"See? And I am so looking forward to that." The rain stopped as suddenly as it had started, leaving the open gutters on either sides of the road swirling with the dirty runoff water of the city. Walking through Rosseau was a hazardous Third World affair, particularly after a storm.

At a small shop they bought a couple of rotis, which turned out to be fat sandwiches rolled up in a pancake-like wrap – chicken for Chloe and curried goat for Tucker, whose interest in trying new foods far exceeded her own. They were inexpensive as well as filling and delicious. Feeling completely sated, they headed back to the Cherry Lodge, marveling at the rainbow that appeared when the sun made a brief appearance during the next shower.

Stretched out on their bed once again, Chloe dug a pen out of her bag and smoothed out a brown paper sack. "What is today?" she asked. Without her phone, she had completely lost track of dates and times.

"I have no idea. Why do you care?" Tucker seemed to be wallowing in their current spontaneous life style.

"Because how else can I figure out how and when we can catch a ferry to St. Lucia or book us plane tickets to Mustique. They are not 747s, you know. They are small with only a few seats."

He did not reply. Instead he closed his eyes and then slid his hand up under her tank top and began to play with her nipple. She pulled away from him, half-laughing. "Don't do that right now. I can't think."

"I know. That's why I'm doing it." He reached for her again and she stood up to escape his grasp.

"Why do I think that maybe you don't really want to ever get there."

"Maybe I don't anymore." His eyelids were still closed.

"Then what are we doing?"

"You tell me. Why are you here? Or better yet, what are you going to do after Mustique?"

"Well, what did you think you were going to do 'after Mustique'?" She threw his question back at him tauntingly.

It was the closest they had come to an argument. He turned his head slowly and locked his hard defiant gaze on hers. "I'm not the one making a plan. I'm just living this life day to day."

"So what do you think is going to happen when my money runs out – have you thought about that? Or if your father the rock musician tells you to get lost? Or – or – or if that sleazebag from Culebra finds us or if my mother..." Her voice trailed off like a small mountain path.

They glared at each other from opposite sides of the small room. "That's completely improbable," he said finally. "So here's my plan." He sat up and stuffed the bed pillows behind his head against the wooden headboard and then leaned back on one long arm to contemplate her. "To never leave each other. No matter what happens."

She felt her angry resolve melting and her vision blurring with tears. She didn't think anybody had ever cared about her this much before, not even her parents. Especially not her parents.

"Okay," she agreed softly, swallowing back her emotions. "That's a good plan." Still holding the pen and the paper bag, she perched lightly on the edge of the bed. "Now help me figure out what the date is today."

She mapped out their strategy on one side of the bag, illustrating it with boxes connected by lines and arrows. From "Ferry to St. L" there was a line to "Fly from St. L to Mustique" which led to "Find Kip K's house" which led to a giant question mark in the middle of the diagram. From there arrows pointed in a number of different directions ranging from "Live happily ever after on Mustique" to "Catch the next boat to Grenada" to "hire out as crew and sail around the world" to "return to Dominica and live in that abandoned cottage on the way to Trafalgar Falls" to "Go home." Tucker circled the choices having to do with world sailing and Dominica, put dotted lines around the options for Mustique and Grenada, and crossed out going home.

"You're my home now." And this time when he slid his hands into her erogenous zones she did not push him away.

Miss Zena was not happy when Chloe began swearing at the computer in the lobby. "Sorry, sorry," she apologized as the woman approached her. There was not much lower she could go in Miss Zena's estimation of her at this point and she could feel the stony disapproval of her long bare thighs as she raced up the two flights of stairs back to the bedroom under the eaves.

"What's going on?" Tucker looked up from the tattered paperback copy of 'Shogun' that he had taken from the hotel's collection of books left behind by other tourists. ("This should last me a while," had been his explanation for his choice.)

"We're fucked. I booked us plane tickets to St. Vincent but then when I tried to book us on a flight to Mustique, the card came up as denied. I didn't use up the balance so I'm sure it's been canceled." In one motion she threw the debit card on the floor and herself onto the bed.

"So what does that mean?"

"It could mean a whole bunch of things. Probably that my dad checked his bank account and realized I was drawing money down. Or maybe the bank thinks the card has been stolen because it's being used in a strange foreign country. In any case it means we'll have to take a ferry to Mustique and we're back to living on jam and bread."

"You hate deprivation, don't you?" he teased her as she pouted.

"Not as much as you hate missing a meal."

"I'm a growing boy," he protested jokingly but something about his statement hit them both the wrong way with its nitty gritty truth.

After spending most of the day indoors, they found themselves attracted by the reverb of reggae music coming from somewhere around the block. "Let's go out," Chloe suggested. "Clubbing on Dominica – I mean, really, who gets to do that?"

She put on the dressiest clothing she had, a nearly sheer white tank top with a little lace trim around the neckline and her short white shorts, brushed her hair and dug out some eye makeup from the bottom of her bag. She couldn't remember the last time she'd worn makeup.

"You look too sexy – I can see your tits right through that shirt," Tucker commented, watching her from the bed. "Why even bother to wear it?"

"You sound like my father." She slid into her flip-flops and handed him his pair. "Let's go."

"Well, at least I'll be the one with the hottest girl. Everyone will know I'm getting some when I get home."

The streets were still wet and dimly lit but it was easy to follow the pulsing music to the nightspot. "Looks like you'll be the one with the only girl," Chloe murmured into his ear as their eyes adjusted to the darkness inside. Black lights gave an eerie purple hue to a small narrow room with a bar along one side that sported a few random bottles of hard liquor on a high shelf and even fewer barstools. The bartender nodded at them but said nothing. Through a door at the back of the room they could see some shadowy figures moving and she followed Tucker as he stepped out into a courtyard where half a dozen men drank beers and bounced up and down in time to the reggae beat.

"Go get us a couple of drinks." She slipped some EC dollars into his hand and backed up into the doorway to wait for him. One of the men immediately approached her. He wore a dark green short-sleeve shirt that reeked of body odor over loose red pants that did not reach his ankles. His short dreadlocks moved up and down when he spoke. "Sa ka fete?" he asked, his bloodshot eyes fixated someplace below her neck.

She shook her head to indicate she didn't understand. He pointed to himself – "Non mwen se Roderique. Sa ki now?" He put his finger lightly on her chest.

194

"Chloe." She took a step back so he wasn't touching her. She pointed to Tucker in the other room. "My boyfriend – mon amour – Tucker."

He nodded and said something else incomprehensible, waiting for her response. Luckily Tucker materialized by her side and pressed a drink into her hand and she held it up to Roderique before taking a long sip. "Rum and passionfruit juice," Tucker replied to her wide-eyed unspoken question at the sweet flavor. "The only juice they had here. Locally made, I guess. I see you've already made some friends."

By the second round, Chloe was loosened up enough to join Roderique and his friends on the dance floor, but Tucker hung back awkwardly, watching from the doorway as she jumped and gyrated to Burning Spear and Yellowman songs with the Dominicans. His presence kept their local style of "grinding" at a respectable distance, and ensured that their hips never actually touched hers as they thrust their groins back and forth with unmistakable universally sexual gestures.

"They might as well be fucking you right there in public," he commented to her when she returned to retrieve her drink from him.

"But they're not." Her face was shiny with sweat, but she was afraid to wipe it off for fear of smearing her eye makeup. "It's dancing, Tucker. And it's fun. You should learn how to do it."

She was definitely intoxicated by the third rum drink, dancing with her eyes closed now, not caring how her damp tank top clung to her breasts or how the river of perspiration felt as it ran down her chest along her belly to her waistband. But she was not the only one who was past her limit; the men were talking louder now, a few staggered soddenly as they stepped, and when Roderique grabbed her roughly and held her against the hardness in his crotch, she knew it was way past time to go.

"Uh – no thanks, pal." She pushed him away and stumbled towards Tucker whose half-shut eyes were staring

195

into his empty glass; he had not even noticed what was happening. "Come on, we need to go. Now."

He reeled to his feet, looking like a drunken superhero who wanted to rescue her but could not quite get his cape on. They said their goodbyes and there did not appear to be any hard feelings except on Roderique's part. He was scowling fiercely as he followed them to the exit and partway down the street, where he shouted a few phrases in patois at Chloe that she assumed probably meant "whore" or "cocktease."

They were running by the time they reached Cherry Lodge, out of breath and consumed with giddy laughter. "Oh my god, I feel like throwing up." And then she leaned over the open gutter and puked in the street.

Pale and dizzy, but feeling so much better, she let Tucker lead her upstairs. He got her as far as the shower in the hall and then, steadying himself against the wall, said, "You're on your own now." She heard his footsteps lurching away and then the creaking of the bedsprings. Without undressing, she stepped under the lukewarm water and let it run over her. It seemed like the easiest way to wash herself and her sweaty clothes at the same time.

They both groaned when Flo's impatient knocking on their door awoke them the next morning.

"Are you guys up? We're leaving in half an hour."

"Holy shit, that was so stupid of us to get drunk last night. What were we thinking?" Tucker held his pounding forehead as he tripped over the little pile of damp clothing on the floor that Chloe had shed after her shower the night before. "What is this? Why are these clothes soaking wet?"

Somehow they managed to dress and get themselves downstairs and into the rental car outside. As it turned out, they could sit quietly in the back seat nursing their hangovers while Joe drove and Flo kept up a running commentary on the landscape and the local culture. By the end of the day they had been to numerous gorges and waterfalls, seen the last real indigenous Caribbean people on the Carib Indian reservation and taken a swim in the Emerald Pool. They had even been able to chill out and nap in the car for a few hours while Joe went birdwatching and by the time they returned to Rosseau at sunset, they felt almost normal again.

"Do you want to go out to dinner with us?" asked Flo. "I read about a great restaurant with the best 'mountain chicken' on the island."

"Um, thanks, we'd love to but we have to watch our budget," Chloe said. "We've kind of overspent our cash and I'm not sure how much is left in my account. We may need to move some money over."

"We can stop at an ATM if you want to check. I need to get some more money anyway. Joe, pull over up there near the Barclay's Bank, will you?"

Chloe was kind of curious to see whether it had just been a fluke yesterday that the debit card had not worked. But this time the machine not only denied the withdrawal, it kept the card. Her legs trembled as she climbed back into the car. "I think we'll still pass on dinner tonight," she announced. "We've got a long day of travel tomorrow and need to get some rest after partying so hard last night. But thanks so much for the offer and for everything. It's been a real fun day."

She shook her head at Tucker's questioning look.

"We have less than $100 left now," she told him the next morning as they climbed to the upper deck of the ferry. "If we take a taxi to the airport in Saint Lucia and then another taxi from the airport in St. Vincent, we may not have enough left for the ferry to Mustique. We probably ought to hitchhike."

"Okay, thanks for the update." Money had become a sore subject between them. "Good thing we have a bag full of bread and a big jar of jam." She could see he was suppressing a smile. They took a seat on a bench along the railing and watched the other passengers as they came

197

aboard. Their white faces stood out among the sea of dark ones that surrounded them.

"I'm nervous about the airport part. Up until now we've been kind of flying under the radar."

"Well, we could always look for another sailboat headed south. I'd like that."

A man wearing tight jeans and cowboy boots had reached the top of the steps. He lifted his wraparound sunglasses and, from beneath a black baseball cap, peered around at the passengers who occupied the open air seating, then quickly dropped the shades back onto his face and went down the way he had come up. Chloe had a strange sensation, a kind of wooshing feeling like being on an elevator that was going down too fast or on a centrifugal amusement park ride.

"Did you see that guy?" She squeezed Tucker's arm. "He looked like – he reminded me of – of someone from Culebra."

"That's crazy. You're just jumpy," he said dismissively.

"No, really. Okay, you're right, I am jitzed up. I must be seeing things." But she could not stop staring at the stairwell.

Tucker was right – she had to be seeing things. There was no way that the man they had seen at the Dinghy Dock two weeks ago could be here on a ferry from Dominica to St. Lucia with them right now.

CHAPTER THIRTEEN

They spent most of the afternoon at a local bar that overlooked the sea so that Elle could satisfy her ongoing need for vodka and a wifi signal. Tyler brought his e-reader so that he could pass the time without depending on the erratic and emotional conversation that seemed to be defining their relationship today. But by the time the sun set he had still managed to lose track of the number of beers he'd consumed. An hour or so later, when a taxi dropped them back at their guesthouse, both of them were too drunk to remember the name of the establishment where they had spent the day.

"Skunks? Spanks! No, Skinks. No, no, Spikes." As least they were laughing companionably about something.

"Slick's. It was Slick's, I'm sure of it," Elle declared, falling backwards onto the bed and pulling Tyler down with her. He was as eager as she was to engage in the one activity in which they always seemed to be in agreement.

A light sheen of perspiration was drying on their tangled spent bodies when a nearly imperceptible ping came from the vicinity of Elle's straw bag. "That could be Hans," she murmured.

In seconds Tyler was out of his sex-and-alcohol stupor, wiping his face on the damp bed sheet, moving to sit on the edge of the bed with her. "What's he say?"

"She used the card twice today – once at an ATM in Rousseau, Dominica and the second time with LIAT to book two airline tickets!" Elle's tone was triumphant, but it only expressed a modicum of what Tyler was feeling.

"That means they are actually on their way south. We can track them with this. Holy shit, we've finally got a break!" He pumped his fist silently in the air. "This is brilliant. It means we are only a few islands ahead of them."

"And he's also canceling the card, effective immediately."

"No, no, tell him to wait – I'll pay him back whatever they spend." He grabbed her wrist. "Let me send him the email."

"No. It's over. He's done with her and with me. All of us." She wrenched her arm away and slid out of the bed.

"Can't we at least find out when and where they booked the flight for?"

But she had already walked into the other room, picking up a silk sarong from the floor and wrapping it around her as she moved away from him.

"Fuck." He threw himself back on the pillows, the elation seeping out of him like a deflated balloon. It was still an amazing thing, he reminded himself. He had guessed it correctly, and even beat them here by a couple of days. Unless they had bought the tickets at the airport... in which case they might be arriving on the evening flight right now...

The idea that Tucker and Chloe could be somewhere on the same island as he was at this very moment made him feel even crazier than before. He tried to think like them but he felt he no longer knew how his son's mind worked. The cautious rational Tucker would never have run away with just the clothes on his back and an SAT test in his near future.

Quietly he got up and moved to the doorway. He could see Elle out on the deck, typing away; her face had an eerie blue cast to it from the light of the phone. Who the hell was she always contacting, he wondered.

Despite the fact that he had not made a sound, she sensed he was watching her. "You checkin' me out, boy?" she asked without looking up.

"What are you doing?" He stayed where he was, at a distance, waiting to see her next move.

200

"Just answering some emails." Her fingers moved furiously – even from several feet away he could tell she was deleting entries. "What are you doing?"

"Wondering where our kids are." His response made it sound like they were a happily married couple, just waiting for their children to come home from a party in surburbia. "Wondering when you are coming back to bed."

She untied the sarong and let it float down around her feet. For the brief second before she turned off her phone, he could see her sitting there naked, like it was the most natural thing in the world. "And I'm wondering why you don't join me out here on the deck. The mosquitos and I would love to feast on you."

Always the seductress, he thought. And I always fall for it.

"You're insatiable."

"Why, thank you. I try."

As he came closer he could see she actually seemed exhausted and worn out and he questioned what her motive really was. "I'm not sure I can do it again tonight. Why don't we just go to sleep? Remember we have to get up early to catch a plane."

"Because I can't get enough of you." She reached for him and began gently stroking him back to life. "And because once those kids come home, this will no longer be our private love fest vacation."

Alice had coffee and croissants ready for them at 6am before she took them to the airport. Somehow Elle managed to put on her travel ensemble again and as they walked out the door, Tyler borrowed a panama hat from a rack on the wall, remembering at the last minute that he might also require a little disguise on Mustique.

"I still feel like I can look right at you and not recognize you when you dress like this," Tyler said to her as they walked into the terminal.

"Here, these will help you remember who I am." She pressed something into his hand, closing his fingers around the silky lace fabric. He knew without even looking that what she had given him was her underpants, and shaking his head, he slipped them into the pocket of his shorts. The woman was out of control.

"So I guess that means you aren't wearing any beneath that tight black dress? I hope there is not any kind of security search here."

Her composure was rattled for only a micro-second. "Well, if so, I guess they are in for a surprise."

The flight took less than ten minutes and there was only one other passenger on the tiny plane, an unsmiling blond man with chiseled cheekbones, impeccably dressed in classic boating attire – polo, khakis and topsiders. Tyler felt more like a beach bum than ever and had to remind himself that at one time he had actually made the choice not to be that man, and that back home, in his "real" life he was well-respected in his community and had a job he liked.

As he had done on St. Vincent, he showed the photo on his phone to the handful of workers in the airport, but they all shook their heads. No one had seen two teenagers traveling alone, and they would have remembered if they had.

Having exhausted that recourse, he turned to Elle. "So if you weren't with me, I would be hitching out of here and then hiking up to Kingsley's house. How do you feel about that?"

"Show me where I stick my thumb out. Want to take bets on which one of us gets us a ride faster?"

Fifteen minutes later they were climbing out of a car at the bottom of the long driveway that led up to Kip's ostentatious modern estate. In the ten years since Tyler had last trespassed on the property, a heavy padlocked gate had been added across the entrance of the private lane to keep cars out, but it was possible for two slim adults to squeeze between one of the stone gateposts and the thick bougainvillea hedge that grew along the main road.

"You're going to end up wrecking your fancy clothes doing reconnaissance the way I do." Tyler waited while Elle extracted a couple of prickly pieces of brush that were caught in her sandals.

"Oh, this old thang?" She brushed the dirt from her black dress and straightened the hem before leading the way up the steep drive. "Y'all think they'll be glad to see us?"

"Keep looking sexy and they might at least be happy to see you. Does the word 'depravity' ring any bells?" Tyler wondered if Kip had cleaned up his lifestyle at all after his drug bust a decade ago. Perhaps he had just become more discreet, installing new security measures and flying farther beneath the radar, if that were even possible.

Even though the early morning sun had barely begun heating the day, they were perspiring by the time they reached the massive wooden front door. Cactus gardens on either side of the entranceway were indicative of the climate; both outdoors and inside, Tyler thought cynically. At this hour there were no signs of life around the household.

"I'm going to hang back. You know what to say, right? Can you be feminine and tearful?"

She pulled her sunglasses down her nose so that he could see the swirl of her wild irises and as he watched, tears began to form along her bottom lids. It was a gift usually bestowed only on extraordinary actresses and he tried not to think about how unnerving it was.

Before she could ring the bell, the enormous door opened and an equally colossal and very black man stepped out, pulling it closed behind him. Tyler did not recognize him; Kip must have hired a new security detail since he was last here. The man was wearing only a pair of red nylon shorts and the visible muscles of his chest and arms left no question as to his ability to literally throw anyone off the property. Just to be sure they understood this, he flexed his pecs as he scrutinized them.

"Yes?" He looked from Elle to Tyler, who was hovering several feet away. "I have two questions for you." His accent was distinctly British. "What can I do for you, miss? And how the bloody hell did you get in here?"

"I'm – I'm looking for my daughter." Elle acted much more abashed than Tyler knew she actually was. "She's the girlfriend of Kip's son and they were coming to visit him."

"Kip's son?" The man snorted. "Ha, that's rich. Sorry, lady, but Mr. Kingsley has no children."

"Actually he does. I've seen this boy's birth certificate and Kip's name is on it. So they aren't here?" Elle spoke with a catch in her throat and removed her sunglasses so that the wetness in her eyes could be seen.

"No, they're not here. So I suggest you go on your way."

"Is Kip Kingsley at home? Maybe he's heard from them in the last few days. I don't know what to do; she said this was where they were coming!" Elle was sobbing real tears now.

The man was not fazed. "Lady, I've seen a lot of fans try a lot of things to get their feet in the fuckin' door, but this is a first. Now do I have to physically remove you from the premises?" He crossed his pumped-up arms across his ripped chest and Tyler thought he looked a bit like a Caribbean Hulk Hogan.

"Wait. Wait, it's true. I can prove it. Honey, where's that birth certificate for Chloe's boyfriend?" With a big sniff, she turned to Tyler imploringly.

Was he really going to let her use that bogus document to gain entrance to Kip Kingsley's house? He knew other ways to get in, if they were still available. But before he could even reply, the guard waved his hands dismissively. "Take it up with your solicitor. Have him contact Mr. Kingsley's solicitor directly. Nobody gets in here today, and especially not some tourists claiming to be the parents of the girlfriend of Mr. Kingsley's nonexistent son."

With her most dramatic gesture yet, Elle threw herself down on the ground weeping onto his feet, her tight dress riding up dangerously high. Tyler's fingers tightened around the lace panties in his pocket. If there was ever a time to show some white arse, this was bloody hell it. "Please, I'll do anything. I need to talk to him. I need to find my daughter and bring her home!"

The man leaned over to try to pry her from his ankles and only succeeding in pulling her dress up, exposing her lack of underwear. It stopped him in his tracks for a minute and he looked up over his shoulder at something. Tyler realized, too late, that of course there were video cameras everywhere. He ducked his head to conceal his face, even though it probably hardly mattered at this point.

Then, with one quick gesture, the behemoth threw her off, sending her sprawling onto her back in the gravel, legs spread wide, dress up around her waist, displaying all. He looked down at her, smirking, taking her nakedness in and Tyler knew, from his past experience with the Kingsley lifestyle, that more impressive nudity than this had surely been used to gain entry to parties and more.

Tyler sprang quickly forward and helped Elle to her feet, tugging her skirt back into place. "Are you all right?" Keeping his face turned away from the house he spoke loudly with a Southern accent. "That man is friggin' bully, darlin'. Give him our phone number and let's get out of here. We'll go to the police. AND our lawyer."

"Yes, please, why don't y'all do that?" The guard mocked his accent.

Elle scribbled something on the back of a receipt she found in her purse. "You will call us if they turn up, won't you? I put my email on there also." She pressed it into one of his hands and then, in defiance of his attitude, stood on her tiptoes to press her lips to his cheek. "God bless you. If you have a daughter someday you'll understand."

Some emotion flickered across his face and for a brief second he seemed to soften before crushing the piece of paper into his fist.

Tyler took her arm and led her away, stumbling, head bent and shoulders shaking. "My phone doesn't even work here," she muttered under her breath.

"Well, your full frontal crotch shot might."

Luckily it was hard to tell from the back that she was laughing instead of crying. "What now?" she asked, stopping to wipe the tears away. "Shit, I've ruined my eye make-up. I need to find someplace to take it off."

"There used to be a path up the cliffs around back with a good view into the house, if I can remember how to find it."

She stopped walking and stared at him with her black-rimmed eyes. "Why would we do that? He's not there."

"I believe he is. That guy was way too defensive."

"And what do you think – that he is holding our kids hostage? That seems a little far-fetched, doesn't it? It seems to me we just figure out where to wait it out now. You know what I'm sayin' cowboy?" She squeezed his arm. "We'll head 'em off at the pass."

He knew she was right. He just didn't know what else to do with himself that might feel useful.

"Isn't there a beach around here somewhere? Let's go find us a resort and pass ourselves off as rich people for a few hours. Someplace that has wifi and a bar."

With Elle it always came back to the same-old same-old. But right now it seemed like a good idea.

"Do you think the airport immigration people will actually contact us at Alice and Nelson's when Chloe and Tucker arrive in St. Vincent?" It was barely noon and he'd had only two drinks but for some reason he was already slurring his words. Maybe it was the hour he'd spent in the hot sun on the pristine white sand beach. And the fact that he hadn't really had any breakfast. From behind his darkened lenses, he peered at Elle through half-closed eyelids. As usual, she was busily typing into her phone.

"Seems like I've worn you out, old man." She did not look up.

"You're as old as me. Why aren't you tired?" She appeared as bright as the sky; her printed sarong tied casually over her bathing suit, shiny wet hair drying on her bare back.

"I must need something to eat. Will you order me a burger or something? I think I'll go stretch out in one of those cushioned lounge chairs. They must be really comfortable." He staggered a little as he got to his feet.

"Are you drunk already?" she laughed. "What a lightweight! Here, let me help you." With an unusually maternal gesture, she guided him to the seat, reclined the back and helped him settle into it.

"Are you acting again? At least your ass is covered this time." The stress must be catching up with him; all he wanted was a nap.

Elle was running her fingers through his hair, stroking his forehead gently, removing his glasses. "I need to tell you something," she said so softly he almost could not hear her. "I'm signing papers on the house on Friday so I have to fly back to Culebra tomorrow."

"Really?" He was so surprised by this that he actually opened his eyes and struggled to a sitting position. The sun was behind her head and blurring his vision and he could not see her face clearly. "You can't postpone it?"

"No, I can't. You know how important this is to me. You can manage – you were originally planning to come without me, weren't you?" She was right. He would miss the sex but it would probably be easier alone. "They'll be here soon and then this will all be over." Tenderly she put pressure on his shoulder so that he fell back against the cushion again. "Take a nap – I'll wake you when your food comes."

Sleepily he took her hand and held it to his lips. "Thanks. Love you."

"Love you too, sweetheart."

"Tyler, it's time to go. Wake up."

The lead ballerina was shaking him, her bare breasts bouncing up and down over a corset of aluminum siding and a tutu made of torn mosquito netting. The rest of the dancers in matching costumes circled him, touching him lightly, leaving cobwebs where their fingers grazed his skin.

"We have to go to the airport. I've called a cab to come get us."

The dancers were floating away now, taking his sybaritic pleasures with them, their pink nakedness and white net skirts disappearing into a cloud of cotton balls.

Tyler opened his eyes. Elle was leaning over him, wearing her black dress, the aroma of vodka wafting off her as usual; behind her he could see blue sky and hear the sound of the ocean. He could not remember where he was or why he had been asleep.

"Come on, sweetheart. You've been out for hours. The stress must have caught up with you." She grabbed his hands and pulled him to a sitting position, putting his glasses back on his face.

He was on Mustique, that was right, at some fancy ass resort, waiting for lunch. His head hurt and his tongue was swollen with dryness. He could not recall the last time he had fallen out like that in the middle of the day. "A cup of coffee and a glass of water," he croaked. "Please."

She held out a bottle and he upended it, draining its contents before coming up for air. "You'll have to wait for the coffee. And I had them pack your burger up to go —you can eat it on the way." She helped him struggle to his feet and led him off, through deck chairs and tables into a dark lobby that led to a parking lot. He felt like an automaton, or a zombie from a B-movie, as he followed her mechanically with leaden feet.

"How long was I asleep? I haven't done that in years. I remember now why I hate taking naps. It makes me feel like shit."

"Nearly four hours. You missed a lovely afternoon at the Firefly with some delightful French tourists. I feel positively tipsy." He could not imagine how much alcohol it would take to make her feel that way, or why she was speaking like she was Audrey Hepburn. Or Katherine Hepburn. One of those high-brow Hepburn actresses. She

208

held open the back door of a shiny dark green car and said, "In here," and he obediently climbed in.

"Well, I feel positively faint from hunger, darling." He hadn't meant to imitate her but he couldn't seem to help himself and it made her dimples appear as she smiled and handed him a Styrofoam container. He had never been happier to see a cold hamburger in a soggy bun and a heaping pile of fries.

The food revived him, although he still felt a bit dizzy, probably from dehydration. But he felt the gears of his brain beginning to work again. He barely had time to use the airport bathroom before they boarded the small plane and took off on the short flight back to St. Vincent.

Elle leaned over to speak into his ear over the roar of the engine. "I called Alice and let her know I rented a car for the next day."

"You did?" He guessed that might make things easier.

"Yeah, since I have to drive back to the airport tomorrow."

He looked at her blankly.

"You don't remember what I told you, do you?" She grinned. "About going back to sign papers for the house?"

They bounced in their seats as the wheels hit the runway; and then the whirring engine became so loud in its effort to bring the plane to a stop that they could no longer converse. Tyler searched his short-term memory for the conversation to which she was referring but nothing came to his muddled mind.

"Remind me," he said to her as they walked across the tarmac to the terminal. As she recounted her plans to return to Culebra early, he felt frustrated and perplexed, and not only by the fact that he had no recollection of these details. Her daughter had been missing for almost two weeks and all she could think about was getting back to buy a house. He felt a rush of some strong emotion he could not identify and did not want to articulate; he thought it might be outrage.

209

"Why don't we put the car in your name?" she was saying now. "Then you can use it after you drop me off in the morning."

He was not in the mood for her upbeat gaiety. He needed a cup of coffee and a shower. He needed his son so, that like her, he could be on his own way home. "Sure. Fine."

"Who's a little bit grumpy?"

He did not reply and she seemed to get the message. They did not chat through the rental process or on the ride back to the guesthouse, during which he consumed two cups of really bad instant coffee he bought at the airport snack bar. By the time they entered the cool darkness of their small apartment, he felt much more clearheaded but no less irritated by Elle's decision. It was not that he couldn't stay on without her; it was just the awareness of her single-minded priorities and the growing suspicion that she was conducting some ongoing business that was not aboveboard.

"I'm getting right into the shower," she announced, tossing her bag, sunglasses and hat onto a chair and then dropping her dress onto the floor with her usual oversexed nonchalance. "Want to join me?"

"No, thanks. I am going to drink a gallon of water and hop in next." As he put the car keys in his pocket, his fingers came in contact with her panties, which he had been carrying around all day, and he threw them on the floor with the rest of her clothes.

He heard the sound of the shower running and then the muffled ping that indicated a new email had arrived on her phone. Glancing nervously in the direction of the bathroom, he quickly fished around in her bag. He had a short window of time and he was going to make the most of it.

A new message had arrived from an unidentifiable source with the Hotmail address of xxyyllmm231. *Ferry llegamos SLU. Al aeropuerto en la manaña.*

He frowned. What the hell did this mean? He marked it as unread and then did a speedy search on "Hans." The

210

three emails she had received from Chloe's father had not been deleted but the return address was "h.erickson71." He scrolled to the last one she had read aloud to him, the one that had mentioned the LIAT airline tickets. His eyes widened as he skimmed the actual words.

"The aforementioned credit card was used for a withdrawal this morning at an ATM in Rousseau, Dominica and then again this afternoon to purchase two airline tickets on LIAT from/to 'SLU-BGI-SVD' for Thursday, March 29th. The bank has now canceled this card and any further charges will be denied, effective immediately. We are violating the terms of our divorce so please do not contact me again unless you do so through my lawyer."

The guy was clearly a prick, but that was not important right now. What mattered was that Elle had known since yesterday morning when Tucker and Chloe would be arriving in St. Vincent and she had not shared that information with him. But apparently she had shared it with someone else.

In the bathroom, the pipes shuddered as the water shut off. He dropped the phone back into her purse and threw himself down on the couch, covering his face with his hands. He had to make sense of all of this, and fast. He did not understand what she was doing, or why, but one thing was for certain; she had been manipulating him for all she was worth and he had let himself be suckered right in. How could he have been so intimate with someone and so unaware? For a moment he wallowed in self-loathing, that he could still be so stupid to be fooled into thinking he knew someone just because he had stuck his tongue in her most private places. It was a chronic theme in his life, like a recurring bad dream.

Bad dream...a nightmarish vision of voluptuous half-naked ballerinas in tattered gray tutus wafted in front of his closed eyes, like dirty smoke that warned of an impending forest fire. With a violent gesture he waved his arms and stood up, trying to chase the image away. It was like he had taken a hallucinatory drug or something.

211

Shit. He was such an idiot. He smacked his forehead and then walked across the room to lean against the bedroom doorframe and stare at the flowered toiletries bag on the dresser.

A wet hand slid under his shirt to rest on the sensitive skin of his belly and he stiffened and shivered involuntarily. "Oooh, touchy, aren't we? It's your turn." Her hand moved downwards, inside the loose waistband of his shorts. "And then it's your turn-on." Her lips touched the back of his neck – he wondered if she could feel the hairs standing on end.

Okay. He had played this game before. He could do this. Act natural, pretend like nothing has changed, think it through, make a plan. Save yourself, he thought. And God help you, save your son.

He turned around and stared into her amphibious eyes; the lovely iridescence now appeared reptilian, like a lizard gleaming in the sun or a snake swimming under water. He kissed her deeply, his mind racing as he held his lips on hers, exploring the inside of her mouth, their tongues twining together over and over, postponing the moment when he would have to figure out what his next move was. Finally she broke away, gasping. "Oh, my god, you are so hot and I am so horny. Go get in the shower –I will be waiting for you in the bed."

He pulled the shower curtain and sagged against the cool fiberglass walls of the stall, letting the tepid water run down his back. Then he squared his shoulders and turned his face toward the stream, as he thought about what he had to do next. By the time he stepped into the bedroom with a towel around his waist, he was a man with a plan.

Stretched out naked on top of the sheet, Elle was propped up on one elbow, checking the messages on her phone again. Casually Tyler threw his towel over the dresser and then ran his hand provocatively down her side. A few minutes earlier he had wondered how she could have been so duplicitous, scheming and withholding information while she shared the intimacies of her body with him, becoming as physically close as two humans could be. But now, as he rolled her onto her back, he understood it perfectly.

CHAPTER FOURTEEN

St. Lucia was much bigger than Chloe had imagined. Everything she had read online had said that Les Pitons had the best beach and most awesome landscape and since they had nothing to do until the following morning, she figured they might as well go there. They were directed to a local minibus for a ride that took upwards of two hours and then it turned out they still had to take another bus to Soufriere.

"Why are we doing this?" Tucker asked her. "We don't even have a place to stay there."

"This is what homeless people do. They ride buses because they don't live anywhere." She was only half joking. It cost two dollars to be squeezed into a rickety van with a dozen local people who reeked from the sweat of a day's labor and a lack of hot showers. On their budget, there was no other way to see St. Lucia unless they wanted to hitchhike.

The light was already fading from the sky as they wandered the streets of the small charming city, looking for a sheltered place they could bed down for the night.

"Act like we're on our honeymoon. This is one of the number one places newlyweds go." Filthy from a day of ferry and bus travel, wearing their same old scruffy apparel and carrying their ragtag possessions, there was little chance that they would be mistaken for anything other than the suspicious vagabonds they were. They passed a few couples walking back from the beach to their lodgings wearing only swimsuits and sarongs or towels.

"Maybe we ought to strip down and act like we've been here a few days. We have great tans; we'll fit right in." It was a crazy but inspired idea, and she was right. The less they had on, the more they would appear to be tourists returning from a day excursion. She already had her bikini top on under her tank top – they took off their shirts and she tied her sarong around her waist and put her sunglasses on her head.

"And we left our wedding rings in the safe in our suite at the La-Di-Da Resort, of course." Tucker slung the pack over his bare shoulder. "Oh, and how do we get back there again? I am so looking forward to relaxing on the terrace by the pool with a martini."

"Too bad we don't have wedding rings. We could be pawning them now so that we could get beds at the local hostel." She gave him a quick kiss. "Thanks for being such a great travel buddy, Tucker Brookstone. Now..." She peered up and down the street. "We need to find a house that looks like it has not been occupied for a while or has been closed up for the season..."

"We're not really going to break into someplace, are we?"

"All we need is a porch with a roof. Preferably in a backyard so that nobody will see us. Even if you look like a honeymooner, you need to think like a professional hobo. Now that you are one." She took his hand.

They strolled casually, eventually reaching the edge of town where the buildings started to thin out. It was nearly dark by the time Chloe finally found what she was looking for – a cottage with its shutters hooked shut and its front porch chairs turned upside down on a small table. A garden path led around to the back of the little bungalow where a screened-in veranda housed a cozy outdoor living area with cushioned rattan chairs, loveseats, and even some padded lounges.

"Oh, my god, we are golden!" she whispered excitedly. The screen door was locked but the ice pick on Tucker's Swiss army knife did the trick.

Tucker sank down on the little couch, spreading his arms out and sighing with comfort. "This is fucking awesome. You are a genius, as always."

The batteries in Tucker's head lamp had long since gone dead, so they sat in the darkness, sharing jam and banana sandwiches on white bread and drinking warm water from a plastic bottle. Later they spread lounge chair cushions carefully on the floor and made up a bed using Chloe's sarong and the stained bed sheet they had been carrying with them since the purple houseboat. With a couple of throw pillows from the loveseat, it made one of the most comfortable sleeping places they had experienced yet.

"The best honeymoon suite for hobos ever." Tucker enthused as he tried it out. "Now come consummate our marriage." She couldn't see him lift the sheet for her but she could hear him patting the cushion next to him.

"Consummate. Use it in another sentence." She undressed and felt around for him.

"I'm going to consummate you until you can't stand up?"

"Oh, my. I can feel that you are ready to do that."

He ran his fingers lightly over her, delicately touching everything from forehead to toes. "I wish we had a light. I love being able to see you and your beautiful body when we make love."

"We'll do it again in the morning before we leave. Now consummate me like you mean it."

She felt his touch in the grayness of dawn but she kept her eyes closed, savoring the coziness of the bed, the closeness of his warmth and the anticipation of how he was going to make her feel. She knew he was watching her nipples grow stiff under his now experienced fingertips and tongue.

Gently he pulled her thighs apart and then crawled down to sit between her legs.

"What are you doing?" she asked sleepily.

"I want to see what it looks like when you come. I want to watch what happens."

216

She laughed. "Is this a science experiment?" The early morning air felt cool on her warmest and softest places.

"I just want to know everything about you." He leaned forward then, changing position so that his cheek rested on her thigh, his eyes inches away from her most sensitive surfaces. "I want to know you better than anybody else in the world has ever known you." He began to touch her in the ways she had taught him, stopping every few seconds to watch the changes taking place. "Because you..." he paused in his motion, seeming to record the intimacy with all his senses, waiting for her to moan her need for him to go on... "you are the best thing that has ever happened to me. And I want to know how to satisfy you. Forever."

His words catalyzed her emotions as much as his actions and suddenly she was sobbing, uncontrollably. "What's the matter? I didn't hurt you, did I?" His arms were around her, his body rocking hers.

"I'm just afraid," she wept. "Afraid of losing you. Of not having this – this crazy life anymore."

"Don't cry. Please. Don't." But she could feel the suppressed shaking of his chest and the wetness in her scalp where his face was buried in her hair.

They sat like that for a long time, until the sky became quite light and they could hear traffic on the road. "We better go. We need to get to the airport." But they didn't move.

When their limbs became so numb from not moving that they could no longer feel their feet, they finally broke their hold on each other. Chloe slipped outside to pee in the grass and when she came back inside, Tucker had already folded up the sheet and put the cushions back in their place. They didn't speak as they packed their few belongings and put the porch back to the way it had been, or while they walked slowly back into town.

Only when they realized they didn't have a clue where or how to get a local bus to the airport did Chloe voice her thoughts. "I think we better hitchhike or we might never get there."

As they stood at the side of the road waiting for a ride, she came out of her morning funk enough to finally become aware of her surroundings. Les Pitons were two steep mountains that defined the landscape with a dramatic beauty that seemed otherworldly. There could be no more awesome spot on earth to stick your thumb out, she thought.

Tucker stood solemnly staring off at some unseen point in space, his eyes still puffy from their earlier emotional bout. She touched his arm. "Look. Look where we are."

He blinked and looked around, taking in the scenery for the first time as she had just done a minute earlier. "Wow. This is a fucking awesome place. We'll never forget it." He squeezed her hand as they gazed at the mountaintops together.

It took longer than Chloe had thought it would to reach the airport and they nearly missed their flight. "Your plane is about to board," the ticket agent informed them superciliously. "Go to immigration. Now."

They ran down the hall, boarding passes in hand, their flip-flops slapping against the tile floor. She did not see the man in the tight jeans and cowboy boots leaning against the wall, typing into his cell phone.

"Passports, please." The uniformed officer behind the desk was stern and unsmiling. Puzzled he looked at Chloe's passport and said, "Where is your entry stamp?"

"Uh, I don't know. It isn't there?" She had not anticipated this part of the plan.

"When did you arrive on this island?"

"Yesterday. We are just in transit. On our way to Mustique."

"Mustique?" He looked at her with curiosity over his reading glasses. "You know that is a very expensive place."

"His father has a house there. He's waiting for us to arrive."

218

"Let me see your passport, please." He put out a hand, waiting for Tucker's documents.

Nervously Tucker slid it over the counter. "And here's my birth certificate too."

"Sir, are you aware that this passport is expired?" The man behind the desk seemed outraged.

"That's why you have my birth certificate there as well. I was told that would be okay."

Chloe was impressed with Tucker's quick response. Over the loud speaker, she could hear a garbled message that sounded like an announcement that their flight was boarding. "Um, excuse me, but we're going to miss our plane."

Slowly and deliberately the man unfolded the piece of paper and studied it. "And your age is what, sir?"

"Um, sixteen. Is that a problem?"

"No, just unusual. Generally a minor needs a parent with him to travel internationally."

"Do you see who his father is?" Impatiently Chloe pointed at the birth certificate. "That is who is waiting for us to arrive in Mustique."

For the first time, the man's expression changed. "You are Kip Kingsley's son?" His previously bored tone was replaced by wonder.

Tucker was taken aback by the shift in negotiations, but recovered quickly. "Yes. And there will probably be some seriously bad press if we don't get on this flight because we were held up by the St. Lucia airport staff." He did his best impression of a spoiled rich boy.

"I will be back in a minute." The agent stepped from behind his desk to confer with a uniformed woman, who looked at Tucker's documents and then up at him with a coy smile on her face.

Chloe held her breath, praying they could pull this off. A moment later the man returned and handed them their boarding passes and passports. "Tell your father he needs to renew your passport immediately. Now please put your

219

bags on the security table so they can be inspected. Your flight will not leave without you."

"Yes, of course. Many thanks, man." Tucker strode coolly to the inspection station without looking back.

"Oh, and if you are flying back this way – bring us a few signed photographs." This last comment was accompanied by a brief flash of gleaming white teeth before his bureaucratic attitude was quickly resumed.

In the end, the only casualty of passing through customs was the loss of Tucker's Swiss army knife. It had been an essential element of their limited equipment, but without any checked luggage, they had to let it go.

"Oh. My. God." Chloe gulped for air as they dashed across the tarmac to the waiting plane. "You were amazing."

"Do you think they will give us free drinks too?" he laughed and nodded patronizingly at the flight attendant at the top of the rolling stairway.

"Don't push your luck. And we still have to change planes in Barbados."

"Well, we better refine our strategy then." He removed her sunglasses from the top of her head and put them on. "Does this make me look more like the son of a celebrity?"

The Barbados airport was bigger and more crowded than any place Chloe had experienced in the last year since moving to Culebra. The transit lounge was chaotic and noisy and it was difficult to hear when their connection was being called. Once again they nearly missed their flight, running to take their place at the end of a line. This time the female agent barely looked at their passports, glancing at the names to make sure they matched the tickets and holding their photos up to their faces.

"You look a bit older now," was all she said to Tucker as she closed the booklet and handed it back to him before hurriedly escorting them and the other passengers to their waiting plane. It was so easy – Chloe and Tucker shared wide-eyed looks of silent amazement as they took the last empty seats in the back row. But not until she felt the wheels of the plane lift off the ground did she relax her tight grip on his hand and rest her head on his shoulder.

"Chloe? What's our plan again when we get to St. Vincent?"

"Umm, I don't know." There was still one gaping black hole in their itinerary, which was where they would spend the night on the upcoming island before catching the final ferry to Mustique the next day.

"Can I count our money?" She dug her wallet out of her purse and watched him count the Eastern Caribbean bills and coins. "How much do we need for the ferry?"

"Twenty-five each."

He put the bills aside and surveyed the small pile that was left. "It's not enough for anything except a little food. And I guess I'll take food over shelter any day."

"You would take food over anything." She closed her eyes – she did not want to think about how dirty and tired and yes, hungry, she felt. She did not want to have to look for another place to sleep on St. Vincent, which, from what she had read online, was still a very poor Third World country. For a few more minutes she wanted to just be in the air, between here and there, without having to care.

It was dark by the time they landed and as they climbed down the steps from the plane, Chloe felt achy and overwhelmed. This must be how refugees feel, she thought. Worn out and wondering if they will be turned away after traveling all those miles.

"You okay?" she asked Tucker as they walked with the other passengers through the warm wind gusting across the runway. "You ready for the next show?"

"Ready to blow their socks off." But he did not look that confident as they got into the immigration line under the fluorescent lights inside the terminal.

Immigration did not go so smoothly this time. Upon seeing Tucker's expired passport, one of the agents pulled them out of the line and made them sit in some plastic chairs against the wall while he unlocked an office and made a phone call.

"Wait, I have this also!" Tucker stood up and waved his birth certificate through the office window, but the man turned around and continued talking into the receiver.

"Please sit down, sir," another officer demanded.

"You don't understand...my father lives here. On Mustique."

"Sit down now, sir."

"His father is Kip Kingsley!" Chloe shouted over both of them. "Look at his birth certificate."

The man laughed like this was a joke. "Yes, and my father was Bob Marley. Just be patient — I'm sure your father's private jet is waiting for you on the next runway."

Tucker held the document up to his face. "Do you see what it says here?" He pointed to the bottom line.

Dark suspicious eyes squinted to read the print and then widened in surprise. "This is true, then?" The officer's expression reframed itself into stern disapproval. "You know the man spent some time in prison here some years ago for drug crimes." His language slipped into a local patois dialect. "Not everyone on dis island love de man like dey love him music. You maybe should na be wavin' dat ting around like a flag."

"Is that true?" whispered Chloe.

"Shit. Yeah, it might be." Tucker bit his lip and looked around. The room was empty now except for the guards; all the other passengers on their flight had been cleared through.

The agent became formal again. "Can I have that document please, sir? I need to show it to the supervisor."

Reluctantly, Tucker handed him the precious certificate, which was now limp and stained from so much handling.

"How long do we have to stay here?" Chloe called after him.

"You are free to go, miss. But your friend will be detained here until we verify his identity." He shut the door behind him.

"Chloe–" The desperate squeeze of his hand said it all. "Don't leave me."

She giggled nervously. "Don't be silly. Where would I go?"

Exhausted and edgy, Chloe and Tucker both jumped when the phone rang in the office behind them. Through the half-open door they could hear pieces of the conversation.

"He is?...What is his name?...Please bring me that letter...And tell him the boy could go to jail for lying about his identity." The receiver was slammed down.

"They're not talking about me, are they? Because I am not lying. They have the proof right there!" Tucker was becoming so agitated that Chloe had to use both mental and physical force to keep him seated and calm.

A new guard appeared in the room, holding an envelope between two white-gloved fingers as he carried it into the office.

"He's holding it like it's an invitation from the queen." Chloe tried to lighten the tension a little.

"Or a summons from the Supreme Court," was Tucker's dark response.

Suddenly they heard shouting from the exit to the baggage claim area; an American male voice was arguing forcefully in contrast to the controlled tones of lilting Caribbean accents.

"Just let me see them. Together we can explain everything!"

Tucker's eyes widened in disbelief. "It's not possible – how..."

"I need to talk to him now. Just listen to me, please!"

"What is happening? I'm so tired... I feel like I am losing my mind." Tucker's gaze darted back and forth as though looking for a way to escape and then he stood up and turned to her. "Chloe, whatever happens–" He saw her face registering something over his shoulder and then her mouth falling open in surprise.

"Tucker – isn't that your father? I mean…" she faltered for words…"your…Tyler?"

It seemed like the world had become a slow motion movie as Tucker rotated around to view the familiar figure dashing across the room towards them. "What is he doing here?"

CHAPTER FIFTEEN

Tyler had stayed awake most of the night, trying to make sense of the situation. He'd taken the car to find some takeaway dinner and come back with containers of conch chowder and curried chicken as well as some beers. He thought maybe if Elle drank only beer, she might need to take something to help her sleep, and he wanted her out soundly. But somehow she had managed to secure a bottle of vodka at the resort on Mustique (he could only imagine at what cost) and although she had no cranberry juice cocktail, the refrigerator was stocked with pineapple and orange juice for breakfasts, as well as a handful of limes.

He opened a beer and pretended to drink it, discreetly emptying it every now and then into the sink or over the balcony, and never letting it out of his sight, even taking it to the bathroom with him so that she couldn't slip anything into it. He did not want to be the least bit inebriated and he congratulated himself on having the will power to be that smart.

He did not think Elle suspected he was beginning to catch on; she was her usual flirtatious and inappropriately suggestive self throughout the meal and through drink after after-dinner drink, laughing and apparently enjoying her own company as much as his. He used the excuse that he still felt cranky from sleeping so much in the afternoon and she seemed to accept that as reason enough for his pensive behavior. He encouraged her to have more alcohol, wanting her to be so drunk that she would pass out and be unconscious for a few hours, giving him time to do what he needed to do before the next day.

As her movements eventually became sloppier and slower, his grew more calculated, appealing to her amorous nature. It did not take much to seduce a woman in her condition who wanted to be seduced and although she wanted him to take her right there in the plastic chair (mostly likely because she didn't want to have to get up), he convinced her she would be more comfortable in bed and then gallantly half-carried/half-walked her into the bedroom. She was intoxicated enough to not notice how distant and disengaged he was as he helped her out of her clothing before starting right in on the business of pleasuring her, hoping she would fall asleep without the need for intercourse; the thought of which now made him loathe himself and his blind carnal nature. When he begged off, she sleepily agreed, murmuring something about "Viagra if you need it," and it was a reasonable assumption that she probably had that in her bag of tricks as well.

He sat on the edge of the mattress, caressing her until he was sure she was soundly out and then cautiously grabbed her toiletries bag from the dresser and slipped into the bathroom. He panicked when a thorough search did not turn up the two "date rape" drugs he had discovered the last time he looked, although the Ambien was still there, as well as a ziplock bag containing condoms and the famous blue pills she had mentioned. He sat on the toilet seat, breathing hard and thinking. If she had slipped him something just that day, chances were that the bottles were in her purse.

Sure enough, he found the Rohypnol1 and Flunitrazepam containers safely zipped into an inner pocket of her straw bag. He had no idea of the dosage needed, but he could look that up online. He emptied half of the contents of each bottle into his pockets, wondering how much she had given him that had knocked him flat for four hours. He didn't have a clue which of the drugs he had ingested or if it had been a cocktail of the two. This was going to take some research. He flicked the switch on the old desktop computer in the hallway and before carefully replacing the toiletry kit where he had found it, he added a couple of Ambien to his collection, just in case.

226

He looked over at Elle, who was still snoring lightly, with one arm hanging limply over the edge of the bed. With her entrancing eyes closed, her weathered cheeks slack and her mouth half open, she did not appear threatening. Or very appealing for that matter. It was hard to believe how quickly his desire had become distaste – but he couldn't think about that now.

Waiting impatiently for the outdated computer to warm up and connect to the internet, he looked around for Elle's phone. He finally found it, still on the table next to the watery remains of her last drink, and scrolled through, looking for the last email he had seen from xxyyllmm231. He was not surprised it had been deleted, but he was able to retrieve the email address just by typing "xx" into the "to" line. Servers had such good memories these days, he thought grimly, as he typed in *"All set. I'll take it from here. Thanks for your help."* He reread it before sending and then remembered that her mysterious communications always seemed to be conducted in Spanish. He used Google Translate to change the language of his message – *Todo está listo. Me lo llevo de aquí . Gracias por tu ayuda.*

Next he looked up the times that flights might arrive in St. Vincent from St. Lucia via Barbados. It looked like the runaways would either be arriving at 6:50 or 9:30; he would bet on the cheaper option which had the later arrival and longer connection, but there would be no taking chances. Then, just in case he might need the information, he looked up what time flights left that would connect to San Juan. If Elle was going to stick with her story of going back to Culebra, she would supposedly be catching the 4:30 to Barbados. Shit, that meant they would be playing this cat and mouse game all day tomorrow...

The phone lit up – a response to his email had already come in. *Usted me debe mucho dinero , coño. Traígamelo a mí mañana.* He reversed his Google Translate to decipher this message – *You owe me a lot of money, cunt. You better bring it to me tomorrow.*

What the hell kind of game was Elle playing?

It didn't matter. The only important thing now was meeting that plane; he could figure out what she was up to later. He deleted the emails and closed down the computer. Then he got into bed and lay awake. Making plans.

He woke her with breakfast in bed, using a woven straw tray he found on a shelf in the living room to arrange the coffee, juice and breakfast breads that Alice always had ready for them, rising at some ungodly hour to prepare it all fresh. He added a healthy shot of vodka to the juice and a lime – a "vodka mimosa" he called it. Might as well get her alcohol levels up to par as soon as possible while setting the standard for the morning.

"I thought we ought to start celebrating early this morning before you have to go. Tomorrow is a big day for you." He clinked his juice glass against hers. "To your new house – and victory at last."

Her eyes sparkled as the drink quickly hit her system. "I love how you think. So what's your plan?"

The question threw him momentarily off guard until he realized she was talking about their morning celebration. "Breakfast, sex, a few drinks, more sex, a few more drinks, sex again and then lunch. How's that sound?" He gave her his most charismatic grin as he bit into a pineapple muffin. If everything went as scheduled, she wouldn't make it as far as lunch time.

"Why stop for lunch?"

"Because we will have worked up an appetite by then and need to recharge?" He took her glass and put it on the nightstand. "And you, my dear, have to do nothing. Because I am going to take care of all your needs." He broke off a piece of muffin and put it to her lips. "Okay, maybe you will have to chew your own food. Now let's get your strength up because you are going to need it."

It was hard to keep his eyes on her at all times and equally hard to keep her eyes off his every move. When he

228

went out to the kitchen to make the second round of drinks, she followed him out of the bedroom.

"Hey, I'm your man-slave this morning, get back in there and let me wait on you!" he scolded.

"Well, I like my slaves naked and well oiled. Get those shorts off while you work, boy." She slipped by him and into the living room, retrieving her purse from the couch where he had carefully replaced it last night. "Everything I need to work from bed is here," she said holding it up. Because he knew exactly what she was talking about, he had to close his eyes and breathe deeply for a second.

"Actually I think you left your phone on the deck," he called after her, as he stirred her drink with a spoon. It looked suspiciously murky – he added more ice and squeezed a couple of lime slices into it, floating the skins on top. Then he made one that was identical in appearance for himself except that all that was in it was orange juice and lime.

She was propped up against the bed pillows, frowning at her phone when he returned with the fresh drinks. "Everything okay?" He handed her the glass and she took a sip without even looking at it.

"Hmm, fine." She made a face. "This taste's a little funny."

"I had to use canned juice; we're out of fresh. It's fine. But it's got enough vodka in it that by the time you finish it, you won't know the difference. Bottoms up, sweetheart! And I mean all your bottoms." He downed his drink, hoping she would do the same.

She laughed lightly and took a big swallow and then another. "Take your pants off – I'm not going to be the only one with a naked bum in the air here." With more merriment, she got on all fours to demonstrate what she meant.

"Now there's a beautiful invitation. But first drink up so you don't get thirsty while I am fucking your brains out. Because there will be no stopping this train." By now, he knew just what kinds of things to say that would push her buttons. She sat down on her haunches and giving him a Marilyn Monroe look over her bare shoulder, she upended the rest of her drink.

"Ugh – I am not a fan of that canned o.j. Maybe make my next one straight up." He could feel the double entendre coming on; she was fun, but so predictable now. "But first there's something else I want straight up."

He didn't know whether he had put enough of the drug in her drink or how soon it would take effect. He wanted to be able to watch her face and couldn't decide if it were better if she was on top or if he was, but she was taking control of this round.

"Wow, this feels so amazing. It's like all of my limbs... are floating away..." she moved up and down slowly, rocking her pelvis back and forth. He took it as a good sign that the crushed pills were doing their dirty work.

But she remained in this semi-conscious stoned state throughout her very sustained orgasm, her language becoming so descriptively lewd that he would have laughed and teased her about it if he weren't so intent on getting her to complete unconsciousness. "Did you come?" she asked thickly, her words slow and slurred but her eyes still open. "Because if you did, I couldn't tell because I was coming so hard..."

Her resistance to drugs and alcohol was way stronger than he had expected. She was definitely experiencing the out-of-body effects of the drug but certainly not the total blackout he'd had. Somehow he was going to have to get another drink into her.

"Oh, yeah," he feigned. It did not take much strength to roll her off him and onto her back. "It was amazing."

"Amazing – that is all you have to say? It was like tripping. What did you put in that drink? Oh, wait." He almost could see a thought slowly making its way through her head. "It's my turn to make you a drink." She struggled to a sitting position, reeling from side to side.

"No, no, no. I told you, you are the lady of leisure this morning. I'll go make us both another." Placing a hand on her chest, he pushed her easily back to a reclining position and then leaped to his feet, grabbing their empty glasses.

"That is not an accept – accept – acceptable answer. Do I sound drunk? I am not drunk. It is not even noon yet."

As he reached the kitchen, he heard a crash and a thud from behind him. "Ouch. Fucking floor."

This was not going as smoothly as it had in his mind. Desperately he filled half a glass with vodka, remembering that she had said she did not want any juice this time. Would vodka alone be enough to disguise the drug mixture?

"Where is my goddam bag? I need my bag." From the bedroom came the smash of dishes breaking as they hit the tiles. "Shit, there goes breakfast!" He could hear her having a laughing fit; it sounded like she was rolling on the floor.

His hands were shaking as he cut limes and squeezed their liquid over the ice cubes. A clinking noise made him look back to find her behind him, slithering across the floor, dragging her straw bag by one handle. "I have to make you a drink. It's my turn. My turn."

She grasped him by the ankle now, trying to pull herself up along his leg. He imagined what Alice would see if she decided to pop in on them right now – a stark naked, raving madwoman climbing the leg of an equally naked lunatic who was trying to keep the glass in his hand upright as he desperately attempted to shake her off.

"Elle! Elle! Honey. Sweetheart." It was easier to come down to her level and he tried not to be overcome by the metaphorical reality as he sank heavily to the cool linoleum beside her.

Still holding the drink aloft, he used his other hand to stroke her hair, trying to calm her down. Her half-hooded eyes were as wild as he'd ever seen them, dilated and pulsing, as some part of her brain registered what was happening. "You're thirsty. Just calm down and drink this and then you can get up and make me one."

"I am thirsty," she agreed, panting a little. With one hand he gathered her hair back from her face, twisting it around his palm like a rope, pulling on it lightly to angle

231

her head back; with the other he lifted the glass to her mouth, tilting it so a little of the vodka wet her lips. With an involuntary reaction, her tongue darted out to lick it away. Then her gaze met his; he did not know what she saw there – his desperation and terror, his disgust or his determination – but suddenly she clamped her jaw shut and pulled back. Some of the icy liquid in the glass spilled over onto her bare breasts but she did not react to the coldness.

"No. You." She tried to push him away and grab the drink. With a primal impulse he put his knee on her soft stomach and then jerked hard on the hank of hair he was still holding. When she howled in pain he dumped the contents of the glass into her open mouth.

She choked and clawed at her throat, trying not to give into the automatic reflex to swallow. He held her head back as she coughed and sputtered. Suddenly afraid that she might suffocate, he released his hold and her body flew forward, knocking him down and sending the glass flying across the room to shatter against a cupboard.

"You fucking bast...." She could not finish the thought and instead she spit at him and a weak splatter of saliva landed next to his nose, gliding down his cheek. She tried to smack him across the face but her brain signals were misfiring now and she no longer had physical control, her hand aimlessly swatting the air next to him.

"Elle. Elle." He repeated her name over and over, coaxing her to lie down next to him, praying that any second she would stop fighting and give in to the oblivion that had to be overwhelming her.

"Fuck me..." she mumbled as she tumbled on top of him with a convulsive tremor and for an instant he thought he was actually going to have to do it with her one more time on the kitchen floor just to calm her down. "Fuck you...fuck...Tyler Macken..."

Her head against his shoulder, she continued to twitch and mutter as she slipped into the netherworld of hallucinogenic forgetfulness. He stayed there for a long time, until his lungs stopped pumping so violently and her muscles had relaxed into soft pliancy. Then, with difficulty, he slid out from beneath her sleeping form and dragged the dead weight of her body across the apartment, heaving it up onto the bed.

Sweating from the effort, he sank down next to her, allowing himself one fleeting second of respite, split equally between self-pity and triumph. And then he was up, moving with lightning speed; there was no time for wallowing. There was broken crockery to clean up, evidence to destroy, packing to do and a flight to be met.

By the time he left the house a few hours later, he had thought only briefly about what would happen when Elle eventually woke up.

At 9:30 that evening, Tyler climbed, for the second time, to the observation deck on the roof of the E. T. Joshua Airport to watch the passengers deplane a LIAT flight from Barbados. He had felt a rush of disappointment when the earlier flight had arrived without any familiar faces. As the hours ticked by until the next scheduled arrival, he became increasingly nervous; at some point soon the drugs would be wearing off and Elle would become conscious again and realize what he had done. If she awoke in time and recalled what was going on, she would find some way to get to the airport. He still did not understand why she had concealed the flight details in the email or what she had planned to do with their children when she met the plane. But he would find out – after he had them safely away from her.

There was a rumbling sound in the air and moments later the blinking lights of the LIAT flight bounced into view at the end of the runway as it landed and skidded to a stop. At nearly the same time he felt a vibration in his pocket and remembered that his final coup as he walked out the door had been to slip Elle's phone into his pocket. He had figured that cutting off her communication would slow her down and hopefully incapacitate her for a while longer.

He looked at the screen – a new email message from the "xx" address. "*Llegado SVD. Todos aqui. Recuerdo, o el dinero o ni hija ni hijo.*"

What the hell was this – had she had someone traveling with them right along? *Arrived at SVD* – Tyler knew this was the code for the St. Vincent airport – *All here. Remember the money or no son or daughter?* Had they been kidnapped and she'd known all this time? Tyler felt like he wanted to throw up from fear. Instead he took a deep breath and shoved the phone back into his pants. He was ready to fight however he had to.

The door of the plane opened and the stairs were lowered to the ground. He held his breath as he watched the passengers descend the steps.

Finally he saw what he had been waiting for – a dark-haired young girl in a sweatshirt and running shorts accompanied by a long lanky silhouette with wild uncombed hair. She was shouting something to him over the noise of the engine and he leaned over to speak in her ear. Then he put his arm around her shoulder and they walked towards the terminal. There did not appear to be anyone with them.

With a whoop of success, he took the stairs two at a time, hurrying to join the throng of taxi drivers and others waiting in the parking lot outside the doors to the baggage claim and customs area.

But after forty-five minutes of pacing, he could no longer contain his sense of urgency. He had seen all the other passengers come straggling tiredly out of the customs area, dragging their rolling suitcases down over the curb to the waiting cars and taxis. Only a man wearing a baseball cap pulled low over his face remained, waiting by the road at the far end of the building. The street light glinted off his oversized silver belt buckle as he rocked impatiently on the toes of his fancy cowboy boots, looking back and forth as though expecting a ride.

Finally Tyler approached the pair of uniformed police officers guarding the door. "Is there another way out?

Because I have been waiting for my son and his girlfriend and I know they got off that last plane."

"This is the only exit. Let me check for you." One of them disappeared into the baggage claim area and then returned in seconds. "You say you are the boy's father?"

"Yes. Is there a problem?" Tyler asked innocently, although he knew exactly what all the problems would be.

"He has been telling us something different. Follow me, please."

The phone in his pocket vibrated again as he walked through unlocked door. *"DONDE ESTAS???"* read the subject line of the new email. *"Estoy esperando. Aeropuerto. Ahora."*

What the hell... he looked over his shoulder, suddenly remembering the lone man waiting on the curb, but the exit had already closed behind him.

At the door to 'Immigrations' the guard turned to him and held up a white gloved hand. "You must wait here," he was told abruptly, but Tyler had had enough of waiting.

"Just let me see them. Together we can explain everything!" His tone conveyed his desperation.

"Sir, have patience. We must follow the law."

"I need to talk to him now." Tyler was shouting at the man's back as he opened the door. "Just listen to me, please!"

Over the guard's shoulder he caught a glimpse of two forlorn figures seated on a bench against the far wall of the room. And then the next thing he knew he was running, past the officers and across the linoleum floor to where Tucker and Chloe were staring at him in dumbfounded amazement.

They were thin and grimy and tired and so, so beautiful. He had thrown his arms around both of them, hugging the reality of their beings. The two stood there, stunned and speechless, a procession of emotions parading across their unwashed faces, before the guards had forcibly pulled him away.

A half hour later, after Tyler sweated it out in a wooden chair inside the office, and Chloe and Tucker waited in bewilderment on the other side of the window, the immigration department felt it had sufficiently scared both parent and child. The decision was made that it would be easier to dispense with the usual Third World bureaucracy and release Tucker into Tyler's care.

"We are only issuing a three day visa. He must depart the Grenadines by that time or you will be in violation," he was told.

"Yes, of course, thank you. We will be leaving as soon as possible. Thanks so much for your assistance." Tyler gathered up all the documents before he was escorted out the door.

"Come on, kids, we're out of here," he announced casually, as though he had been buying ice cream on a family vacation and two armed guards in uniforms were not accompanying them.

Slumped against each other with fatigue, Chloe and Tucker stared at him with fearful wariness and then Tucker straightened up. "I don't have to go with you." He had a newfound look of defiant independence in his eyes.

"Yeah, you do. Unless you want to go to the St. Vincent prison."

"But you're not my father." The rebellious expression on Tucker's face reminded Tyler so much of himself at sixteen that he almost burst out laughing.

In his best Darth Vader voice, he said, "*Luke, I AM your father.* Now let's get out of here – I promise I will explain everything to you once we are on our way."

"Come on, Tucker." Chloe shouldered the daypack and tugged on his arm. "We'll get there, I promise," she murmured into his ear. Reluctantly he stood up and joined the group waiting for him.

"Where are we going?" Chloe asked as they were ushered through the now deserted airport.

"To a guesthouse in Kingstown near the ferry dock." Tyler was glancing nervously back and forth as they exited the terminal. "I have a rental car parked over here to the left; let's go." He walked behind the two teenagers, his presence urging them to move more quickly than their tired bodies wanted to go. He was glad that Chloe was tightly clutching Tucker's hand; the boy's attitude scared him and Tyler was afraid that he might do something stupid like try to bolt.

Just as they reached the car, the three of them jostled against each other as Chloe suddenly froze. "What's wrong?" Tucker was instantly attentive to her shift in temperament; his own self-indulgent sulking had vanished, much to Tyler's parental astonishment.

She was staring at a shadowy figure in a baseball cap, leaning against another car, watching them. "It's that same man – the one I saw on the ferry who I thought…what is he doing here? This can't be a coincidence!" Although she was whispering, her voice began to rise, shrilly and desperately.

Tyler quickly unlocked the doors. "Get in. Now." He had the engine started before their long legs were even safely inside, tearing out of the parking lot and onto the main road. At the first side street he saw, he turned off, driving until the pavement ended a few hundred yards further and became an uneven dirt surface. The silence inside the car was tense as he made a U-turn and then pulled into the long grass on the shoulder of the road, parking against a chain link fence overgrown with vines, before turning the engine off.

"What are we doing?" Chloe ventured timidly.

"I think the term might be 'losing a tail'." Although his answer sounded lighthearted, Tyler's breath was coming way too fast – he could feel his forehead pulsing and his ears ringing – and he felt like he had just run a marathon. "We're just going to sit here for a bit, wait this one out. That okay with you two?"

He turned his body in the driver's seat so he could look at them, but in the darkness he could only make out their unified shape as they huddled together in the middle of the back seat.

"So, Chloe...suppose you tell me who you think that guy back there was and why he is following you." His tone sounded a little more intimidating than he had intended and he could feel the energy bristling behind him.

"So, Tyler." It was Tucker who spoke. In just two words he managed to convey a combative protectiveness of Chloe that made Tyler's heart want to swell and break. "Suppose you tell us first how the hell you just happened to be at the St. Vincent airport."

It was not the way Tyler had pictured their reunion and he knew it sure as hell wasn't the way that Lucy would have wanted him to tell their son her story. But he knew there would be no moving on, in any fashion, until the elephant in the room took center stage. Even if it had to happen in the dark in a parked rental car in a back alley somewhere outside of Kingstown.

Maybe it was better that he couldn't see his son's face as he told him the tale of how, once upon a time his mother, Lucy, had gone off to do a story on Kip Kingsley and Boneyard, and had become romantically involved with the former object of her own teenage music infatuation, leaving Tyler and their long term relationship behind to tour with the band and eventually live with Kip at his London penthouse. A few years later she and Tyler met up so she could hand off a story she had been working on about the underground crimes of another band, Apoplexia, who were good friends of Kip's. It was a dangerous assignment that brought her way too close to home.

Tyler tried to not go into what the accepting of that project had cost him, how five years of his life had disappeared into a rum bottle, and stuck to the parts of the story that were important for Tucker to hear. Although he hesitated before telling him the specifics of the truth – how Lucy had invited him back to the penthouse and, against his better judgment, had seduced him. "Kip was away and I ended up spending the night," was all he said.

238

As it turned out, Lucy had known just what she was doing, timing the event to her ovulation cycle. What Lucy hadn't known was that Kip was infertile, unable to father a child no matter what the circumstances. He didn't tell her this until several months after she had announced her pregnancy; when he did tell her, he used the knowledge against her, inflicting various forms of abuse after she gave birth in ways both mentally and physically cruel.

"Don't ask me to give you details because I won't. Just know that by then she was virtually a prisoner in his compound on Mustique and that her only interest was protecting you, her infant son, from his irrationality. The man was a vindictive monster." Tyler had to stop speaking for a moment, overcome by the memories of his own discoveries of Lucy's ordeal. The response from the back seat was silently respectful.

"Eventually he literally took you away and hid you from her in the house of a woman who worked for him. The woman and her brother helped Lucy escape, not only from Kip's house but from the island, relocating the two of you to Bequia, where you lived under assumed identities. Lucy dyed her hair and changed your names. Maybe you remember that she chose the surname of Mackenzie for both of you."

He heard a sniff from behind him but wasn't sure who it came from. The car suddenly felt stifling and he opened the front windows, Caribbean night sounds filling the air. Dogs barked, confused roosters crowed, tree frogs peeped, and life went on.

"After a few years, her fear of him finding her subsided and she was able to raise you in the idyllic setting of Lower Bay village, until one day she learned that the lead singer of Apoplexia was building a house on Bequia and that Kingsley was coming to the island to play. So you and she moved to the safest, most out-of-the-way place she could remember — West Jordan, Vermont, where she had once come to help me rescue Sa — somebody." He did not want to complicate this story with another sordid tale.

239

"I never knew any of this. I was living on Grenada by then, um, experiencing a ... rough patch." He was beginning to realize how much of his life he had never really shared with his son. "Your mom didn't know where I was. As it turned out, in a quirky twist of fate, I was only a few islands away during your time in the Grenadines but neither of us were aware of how close we were living." He was starting to feel rather emotional himself. "When I finally...learned of your existence, I found my way back to Vermont as soon as possible. So I could be there for the rest of your growing up."

There was real crying being suppressed in the back seat now. "So why isn't your name on my birth certificate then?" Tucker choked out. "Why didn't anybody ever change it?"

"I never saw it until we left on this trip." Tyler's answer was completely truthful. "I guess I would have to take a paternity test to prove it. And I promise I will when we get home." He smiled in the dark. "But one look at you and there was never any question."

"See – isn't that what I said?" It sounded like Chloe was the one who was really crying.

"Oh, shut up." But Tucker's tone was affectionate. "So can we still go to Mustique? Because I'd like to punch Kip Kingsley in his ugly face."

Tyler laughed. "Yeah, maybe." But his light mood darkened instantly. "But right now we have a much bigger issue." He started the engine and slowly pulled the car out onto the road. "We are going to a hotel room I reserved in town, if they will still let us in this late, and then Chloe, you are going to talk to me."

"What's she need to talk to you about?" Again that endearing protectiveness.

"The man at the airport. And her mom." He stopped the car at the corner and peered cautiously in both directions. There were no other vehicles that he could see. "Who also happens to be on this island."

"What?!" she squeaked. "What is she doing HERE?"

Besides trying to kill me, he wanted to say, but instead said aloud, "That's what we need to figure out."

CHAPTER SIXTEEN

The first challenge presented itself after he had unlocked the door to their hotel room. Chloe and Tucker had immediately thrown themselves down onto one of the two double beds covered in cheap flowered spreads and he felt his parental terror click in again.

"Okay, okay. Listen." He was speaking as much to himself as he was to them. Two pairs of eyes turned to look at him but their heads remained on their respective pillows. "I get it – you've been sleeping together every night for two weeks now." He had not heard the particulars of their journey yet and whatever he was imagining, he did not want to think about this part of it. "But – I am your father and I am sharing a room with you. So..."

In another world at a different point in time he would have insisted that Tucker share the bed with him and that Chloe sleep alone. But right now that seemed like a futile exercise in drawing imaginary lines.

"So?" Tucker was having trouble keeping his eyes open but Chloe's frightened gaze was steady. They had not discussed Elle yet.

"So you can sleep in the same bed, but no sex. Got it?" It was the best he could do. He sat down heavily on the other bed. "Even if I were just your friend, it wouldn't be polite. That's just basic etiquette."

"Duh," Tucker managed to say before falling into a deep immediate slumber in the way that only growing teenagers can.

"Tucker." Chloe slapped him lightly on the arm. "Thanks," she said to Tyler. "For being cool about it, I mean. I know it must be weird for you."

Weird did not begin to describe it. He shuddered inwardly at the thought of the dangerous adult game he had been playing with this lovely waif's mother. A few days ago he had imagined it would be the two of them here, he and Elle, welcoming their children... he did not even want to consider how uncomfortable that situation would have been.

"Chloe–" he began.

"Can we talk about my mother in the morning?" She closed her eyes now, mechanically crawling under the bed covers, shutting out reality, her young face etched with the effects of physical and mental fatigue. She had barely a passing resemblance to Elle, whom he had also watched fall asleep just hours earlier, albeit under very different circumstances.

"Yes. But first thing. And we are getting up early. To catch a ferry." He was talking to himself again now, both teenagers already in dreamland. He continued to sit there for some minutes more, savoring the sight of them, safe for the time being. When he finally allowed himself to rest, his last thought was that he had not had a drink all day.

Of course he was awake before they were. At some point in the night, Tucker had joined Chloe under the sheet and Tyler could see that his arms and legs were wrapped around her body like vines on a trellis. He slipped quietly out the door, grabbed a cup of coffee from the dining room, made a few inquiries and was back in moments. He was not sure which he was more worried about, the dangers that lay outside of the room or within it.

If possible it seemed their bodies were more entwined than when he left, the sheet twisted between Chloe's limbs, Tucker's dirty bare feet hanging off the edge of the mattress. The eventual separation of these two might be the most difficult task of all those that lay ahead of him.

"Time to get up, guys." He pulled the curtains back, flooding the room with the soft sunlight of early morning. "We have to be out of here in less than an hour."

Tucker groaned and tightened his hold around Chloe's waist. "Why?"

"We're catching the ferry to Bequia. From there we'll hire a boat to take us to Mustique."

As expected, this news jolted both of them to upright, wakeful positions. "What? Really?"

"Yes. So take a shower – ALONE – and we'll grab some breakfast and get out of here as quickly as possible." At the word 'shower,' Chloe had already slid out of bed and was headed towards the bathroom. "Uh, Chloe first."

Yawning, Tucker rubbed the sleep from his eyes. "Wow, Bequia. Are we going to stay there?"

"We'll have to spend the night, I'm sure." Tyler's plan was still not completely formulated beyond getting the three of them off the island as soon as he could. "So you and Chloe seem pretty...uh...solid."

Tucker blushed a little, his teenage bravado having not yet kicked in for the day. "Yeah. I'm thinking of maybe not going back to Vermont."

Tyler sipped his coffee, trying to play it cool. "Oh, really? And what would you do instead?"

"Work on a boat down here. Maybe crew on a sailboat. Turns out I really like that stuff. A lot more than I like sitting in a classroom." He stared out the window, somehow appearing both dreamy and defiant.

"Well, you did miss the SATs last week so a college education may be farther away than expected." Lucy would kill him if he didn't bring Tucker home.

Tucker looked at him blankly. "I did? Oh. Huh. Oh, well." He shrugged. "I don't think you need a good SAT score to rig a sail."

"What about Chloe? Is she down with this plan?"

Tucker grinned. "Well, she gets kinda seasick. But if she wears one of those patches she's okay." His expression turned serious. "You do get it that we're in love, right? That this is not just a casual hook-up."

244

"Oh, yeah, I get it." They could hear the shower still going full blast in the bathroom. "So, let me ask you this – do you know who that guy was at the airport last night?"

Tucker frowned and glanced towards the bathroom door before replying. "Chloe says she saw him on the ferry from Dominica to St. Lucia."

"Dominica to St. Lucia, huh? You've been doing some traveling, haven't you?" Tyler decided to act like he didn't know where they had been. "Does she know who he is?"

"Well, that's the thing. She thinks he is a guy we saw in Culebra the night we met." Tucker began nervously picking at a mosquito bite on his arm and Tyler had to resist the urge to pull his hand away.

"And? So why is she so afraid of him?"

"We saw him – well more like heard him – do something. And then he saw us seeing him." With a sudden movement, he kicked off the sheet and started scratching at his ankles.

"Like what was he doing?" When Tucker did not reply, Tyler repeated himself. "Tucker, what was he doing – selling drugs? Stealing something?"

"No, nothing like that." The water had stopped running now and once again the boy's eyes moved anxiously in the direction of the shower.

"Then what. You have to tell me. This is really important."

"I know, I know!" Tucker closed his eyes. "It was worse."

"Worse."

"Than those things. He was drowning someone."

The bathroom door opened to reveal Chloe with a white bath towel wrapped around her wet body, her eyes wide and frightened. She stood there, ignoring the rivulets of water that dripped from her dark hair and ran down her shoulders and back, her gaze darting back and forth from one of them to the other.

245

Finally she said, "Your turn." Then, tucking the end of the towel tightly under her arm, she propped up her pillow and sat down on the bed.

Without a word, Tucker got up and went into the bathroom, shutting the door behind him. They heard the thump of the toilet seat being lifted and then sounds of peeing that seemed to go on forever.

"So you witnessed this man 'drowning someone'?" Tyler tried to keep his voice calm as he continued the conversation, assuming that Chloe had heard the end of it.

She crossed her arms defensively over her chest. "We heard it more than saw it. But yes, afterwards we saw him and he saw us." Tyler could see that she was trembling a little.

"Do you know his name?"

She shook her head, suddenly unable to speak. "But I'd seen him before. My – my mother knew him."

A few pieces were clicking into place now. "And so that's why you disappeared? Why you and Tucker ran from Culebra?"

"Yes. Partly." She was almost whispering now, clearly afraid of something.

"Did you know the person he drowned?"

"Perry? The real estate guy?" Her voice was barely audible and a tear was forming in the corner of one of her eyes and she blinked several times.

"I'm sorry – was he a friend of yours?" Tyler wasn't quite sure what was going on here.

"No. It's not that. It's just–" She shivered suddenly and pulled the bed covers up over herself and the towel, using the edge of the sheet to wipe her cheeks. "It's my mom." She looked up at him with genuine fear in her gaze. "Tyler, why is she here?"

His answer came slowly. "I'm not sure." It was his turn to be nervous again. "She came with me to look for you. But I don't think it was for the same reason I originally thought it was."

"You came here *together?*" Her pitch hit that characteristic squeak of surprise again. She looked around the room in terror, as if Elle might jump out of the closet or from under the bed. "Where is she now?"

He did not understand her reaction – but then again, he did. "I don't know. Chloe, to my knowledge she has no idea where we are." His hand closed around the phone in his pocket; he wasn't sure how much to tell her. "But I think she is involved in – something...kind of bad."

Chloe nodded, the tears streaming down her face again. "She was there. That night. At the Dinghy Dock." She choked on the words.

Tyler felt as if a cold wind had just blown through the space between them. He stood up abruptly, crossing the room to turn the air conditioning off, but it already was off. He leaned back against the wall, looking at Chloe curled over herself on the bed, her shoulders heaving as she tried to control her emotions. He wanted to take her in his arms and console her, but there were too many dangerous lines he would be crossing to do so. Instead he said, "You saw her?"

"No, sort of, but mostly I heard her. She was arguing with Perry a few minutes before it happened. I know her voice. And then there was like this thud. And then she was speaking Spanish to someone else. A few minutes later there was all the noise in the water." She finally looked up at him. "I don't think it was a coincidence that she was there."

He stared at her, a memory coming back to him. Of the morning that he and Elle had received text messages. What had Chloe's said? "*I know, Mom.*" Elle had blown it off as a 'mother-daughter thing.' But it had not been that at all. Not unless you were the kind of mother that ate her young...

He moved quickly to the window of the room and peered out at the street, unsure of what he was even looking for, just knowing that he had to be wary. And that he had to get them away from here. Fast.

"I don't think it was a coincidence either. Now I am going to grab some breakfast for you two and when I get back, you both need to be dressed and ready to go. Okay?"

"Tyler?"

He stopped with his hand on the doorknob.

"She's in trouble, isn't she?"

It was a simple statement that didn't begin to cover everything that had occurred or was yet to happen. "Yes. I think she is. But right now so are we."

He was a nervous wreck until he heard the creak of the chains and the gnashing of metal on metal that meant the ferry ramp was being raised and the boat was underway. Watching Kingstown recede into the distance, he knew it was only a matter of time until safety became an illusion, but it gave him a window of opportunity to come up with a plan.

When they hit the rough seas in the channel between the two islands he turned to Chloe. "Keep your eyes on the horizon," he started to advise her.

"I know. I am. Besides, I think the patch is good for three days." But the tight grip of her hands on the railing and her vision focused on the approaching shore told a different story.

Even after ten years away, the bustling activity of Bequia's ferry dock still took him by surprise, and he had to summon all his Caribbean know-how and experience to not be overwhelmed. Finding a familiar taxi driver helped and soon they were on their way over the hilly coastal road and driving down into the peaceful village of Lower Bay.

"Wow, I totally remember this." The look on Tucker's face as they came around the final hairpin turn on the steep slope to the seaside cluster of houses made everything seem worth it. "Wasn't there a restaurant right on the beach here? I am so ready to eat again."

Tyler set up the two of them with burgers, fries and sodas at De Reef and then went in search of old friends and acquaintances who could help him on his current mission.

The rest of their short overnight trip had gone as well as could be expected, maybe even better. He reunited with a few old friends and relaxed enough to allow Tucker and Chloe to do some exploring on their own of the beach and town. He spent some time getting to know Chloe and gaining her trust. She told him about how dysfunctional her life had become since the age of twelve, when her mother had left her father and abandoned her teenage daughter to go "live the life she had always imagined" on Culebra.

"Really I don't know how they stayed married that long," she commented. "My mother is loco and my father has no sense of humor at all." He'd had no clue how to raise a wild girl rebelling against an unhappy home life — by fifteen she had been shipped off to boarding school. Before she turned seventeen, she had been kicked out.

"I was Honor Society, taking all AP classes, but hanging out with some real bad-ass kids." She was vague about why she had been expelled, something to do with drinking and "some other stuff" in the boy's dorm; Tyler wasn't sure if she was embarrassed to talk about the details in front of him or in front of Tucker. Her father couldn't deal with the situation; he bought her a one-way ticket to Culebra where she had basically run wild for the last nine months or so under the unwatchful eye of Elle. The most motherly activity that Elle had engaged in was looking for a bigger house, which had resulted in her compulsive preoccupation with buying the bungalow; once she found it, "she HAD to have it," and nothing was going to stop her.

"I wasn't really expecting this to happen." She made a gesture that indicated her feelings for Tucker. "I mean, I didn't go to the bar that night looking for like, a real relationship. But then all that shit went down...and we decided it made sense to...take a trip together."

"For what it's worth, I think that having you on the island was what inspired your mother to find a house to buy. I think she wanted you to have a room of your own. Get out of that tiny one-bedroom cottage."

"Yeah, but believe me, any motive she had was purely selfish. She just didn't want me to be in the way when she brought..."Chloe's cheeks flushed suddenly. "You've been to where we live then."

It was Tyler's turn to redden. "I have."

"And you're still drinking beer." Her tone was bitter and he looked at her questioningly. "The last two guys who came to our place both drank as much vodka and cranberry as she did." Instinctively she clapped her hand over her mouth and then covered her purposeful gaff with a sarcastic laugh. "Ooops. I didn't really mean to say that."

Somewhere in the back of his mind a couple of puzzles pieces fell into interlocking places but he was not ready to speak the astounding possibility aloud. "Well, that's all history now," he said briskly.

"Yes, come along, children. Spit-spot. Best foot forward," she remarked brightly in a Mary Poppins voice. "Well, too bad you didn't show up sooner. You might have been a good influence on her and our lives."

His embarrassment and guilt about how untrue her statement was forced him to change the subject immediately. He asked the first question that came into his head. "So, Miss Chloe, what do you want to be when you grow up?"

"Dad." Tucker, who had been studiously looking uninterested, admonished him. "Uh, boring family dinner conversation, maybe?"

But Chloe had a faraway look on her face now. "I wanted to study geography and earth sciences. When I was in eighth grade I was a finalist for the state levels of the national geography bee. And I used to run track." The wistfulness of her words hung awkwardly over them for a few seconds.

Then Tyler sat up straighter. "Really? Can you still run fast? Because that just might come in handy."

The Lower Bay Guesthouse was the cheapest available place to find a room on such short notice; unfortunately there were none with two beds so he had to book two rooms. He knew it was ridiculous to stand on ceremony at this point, but to maintain his parental dignity he decided to say nothing and left Chloe and Tucker at the guesthouse alone that evening. He had a few beers with his old buddy, Calvin, arranged for a boat that would take them to Mustique in the morning. When he returned a few hours later, he found them sleeping soundly in one of the rooms, wrapped as tightly together as any two naked bodies could be. Sighing heavily, he tucked in a loose corner of the mosquito net that covered their bed and then retired to the room next door.

They traveled by motorboat the next morning to the neighboring island; after that the trip to Kip's seemed as though it would pretty much be an exact repeat of the one he had done a few days earlier with Elle. The same burly bodyguard gave the same answers and was again less than impressed with the birth certificate that Tucker showed him this time. It was clear within a few minutes that nothing was going to get them past the front door and that Tucker was probably not the first person to claim to be some blood relation of Kingsley's.

"If I leave a message, will he know my name?" he whispered to Tyler.

"Oh, I think the Brookstone name will ring a few bells that he might have hoped to never hear again. Sure, leave a message. Just don't tell him where to find you. I know your mother never wants to see him again." Tyler handed him a pen and a piece of paper torn from his notebook.

"This is not how I pictured this going down." Tucker was speaking more to Chloe now.

"Did you really think he was going to welcome you into his house and take care of you? Like he never even did when you were living here as a baby?" Tyler could not keep the disgust out of his voice.

"Well, yeah. I guess I did."

The bodyguard frowned as he listened to their conversation. "You saying you actually lived in this house?"

"So I've heard. They tell me I spent the first few years of my life here." Tucker was scribbling something on the paper now.

"Till you were three actually. From what I've heard, I'm not sure you would want to remember any of it though. It wasn't exactly a PG movie for kids." Tyler was ready to be done with the Kingsley security show and the sordid past lives of aging rock stars. He had some other serious present-day issues that needed to be dealt with in real time.

"And what was your mother's name?"

Tucker glanced at Tyler who, after a second, gave a brief nod. "Lucy Brookstone."

"Well, hang on, hang on. Just a minute, then." The man disappeared inside the house, shutting the door behind him.

"Did what I think just happened just happen?" asked Chloe in a daze. "Are we actually going to get inside?"

Tucker finished his note and folded it in half. "I'm not sure I care anymore."

"What's it say?"

He handed it to her and she read aloud, " 'Dear Kip Kingsley, You are such a loser. Fuck you. Tucker Brookstone.' Really?"

Doubled over with laughter, Tyler did not even notice the door opening again. When he finally looked up he found himself staring at the pale pinched face of a withered elderly man. His long wispy white hair and colorless cold eyes were the only familiar features that Tyler could identify. His rail thin shoulders seemed to be permanently hunched over from decades of playing electric guitars; a white t-shirt and linen shorts hung loosely on his skeletal body like empty clothing on a hanger.

His gaze darted back and forth across their three astounded faces, lingering for a few seconds longer to do a reflexive and lecherous once-over on Chloe, and then came to rest on Tucker. "Your mum didn't come with you, then?" His voice was like tires on gravel. "Where is she these days?"

Tucker's mouth opened as if to speak but no sound came out. From Kip's throat came a wheezing noise that seemed to simulate laughter, but quickly dissolved into a coughing fit. Instinctively they backed a few feet away and moved closer together.

"I can't believe that's him," Chloe murmured. "He's...antique."

Kip regained enough composure to resume what he must have thought still constituted an arrogant stance. "You do know," he smirked, "that, no matter what that certificate says, I am not actually your father, right?"

Tucker nodded, apparently still unable to attach words to whatever was running through his brain.

"And that your mother was really just trying to get her hands on some of my hard-earned fortune. Where'd you say she was again?"

"In a way better place than you. And she never wanted any of your fucking money." Almost simultaneously Chloe and Tyler each grabbed hold of Tucker's hands that were clenching into fists.

"He's not worth it," Chloe said. "Let it go." She stepped in front of Tucker, and glared defiantly at Kip.

"Who's this spunky chick, lad? She looks like she has a hot little twat—"

The words were barely out of his mouth when Tucker's fist collided with it. The second blow landed the frail old rocker flat on his front step before Tyler and Chloe were able to restrain Tucker. "You're a fucking asshole!" Tucker shouted. "And I hate your fucking guts."

"I think we better go." Tyler forcibly pulled him away, backing down the driveway with both arms tight around the raging angry teenager.

"And your music sucks as much as you do!"

As the massive silhouette of the bodyguard filled the doorway, the three of them turned and ran down the length of the steep driveway to tumble into the rented car parked just outside the gate. Some unfamiliar emotion filled Tyler's heart as he started the engine and drove swiftly away. Then he realized it was pride.

"Can you pull over?" Tucker croaked tightly. "I think I'm going to puke."

They had driven directly to the tiny Mustique airport to wait for the next plane out. Fearful of flying back through St. Vincent, Tyler had discussed the options at length until the gate agent convinced them that they did not have to deplane but could stay in their seats during a stopover that would go on to Barbados.

"Good thing you're not going to college now," he remarked offhandedly as he pocketed his credit card. "Because I'll be paying off this extra-curricular excursion for years." He knew it was a cynical comment at a time when his son was still shaken from the experience of the last hour, but he could not keep the harsh truth of the reality to himself.

"Sorry. I'll pay you back. Someday."

The pallor of Tucker's face kept Tyler from adding the observation about how long that would take at the wages earned by someone without a high school diploma. "It was totally worth it. How's your hand?"

"It hurts. But in a good way."

"You know I don't condone violence."

"I know."

"Umm... Tyler?" Chloe's voice broke timidly into their conversation. "Where are we going now?"

It had been hard to convince her to get on the plane with them back to Culebra. "Chloe, you can't stay here." He was still not used to dealing with the fragile emotional state of a female adolescent. "I need your help. You are a major player in what we have to do next." He wasn't sure this was entirely true, his plan was only loosely formed.

"But I can't go home. Not now," she wailed.

254

He knew she was right. "You'll come with us to the campground. It'll be okay. I promise. You guys will be together."

This calmed her down a little but she was soon worked up again. "But I know she'll find out I'm there. HE'LL find out I'm there."

It was what Tyler was counting on. But he couldn't tell her that just yet. "We'll keep you safe. It'll be okay." He shot Tucker an appealing gaze and the boy totally got it. He wrapped his arms around Chloe and walked her to the outside of the airport, and then they disappeared from view.

Fifteen minutes later when he went to call them to come in for boarding, they were standing in the shade of the building, lip-locked in a passionate embrace, the adult eroticism of their body language making him extremely uncomfortable.

"Uh, kids, time to go!" he called, realizing at some point soon he would have to stop thinking of them as children.

Completely unselfconscious, Chloe and Tucker stepped apart and followed him to the gate.

It took five take-offs and landings to reach San Juan. It was nearly midnight by the time they walked stiff-legged into the terminal. After the fourth island of the day, Tyler had lost track of their connections and once it got dark there were no more visual cues. As they deplaned for the final time, the prospect of finding another hotel for the night was daunting.

"We'd be okay with just sleeping in the airport, you know," Tucker informed him rather proudly. "We've spent the night in much worse places. At least there won't be any mosquitos."

It did seem like the easiest solution. In a quiet corner of a newer terminal, Chloe spread their well-worn sheet on the rug between two rows of plastic seats and made a bed for Tyler out of her sarong. "How cozy is this?" She gave him a tired grin.

But before he stretched out on the floor, he plugged his cell phone into a nearby wall outlet. It had been days since he'd had access to his calls but for now he still ignored the voice mails and messages that had accumulated. Instead he keyed in two texts; one to Lucy and another to Sam.

He rested more than he slept in the next few hours, but it felt good to be flat on his back with his legs extended. Chloe and Tucker had wrapped their sheet around themselves like a cocoon, covering even their heads, the bodies forming the single amorphous shape that he now knew as their nightly norm. He tried not to think about how he was going to keep them safe for the next few days.

Around 4am he sat up and started making notes on the back of a boarding pass. When he reached into the front pocket of his pack to look for his notebook, his hand came in contact with Elle's cell phone. He had forgotten that he had stashed it away. He exchanged it with his own on the wall charger and watched it power up, wondering what she was doing without it. Seventeen voice mails had arrived since she had last checked it; without her password he couldn't listen to those. But he could check her email and see if anything more had come of the exchange he had been having with the xx address.

He was stunned by what he saw and stared at the screen for some time before he realized what had happened. The last email that he recalled seeing had been in the airport parking lot. "*Estoy esperando. Aeropuerto. Ahora.*" *I am waiting. Airport. Now.*

He had not thought about the fact that Elle would be able to also access her email account through another device – probably the computer at Alice's apartment.

Her reply had been sent a few hours later, at midnight that same evening, and he quickly ran it through Google Translate to make sure he understood what it said. *"Lost my phone and I cannot get to the airport tonight. Did they arrive?"*

He scrolled down to read and translate the reply. *"You've wasted a lot of my time, bitch. I want that money now."*

Did she owe him or was he trying to extort it from her?

Her answer was short. *"Sorry, trouble here and plans have gone all wrong. Where is my daughter?"*

His eyes widened in disbelief when he read the next response. *"Tengo tu hija y nos vamos a volver a Puerto Rico. La verás cuando veo mi dinero por mis servicios."* He rapidly checked the translation. *I have your daughter and we are going back to Puerto Rico. You'll see her when I see my payment for services rendered.*

What the hell? Who was playing whom here?

Suddenly fearful, he leaped up, quickly glancing over at Chloe and Tucker to make sure the girl was still really there. He was reassured to see a slender tanned foot, with chipped black nail polish and a silver toe ring, sticking out from the mummified bodies wrapped in the bed sheet.

He sank back down and leaned against the wall to translate the final message in the email thread. *"I'll get you your money. On my way to Culebra in the morning. Will go to bank immediately. Please. Don't. Hurt. Her."*

Elle was in way more hot water than he had even imagined. And his plans were going to have to be way more extensive.

CHAPTER SEVENTEEN

Tyler could not calculate how long he had been gone –
five, six, seven days? – and, in fact, he realized he had no
idea what day of the week it was, let alone what the actual
date of the month was, but somehow landing in Culebra felt
a little bit like coming home. His phone told him it was a
Sunday morning in early April, Easter Sunday in fact. They
probably couldn't have picked a worse day to fly in but
somehow it all worked out.

Maybe it was because Sam was there to greet them,
sleepy-eyed and slightly hung over, but freshly showered
and smiling, with his hair tucked up neatly into his man
bun and wearing a semi-clean t-shirt. And then Tyler
realized it was not just Sam, but a whole group of people
who surrounded them, only a few whom he recognized.

"Hey, welcome back, man. Thought it might be safer if I
brought a crowd. We were bringing them to yoga anyway."

"Hey, welcome back! Welcome back!" A half dozen men
and women he didn't know clapped them on the shoulders
and then began moving en masse across the small terminal
to the exit. Tyler saw Sam's grin become devilishly gleeful
as he realized how well his quickly improvised idea had
worked.

They were herded across the parking lot to a white van
that sat waiting with the back doors open. As they all
climbed in, Sam hastily introduced the driver, a stocky man
with a shaved head and a bristly mustache. "This is Pete.
He comes to the campground every year about this time and
he leaves the van here. He's from Maine and always hosts a
Down Easter party where he and his buddies play music.
Maine, Down Easter – get it?" As always, Sam enjoyed a
good pun.

Tyler realized that the women sitting on the floor around him were actually wearing yoga pants and holding rolled up mats and a few minutes later the group all disembarked at the library, profusely heaping thanks and blessings on Pete for giving them a ride.

When they were finally alone and headed back to Flamenco Beach, Sam turned to Tyler with a triumphant look. "So I was right?" He nodded meaningfully towards Tucker and Chloe.

"Spot on," Tyler admitted. "And if I were still an investigative journalist, I'd hire you."

"So Tucker, good to see you, man. I hear you been doing some island hopping the last few weeks with uh, Chloe." Sam seemed to focus in on Chloe for the first time, clearly making note of her short shorts, long legs, and pierced navel. "Elle's daughter, right? Where you guys been?"

"Around." Tucker tightened his grip on Chloe's waist, so clearly staking out his territory that Sam burst out laughing.

"All right then. Can't wait to hear about it. You picked a good week to be away, Tyler. The beach has been a zoo this past weekend but most of them should be leaving by sundown tonight."

"That's okay, we just want to lay low today anyway." Even as tightly wound as he was, all Tyler could think about was sleeping for a few hours. "And you and I need to talk. A few new developments have come up."

Tyler had been thinking that the little tent was going to be tight quarters for the three of them so he was surprised to find a much larger three room tent pitched on his site. He immediately recognized it by the duct tape repairs that ran the length of one side.

"Surprise," Sam exclaimed merrily. "We scored this a few days ago when Alejandro left so we relocated it and moved your stuff in. I figured you wouldn't mind the upgrade. It's obviously got a few issues and one of the windows doesn't zip up, but I've been enjoying it while you were gone – it's like a fucking mansion after living with Leo all these months."

"Wow, this is awesome." Chloe unzipped the screened middle section and stepped into the space on the right. "This is the closest I've had to my own room since I've been on Culebra."

"Well, I'd like to take all the credit, but it's mostly thanks to Cassidy really. That man's a scavenging genius." As he threw himself into one of the camp chairs, Tucker slid past to join Chloe inside. Seconds later they heard the sound of the zipper that indicated the privacy panel closing.

"They haven't had much time to themselves in the last few days," Tyler explained as he inspected the new accommodations. "I rarely let them out of my sight and I won't let them have sex when I am in the room with them."

"We're not in the same room with you now!" Tucker called from inside.

Sam gave him a high five. "I think your parenting skills are magnificent, dude."

Tyler gave a start as a buzzing began in his pocket. It was a call from Lucy. "Sorry, I think I better take this. Hey, Lucy... We're back on Culebra...He's fine. THEY'RE fine. He's kind of become a they..." Now Sam was giving him a thumbs-up. "Mustique? Yeah, yeah, he did. WE did, I should say... It actually went perfectly. I'll let him tell you about it... Oh, he hasn't had a chance to charge it up yet. If anything good has come out of this, it's that he's not addicted to his phone anymore."

"Yeah, he's addicted to something else," Sam mouthed silently, making an obscene hand gesture. Tyler swatted him away and tried to focus.

"I don't know – hopefully by the end of this week... I know, I know. Well, he just might have to repeat this year..." Tyler rolled his eyes and held the phone away from his ear. "Look, I found him, okay? He's safe and healthy and in love... You know what – you can talk to him yourself. Tucker! Your mom is on the phone!"

The sound of the tent flap zipper preceded the sound of the zipper on Tucker's shorts as he appeared at the screened entrance, scratching his bare chest. "Right now?" he whispered.

"Yes! Come out here and take this thing. You remember how to use it, don't you?" They watched as the boy moved away from them and bent his head to speak privately. With her face pressed against the screen window, Chloe's eyes were also following him, and from her bare shoulders Tyler guessed that all she was wearing was a worried expression.

He leaned forward, wearily resting his forehead on his knees. "I think you can take back that parenting award."

"Oh, come on. I've been looking forward to hearing you say it – 'I'd like to thank the academy and everyone else who helped make this dream a reality, especially my friend Sam in Section E'..."

Although Sam kept things light, Tyler knew they were going to have to get serious soon enough. Eventually Tucker returned and handed him his phone. "You good?"

"Ha. Yeah, never better."

"Your mom supportive of your plans?"

"Oh, sure. Totally."

"Supportive like 'I never want to see your ass again and have a great life as a beach bum on Culebra'?" he called after him. The sound of zipping and unzipping was his answer.

Hey, some of us are good with that," Sam protested.

Tyler stood up, reeling with exhaustion. "Let's go over to your site for a few minutes. I need to talk to you privately."

"You know it's not exactly private over there – it's like Beach Central Station this weekend. But come on. We'll find somewhere."

They sat at Cassidy's picnic table because Sam said he had gone kayaking for the morning and wouldn't be back for a few hours. Over a couple of pre-noon beers, Tyler laid out everything that had occurred during the previous days

261

– how they had tracked Chloe and Tucker through the credit cards, Elle's strange emails and texts, the first trip to Mustique. When he got to the part about her drugging him, Sam choked on his beer.

"Are you fucking kidding me? Go on, go on."

He could barely sit still when Tyler described how he had used her own strategy against her so that he could get to the airport and rescue their children and how they eluded the man who had been shadowing Chloe for Elle. When he got to the part about the visit to Kip Kingsley, Sam literally threw himself into the sand hooting and kicking his feet.

"Oh my god, oh my god, this is amazing. Okay, okay, I'll be cool." He stood up and brushed himself off. "What happened next?"

When he told him about the email exchange he had read this morning, ("And oh, yeah, I took her phone.") and how the guy who had been working for Elle was now working her over with his lie about having Chloe, Sam shook his head in complete disbelief.

"We need more beer and then you tell me what you think is going on here." He was back in thirty seconds with a couple of lukewarm Medallas. "Best I could do. So before you go on – do you think Chloe is in, like, serious danger?"

Tyler grimaced and passed a hand across his forehead. "Yeah, maybe. But I'm not sure from whom. She doesn't know that this killer has claimed to have kidnapped her but she is afraid of her mother whom she believes had a part in Perry's drowning."

He then explained to Sam what Chloe had told him in the hotel room on St. Vincent. "I'm not sure what Elle's intention was if her plan to drug me had worked and she had gone to the airport alone to meet them. And how this other guy was supposed to fit into that picture. I'm still not sure if she wanted to silence Chloe or save her. And god knows where Tucker would have fit into the picture." He shuddered involuntarily.

"You're killin' me, dude! Sorry, bad pun – but now you tell me you've been sleeping with a freakin' accomplice to a murderer? Shit, what are we gonna do. Elle. Jesus."

Tyler covered his face and shook his head. "I'm such a fool when it comes to females."

"Aren't we all. But look what you did. The kids are all right. And so are you."

"For now. But there are two snakes out there, ready to strike again as soon as they can." Overwhelmed, he took off his glasses and leaned forward, resting his cheek against the rough wood of the table.

"So what's your plan? I know you have one."

He opened one eye and looked at Sam sideways but with his blurred vision he could only sense his eager expression. "We're going to get her," he whispered. "We're going to trap her at her own game. Literally." The combination of beer and exhaustion had taken over now and he felt too sleepy to even get up and go back to his tent.

"Like how?"

"Nines at eight…"

Somehow Sam got him back to the tent and onto his air mattress. "Sam, thanks…listen." He hoped he was actually mumbling and not just dreaming that he was talking. "I'm only going to sleep for a few hours. Watch them for me. Don't let them go anywhere."

He thought he heard Sam say, "No worries. We'll be cool."

It was not sound or light that eventually woke him but his sense of smell. There was fish barbecuing somewhere and he was starving. He had no idea what time it was but if his phone was correct he had slept for nearly five hours. Abruptly he sat up, wondering where Tucker and Chloe were. When he called out, there was no response.

He staggered out of the tent and after a quick trip to the toilet quad, he traveled the pathways to various nearby sites, noticing along the way that there were several fewer camps than when they had arrived that morning. Following his nose, he ended up at Antonio's outdoor kitchen. Antonio, a longtime long-termer had a cooking set-up that was the envy of all the other campers because it included not only a four burner stove top, a full set of pans and utensils, but also a propane-fired oven where the veteran camper actually baked whole grain bread which was nearly impossible to find on Culebra. To be invited to dinner at Antonio's was a coveted honor, shared with only a select few.

But here was where he found them, along with a half dozen other acquaintances. Chloe with her hair wet and slicked back, wearing only a tiny white string bikini, was chopping vegetables for salad beside Antonio's partner, Ramone, along with an equally sea-salty Tucker, who was cleaning the catch of the day.

"Octopus salad," they informed him, obviously happy to be helping to create such exotic local cuisine. "Sam and Leo took us out spearfishing with them and this is what we came back with. And a couple of snappers."

The reef was probably the safest place they could have gone for the afternoon, in addition to being the most exciting. Now that he was rested, Tyler felt a great sense of relief that he had this family of campers to watch his back. Cassidy greeted him with characteristic warmth as he passed by carrying a pot of cooked pasta for the salad; Tom and Lisa were running the bar, as usual.

"Tomorrow is our last night," was Lisa's forlorn update. "So this is kind of our going-away party."

"You mean our drink-up-all-the-liquor party," Tom corrected.

"Seems to me you guys do that every night," Tyler laughed.

"Well, nothing wrong with that!" Tom toasted himself with another shot of whiskey.

"Don't forget, tomorrow night we're doing a Nines at Eight party, right?" Sam looked up from the grill at Tyler, shrugging his shoulders and widening his eyes. He was clueless but willing to go along with whatever Tyler was scheming.

Tyler nodded vigorously, his mouth full of guacamole. "Mmm, yeah. Anybody seen Elle around? We need to invite her."

Chloe's head whipped around in alarm. Realizing his thoughtless mistake, he gave her the most reassuring look he could.

"I heard a rumor she's back," said Cassidy. "Didn't you two leave here together?"

"We did, but we, uh, sort of split up. She came home on her own." He crossed the few feet to stand next to Chloe who had gone quite still. "It's okay," he murmured, leaning over the salad bowl and popping a tomato in his mouth. "This is all part of the plan. I'll explain later. Don't worry."

"I tried calling her last night after someone said they saw her at the Sand Bar but she didn't pick up." Lisa cleaned the top of her beer can with the hem of her shirt, self-consciously keeping her eyes down. "I'd like to say goodbye to her."

"I bet you would."

Not tonight, you two!" warned Antonio. "Not in my camp anyway. This is a peace, love and octopus gathering." Despite his white hair and gentle nature, he was a large man with an imposing presence and was regarded with respect for his decades at Flamenco and his impressive array of camping conveniences. Undoubtedly Tom did not want to lose the privilege of being invited to dine at Antonio's table.

Ramone cleared his throat. "Actually I saw her walking the beach early this morning." The group became instantly silent, all eyes staring at him. "I didn't know it was important to anyone. She chatted with me for a bit but no one else was around so she left. What?"

"Nothing. It's fine. We'll all see her tomorrow," Sam replied hastily. "Who wants another beer?"

Slowly Chloe put down the knife she had been holding and gripped the edge of the table. Tucker materialized at her other side and whispered, "You want to go back to the tent?"

Putting an arm around each of them, Tyler moved out of the clearing to the privacy of the path. "I think it's better if you guys stick with the crowd, especially tonight. Chloe, I know this is scary, and I shouldn't be asking, but I am going to need your help in the next twenty-four hours getting some closure on this crazy thing." He realized that she was shivering, maybe because she was still damp and nearly naked at nightfall. "Tucker, will you go get her sweatshirt?"

Somehow the boy managed to step between them, forcing Tyler to take a step back. His eyes were as wild as his hair had become, his dilated pupils vacillating between pinpricks and large black holes, and Tyler suspected he must be very stoned. "You can't make her do something dangerous."

"I'm not making her do anything."

""But nobody is as manipulative as you and you make a lot of bad choices."

The truth of Tucker's defiant words made him flinch. Regaining his composure, he replied, "Oh, I think Chloe's mom has me beat on both those accounts. Now please get your girlfriend something to cover up with. She's freezing."

When he stormed off, Tyler turned to Chloe. "Sorry I said that."

Her fearfulness dropped away for a second to let the old, self-assured Chloe through. "For what?" she snorted. "You are totally right. But..." Her confidence was gone as quickly as it had come on. "Is she going to end up in jail?"

"Sweetheart, she needs help. I think you know that better than you let on." He waited while Chloe bit her lip and then nodded in agreement. "But even if she is a little crazy, I do believe she loves you, in her own misguided way. So..." and yes, now he was going to be as manipulative as his son said he was, but hopefully with a good outcome, "I might need to use you as bait tomorrow But I promise, nothing bad will happen to you. I'll make sure of that."

Later, as they all sat around in their assorted folding camp chairs, feeling satiated and listening to Pete play his guitar, Tyler and Sam spoke quietly regarding the plans for the next day.

"Do you think it's safe for the two of them to stay in the tent tonight?" Tyler looked over at Chloe and Tucker who were accompanying Pete's music on some random percussion instruments he had handed out.

"I think the smartest thing I ever did was switch out your old small tent with the big one. If Elle came by looking for you this morning, she probably assumed that we took your stuff away and someone else had taken your site. It's like hiding in plain sight. Get it – 'sight' – 'site'?" As usual, Sam easily entertained himself.

"So you need to invite her to come tomorrow night. But you'll have to go find her because, remember – I've got her phone. Which kind of totally complicates things." Tyler frowned, realizing part of his strategy had involved contacting Elle.

"I'm guessing she must have gotten a new one by now, even if it is just a temporary disposable. She might even have switched her number. She could do that, you know." He pulled out his own cell and then said, "That reminds me. I wanted to show you this. I totally forgot I had actually taken a video of this night."

He touched the screen a few times and handed it to Tyler.

"What am I looking at?" he asked as he saw a close up of someone's hand holding playing cards. Then as the camera zoomed out, he understood. It had been shot at Sid's table during a game of Nines. Elle was laughing and mugging, leaning close to a man with sharp features whom he didn't recognize. She put her cheek against his and held the cards up in one hand and her drink in the other.

"See? We share everything," she was saying. She put the cup to her own mouth and then to her companion's, who

267

drank greedily, smacking his lips. "Now what card should we play, Ivan? You pick."

"Ivan? That's who that is? When was this taken?" Tyler's pulse quickened with excitement.

"You know. It was that night – this is historic shit, man. The last footage ever taken of him. Last time he was seen alive."

"Sam, this is more than historic...Let me watch it from the beginning again."

Tyler stood up and walked off into the shadows with the phone to watch the short movie. It was all of sixty seconds – but it was everything he needed.

And now he knew exactly what had to happen. If they could pull it off.

"Can you send this to me?" he whispered.

"Nah, the file's probably too big, it would take forever from here and run down my battery. But let me see what I can do – maybe I can compress it and save it to the cloud in the morning." As Sam began fiddling with his phone, Tyler looked around at the faces of the others, dimly lit by solar-powered lanterns. How many of them could they trust to be in on this? There were a few key players he desperately needed.

"Hey, I'm looking for Elle. I wondered if she happened to be around," he heard Sam say; he looked up and mouthed, "I'm calling the Sand Bar," and then a surprised, "Hey, Elle, you're back. Uh, how'd it go?"

Tyler felt himself start to twitch – he had not expected Sam to do this without discussion. Quickly he pulled him by the arm and they stepped out of the circle of light onto the path.

"Oh, sorry to hear that. So is Tyler with you?" He gave Tyler a hand sign to indicate he had the conversation covered. "No, we haven't seen him. I thought you guys were together...Really, huh. Well, listen, we're having another last Nines party tomorrow and we need you to be there..."

He listened while Sam used all his flirtatious boyish charm to convince her to attend. He finally sealed the deal with the promise of a "vodka and cranberry" theme and the agreement that he would go out with her after the game was over.

"Phew, she's so intense. I don't know how you did it." He turned to Tyler. "Now tell me again – why did I just invite her to that?"

Long after the campground had quieted down for the evening, they were still strategizing. They sat in Tyler's side of the three-room-tent, speaking softly. Tyler was afraid to leave Tucker and Chloe alone, especially at night, Even if Elle did not actually know they were here; it was a small island and word traveled. He knew the two of them were trying to be discreet but it was hard not to hear their activity through the nylon walls and open screens.

A few times he swore and finally said, "I don't want to listen to this," but Sam restrained him and then took him outside for a short stroll and a few quick puffs of the weed pipe.

"You're pretty much not letting them do anything else, dude. It's like you have them under house arrest with no diversion but their hormones. And they seem to be pretty solid. I say let it go. But, hey – I live with Leo the chick magnet. I know how you feel."

"Yeah, but he's not your sixteen-year-old son." But he knew it was true; he was keeping them confined and guarded and at least they were entertaining themselves the way they knew best.

When they finally returned, the activity seemed to have calmed down and after a little more discussion and dividing of tasks, they parted for the night. Still nervous and on the defensive, Tyler left the panel to his side of the tent unzipped so he could hear more easily if someone unwanted tried to enter. Finally he realized this was absurd – there was merely a rip-stop wall protecting them from intruders and kidnappers. This tent had already been slashed once; in the grand scheme of probability, did that lower the odds of it happening again?

He berated himself for bringing Tucker and Chloe back here; what had seemed like a halcyon haven was merely camouflage for a dangerous snake pit.

The best laid plans were nearly undone shortly after dawn the following morning. As he strolled away from Rosita's kiosk with his coffee and a bag of toasted bagels to share with the kids, there was Elle coming in from the parking lot. Her loose hair was bright in the early sunlight, and her gauzy white dress floated around her in the morning breeze as she headed towards the beach. His inevitable sense of attraction was quickly suffused by nauseating fear; he stood still as though he was hunted prey in the wild woods and maybe his predator would not notice his presence.

She stopped in her tracks, as momentarily confused as he was by this unexpected encounter, staring at him with uncertainty, her eyes hidden behind her oversized sunglasses. He thought it might have been the first time he had ever seen her less than completely self-assured. They studied each other and once he got over his initial impression of angelic beauty, he realized that the vibration he sensed was not energy but exhaustion. A slight twitch of her cheek, a tremor of the hand that clutched her sandals, it all revealed how close to the edge she was.

"Tyler." The mistress of manipulation had regained her composure first. "I didn't expect to see you back here."

"Elle. I might say the same for you." Frantically he tried to claw his way out of this strange and uncomfortable confrontation. "You were in pretty rough shape the last time I saw you." He was warming up to the situation now. "We had some harsh words."

She took her glasses off to scrutinize him better and the weighty bags beneath her crazy eyes told him everything he needed to know. "Really. Because I don't remember much of anything that happened before I woke up alone in that apartment." She started towards the path that led to the beach. "Walk with me," she commanded as she sailed past him and he hurried to catch up. When they reached the sand, he took her arm and steered her to the right, in the direction opposite the campground, towards the Shark Tank. The white crescent of Flamenco was deserted and beautiful at this time of day.

"You had a lot to drink. It got pretty weird." He was leaving much unsaid and the truth hung between them like a tether ball to be bounced back and forth. "You made it pretty clear that you didn't want to see me again." That was not a lie at all.

Her eyes narrowed so much that he almost thought she might have fallen asleep if she hadn't been walking and then she said, "Where are they?"

"The kids?" Shit, what could he say here...he had not been ready for this at all. "I don't know where your daughter is." Okay, now he was lying. Big time. "I went to the airport and picked up my son. He said they weren't together anymore."

She stopped moving and turned to stare at him in disbelief. "What?"

"I sent him home to Vermont and came back here to get our stuff." Despite the fact that she was standing still, he kept walking. He wanted to get her as far away from Section E as possible.

Barely missing a beat, Elle was back at his side. "What the hell do you mean they weren't together? Where is she then?"

"How should I know? It was a fling – they probably had a fight and she didn't want to go with him on his odyssey to meet his 'dad' anymore. I'm assuming he left her on one of those other islands – St. Lucia, maybe? I didn't ask and I didn't care. I was happy to find my son and send him safely home." He was in it deep now. "I'm sorry if you haven't heard from her."

He turned when he realized she was no longer keeping up with him. She had sunk down into the sand, her shoulders slumped over, her head resting on her knees. For a fleeting second he felt badly about the story he had fabricated, until he remembered who he was dealing with.

"Look, if you want I'll call him and ask him if he can give us any other details about where she might be headed."

She looked up at him, the hope briefly flickering across her face quickly erased by the reality of what she thought she knew. "No, that's okay. What's the point." She said it flatly, not as a question.

He had to act like the Tyler who really didn't know that Chloe was actually wrapped cozily in the arms of her boyfriend, his son, only a fifteen minute walk away. "No, really, let me call him. Maybe it will help."

He pulled out his phone and dialed Sam's number.

"It's early, dude."

"Hi, Tucker," he said in response to Sam's statement. "How is everything at home?"

"What? You butt dial me or something?"

"Good. Good. I'm here sitting on the beach with Elle not too far from the Villas. Elle, that's Chloe's mom, you remember?"

"Holy shit. You all right? You want me to come down?"

"No, that's okay. Yeah, well, she just wants to know if Chloe might have said where she was going to when you guys separated."

"Um, what do you want me to do here? This is a fake conversation, right?"

"She thought she might go back to Dominica? By ferry? Okay, well, if you think of anything else, give me a call. And hey — remember, keep an eye on the chickens for me — there's been a fox around in the neighborhood lately."

"Got it. No worries. Make sure she's coming tonight if you can."

"Good luck with school today. They can call me if there are any issues."

"Yeah, love you, Dad."

Tyler laughed. "You too, bro." He turned back to Elle, who was watching him warily. "Sorry, that's the best I can do. She's resourceful, right? I am guessing she'll be fine.

Maybe you should text her and let her know you signed on the house."

She appeared perplexed. "Signed? Oh, no, that didn't happen yet. There's been a hang up with the...financing." Suddenly she was on her feet and heading towards the end of the beach again.

She's a land mine, he thought as he matched his stride to hers. Step on her and she might go off. She should be wearing a 'Peligro' sign like the rest of the unexploded bombs on this island.

"So where were you last night?"

"What?" He thought he hadn't heard her right.

"Where'd you sleep? I talked to Sam and he hadn't seen you."

Shit. There was no saying "I got in late" on Culebra. The last flight arrived before dark and the final ferry was in by eight and she would have been watching the ferry from the Sand Bar. "Yeah, I didn't see him until kind of late. My tent had been taken down and it turned out that Cassidy had all my gear. Like just in case I never came back, he would score." Keep making it up, he coached himself. "So I just slept on his floor. It seemed the easiest thing to do. I'm only staying until tomorrow."

Elle nodded as though she understood. Then, still focused on their destination at the end of the beach, she said emotionlessly, "You're welcome to stay at my place tonight."

Right. Her invitation was probably as coldblooded as it sounded. "Uh, thanks. Probably not a good idea. But I heard there is a game of Nines tonight here. You coming?"

She shrugged. "I don't know. I'm feeling kind of stressed. I have to straighten out my financial issues. I'm waiting for the bank to open."

He knew her money problems had nothing to do with a home mortgage today. But, hell, he was going to have to do something to make sure she came to the campground and he knew what it was. The thought made him queasy.

They didn't speak again until they reached the picnic table under the pavilion by the Shark Tank where they sat to rest. There was no wind and the water seemed almost motionless, like the calm before a storm.

"How about a swim?" he suggested. "You always say it changes your perspective for the better."

Still and silent, she stared out to sea and he sat there beside her, knowing both of them were calculating their next moves. Then she stood, shedding her dress like a discarded snakeskin, and slipping swiftly across the sand to the water's edge. She wore a simple gray tank suit of some shimmery iridescent fabric that looked almost like fish scales, more like a dance leotard he realized when it began to get wet, displaying the unconfined outlines of the body he had known so intimately.

She turned back to him, her breasts bouncing as freely as if she were naked. "Coming?"

He did not want to swim with her, but he wanted to keep her at this end of the beach for a while, wear her out so that she would not think of walking to the other end to check in with her buddies at the campground. "Coming," he called, as he began to empty his pockets onto the table — wallet, cell phone, knife, Elle's cell ...

Shit. What if she saw it? He turned his back, blocking her view as he slipped the pilfered phone into the bag of bagels. Whipping off his t-shirt, he threw it protectively over his possessions and then followed her footsteps into the sea.

He swam the short distance to where she was standing, arms outstretched on the surface, face turned up to the sun, her hair hanging in thick wet clumps, heavy down her back. Medusa, he thought, and then he was unable to push that violent image from his mind.

As he knew she would, she reached for him, pulling her body through the warm water to press her nipples, so hard they were almost sharp, against his chest, and pushing her salty tongue into his mouth. And as she knew he would be, he was nearly overcome by the sensuous sensations of her.

"Let's do it," she gasped, grinding her crotch into his. "Here, now, in the water."

An instinct for survival helped him resist the primal temptation of her; pulling himself away was like detaching a strong magnet from a huge hunk of metal. "No. I can't. Not now. Later. Tonight."

She twisted around so that instead of pushing her away, his hands were instead grasping her breasts, her own hands over his and she rubbed herself against him. "Please. Please. I need this so bad."

"Tonight." He whispered into her ear. "After Nines." He knew that the promise of sex would help to ensure she would be there, like nothing else would. Gently he squeezed the soft flesh beneath his fingers and she groaned and melted back against him.

"Both," she pleaded. "Now and then." Beneath the water she reached for him, trying to get her hands inside his shorts and he released her, kicking away and backstroking in the direction of the shore.

"It's something to look forward to!" he called to her. Even from a distance, through the water spots on his glasses, he could see the tears of frustration welling in her eyes.

He hesitated on the beach, not sure if he should make a dash for the campground while she was still in the water or stay and make sure she got safely on her way to town in the golf cart. He knew she would try to seduce him again if he stayed, but the memory of his altercation with her on the kitchen floor strengthened his resolve; she was a deadly madwoman and he would not let her get to him.

His chest heaving, he sat down on the bench to wait for her. When she finally emerged from the water, she moved slowly until she stopped in front of him, their eyes locking in an intractable gaze.

Without blinking or looking away, she stripped off her swimsuit and stood there, wet, naked and defiant. In his peripheral vision he could see the water glistening in her pubic hair and dripping off the ends of her erect nipples. Without breaking his stare, he picked up her dress and held it out.

"You know this is not a nude beach."

"It can be if no one is watching." She took the dress from him, using it to wipe the water from her face, and then with a coy smile, ran it between her legs to dry the dampness there before pulling it over her head. And then, as quickly as her seductive self had materialized, it disappeared into her tangled miasma of nefarious responsibility.

"What time is it – I need to get to the bank. And get a new phone."

"Then let's go." He put his arm around her shoulder and steered her back up the beach, moving aside when he was sure she was in motion again. As they neared the kiosks, the atmosphere between them returned to its former strained silence and he was relieved when he was finally able to help her into the golf cart.

"See you tonight then." To seal the deal, he forced himself to give her a warm and promising goodbye kiss.

"I'm looking forward to it." A little bit of her usual carefree character surfaced for the time it took to wink at him.

"Me too."

She had no idea how much.

CHAPTER EIGHTEEN

By the time the sun went down, the stage was set for the evening's activities. As it was growing dark, Tyler took a last look at the screened pavilion erected at the end of the beach, just beyond the painted tank. Inside, strings of white solar lights ran back and forth; palm fronds decorated the corners and roof line. A picnic table occupied the center of the space; a bar made of driftwood and milk crates sat against one wall.

Rezipping the only entrance behind him, he surveyed the rest of the area. The beach had a post-holiday peacefulness that was reassuring for the moment. Lighting was in place, the tank itself had been discreetly "outfitted," and all supporting props were concealed.

Most importantly, Lisa had been dispatched on the mission of ensuring that Elle arrived on schedule.

Tyler himself had sat down with each of the players that needed to be involved, carefully explaining the situation and what had to happen. Starting with Chloe, and inevitably her protector, Tucker, he outlined the role that had to be played with utmost buy-in. He hated putting the two of them in danger, but their complicity was key to the success of the operation.

"I'll be there, don't worry. And you don't do anything until you see me, understand? You'll take your cues from me."

And then, much to their distress, they were shipped off in Pete's van for the remainder of the day to a "safe house," which was really Sadie's guesthouse on the far side of the airport. It was unlikely that Elle might accidentally (or purposefully) discover them there.

Cassidy was a wild card, mostly because it was so difficult for him to process how the theoretical chain of events had occurred and Elle's diabolical responsibility for their occurrence. "Are you kidding me, man? I mean, I know she was kind of a tricky chick who liked to get her way, but really? I mean, I just can't believe..." At first he didn't want anything to do with the plan, but when he heard that pretty much everybody else was in, he agreed. "As long as I don't have to play Nines. I really suck at Nines."

He'd let Sam handle Leo and Antonio, who readily agreed to take on the task requested of them. "Make sure they know that it's a last resort, only if needed," Tyler reiterated when Sam had reported back that they were totally "stoked" about participating. Once Antonio was in, Ramone was easy to convince.

It was such a crap shoot working with so many people; there were too many details that could go wrong, but it was really the only way. Tom had not been a problem; he was ready to serve up Elle's head on a platter just for the crime he felt she had committed against him. Lisa had been tougher; Tyler had taken her for a long walk on the beach and let her have a good cry. "You are a key witness," he had assured her and eventually she too had to admit that all the evidence pointed in one direction and her sense of justice had kicked in. She had agreed to take the risk of going to town to guarantee an on-time arrival.

"Don't worry – I know I can get her here. Maybe with a little detour?" she added wistfully.

"Nothing that will put you in a compromising position. Okay, you know what I mean." But at least she had given a rueful hoarse laugh at his unintentional joke.

Even Alejandro had been called into absentee service from his family reunion outside of San Juan. He was the only one who actually had a few insider connections to the Puerto Rican police force, and although Tyler was dubious as to how he might have earned those associations, he appreciated the information that Alejandro was able to obtain regarding the autopsies of the two recent murders on

Culebra. "Muchas gracias, amigo," he said when Sam handed him the phone. "I owe you a few turquoise drinks next time I see you."

"I will not forget that!" Alejandro assured him. "Glad I could help and buena suerte with whatever it is you are working on."

Now, as darkness began to seep into the corners of the campground, Tyler paced nervously, hoping it would all work out. He passed Cassidy, carrying the last of the solar chargers down to the beach. "They're as good as they're going to get. Let's hope they last."

"Tyler, I need your phone," he heard Sam call. "It's time."

He checked his messages as he headed up the path. *"All A OK. On our way,"* had come in from Lisa and *"At parking lot. Be there in a few,"* from Pete.

It was happening.

An hour later, inside the screen house it was game on. Unsurprisingly, Elle had arrived carrying the traditional to-go cup and despite her semi-inebriated state, she seemed abnormally jitzy. Her iridescent eyes did not display the customary languid self-confidence, but instead darted furtively from corner to corner as she conversed and the laughter that punctuated her sentences seemed forced and unnatural. Most strangely of all, she was not wearing the usual flowing dress but black leggings and a black t-shirt. Tyler could not remember seeing her outfitted like this before, but then again, this was no typical night.

"Wow, you look..."

"Sexy?" She gyrated her hips and threw him a challenging grin.

"Yeah, that too."

They sat next to each other on the bench that faced the ocean; Sam, Pete and Ramone shared the bench opposite them.

Tom sat on a stool by the bar with Lisa half-perched on his knee, one arm draped possessively around her, the other cradling a bottle of Jack Daniels. When Cassidy reminded him of the no glass bottle rule, he snorted and declared, "Fuck that. I'm leaving in the morning, what are they going to do, throw me out?"

"I'll have what she's having," Tyler announced and now his drink matched Elle's.

"Really?" At his unexpected choice, she peered at him over the rim with a provocative raise of her eyebrows.

"It's our last night too." He clinked his plastic cup against her own and then pressed his thigh against hers to reinforce the suggestiveness of his gesture.

"I'm not – I can't – I've got to leave in a couple of hours." Her flustered response was so atypical that everyone inside the tent had a hard time concealing their surprise.

"Well, then we better play faster." As Sam slapped a couple of cards down on the table, his eyes met Tyler's.

The accelerated pace of the game alleviated some of the tension in the air and occasionally the players could even forget why they were there. It was no accident that Elle seemed to be on a winning streak and Tyler knew it especially pained Sam to throw hand after hand.

Pete had brought his box of percussion instruments which he suddenly produced and placed at the end of the table. "We're going to make some music after this. So you all get to choose your weapons."

"Ooh, that's a bad choice of words," Sam murmured as he poked through the assortment. "Okay, I claim the tambourine." He gave it a few lackadaisical shakes before laying it down beside his seat. "Ramone, you know you like this thing – what's it called?"

"La cabasa." Ramone fingered the chain of steel balls wrapped around what looked like a wooden mallet. "Yes, my favorite."

Lisa picked up a couple of castanets for herself and tossed a little bongo drum to Tom. "Beat on this, baby."

280

Tyler peered into the box – all that was left was a pair of maracas. "I guess we'll have to share." He gave one to Elle and half-heartedly rattled his own.

"I probably can't stay for the music anyway." She glanced at her watch, a large gold affair with a flashy neon orange band, which he'd never seen before.

"Wow, who wears a watch on Culebra," laughed Sam.

Someone who has no phone, Tyler answered him silently with a meaningful glare.

A short while later, Tom began to act very wasted and Lisa got angry with him, and although this had been planned, Tyler wasn't sure if any of it was really an act. Before long they staggered off, saying their goodnights, with Lisa blowing Elle a kiss and an apologetic look.

Tyler held up his empty cup. "Oh, no bartender, guess I'll have to share yours for the rest of this round." He lifted Elle's drink to his lips.

"Wow. Déjà vu." Sam stared at them a little too blatantly before saying, "Just don't start drinking out of the cup at the same time."

"Like this?" Tyler put his face next to Elle's and held the cup up. "Come on, show him we can do this."

She giggled oddly and then hesitated, a frown wrinkling her brow. "Who's turn is it?"

"It's mine." Pete laid down an ace, clearing the cards off the table.

The rest of the round moved quickly and then Ramone stood up abruptly. "Too much beer; I've gotta take a leak."

"Me too." Pete followed him out of the tent.

"Well, this is awkward," said Sam, now alone on the facing bench. "Why don't I give you two lovebirds some space? We'll all come back in a little bit."

"Lovebirds? You're so quaint, Sam!" Tyler called after him and then put his drink down. "All this talk about peeing – I need to relieve myself also. Just stay where you are; do you mind? I'll be back in a second."

"Okay, but I'm going to make you your own drink while you're gone. No more of this sharing business." Elle stuck her tongue out at him and then provocatively licked first her top lip and then her bottom one.

Once he was out of the tent, Tyler took a deep breath. Perfect, he thought. He walked a few feet and turned back. The vented walls of the screen house displayed the lighted interior like a television set; he could see Elle clearly, sitting impatiently, drumming her fingers on the table, looking in his direction. Then she jumped quickly to her feet and ran over to the bar, and, with the ease of a professional bartender holding a bottle in each hand, she poured a stiff drink in one of the empty plastic cups.

If he had not been watching so carefully he probably would have missed what happened next. It was almost a sleight-of-hand trick, the way her fingers dipped briefly into her purse and then covered the rim of the cup, how she casually stirred the ice with her pinkie finger, her eyes never leaving their vigilant lookout for his return.

He gave a silent fist pump in the air, composed himself and then strolled nonchalantly back into the tent. A few hundred yards down the beach, over the light crashing of the surf, he could hear a guitar tuning up and a couple of random drum beats.

Elle looked up at him brightly and patted the seat next to her as he reentered the space.

Straddling the wooden bench, he gave a long exhale and reached for her hand. "Now where were we?"

"Well, you can start here." She pushed the new drink towards him, the rosy-tinged contents sloshing dangerously, like high waves in a stormy sea. "How about a toast to us?"

Tyler eyed the lethal liquid warily and then picked it up and twisted his arm around hers. "Okay, you drink from mine and I'll drink from yours. Like blood brothers or as if we were feeding each other wedding cake."

She laughed cautiously and tried to pull back. "Ha – I'm not interested in marrying you, Tyler Mackenzie."

"So what is it you are interested in, Elle? Besides making me victim number three?" He could feel her arm trembling now as she tried to wrest it away from his stronghold.

She blinked rapidly a few times and then gave a harsh titter. "Believe me, there have been more than three boyfriends in my life."

"But how many have you offed this way?"

"Offed? What are you talking about?" She froze and he suddenly thought how ironic it would be if he was unable to release himself from her rigor mortis grasp.

Without breaking eye contact, he slowly unwound his elbow from hers. "You must have a low opinion of my intelligence if you thought I would fall for this twice." When her expression continued to register incredulity, he went on. "First on Mustique. When I supposedly fell asleep in the sun. I know you were testing my tolerance that day."

"Well, you are testing MY tolerance right now." Abruptly she stood up. "I don't have to listen to this."

"I know this is how you did it with Ivan."

Another snicker of disbelief. "You have such a vivid imagination. What do you think I 'did with Ivan'?"

"I think you killed him."

"Ha, that's so absurd. I was with Lisa that night. Just ask her; it was pretty unforgettable – or better yet, ask Tom." Elle crossed her arms smugly.

"Yeah, so I know all about that. That turned out to be a super-convenient alibi, didn't it?" Tyler got up now and moved between Elle and the screened entrance, just in case she was planning to make a run for it.

"You're insane, Tyler Mackenzie." Out of habitual nervousness she reached for her drink and then stopped in confusion, unsure of which cocktail was which now.

"Probably a little bit," he agreed. "But let me just run this crazy scenario by you. Here's how I think it went down. Ivan had just outbid you on the bungalow of your dreams and money was no object for him. He wanted that house just as much as you did."

"Ridiculous. How would you even know that?" she scoffed. She stared at the two cups in front of her for another few seconds before choosing the one that was only half full.

"It's a small island? So you decided to take him out of the running with a "super cocktail" of your own design. At a game of Nines, just like tonight. It was easy – he loved vodka and cranberry juice as much as you, so you pretended to share. You know they call these things Cape Codders where I come from?" He held up the tainted drink that had been left on the table.

"You'd already slept with him," Tyler went on. "So it was not improbable that you two would leave the card game together for an amorous roll on his air mattress. But he probably passed out before you got to the amorous part – and then a pillow over his face was really easy."

"That's absurd. I told you I was with Lisa." She glanced nervously at her big watch.

"Who you inconveniently met coming up the path to Ivan's tent as you were leaving. Because apparently she had her own plans to jump Ivan's bones that night. Although I don't know what you girls saw in him. I've heard he was a real prick. Anyway, your quick thinking turned that problematic situation into an advantageous alibi, in case you needed one. How am I doing so far?"

Elle spat out an ice cube in a show of skepticism. "Pure conjecture. You can't prove a thing."

He shrugged. "Maybe not. Or maybe yes. The toxicology report was pretty clear. And you didn't exactly wipe down your fingerprints." Okay, he didn't know anything about fingerprints, but he was sure it was true.

"Doesn't mean anything – like you said, I'd been there before." But her show of confidence was clearly eroding. She fumbled in her straw bag for something as she spoke. "I don't get it, Tyler. I thought we were besties – why are you throwing me under the bus?" She pouted a little, apparently trying to elicit some sympathy. "Oh, wait, you're jealous, aren't you?"

He tried to ignore that illogical rationalization, but she was approaching him now; maybe she was going to try to get by him and escape to the beach. He couldn't let her leave yet, not without a confession. He opened his arms and was a little surprised how willingly she came to him, thinking she had correctly guessed his motives. She pressed her body against his in a sensuous embrace, placing her head against his shoulder.

"I don't want to fight with you, baby," she murmured. Then, placing her hands on the back of his head, she pulled his face towards hers and began to kiss him, passionately, almost ferociously, thrusting her tongue into the deep recesses of his mouth in a long and thorough exploration.

Suddenly he felt something else against his palette, a couple of small hard objects and he thought perhaps he had broken a tooth. He tried to pull his head away but Elle held on, her lips locked on his and he realized she was pushing at the objects with her tongue, forcing them towards the back of his throat.

At the horrific realization of what she was doing, he lashed out, trying to get her off of him, but she was wound around him now, tightening her grip, a boa constrictor with her prey.

When he finally managed to shove her away, he fell to his knees gagging, trying to cough up whatever it was she had compelled him to swallow. "You bitch!" he choked. Whatever pills she had introduced into his mouth were stuck in his throat now, going neither down or up. He looked up in time to see her take a swig of her drink and swish it around inside her cheeks, cleansing her own mouth before spitting it out on the floor of the tent.

He hacked violently and it was a gut reaction to take a big swallow from the cup she so slyly handed him. At the first mouthful he realized his mistake but by then it was all too late.

"What was that?" he whispered hoarsely.

"Oh, nothing to worry about sweetheart, just a few Ambien to make you sleep soundly. I just can't have you interfering anymore tonight. I have some important business to attend to." She slung her bag over her shoulder and tapped her foot impatiently like she wanted him to move aside.

Somehow she had managed to foil him the same way he had incapacitated her in St. Vincent, exacting purposeful revenge even as she lay in the crosshairs.

Shit, this was not what was supposed to happen, he thought, his heart racing as fast as his brain. He figured he still had fifteen minutes before it began to affect him. That was probably all the time he needed if he used it efficiently – he would have to trust the others to take care of the rest of the plan.

He stood up, clearing his throat and reminded himself that nothing was wrong with him. Yet.

"Hold on. We're not finished here." He put his hands on his hips and assumed what he hoped was a threatening pose. She watched him with a vaguely amused smile and a superior attitude.

"Let's talk about Perry."

Her smile faded slightly. In the near distance he heard the beating of congo drums start up and then the strains of guitar music, signaling him that, no matter what happened to him, the gears had been set in motion.

"You thought you were all set and you really didn't want to lose that house, so you barely waited a day or two before you started pushing Perry. But he suspected, didn't he? He knew how competitive you were with Ivan on this one and he started giving you some shit about it. And you were so sure of your success that you decided to try it again, especially since you had one other lucky break going for you. Perry's favorite drink was also your own."

Her jaw dropped this time. "You have actually been freakin' investigating this, haven't you?"

"And the toxicology reports on Perry and Ivan were unsurprisingly similar. The real difference was that this time you asked someone else to help you with the dirty work. Someone with even less ethics than you. What's his name again? The one you owe all that money to for his 'servicios'?"

Elle's posture stiffened defensively. "You can't possibly know about that."

"Actually there were two differences this time – there was also an eye witness. Your own daughter. And when you found that out, you wanted to get to her before I did, to find out exactly how much she knew."

She was backing away from him now, her eyes wide and frightened. "Don't you bring Chloe into this," she sputtered. "I've done all of this for her."

"Oh, right. Saint Elle, the selfless mother and martyr. They should name an island after you. But remind me again, before I forget. What's the name of the guy – the one with the cowboy boots and silver snake belt buckle who you asked to tail our kids around the Caribbean and who then turned around and blackmailed you?"

He sensed rather than saw her hand close around the nearest available weapon and then, with a hiss, she lunged at him waving one of the wooden maracas in the air, the seeds inside rattling loudly. She stopped short when she saw what he held up in front of her face.

"It's all on here; your emails, your texts, and this whole conversation. And Sam's video of you and Ivan? That's on Youtube." The red 'Record' button at the bottom of the screen on her phone glowed ominously. "Oh, and also – five other phones have been videoing your every move here tonight from five different angles."

Immobilized by his words, her eyes darted around the space, and then she turned helplessly in a circle, wielding the maraca, as if she might actually fight off a warrior army that surrounded her.

"So I know it's a lot to take in right now, and you are probably confused, but yes, I have been impersonating you in your emails to... the one you told me about once. Who left his mark on you. Serpico? It was something like that." He tried to snap his fingers but couldn't quite manage the simple skill required. He was definitely starting to feel woozy and hoped he could get to the finish. "Serpentino, that was it. And vice versa. I mean I sent emails from him to you, too. Ha,ha." Hell, he was really feeling it now. "And that's why he's waiting for you on the beesh – I mean beach."

Suddenly the phone in his hand began to vibrate and ring. They both stared at the screen; *unknown caller*. But even with his alertness fading, Tyler recognized the Puerto Rican number. "Less put this on schpeaker and anzer it, shall we..." He could feel sleepiness reaching up to strangle him as he touched the button.

"Mom? Mom? It's me – Chloe."

Elle wrested the phone from his unresisting fingers. "Chloe? Oh, my god, where are you?"

Tyler tried to widen his eyes to combat the drowsy wave of blackness that threatened to knock him to the ground. He needed to find some place to lie down.

"I'm here at the tank. On the beach. With a guy who says he's waiting for you. He's got a gun."

Tyler lifted his head at these words, unsure how he had ended up stretched out on the picnic bench, but conscious enough to know that something had gone wrong. "A gun?" He called out in the direction of the phone. "Chloe, that was not part of the –"

"He says he's going to hurt me if you don't show up soon..."

"Tino? Tell him I'm on my way! Do you hear me? Tell him!"

The hysteria of her voice and a jolt of fear brought him to a fleeting state of wakefulness. He heard the sound of the door being unzipped and her footsteps fading. A semi-conscious thought floated past him...she had not rezipped the flap; mosquitos would get in and eat him alive...and with great effort he pushed it from his mind. What had Elle just said to Chloe? Tino? Serpen...tino... An image of a sinuous handcrafted belt buckle came almost to the forefront of his brain and then dissolved.

He tried to remember where his own phone was. Duct taped to something, wasn't it? He saw it now, beneath the makeshift bar, shimmed with pieces of cardboard so it would point at the table. With some tour d'force of automatic instinct, he launched himself off the bench and lurched for it, landing hard on his shoulder and banging his head against the metal leg of a folding chair. With his current lack of coordination, there was no way he could remove the phone from where it was mounted. His eyes could not seem to focus and he realized that somewhere between standing, laying and falling he had lost his glasses.

The phone was still recording, he realized. He walked his slow brain through the steps he need to accomplish and willed it to send his fingers the message...get to home screen...touch the call icon...speed dial #2...

"Dad? Where are you?" Tucker's voice was faint.

"Are you...with...Chloe?" His tongue felt thick and stuck against the back of his teeth.

"What? You sound weird. I went back to get the bug spray. Chloe's waiting at the tank; I'm heading back over there now."

"Wait. No. He's got her. And a gun."

"Oh my god, what? Chloe! I'm coming!" He heard Tucker yell.

"Don't – no – don't... you... go..." Tyler's own words floated above him for one last second and then he tumbled down the black hole of oblivion.

CHAPTER NINETEEN

"Under different circumstances, this could be very romantic." Chloe tried to smoothe out the beach towel they were lying on, but then realized that the uncomfortable bump was actually part of the rusted metal beneath them. "I mean, a girl, a boy, the sea, the stars, an old army tank..."

"Navy actually. Whatever. Just sayin'." Tucker sat up and then stretched out again, unable to relax or find a position that did not hurt his lean bones. "We should have brought some pillows. This is torture. Only my father would think this up."

"Here, lie on your back like this. Bend your knees, cross your arms over your chest. When we're down we can't be seen."

"How about I just get on top of you and you can be my pillow?" He laid his cheek against the swell of her breasts, threw a leg over her, and rubbed up against her hip.

"How can you get a boner at a time like this?" she laughed.

"I'm a teenage boy; I can get a boner anytime." He put his lips against hers and then smacked at his ankle. "Damn sand flies. No see-ums. Whatever the hell they are."

She held him close, suddenly aware of the ephemeralness of the moment. "We're making too much noise. Shh."

"Ouch, watch my sunburn. Painting that wall today at Sadie's was killer on my shoulders. I probably should have worn a shirt but it hurt too much."

"Sorry." She kissed the hot bare skin as he swatted at his rib cage. "We probably should have brought some insect repellent too."

"I can't stand it." He sat up again. "I'm going back to get some."

Alarmed, she reached out for him. "You can't go now."

"We've got time. I'll be quick. I'm not going to be able to be quiet otherwise." He gave her a quick peck on the lips. "Maybe I'll grab a condom too."

"Don't be ridiculous." She could not see his face in the near-to-complete darkness but she knew he was grinning. "Just hurry."

He lowered himself over the side of the beached tank into the shallow water. The night breezes had picked up since they had arrived and the surf lapped almost to his knees now.

"Tucker–" she wanted to tell him not to leave her alone, that she was frightened, but for some reason she couldn't. Instead she hoped he would think she was strong and brave. "I love you. Now go fast."

The night seemed to wrap its arms around her, enveloping her aloneness with its velveteen blackness. She took comfort from the soft light of the camp lanterns that peeked through the foliage of Section E and from the faint strains of music she could hear a short distance away. She knew that Tom and Lisa were camped close enough on their "beachfront property" that they could probably hear her if she shouted, but she wasn't sure they were even there now.

It felt strange to be by herself, even just for a few minutes. She almost could not remember what her life had been like before Tucker, when she had nearly always cruised alone. She'd been suspended in time for the last few weeks and nothing about her world would ever be the same, especially not after tonight. Was she even still the same person inside? What was going to happen to her? What if Tucker was forced to go back to Vermont and leave her here – what would she do?

She sat up, suddenly more scared of the future than she was of the present. The rapid pounding of her heart was so loud she thought it could probably be heard fifty feet away.

A dark silhouette could be seen hovering on the beach nearby.

"Tucker?" she called softly.

The shadowy figure moved swiftly, covering the distance between them in just a few seconds.

"Is that you?" her voice quavered, full of fear. She heard a few sloshing noises and then the thud of a body hitting metal. Groping for the small flashlight she had placed next to her on the towel, she flashed the beam in the direction of the sound.

"Apaga la luz. Ahora."

She froze, not understanding. Then something hard struck the flashlight out of her hand, the reverberation of the blow going up her arm into her shoulder; a small plopping sound told her the light had landed in the water. She gasped and tried to back away, but her escape was immediately blocked by strong fingers that gripped her hair at the base of her neck. As she struggled to free herself, something cold pressed against her temple.

She froze. This could not be happening. Tyler had promised nothing bad would happen to her.

"Finalmente. La hija." Her two years of high school Spanish were enough to translate this declaration — "Finally. The daughter."

"Who are you?" she gasped nervously. "What do you want from me?" She fumbled for the words. "Quien es? Que quieres?"

"Dónde está su madre? Mi amiga vieja, la puta mentirosa?" He pulled tighter on her hair as he stepped down into the open cockpit where she was kneeling, his shoes making wet, squelching sounds.

"My mother? She is coming." Chloe could barely breathe, let alone think of how to speak Spanish. "Ella arriva soon. Uno momento."

"Llama. Ahora." A beam of ambient light illuminated her face and glinted off something shiny at his waist. A silver belt buckle in the shape of a serpent; and then she knew who it was. "Llama a tu madre." He had shoved his gun into his belt and was holding his cell phone in front of her, the number pad ready for dialing.

"But..." Tyler had her mother's phone. If she called the number she might be able to let him know she was in danger.

She had only keyed in the first few digits when the number came up automatically on the screen from memory, sending a tremor of terror through her already shaking fingers.

"Mom? Mom? It's me – Chloe."

Expecting Tyler to answer, she was unprepared when Elle's voice came through the phone. "Chloe? Oh, my god, where are you?"

Her assailant twisted her hair tighter and she was not sure if the tears that filled her eyes were from pain or emotion. "I'm here at the tank. On Flamenco. With a guy who says he's waiting for you. He's got a gun." He growled something about " más dolor" and she whispered weakly, "He says he's going to hurt me if you don't show up soon..."

"Tino? Tell him I'm on my way! Do you hear me? Tell him!" Elle's vocal desperation seemed to satisfy him, and in one swift motion, the phone was gone and the gun had returned to his hand.

"Vamonos." She cried out as he jerked her to a standing position and then switched his iron grip to an arm around her waist. Pushing her in front of him, he forced her to make the awkward decent over the edge of the tank into the water a few feet from shore, holding her so tightly against him that her feet barely touched the sand when they landed.

Wet from the waist down now, she shivered as much from cold as from fear. She was surprised to realize that, aside from her own perilous reality, nothing had changed in the last few minutes at Flamenco – music was still playing, campers were still in their tents, the stars still shone overhead and the plan was still on. But where was Tyler? He was supposed to be doing the negotiating. He must be on his way. The thought calmed her a little bit until suddenly they heard the thud of footsteps running towards them from the far end of the beach.

It was her mother, out of breath, fair hair barely visible as it flew out behind her in the faint half-light of the moonless night. "Tino – No! Leave her be. Es bastante!" Elle could barely get the words out as she gasped for air.

Chloe could feel something shift in the man her mother had just called Tino, a constriction of muscle, a flexing of strength. But also a relaxation that came with a sense of control and the knowledge that he had the upper hand now.

"Tienes mi dinero?" His strong fingers squeezed Chloe's rib cage so hard that she could feel the bruises forming, and then, in a machismo display of domination, his thumb moved upwards to rub roughly over her nipple. When a sob escaped her, he laughed cruelly. "La tetas de la hija son más bonitas que las de la madre."

What had he just said? That her tits were nicer than her mother's? Had her mother slept with this monster?

"Tino. Bastante! Quieres el dinero o no?"

Regretfully he gave one last long painful squeeze with his thumb and forefinger that made Chloe wince with pain and then released her, still holding the pistol against her head. With his free hand, he flicked on a small penlight and shone it in Elle's direction.

It had only been a few weeks but her mother looked different; she seemed smaller, older, crazier and much less self-assured. Shielding her eyes, she was trying to see beyond the circle of light.

"First show me my daughter." Just speaking the words seemed to make her posture more defiant.

Despite the fact that he spoke no English, Tino seemed to understand it well enough. He turned the light towards Chloe, shining it on her throbbing left breast which he now probed at with the end of the cocked pistol. "Tan bonita," he sneered.

"Mom. Please!" She tried to hold still and not wail.

"Okay, okay! You bastard. Look, here it is."

Tino trained the beam on Elle's straw bag which lay open on the sand at his feet. He kicked it over and the contents spilled out on the ground. Along with a pile of personal belongings were several bundles of bills.

"Esto es todo? Cuéntamelo!" He was ordering her to count it in front of him. As Elle got down on her knees, Tino grabbed Chloe's hand and closed her fingers around the flashlight, indicating that she should hold it. Then with his free hand he pulled her back against him so she could feel the hardness growing in his crotch as he muttered foul things in Spanish that made Elle tremble and lose her place.

"Voy a chingarle tu hija, puta," he sang out, loudly and repeatedly snapping the waistband of her shorts. Chloe knew the word for "fuck" and when he actually began to pull her pants down, she could not keep herself from screaming. Dropping the light, she clawed at his wrist, bucking and trying to twist out of his grasp.

And then suddenly everything went white and she ducked her head to keep from being blinded by the glare. Tino froze, changing his grip to a stranglehold with his arm around her neck, using her head as protection for his eyes until they became accustomed to the brightness.

When she finally looked up, she could see the whole area of the beach surrounding the tank illuminated by spotlights, as bright as midday. Elle was cowering face down in the sand, flattening herself to the ground as though a bomb had dropped. But she was alone. Something was wrong with the plan, Chloe thought abstractly, knowing that the plan had gone awry a long time earlier.

"Let the girl go!" boomed a voice from the trees. It sounded like someone using a megaphone.

Tino began to back away, using Chloe as a shield, the pistol still pressed to the side of her forehead. Her throat hurt, he was clutching her neck in the crook of his elbow and she worried that he was crushing her windpipe. She saw Elle lift her head and look around but nobody appeared on the beach. And where was Tucker? He should have been back by now.

"We said let the girl go! NOW!" She couldn't identify who was shouting the words which seemed to have no effect on Tino who was waving the gun at Elle as she scrambled back onto her hands and knees, trying to hide the pile of bills as she struggled desperately to scoop them back into her bag.

"Recoger el dinero y traígalo aquí. Vamonos," he growled at her. "Va a venir con nosotros, vieja." If anything, the heightened sense of danger had made the man act even more demanding and impervious. He was commanding Elle to bring the money and go with them...where? She was shocked to see her mother scurrying to obey – what hold did Tino have over her?

There was an unexpected whoosh of air as something seemed to zing by her left leg and then Tino let out a horrible howl. He lowered the gun but at the same time his hold seemed to tighten on her and he twisted her head painfully against his shoulder.

Another whistle of air came from behind them and Chloe felt Tino's body stiffen reflexively from some sort of impact. This time he screamed and jerked as the arm that held her released its death grip around her neck. As she fell awkwardly to the sand, she saw him clutching with one hand at something stuck in his foot while reaching the other hand around his back.

Still trying to register what had happened, she saw a figure emerge from the water at the side of the tank and another step from the underbrush beneath the trees. Both wore sleek black wet suits and carried spear guns.

Leo and Antonio stood silently at the edge of the lighted area, still training their weapons on Tino, surveying their work, while Sam sprinted across the beach, sweeping Chloe off her feet and carrying her to the safety of the sidelines.

"You're okay, right?" he asked, giving her a quick squeeze before transferring her to the care of a rather stunned-looking Tom and Lisa. Speechless, they all stared as he ran back towards the spectacle happening on the shore.

Tino was writhing on the ground, struggling to remove the arrow that had impaled his foot, pinning it to the soft sand like a tent peg, at the same time trying not to put any weight on the spear that was lodged in the back of his hip. Sam rushed towards him, diving for the dropped handgun. But with the increased alertness of a wounded animal, Tino sensed Sam coming. Gritting his teeth he grabbed for the gun, firing a wild shot that ricocheted off the rusted metal of the tank and caused Sam to freeze.

"Uh, dude." Sam cleared his throat nervously. "You've already got two arrows in you and the police are on their way." And then he seemed to realize that Tino was not aiming at him but at a target behind him. Sam stole a glance over his shoulder and all eyes followed his gaze to where Elle was surreptitiously backing away towards the trail leading up to the campground, her straw bag clutched in her hand.

Damp sand clung to the front of her clothing and to one side of her face from when she had fallen a few moments earlier, the asymmetrical effect escalating her usual wild-eyed appearance to that of a maniacal madwoman. She was moving slowly and stealthily, about to slither soundlessly into the cover of night.

"Elle – wait! Damn, where the hell is Tyler?" Without moving, Sam's eyes went back and forth between the two crazy people on either side of him.

Suddenly a shape flew off the bank behind her accompanied by a primal war cry. The long-limbed form knocked her body to the ground and then, holding a container of something above her head, sprayed it into her face.

"You fucking witch! What did you do to my father?! If he dies, I will kill you!"

Elle screeched and clawed at her burning eyes as Tucker continued to empty the can of insect repellent in her direction. Chloe tried to run to him, but Tom and Lisa restrained her from both sides, holding her firmly at bay.

Then they all stared as a shiny silver cleaver sailed heavily out of the trees and struck Tino's hand with a resounding thwack. Both the cleaver and the pistol skidded several feet across the sand. As Tino shrieked at the blood gushing from his fingers, yet another person jumped from the trail into the fray.

Cassidy tackled Tucker and wrapped himself around the furious boy, pulling him away from Elle's flailing arms and legs. "Hey, hey, hey..." he yelled in an attempt to calm the situation but Tucker tried to push him angrily aside.

After a second of awe-struck silence, everyone began shouting at once. In the confusion that followed, Tino began crawling down the beach, still refusing to give up. Leo, Antonio and Sam ran to suppress his escape and Cassidy turned his attention to the still raving Tucker.

"She poisoned him! We have to find out what she gave my dad!"

"Elle, what'd you give Tyler?" Cassidy bellowed over his shoulder as he attempted to hold Tucker's arms behind his back.

When there was no response, they both looked in her direction. She was now scuttling across the sand like a crab, peering through the narrow slit of vision she somehow managed to maintain through swollen, tearing eyes. As they watched, she stood up and began running full tilt, bypassing the group who were working to confine Tino, heading into the darkness towards the central part of the beach and the parking lot.

"We've got to get her!" Desperately Tucker tried to tear himself from Cassidy's grasp.

"No worries, young man. She's not going anywhere. Wait for it – wait for it...There. Now let's go."

From the shadows ahead came a desolate wail of frustration, followed by a raging torrent of swearing and screaming. As Tucker ran towards the noise, Cassidy held up a powerful flashlight to illuminate the area beyond the floodlights. They could see Elle – she appeared to be clawing at the air around her, unable to move.

"Hold up, man. You don't want to get caught in it," Cassidy warned.

"Please. We have to go too," Chloe began to plead with Tom and Lisa but they were already on their way, dragging her with them, as anxious as she was to see what was happening.

Tucker had stopped short of Elle's flailing body, staring in puzzlement. "What the fuck–"

"Fishing net. Strung from Tom's camp to that pole pounded into the shoreline. Extra precaution for the ones that try to get away." Cassidy coughed violently, bending over at the waist. "Damn, I'm too old for all this exertion. Elle, old girl why'd you have to go and cause all this trouble?"

Out beyond the reef they could see a motorboat with flashing red lights and powerful search lamps heading into Flamenco Bay.

"Looks like the coast guard will be getting here first," Tom commented, stamping out his cigarette. "Better go make sure we got all our illegal shit put away."

"Don't worry, we're all packed," Lisa called after him.

Chloe took the opportunity to run to Tucker's side, but backed away as she realized he was still seething with fury, focused on the forlorn heap that was her mother, writhing at his feet.

More tangled in the net than before, Elle was now curled up in a ball, whimpering softly. Tucker loomed over her menacingly. "Tell me what you drugged him with." He kicked out at her and then, unable to control his anger, fell to his knees and began beating her with his fists. "Tell me, goddam it!"

"Ambien, alright? Just an extra strong dose. He's only asleep, that's all. He'll be fine in the morning, you raving lunatic! I didn't hurt him," she sobbed. "I didn't hurt him. I didn't!"

Tucker continued to rain blows on her until Chloe came forward and threw herself on his back, pulling him away from her mother and down into the sand.

"Whatever you did do to him, Elle," Sam's voice came from a few yards away, where he was helping to hold a weakening Tino down. "It's all on video. So get ready for your fifteen minutes of fame."

CHAPTER TWENTY

"Chloe! Tucker! The chickens are out again!"

Fresh eggs just weren't worth the trouble, Chloe thought as she put down the heavy textbook she had been studying. She wasn't sure which was more boring, European History or taking care of chickens, and then chided herself for being negative. Her life was better now than any time she could remember and even if she thought Tyler's "responsibility program" was over the top sometimes, she would not complain. He was being a better parent to her than either of hers had ever been.

"Let's go, Mr. T." She stood up on the quilt-covered futon mattress and looked around for something to wear, finally digging through the chaotic heap of clothing that covered most of the floor of the tree house. She didn't care how messy it was; the tree house was their sanctuary and the only place she and Tucker could truly be themselves. For the better part of the summer they had climbed the ladder and shed their clothes at the door, the way most people left their shoes on a doormat. Tyler didn't know that on cool mornings they actually plugged in an electric heater so they could still live like they were on a tropical desert island.

She turned around when Tucker didn't respond. He had fallen asleep with the Anthology of English Literature open on his lap, victim to the mid-day heat of the cramped but cozy space. She didn't wake him – they had to go to work in a few hours at the West Jordan Inn, where he washed dishes and she waited tables, and he needed the sleep as much as they needed the money from their part-time jobs. Between that and studying for their high school GEDs, working for Tyler at the newspaper and doing all the "chores" he came up with for the two of them, Chloe and Tucker had very little time for just hanging out. But until the weather turned cold, at least they had the tree house.

Frustrated with navigating the clothes pile, she grabbed a pair of exercise leggings and one of Tucker's t-shirts, and was still putting them on as she ducked through the arched doorway to the tiny ledge they called their front porch. From this elevated vantage point she could view the entire yard, where two dozen brown and black hens were busily pecking their way to the free world beyond the driveway. She could also see Tyler at work inside the newspaper office, the large bay window framing a picture of him sitting at his computer, looking at her over the glasses pushed down on his nose, and shaking his head ruefully as he watched her finish dressing outside before descending to the ground below. She flashed him a peace sign and a grin as she walked by and he gave her a thumbs up.

"Thanks for putting pants on this time!" he called. "The neighbors love you for it!"

"Only because it makes you happy!" she responded.

Three months had passed since she had flown back to Vermont with Tucker and his father to start what Tyler had told Tucker's mother was a "creative solution to the problem at hand." The plan had been that Chloe would live with Tucker at Tyler's house and they would both go to high school, finish up and get their diplomas. They were nearly at the same level, since Chloe still had another year to complete. But it turned out that Tucker was going to be held back for missing so much time and that Chloe could not enroll until she turned eighteen in a few months. Also Tyler was not actually her guardian, a situation which threatened to open up a can of worms that Tyler had been working hard to sidestep.

After several acts of teenage rebellion and a few visits to a mediation service, they came up with a new strategy that satisfied everyone. Except maybe Lucy. Tucker would go to summer school to make up his lost credits, and the two of them would study for their GEDs. To earn their keep, they would work for Tyler, reporting and writing articles for the paper and helping with distribution and social media marketing. In addition they would stack a winter's worth of firewood, learn to cook real food, plant and tend the vegetable garden, and most importantly, learn how to "act responsibly."

Taking care of the chickens was a chore that had been thrown in as an afterthought, and although Chloe had thought it sounded like quaint country fun, it actually was really a pain in the butt. And there was nothing Chloe hated more than shoveling chicken shit out of the henhouse.

"Isn't this called slavery?" Tucker had grumbled. He had never worked so hard in his short life, but if it meant that Chloe could stay and that they could pursue their dreams together, he would go along with anything.

Fixing up the tree house was really what had made it all work. Chloe had been enchanted by the childhood play space that Tyler had built for Tucker years earlier; she'd never had anything like it herself. At first, the prospect of sharing a single bed in a tiny bedroom, formerly used only on weekends, seemed like it might put a strain on their relationship. But one night, Tucker's best friend, Myles, had shown up with some killer pot to share, and they had retreated to the tree house for some privacy to smoke a bone.

Myles was a sweet skinny guy with blonde dreadlocks and a smile full of wonder and envy at Tucker's turn of fortune.

"Bodacious girlfriend, no more high school – you're livin' the dream, dude!" They had grown up together at the West Jordan Inn, Myles was the son of Tyler's former girlfriend, Sarah – "Yeah, we are kind of a convoluted, extended family unit" – and up till now they had shared pretty much everything. "I mean, we still could, if you're into it," he had suggested once they were all relaxed and high, stretched out on the worn Oriental rug that covered the floor.

303

"Ha, ha, dream on," had been Tucker's reply, but sometimes Chloe found herself wondering what "sharing everything" might've been like.

At that moment, however, she had been more interested in spinning the possibilities of turning the tree house into a tree home. She could see that, with a few improvements, the rough wooden structure could become a cozy hangout.

They replaced a few rotten boards and roof shingles, stapled some wire screening over the windows and dragged an old mattress out from the house. A few cushions, a string of Christmas lights and a couple of long extensions cords later, they moved in and when not working, only left their safe haven to use the kitchen or bathroom. It was like camping, only more permanent, and suited the minimalist perspective they had acquired in their Caribbean travels together, reveling in their growing scruffiness and the simplicity of a world that mostly revolved only around each other.

"Maybe we should let our hair go dread like Myles," she proposed one day when she could not find her hairbrush and Tucker had been delighted by her suggestion. These days he was always up for defying convention, and by mid-summer their tangled tresses were now well on their way to dreadlock status.

They propelled themselves through the drudgery of studying by keeping their "eyes on the prize" as Tyler frequently reminded them. Once they both passed the GEDs, they were free to go, and go they would. Old National Geographic maps of the world covered the pine board walls of the tree house, as well as a few nautical charts of the Caribbean that they had ordered on e-Bay. By the time winter set in, they vowed to be on their way, backpacking to some place warm and exotic. Chloe was voting for Southeast Asia, where they could live and eat for cheap; Tucker wanted to go someplace where he could work on sailboats, maybe the Caribbean or the Mediterranean Sea. They had signed up at a few online "work-your-way"

304

sites and the possibilities now seemed endless, with the list including eco-farms in Costa Rica and hostels in Argentina.

Of course, really Chloe would be free to do whatever she wanted sooner. Her eighteenth birthday was just a few weeks away, and from then on no one could tell her what to do. But late at night, sitting astride Tucker, moving in rhythm with him warm and large inside her, in the cozy tree home lit by the colorful strings of lights, she could think of nowhere else she would rather be.

Lucy had been rip-shit at first, but as Tyler had predicted, she eventually calmed down and, in order to see more of her son, sometimes even pretended to be supportive when Chloe and Tucker went to her place for dinner. But she was clearly not happy with anything that was going on or with their plans for the future.

"I thought I would have a few more years of him yet. I'm not really ready to give him up to another woman," she said at first, patting his hand fondly.

Chloe was surprised by Lucy's tiny size — a petite powerhouse with a personality that threatened to conquer all, her appearance was dominated by a full mane of long curly hair that seemed to be rapidly changing from pale auburn to pure white. The idea that her only child was blowing off a college education to be a world-class vagabond with some dark-eyed ragamuffin he had hooked up with on vacation did not sit well with her at all, and there was rarely a visit to her house where the subject did not come up. It was hard to imagine that this overprotective and disapproving woman had, at one time, thrown away a successful career as a journalist to run off with the lead singer of a heavy-metal band for a life of depraved debauchery which had not ended well.

Chloe also thought Lucy was worried that Chloe might have inherited the insanity gene. She often asked her how her mom was doing, but Chloe had no clue what was going on with Elle now. She hadn't seen her since that last awful

305

moment on the beach before the police had cut her out of the net and taken her away.

Tyler had learned that Elle had been put into a psychiatric facility on the big island of Puerto Rico. It was unclear whether she was going to have to stand trial for the murder of Ivan or as an accessory to the murder of Perry. He didn't think there was enough evidence for the first and they only had Tino's testimony on the second. Although the police did have possession of three phone videos of Elle's confessions to Tyler and of her doctoring his drink which was probably enough to convict her of some of the crimes committed. He'd thought it made sense to get Chloe away from Culebra as soon as possible, before she might have to testify, and apparently it had already been in his mind to bring her back to Vermont. He also thought it wasn't a bad idea if she disappeared on a backpacking trip around the world for a while, in case she was subpoenaed to appear in court regarding the incident with Tino on the beach. Tyler thought it could get really messy and she kind of agreed with him.

He hadn't wanted to tell her the story he'd pieced together about her mom and Tino, but finally he did. It turned out that when Elle had first gone to Puerto Rico, she had rented an apartment in Fajardo from Tino and his wife. Tino's other income was small-time drug dealing, Elle and Tino had an affair, Elle started drinking a lot, Elle needed money...etc. etc. The blanks Tyler left in the story were easy to fill in. One weekend they went in Tino's motorboat to Culebra. Elle fell in love with the island and decided to move there and Tino set her up in business; they became partners but he was the one with controlling interests. He was going to front the money she needed to buy the house and agreed to help her out with the "roadblocks" she was encountering, as long as she made it worth his while. But things got really messy for both of them when Chloe caught them in the act at the Dinghy Dock.

"He was a sadistic macho bastard. But I guess you know that." He wouldn't say more.

She knew she was probably the key witness who could ensure that he was put away forever and she felt very conflicted about that. "Don't plan your life around it," he advised her. "You guys go do your vagabonding thing; this could take years." Sometimes she thought he actually seemed a little anxious to see them gone.

"What do you think she would have done if she had gotten to us before you at the airport in St. Vincent?" she asked, still experiencing anxiety over the "what-ifs."

Tyler had considered the question for a long moment before answering. "I don't know. Talk to you before I did, find out how much you had really seen, ensure your silence somehow. And I think she also wanted to protect you from Tino, who was proving to be more of a risk than she'd anticipated. As self-serving as she may seem, I think she still has some maternal instincts."

But Chloe was not so sure. She had not argued when Tyler suggested she start talking to a therapist once a week, but she found it a depressing and painful experience to talk about her mother, and mostly she was much happier not thinking about how fucked up and dysfunctional her previous life had been.

Tyler had kept to himself pretty much since they'd been back, not going out except if there was a story to cover for the paper or if he had to take Chloe and Tucker somewhere. She thought he could probably use a little therapy himself. The only time he'd come out of his anti-social funk was when Sam and Leo had come up from Virginia to visit in June for a weekend and they'd all had a big campfire party in the yard, reminiscent of Flamenco Beach. It had been a relief to see Tyler relax a bit and she had been glad to hear them partying far into the night, long after she had gone to bed.

"I'm glad you came. He's been kind of depressed," she confided in Sam when they were saying their goodbyes. In her mind Sam was a white knight who had literally swept her off her feet and rescued her from an immoral villain; the image did not quite jive with the slim curly-haired

307

jester standing in front of her, wearing a ragged Hawaiian shirt and a flippant grin.

"Oh, he just was missing his Section E bros, that's all. I think I've convinced him to come back and camp with us for a while next winter. He'll have that to look forward to. And maybe you two kids can put us on your world tour too."

But Chloe didn't think she would be going back to Culebra any time soon.

After she had chased the last wayward hen back into the pen, she saw Tyler was now standing at the side door, waiting for her to finish. He motioned for her to come to the house. "I have something for you."

He handed her a mailing envelope; inside its wrappings was a short white summer dress. She held it up questioningly – made of some stretchy fabric, it was a simple style with halter straps that tied around the neck.

"For the Mackenzie family reunion on Long Island this weekend," he explained. "My brothers are not quite as open-minded as I am."

"Oh, I didn't think I was going with–"

"Of course you are. You're part of this family now. Go in the bathroom and try it on."

Flushed with emotion and confusion, she did as he said. Intimidated by the idea at first, she was surprised at how comfortable the design was and how easily it transformed her from dirty duckling to sophisticated swan. Using a rubber band she kept around her wrist, she tucked her disorderly hair into a high bun on her head and surveyed herself in the mirror. She had put on a little weight since settling into this rural lifestyle and she filled the dress out well. She and Tucker laughed about how they were both still growing – it seemed as though he had grown another inch taller and her breasts had actually gotten bigger. But that might have been because of the birth control pills she started taking.

"You did good, Tyler Mackenzie. Right size and everything. Even a built-in bra." She laughed. "Because you knew I wouldn't wear one otherwise, right." She twirled in front of him so he could admire his choice. "But white? How am I going to keep it clean until Saturday?"

He handed her a hanger from the hall coat closet. "Try this. You'll be surprised how well it works."

"Thank you." She gave him an impulsive hug before leaving. As she walked across the lawn in the airy little dress, she saw Tucker emerge from the tree house to stand naked on the edge of the porch to pee over the side.

"Hey, what did I tell you about that?" Tyler yelled from behind her. "The yard is not your urinal! And put some frickin' clothes on!"

"Okay, okay! I woke up and had to go really bad. Sorry!" Tucker's disgruntled expression changed as he looked at Chloe. "Whoa, what's this all about? Who is this imposter and what have you done with my real girlfriend?"

"Your dad bought it for me to wear to New York. What do you think?"

He beat his chest and let out a jungle shriek. "Tarzan think Jane look pretty hot. Want Jane to come up here now so he can rip her dress off and have ape sex on back deck."

"No ripping the dress off!" came the muffled shout from the office. "And no sex on the back deck! And remember you're leaving in half an hour for work. I've got to drop you off early so I can cover that zoning board meeting."

Chloe had climbed the ladder by this time, Tucker reaching his hand down to help her up the last step onto the platform. "He can't see what we do back there. Come on, you sexy thing, you." They walked nimbly, single file, along a narrow plank that led to the rear of the tree house where they had extended the platform with a half dozen wide pieces of pine that stuck out from the edge like an extra-wide diving board, creating a space that was just wide enough for them to lie down for sunbathing or for looking at stars and other carefully balanced activities. The dense woods surrounding the back of the property gave them all the privacy they felt they needed.

She started to untie the straps of the dress, but Tucker stopped her. "Wait, let me admire you in it up close. You actually have cleavage in that thing."

"I know – how amazing is that?" She shimmied her shoulders a little at him before slipping the dress off and folding it carefully over the hanger.

"Oh, here, let me hang that in the wardrobe for you." Tucker reached up and hung it on a limb of one of the big trees that supported their lofty refuge.

"You don't think he knows we're doing this?" she teased him as they wrapped their arms around each other.

"I don't care what he knows. He's not the boss of us." His fingers searched through her hair for the elastic that confined her disheveled locks.

"You're too tall now for us to do this standing up, Tarzan. Unless you think I am going to swing like a monkey from this big thick vine of yours."

"Well, I wouldn't want you to get splinters in your lily-white girl butt, Jane." He pried up a loose corner of a window screen and reached inside for the old Mexican blanket that they always kept within reach.

"That's not how Tarzan talks," she laughed as they spread it out on the rough boards and sat down.

"No, this is how he talks," Tucker said, putting his mouth on hers.

ABOUT THE AUTHOR

A lifelong lover of travel, mysteries and creative expression, Marilinne Cooper has always enjoyed the escapist pleasure of combining her passions in a good story. When she is not traveling to warmer climates around the world, she lives in the White Mountains of New Hampshire and is also a freelance copywriting professional. To learn more, visit marilinnecooper.com.

ALSO BY MARILINNE COOPER
available at amazon.com

Night Heron
Butterfly Tattoo
Blue Moon
Double Phoenix
Dead Reckoning
Snake Island

Jamaican Draw